To Love
and to
Cherish

To Love and to Cherish

Lyn Andrews

headline

The right of Lyn Andrews to be identified as the Author of the
Work has been asserted by her in accordance with the
Copyright, Designs and Patents Act 1988.

First published in 2010
by HEADLINE PUBLISHING GROUP

This edition published in 2011
by HEADLINE PUBLISHING GROUP

1

Cataloguing in Publication Data is available from the British Library

Royal hardback ISBN 978 07553 7181 5
Demy hardback ISBN 978 0 7553 7182 2
Trade paperback ISBN 978 0 7553 7199 0

Typeset in Janson by Avon DataSet Ltd,
Bidford-on-Avon, Warwickshire

Printed in the UK by CPI Mackays, Chatham, ME5 8TD

Headline's policy is to use papers that are natural, renewable and
recyclable products and made from wood grown in sustainable forests.
The logging and manufacturing processes are expected to conform
to the environmental regulations of the country of origin.

HEADLINE PUBLISHING GROUP
An Hachette UK Company
338 Euston Road
London NW1 3BH

www.headline.co.uk
www.hachette.co.uk

DEDICATION

In memory of my dear friend Anna Lagaras (née Romney) who died in Athens in June 2010 after a seven-week illness. She was the third close friend I have lost to cancer but almost miraculously she didn't suffer for a prolonged period of time. The last time I spoke to her she said, 'Lyn, I have never been ill in my life before,' and she hadn't, thank God. My thoughts and prayers are with her husband Stelios and sons Marcus and Andreas. We all miss you so much, Anna.

Lyn Andrews
Rahan, 2010

Part I

Chapter One

———

Liverpool, 1925

'WILL THE PAIR OF you try and look as if you're delighted that your da is home at last! He's been away for the best part of a year!' Sal Jenkins urged her two daughters while adjusting the fox fur that was draped around her neck and shoulders. All three stood with the small crowd of wives, mothers and girlfriends of the crew of the SS *Amazonia*, which had just docked. It wasn't a very big ship; in fact it was tiny compared to the huge passenger liners of both the Cunard and Canadian Pacific Lines, but then ships as big as those could never have sailed up the Amazon. Sal knew from experience that its passenger accommodation was equally as luxurious as that of the big liners. Not that she had ever sailed on the *Amazonia*, but as the wife of its Chief Steward she had been welcomed aboard many times.

'Mam, why did we have to get here this early? You know it takes them ages to get tied up and clear the Customs formalities and then get a gangway down and it's not as if we have to wait until the crew comes ashore. We're always allowed on board. We could have stayed at home for at least another hour,' Gloria, Sal's eldest daughter complained. At sixteen Gloria was the beauty of the family: a tall, willowy girl with thick, dark hair cut in a fashionable bob and large brown eyes fringed with lashes that did not need the aid of Vaseline to make them curl. It was a dank, miserable November day and the wind coming down the Mersey estuary was freezing. Even though she had on her best royal blue wool coat and matching cloche hat over a knitted long-line jumper and pleated skirt she was already shivering.

Sal ignored her complaints. Harry's arrival home after a nine-month voyage was the highlight in her year, an occasion to get dressed up to the nines and come down here to be admired and envied by most of the waiting crowd as she and her daughters were escorted aboard to greet Harry while everyone else had to stand and wait for their menfolk to come ashore. And there was always plenty of money when he got paid off too. Of course he left her a generous allotment, which meant they didn't go short for the nine months he was away at sea, but he was always over generous while he was home and he always brought gifts too.

She considered herself to still be an attractive woman even though she was nearing forty, which was considered middle-aged. She was tall also, and she had kept her figure; her reddish-brown hair was thankfully devoid of any encroaching strands of grey. She took care of her complexion too, although she wore little make-up – just a faint dusting of powder, a touch of rouge and of course lipstick. She wore a mustard-coloured coat with a deep shawl collar and wide cuffs, which was the latest fashion, and a dark green cloche hat with a green and mustard striped ribbon bow attached to one side. She had matching gloves and shoes and her real crocodile handbag, which Harry had brought home for her last year, and of course her treasured fox fur. She knew she looked smart and elegant, which had been her objective; after all Harry had a very good position and she always made sure that both she and her girls didn't let him down, at least in the matter of appearances.

She tutted impatiently, leaning forward to tweak the collar of Betty's coat into place. Her younger daughter was a bit of a harum scarum, unlike Gloria, and always managed to look untidy.

Betty frowned mutinously at her mother. She was a small plump girl of fourteen with Sal's blue eyes and reddish-brown hair and she hated having to dress up like this. Her hair, cut in a similar style to Gloria's, had a natural wave and would never lie flat and smooth like her sister's, and her small pink and brown hat felt tight and uncomfortable. It matched the pink and brown checked coat she wore but she would have felt more at ease in her navy gabardine school coat. She also hated the fact that everyone was staring at them, a couple of girls of her own age with ill-concealed envy. Neither did she think it very fair that they could just

5

waltz on board while all these other people had to wait on the dockside in the freezing cold. She couldn't understand either her mother or Gloria's attitude. Her da was a member of the crew like everyone else. True, he was Chief Steward, but he wasn't the Captain or the doctor for heaven's sake, and they didn't live in a big house in a smart part of the city. They lived in a rented semi in Aintree near the Blue Anchor pub. It was a great deal nicer than many parts of Liverpool but it wasn't what you would call 'posh'. She pushed her hands deeper into the pockets of her coat. At least she agreed with her sister about getting down here so early. By the time they finally did get on board they'd be frozen stiff; she could hardly feel her feet now.

Sal checked her watch, hoping they wouldn't have much longer to wait. It was a thoroughly miserable morning and they'd been up since six. Betty had done nothing but complain, saying she would have preferred to go to school, but Sal had refused to listen. She'd sent in a note to the headmistress earlier in the week, explaining the position, so there would be no concern over her absence. It was one day in a year, she had reiterated, a big occasion, so Betty could stop moaning and get a good wash and put on her best clothes. She'd had no such complaints from Gloria, who was happy to be leaving school in a few weeks' time. She had already had an interview for a job as a junior clerk in the offices of the Inland Revenue and was very hopeful of being taken on. Sal smiled to herself. The fact that Gloria had obtained an interview at all was entirely due to the fact that Richard Mostyn, Harry's sister's husband, was a member of the Masonic Brethren and had used his influence. Richard had his own business and was very successful.

'Well, thank goodness for that! It looks as if it won't be long now, Mam. They appear to be getting the gangway sorted out,' Gloria announced and they all watched as the gangway was manoeuvred into place.

'Customs will be first aboard but they usually don't take long,' Sal said thankfully, pulling her hat further down over her ears, which were starting to tingle with the cold.

'I shouldn't think there would be much of a problem with the stuff they carry,' Betty remarked flatly. She couldn't see that sides of frozen beef or planks of mahogany would excite much interest in Customs.

'They have to check all the documents, you know that,' Sal reminded her, thinking that a hot cup of tea would be very welcome indeed.

It was almost another half an hour before there was any sign of the officials leaving and everyone was chilled to the bone. Betty's nose had started to run and she was sniffing audibly.

'For heaven's sake, where's your handkerchief?' Sal snapped.

'I forgot it,' came the sullen reply, accompanied by another sniff.

Gloria delved into her handbag. 'Here, use mine and stop making a show of yourself.'

'And us!' Sal added tartly, then, catching sight of a deck steward coming quickly down the gangway and beckoning to them, she smiled broadly. 'Right. Come along, the pair of you, and for the love of God put a smile on your faces.'

The two girls glanced at each other; Gloria shrugged and then smiled obligingly.

When she stepped aboard Sal sighed. The ship was so warm that she felt better already. She knew the way well enough, she thought as her feet sank into the deep pile of the carpet, but she dutifully followed the steward. The walls of the companionway were lined with beautifully polished woods and then it opened out into a small circular lobby where carved and gilded tables and chairs were tastefully placed and firmly secured. On the tables were Wedgwood urns and vases, firmly stuck to plinths. Beyond this was a very elegantly furnished lounge, again panelled in polished woods with oil paintings of the ships of the Porto-Brasilia Line hanging on the walls; a large chandelier was suspended from the ceiling.

It wasn't at first noticeable but on closer inspection it was possible to see that the blue and gold brocade-covered chairs and sofas and the highly polished inlaid tables were all firmly anchored to the deck. The *Amazonia* sailed from Liverpool to Lisbon, crossing the notorious Bay of Biscay, then on to Madeira and the Canary Islands and finally across the treacherous Atlantic Ocean to South America before sailing one thousand miles up the River Amazon to complete the voyage at Manaus, the city in the heart of the jungle. Sal smiled to herself as she noticed that one of the tables was set with white bone-china cups and saucers and plates banded with gold, silver cutlery and thick white damask napkins. A solid silver sugar basin and milk jug were also set out.

She knew they were solid silver and not merely plated for she had just such a set at home; Harry had brought them, informing her that one set wouldn't be missed.

The two girls had followed in silence; they had been aboard many times and were used to the opulence. Their father's working life was spent in far grander surroundings than the rented semi in Aintree. They were never taken to his cabin-cum-office, although their mother had visited it. She had told them it was very comfortable and neat but not really big enough to entertain his family in.

Harry Jenkins walked towards them smiling. 'Sarah, my dear! No need to ask how you are, you look wonderful!' He greeted his wife warmly and embraced her. He was a small, slight man with dark hair neatly slicked down, dark eyes that missed nothing, a small waxed moustache and deeply tanned skin. In his immaculately pressed uniform, pristine shirt and tie and highly polished shoes he was a dapper and some would say handsome man.

'Henry, it's so good to have you home again, safe and sound.' Sal beamed at him, kissing him on the cheek.

Betty shifted impatiently from foot to foot. She hated all this. It was all for show, this 'Sarah' and 'Henry' performance. At home they called each other Sal and Harry. Who was there to witness all this play acting anyway? The deck steward had disappeared and his place had been taken by a waiter in a white jacket and dark trousers, standing beside the door at the end of the lounge from which her father had emerged.

'The girls have been so looking forward to today,' Sal continued, turning and smiling at them both.

'And don't you both look so grown up. Gloria, quite a fashionable young lady now.' Harry stepped forward and embraced his eldest daughter.

'Welcome home,' she said, smiling.

'And Elizabeth.'

Betty was then embraced and muttered, 'Welcome home, Da— Father.' She quickly corrected herself, prompted by her mother's frown of disapproval.

'Was it a good trip, Henry? No bad weather or storms?' Sal asked as her husband indicated that she should sit and the waiter rushed forward to assist her.

'Nothing of any major significance. We had a few uncomfortable days on the Atlantic, which isn't unusual at this time of year.' He glanced sharply at the waiter who disappeared and then reappeared bearing a tray on which reposed a silver teapot, a silver hot-water jug and two plates of dainty little sandwiches with the crusts cut off. Another waiter followed bearing a three-tiered silver cake stand complete with a variety of fancy cakes.

The two girls said little, leaving their mother to make conversation, but both were glad of the tea and sandwiches and Betty had her eye on a cream and chocolate éclair.

'And your passengers? Any difficulties there?' Sal asked, sipping her tea.

Using the silver tongs Harry dropped two sugar lumps into his tea and then fastidiously rearranged his napkin. 'We only had three ladies this time so Miss Ellis was well able to cope, although two of them were sick for a couple of days during the bad weather.'

Sal nodded. They carried only half a dozen passengers and the ladies were treated like royalty. Even Miss Ellis, who was the only stewardess, was treated like a lady. It wouldn't have been her who had cleaned up after the two seasick passengers but a steward. She wouldn't have been expected to soil her hands or her starched white uniform. Sal had met the woman a few times and had thought her insipid-looking and very stand-offish.

When they'd finished the refreshments Harry got up, smiling broadly. 'Now, I think a glass of Madeira is in order for your mother while I show you girls what I've brought you this time.'

Sal sat back in her chair and relaxed; this was all part of the ritual. She would enjoy one or two glasses of the sweet wine served in Waterford crystal glasses and Harry would distribute the gifts. Then he would escort them to the dockside where a taxi would be waiting to take them home and he would follow later in the day. He was very generous and enjoyed giving them treats. Of course, like any man he had his faults, the main one being his quick temper.

'You know how much he enjoys buying you things,' she reminded her daughters.

Both girls nodded and looked excited as their father reappeared, his arms full of boxes.

Sal exclaimed in delight at the bottles of expensive perfume, the emerald ring in its velvet box and the beautiful soft leather gloves he'd given her. Gloria smiled and thanked him profusely for the half-dozen pairs of silk stockings, the gold pendant and bracelet and the real crocodile-skin purse. Betty also thanked him, uttering a cry of delight when she opened the intricately carved jewellery box, inside which was a brooch shaped as a butterfly and set with semi-precious stones.

'You need somewhere to keep all the jewellery you no doubt will acquire in the coming years,' Harry said affably.

'Thank you, Father. It's really lovely,' she replied before turning her attention to the other two boxes on her lap. Of course she was pleased with her gifts but she would be glad when it was time to go home. She hated all this pretence.

Chapter Two

———◆———

WHEN THEY RETURNED HOME Betty was glad to be able to take off the hat and coat and get changed into what she considered to be more comfortable clothes.

Sal covered her dress with an apron and began to set the table while Gloria went upstairs to put on a pair of the silk stockings with which she was delighted.

'Don't just sit there, milady, you can give me a hand,' Sal instructed Betty as she tried to decide which of the two beautifully embroidered tablecloths to use. When Harry was home she made far more of an effort at mealtimes. He was a bit of a martinet where table settings and meal presentation were concerned. She supposed it was only natural; it was after all part of his job to oversee things like that. He'd brought all her best tablecloths and napkins from Madeira where the nuns spent hours making and embroidering them

13

and then sold them at what Harry had said was a very reasonable price. Her best china was always used when he first got home, but as time went on she reverted back to using her everyday dishes. She liked living in this house, she mused. There had been some discussion a few years ago about them moving; Harry had said they could afford to buy a house if they saved more, but she hadn't been in favour of that. This was a quiet, residential suburb of Liverpool and although the houses were situated on a main road there wasn't a great deal of traffic, and the Leeds to Liverpool canal, which was quiet and pleasantly rural on this stretch of its route, ran at the back of them. The houses were semi-detached, with lovely bay windows and a garden front and back. She had it well furnished with every modern comfort and she didn't want to have to start watching every penny, the way she'd done when she'd first been married.

'Mam, when I've finished this can I go and see if Rose is home from school yet?' Betty asked, carefully setting out the cutlery.

Sal nodded, checking that everything looked right before she went into the kitchen to make a start on the meal. 'Oh, I suppose so but don't be there for hours. Your da won't be very pleased if you're not here when he gets in.'

Betty thankfully escaped next door to where her best friend Rose Cassidy lived with her widowed mother Dora, who was a great friend of Sal's. Their house, while being identical in layout to her own, looked very drab by comparison. Dora had no good carpets or rugs, just the peg rugs made from scraps of material she'd made herself. No heavy maroon-coloured chenille curtains hung at the windows; the furniture (although well polished) was dark and old-fashioned. The material that covered the sofa and armchairs was faded and worn and Dora, unlike her mam, had very few ornaments, pictures or lamps.

Rose was just taking off her school coat and she grinned at Betty. 'They let you out then?'

Betty nodded. 'He's not home yet but I don't suppose he'll be long so Mam says I've not to stay for hours. Is there much homework?'

Rose rolled her eyes expressively. She was taller than her friend and thinner. She had curly fair hair and blue eyes and was possessed of an easy-going nature. 'Mounds of it. I brought home the books you'll need.'

'You needn't have been so thoughtful,' Betty answered, pulling a face.

'Why don't the pair of you go up to Rose's room while I start the tea? You'd give anyone a headache with your chatter and I think I've a cold coming on,' Dora Cassidy urged.

'Was it the same as usual? All that "Sarah" and "Henry" stuff?' Rose asked, dumping her satchel on the bed and sorting out the books she'd been instructed to bring home for her friend.

Betty sat on the bed. 'Yes. It's all so *stupid*! The minute he gets through the front door it's back to Sal and Harry.'

'What did he bring you this time?'

'A jewellery box, a brooch, a real silk scarf that I'll never wear and some posh talcum powder and soap. "Attar of

Roses", it's called. I said our Gloria can have the scarf and the toilet stuff, it's more her style.'

Rose nodded and then frowned. 'You'd better tell her not to let him catch her with them or he won't be very pleased.' She sat down beside her friend. Her da had died when she'd been a baby, she didn't remember him at all, but despite the fact that Betty had so much more in the way of material things than she did, she didn't envy her at all. Harry Jenkins was something of a Jekyll and Hyde character. All good humour and generosity when he got home, then irritable and snappy when he got bored. They often heard the rows through the walls.

She changed the subject. 'I suppose you'll have your Aunt Sybil visiting now your da's home.'

Betty nodded, pulling a face as she thought of her da's sister. 'Not too often, I hope. She really doesn't like me, Gloria's always been her favourite, and I don't like her much either.'

Rose squeezed her hand. Sybil Mostyn's attitude towards Betty seemed terribly unfair to her and like her friend she didn't like Harry Jenkins's sister one bit: Sibyl was an out-and-out snob. Oh, she had plenty of money and lived in a big posh house in Formby but she'd only come from a two-up, two-down terraced house in Anfield like Betty's da. She had no children and still worked part time. She was the buyer for a big millinery wholesaler in town that supplied hats to all Liverpool's most exclusive shops, which was why Sal and Gloria and Betty always had the most stylish and expensive hats – they were 'samples'. 'Christmas is in four weeks, that might keep her so busy she won't have time for much visiting.'

Betty nodded and looked more cheerful. Her da hadn't been home for Christmas for a few years. Perhaps she should suggest to Mam that they put off the big party they always had when he came home until nearer Christmas. He always enjoyed organising it and being the life and soul of it too and then Mam could take him Christmas shopping. Most men hated shopping but he seemed to enjoy it. That would keep him occupied.

The following day was Saturday so there was no school and Harry had informed them the previous evening that he had to go down to the company's offices in the Royal Liver Building at the Pier Head as he had some business to attend to. Both girls were relieved because Gloria wanted to go into town shopping with a friend and Betty and Rose wanted to go to the local cinema's weekly Saturday morning show. Usually on his first full day at home, if it was the weekend, they were expected to spend it with him.

Sal hadn't finished her morning chores and was still in what she termed her 'housework' clothes, which consisted of an old dress and cardigan covered by a cross-over pinafore and her old slippers, when her sister-in-law arrived. Hastily dragging off the pinafore and running a comb through her hair she went to open the door, having seen Richard Mostyn's Austin 10 pull up outside.

'This is a bit of a surprise Sybil. Richard, it's good to see you.' Sal smiled at her brother-in-law, whom she genuinely liked. He was a tall, slim man now in his forties with dark hair that was greying at the temples, and as always was dressed in a dark well-made business suit. He was what she called a 'thorough gentleman', being courteous, considerate and generous. She turned back to Sybil. 'I wish I'd known you were coming.' As usual her sister-in-law was well dressed in a beautifully cut charcoal grey herringbone tweed costume with large black buttons on the jacket and cuffs of the sleeves. A bright scarlet cloche hat with a black bird of paradise feather curled around the brim covered her neatly set short dark hair. Her shoes and bag were of black patent leather and she carried black kid gloves.

'Richard has to go in this morning, something to do with the stocktaking.'

Richard smiled and shrugged. 'It's a busy time so I have to be there, but I promised to drop Sybil off. Well, I'll leave you two to chat. I'll pick you up later, Sybil.'

'Is Harry home?' Sybil took off her hat and jacket, revealing a pure silk blouse in scarlet and black stripes decorated at hip level with a sash and a floppy bow, and sat down on the sofa.

'Yes and no,' Sal answered, sitting down in an armchair opposite her and wishing she had changed out of these awful-looking clothes. 'Yes, he got home yesterday and no, he's gone down to the Royal Liver Building on business or something. Although he did say he'd be back at dinner— lunchtime,' she hastily amended. 'Can you stay for lunch?'

Sybil shook her head. 'No, we're going into Southport

this afternoon to start the Christmas shopping, but thanks for the offer.'

'I'll put the kettle on, you can have a cup of tea at least,' Sal said, getting to her feet.

'I'd love one.' Sybil smiled.

'How does he seem?' Sybil asked as Sal handed her the china cup and saucer.

'Fine. He brought me a beautiful emerald ring and perfume and gloves and lovely gifts for the girls.'

Sybil nodded; Harry seldom saved, he preferred to spend; he was often generous to a fault. He had a very good life, the best of both worlds, and in her opinion he should think himself very fortunate and put something by for a rainy day. 'Has Gloria heard any more about that job? I know Richard had a long talk to Bradley Wilkinson about her, he's quite high up in the Revenue and he's Worshipful Master this year.' Sybil tapped her nose and smiled knowingly. 'It's not what you know but *who* you know that counts these days, Sal.'

Sal shook her head as she sipped her tea. It was something Harry was always saying but he'd never been inclined to become a member of the Masonic Brethren and so had had to make his own way in the world. Yet he'd done well enough for himself, she mused. When they'd first been married and the girls were babies his trips had been much shorter, but he'd only been a second-class steward then with Cunard. He'd always been very ambitious and had finally got the job he wanted, that of Chief Steward, but it had meant these very long trips – which in turn led to much longer stays at home between voyages. She frowned, after the first few weeks at home he would begin to get restless and bored, becoming more and more irritable and the atmosphere in the house would change. Not wanting to provoke an outburst of temper they were all careful of what they said and did; it was like walking on eggshells.

Sybil noticed her change of expression and knew what she was thinking. 'I just honestly don't know why he gets so bored. You'd think he'd enjoy having less responsibility for a while, enjoy being at home more,' she remarked.

Sal shrugged. 'I know. I keep telling him to relax, but you know how seriously Harry takes his job.'

Sybil sighed. 'I do.' She was only too aware of how much he valued his position, in fact she thought he gave himself airs and graces far in excess of his station in life, which was why Sal had to go through the pantomime of being so terribly formal and 'correct' whenever they went on board. Something to do with maintaining the respect of the crew, he'd once told her.

'I don't suppose you'll change him now, Sal,' Sybil said.

Sal had to agree. Although she missed him when he was away she had become accustomed to it and she enjoyed her life. She did her chores in the mornings, then she got changed and either went to the local shops or got a tram to Walton Vale for her shopping, and two afternoons a week she went to a tea dance in the local community hall. She enjoyed that and she was always the best dressed woman there. She wasn't short of money; she went to the hairdressers every Friday. At the weekends she often went into Liverpool to shop, taking the girls with her, and then on a Sunday evening she and Dora would go to the cinema. It was always her treat for poor Dora had to manage on the small pension Bill's firm had paid her ever since he'd been killed in that terrible accident, and the even smaller amount of money they'd managed to save before he'd died. She sighed as she finished her drink. She didn't know what she would do if she didn't have Dora, who was a close friend as well as a good neighbour.

Chapter Three

———◆◆◆———

SAL THOUGHT IT A great idea when Betty, urged on by Gloria, suggested to her that they delay the home-coming party until a week before Christmas.

She mentioned it when they were all sitting in the living room after supper the following day. The heavy maroon chenille curtains were drawn across the window, shutting out the bitterly cold frosty night, and a good fire burned in the hearth, making the room warm and comfortable. The wireless was on low; a concert was being broadcast from the Royal Albert Hall in London and Harry thought it would be suitably 'improving' for the family to listen to. Even though he was only spending the evening at home with his family he was immaculately turned out in a shirt and tie over which he wore an expensive fine wool cardigan. The creases in his trousers were razor sharp and his shoes were polished; he flatly refused to wear slippers. He was studying the *Journal of Commerce* for he had a keen interest in the movement of all the shipping in and out of the port. Sal was knitting, Gloria was half-heartedly reading a book on etiquette that Sybil had insisted on lending her (it was dull but she knew it would please her father), and Betty was sticking the picture postcards Harry had brought into an album, something which also pleased him.

'What do you think about Betty's suggestion, Harry?' Sal asked him.

He put down the paper and appeared to be considering it. 'Won't it all be a bit much for you so close to Christmas?'

'Not at all,' she replied brightly. 'All I have to do is see that the food is set out nicely, you know how good you are at organising everything. And it will be a double celebration this year. Your home-coming and Christmas. You've not been home for the holiday for two years.'

'It will be great, Da. We'll have all the Christmas decorations up by then and the tree,' Betty urged. 'By the way, I've already got one of the Opera House in Manaus and one of the statue of Christ of the Andes, so can I give these two to Rose?' she added, holding up the postcards. Both she and Rose spent a good deal of time sticking things in their scrapbooks.

Harry nodded. He really must make a list of all the postcards she had in her album. There was no sense at all in buying duplicates and then having to give them away.

'The place will really look more festive than usual, Da, and we can have crackers and party hats,' Gloria added, wondering if this year, seeing as she'd have left school and was soon to have her first job, she could persuade her mam to buy her her first grown-up evening dress.

'You know how much everyone enjoys themselves, Harry. Even your Sybil says it's one of the best parties she ever attends; nothing is left to chance and everything is of the finest quality. She told me that even at Richard's golf club they don't do things in such style.'

He smiled, looking pleased and smug. The party took very little effort to organise compared to the task of ordering provisions for all the meals, drinks, cocktail parties and similar functions for a nine-month voyage, to say nothing of keeping a check on all the crockery, glass, cutlery and linen that was in use and making sure his staff of chefs and kitchen workers, laundry personnel, stewards, waiters and barmen did their jobs properly. He was good at his job and he enjoyed it. His position gave him the status he had always wanted; he was respected, and not only by his staff but by the Captain and officers as well, and he enjoyed meeting and conversing with the passengers they carried. His days at sea were always full and busy and in the foreign ports he always managed to find time to get ashore to take in the sights and do some shopping. It was just when he got home for this long and relatively inactive leave that he found life tedious. On board ship he was 'somebody', here at home he was virtually 'nobody' and that rankled deeply, as did the fact that they coped quite well without him.

He pushed aside these unsettling thoughts and turned his mind again to the party. It did seem the sensible thing to do.

His home-coming party was very lavish, with the best of everything, but in reality it cost him very little because of his 'perks': the gifts and discounts he received from the companies who supplied goods and services to the *Amazonia*. It would be a fine way to celebrate Christmas.

'I think you're right. We'll have it just before Christmas but this time, Sal, don't invite those people from further down the road; they don't know how to behave in decent company. Last time she asked me did we have no sheets of ribs or pig's trotters, would you believe? She said a "do" wasn't a proper "do" without them. I give them smoked salmon and Parma ham and *she* asks for ribs and *trotters*! And she had the nerve to pester Richard, asking him did he have a job in his factory for her husband and son.'

'They've moved,' Sal replied.

'They were thrown out for not paying the rent,' Betty informed him.

'It doesn't surprise me,' Harry said with some satisfaction, not bothering to wonder if the fact that the woman's husband had been looking for work had resulted in their eviction. He seemed oblivious to the hardships that other people were increasingly suffering; these were difficult times.

'And then after we get the party over we can go shopping, Harry, for Christmas presents. You always know what Sybil and Richard would like. You've far more idea than I have. I never know what to get and you do have such good taste,' Sal added.

He nodded, looking pleased, and was about to pick up the

Journal again when there was a knock on the front door. He looked impatiently at his wife.

'Betty, go and see who it is. If it's anyone selling anything we don't want any,' Sal instructed.

Betty did as she was bid and returned with a worried-looking Rose.

'Mrs Jenkins, I'm sorry to disturb you but could you come and have a look at Mam, please? She's not a bit well.'

Sal instantly got to her feet. 'What's the matter, Rose? I know she's had a head cold but I didn't think she was too bad.'

'She's got a bad cough now,' Rose informed her.

Sal pulled on her heavy cardigan and followed Rose out, casting an apologetic glance at Harry, who was looking far from pleased at the interruption.

Dora was sitting in a chair by the fire and she really didn't look at all well, Sal thought. She looked feverish and seemed to be struggling for breath.

'What's wrong, Dora, luv? How long have you been like this?'

'Since this afternoon. I've had this cold for a few days but I feel all hot and my chest feels tight,' Dora replied before being overcome by a spasm of coughing.

Sal placed her hand on her friend's forehead. It was very hot. 'I think you should at least be in bed, Dora, and perhaps we should get the doctor in to see you?'

Dora shook her head. 'No, I'm not that bad, Sal, and you'd have a job to get a doctor out at this time. Anyway, I dread to think what he'd charge.'

'Oh, don't you be worrying about that. I'd be glad to pay him.'

Again Dora shook her head. 'No, it's just a cough and a heavy cold.'

Sal sighed. 'You can be so stubborn, Dora. Rose, luv, get a hot-water bottle and fill it and take it up and put it in your mam's bed. Then go next door and get our Betty to give you the pot of honey from the larder and ask Mr Jenkins for some whisky, I know there's plenty. I'm going to make her a hot toddy; it should help. And ask our Gloria to get the packet of Beecham's Powders from the cabinet in the bathroom.' She turned back to Dora. 'And if you're no better in the morning then you're having the doctor and no arguments.'

It was a good hour later when she returned home after having seen her friend to bed after a Beecham's Powder and a hot toddy.

'How is she now, Mam?' Betty asked, looking anxious.

'I hope she'll sleep, it will do her good. But I've told her if she's no better tomorrow she's having the doctor. We don't want it turning to bronchitis or even pleurisy.'

'That woman should take better care of herself,' Harry remarked.

'I know but she finds it hard to make ends meet,' Sal replied. She knew Dora couldn't afford to keep a good table which was why at least once a week she asked her friend and Rose in for supper – when Harry was away of course. Otherwise there would be remarks about 'feeding the neighbourhood', which was rich considering what he must spend on giving a party every time he came home, a party to which not only friends and family were invited but half the neighbourhood as well.

The following morning Sal went in to see Dora after she had got the girls off to school. She found her friend up but sitting hunched in a chair beside the fire. The breakfast dishes were still on the kitchen table and the room was untidy, which wasn't like Dora at all. She kept the place spick and span.

'You shouldn't have got up. Rose is well able to get her own breakfast and get herself out to school.'

'I can't be lying in bed all day, Sal,' Dora replied.

'You can. Now, I'm having no arguments out of you, Dora. You're having the doctor. I'll go and ask Harry if he'll call and see him. You get yourself back up to bed now. I'll nip back in and tidy up,' Sal said firmly, helping Dora to her feet. She was worried about her.

Harry had started to make a list of everything they would need for the forthcoming celebration, intending to get in touch with the various suppliers in the following days. Being occupied and busy had put him in a good mood.

'She's not at all well. Harry, would you do me a huge favour, luv?' Sal asked.

'Of course,' he replied amiably.

'Would you pop into the surgery and ask if Dr Foreshaw could call in to see Dora when he's finished surgery? I'd go myself but I promised her I'd tidy the place up before he comes.'

'Is she that bad?' he asked.

Sal nodded. 'I think she is and I don't want her to be ill and have to miss the party. She really enjoys it.'

Thus appealed to Harry left his lists and got up. It was a cold but bright sunny morning and he wouldn't mind the walk. Dr Foreshaw was bound to ask him about his voyage, he usually did on the infrequent occasions he saw him, and Harry had always found him to be a pleasant and interesting man. He'd take him a bottle of the good Napoleon brandy he'd brought home.

Sal had tidied up both Dora's kitchen and living room and had made sure that her friend was tucked up in bed before the doctor arrived. When she saw his car stop outside she informed Harry that she would just pop next door to see what he said.

'Is there anything I can get for her, doctor?' she asked as he came downstairs.

'If you could take this down to the chemist, Mrs Jenkins, please. It's for a linctus which should loosen the cough,' he replied. It was always a busy time of year with colds and influenza.

'Is it just the cold or is it something else?' Sal enquired. 'You know she has no one except Rose and she's always been a great friend to me.'

'It's bronchitis, Mrs Jenkins. But the linctus should help and I've told her to stay in bed and keep warm.'

Sal nodded, thankful it wasn't anything more serious. 'I'll make sure she does. I'll see to Rose, Dora looks after our Betty often enough. How much do I owe you, doctor?'

He shook his head. He knew Dora Cassidy's circumstances

and it was generous of Sal Jenkins to offer to pay his fee. 'I think the very fine bottle of brandy your husband left me is payment enough, Mrs Jenkins. It was very generous of him. It's something I wouldn't dream of buying for myself.'

Sal smiled. 'Oh, that's Harry down to a tee. Always generous and always the very best of everything. Thank you, I'll take this to the chemist myself. And I'm sure she'll soon be on the mend.'

When he'd gone she went up to see Dora. 'You're to stay in bed and keep warm. I'm going to the chemist for this medicine he's given you and you're not to worry about anything. I'll give Rose her tea and she can sit with our Betty and do her homework, then she can come back in to you. I'll get what shopping you need, you just concentrate on getting better. You can't miss the "event" of the year, Dora. I'd never forgive you.'

Dora managed a smile. 'Thanks, Sal. How is Harry?'

'Fine. He's got plenty to do and then with Christmas nearly on us I'm hoping this leave he won't get bored. Our Gloria is waiting to hear if she's got that job and if she has then she'll need some smart office clothes. I'll send him off with her and Sybil to buy them, and then he can take them somewhere posh for lunch. He likes doing things like that.'

Dora nodded. She hoped for Sal's sake that all these distractions would keep Harry Jenkins in a pleasant enough mood until he sailed again. She'd seen how when his mood soured it affected the whole family. It was as if a black cloud descended on them.

Chapter Four

———◆———

IT WAS A WEEK later when Gloria received the letter informing her that she had got the job she'd been interviewed
for. It was waiting when she got in from school.

'There's a letter for you,' Sal announced, holding out the
envelope. 'It came in the lunchtime post.'

Gloria hesitated before opening it.

'Go on, I can't stand the suspense,' Sal urged.

Gloria ripped it open and scanned the lines. 'Oh, Mam!
I've got it! I'm so relieved. I was beginning to wonder. It's
been ages since the interview.'

Sal hugged her. 'I knew you would. Your da will be
in soon and I know he'll be just as delighted.'

Gloria took the letter upstairs with her to reread it while
she changed out of her hated school uniform. Oh, now
she felt really grown up and she was looking forward to the

future. She'd applied for three clerical jobs and had got an interview for two but they had both been on the same day and both in the morning. As her Uncle Richard had gone to some trouble on her behalf, her mam had said she should give preference to the interview at the Revenue office. As far as she had been able to ascertain her duties would consist mainly of opening the post and distributing it to the appropriate people and doing the filing, of which there was a considerable amount. It didn't sound terribly exciting but she had to start somewhere and she would be earning her own money at last. It wasn't a great deal, in fact only ten shillings, but she was a very junior clerk – in fact *the* junior clerk – but it would increase in time. Surely now Mam couldn't refuse to let her have a proper evening dress?

When Harry arrived home the table was set for the evening meal and Betty and Rose were helping Sal to put it out. He'd been to see one of his more important suppliers and had spent a very convivial afternoon being entertained in the Adelphi Hotel. He'd had a couple of glasses of Scotch, which was his limit when discussing business matters, for you had to keep your wits about you and it certainly didn't impress anyone if you started slurring your words or laughing raucously.

'Gloria's had some good news, Harry,' Sal informed him, smiling at her eldest daughter.

'I got the job, Da. I start after the Christmas holiday,' she announced.

He smiled at her and nodded. 'I knew you would. It's a good position, very respectable indeed.'

Betty exchanged glances with Rose as they sat down at the table. Everyone knew that it was due to Uncle Richard's influence. Influence that she very much doubted would be used to obtain such a job for her, not if Aunt Sybil had anything to do with it.

'Have you thought about what you want to do when you leave school, Rose? It's not that far off, you know,' Harry asked as Sal poured the tea.

'Not really,' Rose replied.

'You should, Rose. After all, you have to think of your mother. She's struggled for years bringing you up. You should aim for something that pays a good wage or has prospects. In fact now that Gloria's starting work, you should start and think about a job too, Betty.'

Betty shrugged but Rose nodded. She didn't need to be reminded that she needed to help pay for her keep. 'I don't really mind what I do as long as I can earn some money to help Mam out.'

'Plenty of time yet before you two need to worry about jobs. Thank goodness your mam is on the mend, Rose. She got up this afternoon for an hour,' Sal informed them.

'And she's not coughing as much now.'

Harry changed the subject. Talk of illness always depressed him. 'So, Gloria, I suppose you are going to need some new clothes? We can't have you starting work looking drab.' Indeed not, he thought. It would be a bad reflection on both himself and Richard Mostyn.

'She will, Harry, and I was thinking that maybe Sybil could take her into town and you could accompany them or meet them afterwards and take them to lunch somewhere . . . nice,' Sal suggested. 'If, of course, it won't interfere with anything you have planned,' she added.

Although Gloria was delighted at the prospect of new clothes she would have preferred to have gone to choose them with just her mam and then gone to either Lyons or the Kardomah for something to eat, but she said nothing. By the time Aunt Sybil had finished with her she would be the most stylish and expensively dressed girl in the office, which was a bit ludicrous seeing as she was only a junior clerk, and she wouldn't enjoy lunch very much for she would have to watch what she said and did.

Harry nodded. It was a good idea. Sal sometimes showed flashes of inspiration. Sybil was well known in all the best shops so they would be treated with deference and would most probably get a discount too. He beamed approvingly at Gloria. He wanted her to do well. He loved both his daughters but he had to admit that Gloria was by far the more attractive and academic and with Sybil's influence and guidance he hoped she would go far. Sal could be a bit lackadaisical in these things. Gloria would do well to emulate her aunt, he thought. She would have a good job, as his sister had, and hopefully she would also marry well, just as Sybil had done. 'I think that's an excellent idea, Sal.' Then he frowned, thinking about contacting his sister to make the arrangements. 'You know I really think we should have a telephone of our own. It's most inconvenient having to go and use the public phone boxes. All that fiddling about putting pennies in and then pushing Button A and having to put more pennies in when the pips go. I'll go into the General Post Office in town and ask them how to go about getting one installed. We want a private line; we don't want to have to share one and have someone listening in to our conversations. I'll find out how long it will take and how much it will cost.'

Betty had to stop herself from raising her eyes to the ceiling and from looking at Rose in case they burst out laughing. Her da just hated people to see him using the public telephone. He was as much a snob as Aunt Sybil was.

Sal was looking quite pleased. 'I've been thinking along the same lines myself, Harry.' It would certainly be more convenient, she thought.

The days that followed were busy for everyone. Rose insisted on doing the housework and the shopping for the weather hadn't improved and she didn't want her mother to go out on the bitterly cold December days. Dora was improving although Sal thought she should be recovering more quickly. When she'd commented as such to Harry he'd said, off-handedly, that she probably would have done if she had a stronger constitution and ate properly. Betty helped both Sal and Rose as much as she could and she'd gone with Gloria to choose the Christmas tree and get the holly. Sal had said it wasn't worth Dora wasting money on a tree or extra food for she intended to have both Dora and Rose in for all their meals over the holiday, but Betty had got a few extra bunches of holly out of her own pocket money. As she'd said to Rose, you couldn't not put some kind of decorations up.

Gloria's outing to Liverpool had been what Harry considered to be a great success. Sybil had actually made appointments in both Hendersons and Cripps so they wouldn't have to hang around at this busy time, waiting for assistance, and so he had decided to accompany them. Both establishments had commissionaires on the doors, something he greatly approved of for it kept the riff raff out. Once inside they were shown to the appropriate departments and were attended to by at least two assistants, while he had been escorted to a seat. Sybil had picked out what she considered to be the most flattering yet suitable garments, Gloria had tried them on and after they had been approved and duly wrapped, he had paid for them. It was a very civilised and satisfactory way of shopping, he'd thought. It was certainly better than all that rummaging around and then trying to find an assistant. Gloria now had a well-cut dark green winter coat and two stylish costumes, one grey and one chocolate brown. She had three very pretty crêpe-de-Chine blouses in pastel colours and two smart tailored skirts.

As they were leaving Cripps he had seen Gloria glance longingly at an evening dress displayed in the window. It was just gorgeous, she'd enthused. It was of peacock-blue chiffon with a handkerchief hemline and the bodice and tiny straps were embroidered with bugle beads that sparkled like diamonds. She'd look like a film star in something like that, she'd thought.

'Beautiful, isn't it? Of course it's much too old and sophisticated for a young girl like you, Gloria,' he'd said but he'd raised an eyebrow enquiringly at his sister.

'Not at all suitable, Harry, but don't you think perhaps . . . something else?' Sybil had suggested.

'Oh, please, Da? I've had my heart set on a real grown-up evening dress,' Gloria had pleaded, ignoring her aunt's look of annoyance at her use of the hated 'Da'.

' "Father", or at least "Dad",' Sybil had muttered.

Gloria had ignored her but had continued to look pleadingly at Harry.

'Well, why not? You are a young lady now and lunch will wait for another half an hour or so,' he had agreed and they had gone back inside.

Sybil had chosen a dress in pale pink silk which had the fashionable short skirt and dropped waist around which was a sash of darker pink satin, but the neckline was quite high and it had short cape sleeves. Gloria did have to agree that it looked lovely on her. Sybil had also picked out a headband adorned with a pink feather that matched it perfectly and looked good over her short dark glossy hair.

'She'll be a credit to you, Harry,' Sybil had said.

'And she'll be the talk of the entire neighbourhood for weeks. Now, let's finish the day off with a good lunch,' Harry had added affably as he'd escorted his sister and daughter out into Bold Street.

Rose was in Betty's house when Harry and Gloria arrived home. Gloria was excited about all the things Aunt Sybil had picked out and her father had paid for, but she was in raptures over the evening dress and Harry insisted she try it on for them.

Sal said she had never seen Gloria look so elegant and grown up and Gloria blushed with pleasure. Betty said it was gorgeous and the colour really suited her and Rose added that it looked lovely, but when Betty went back next door with her friend to help Rose to bank up the fire and make sure her mam was all right Rose said she thought it was very unfair that so much had been spent on Gloria.

'I don't mind, honestly, Rose. I mean she's got to have some grown-up-looking clothes to start work.'

'But so many? And that evening dress – it must have cost your da a small fortune. I really don't think it's fair,' Rose protested.

'I definitely wouldn't want a dress as fancy as that. Could you see me in pink silk and satin?' Betty replied, being absolutely honest.

'Well, maybe not, but they could at least have bought you *something*,' Rose persisted.

'I don't *need* anything, Rose.'

Rose shook her head and went to put the kettle on to make Dora a cup of tea. Betty really didn't seem to mind but she thought that in some ways Gloria was very like both her father and his sister. Selfish and thoughtless.

Next day Betty helped Rose to decorate their living room with the holly and some paper chains which Rose had found in a box in the cupboard under the stairs. She was glad of the excuse to escape from their house; things were a bit chaotic, she confided to her friend.

'Mam is getting in a bit of a state about all the stuff that's being delivered. She says she doesn't know where she's going to store it all.' Betty was balancing on a chair, trying to make sure that the large sprig of holly she'd stuck behind the mirror didn't fall down.

'I thought your da had everything sorted out,' Dora remarked. She was sitting by the fire, a blanket over her knees, watching the proceedings. 'Maybe you'd better use a few drawing pins or a bit of sticky tape, Betty,' she added.

'He's ordered everything. The food won't be delivered until Saturday morning so that's not a problem. Mam will just have to set it out on all the dishes. It's all the drink, the bottles and the glasses and things like that. Mam says there just isn't room. We'll be falling over everything and the place will look untidy.'

'Tell her to bring it all in here, Betty. I don't mind a bit of clutter and it's only for a few days. I know she will have her work cut out rearranging the furniture and taking up the carpet in the living room. She told me she wasn't leaving it down, not after the last time. She had to get down on her hands and knees and scrub it, so much had been spilt on it.' Dora sighed. 'I wish I could be more help to her. At least if I—' She broke off as a bout of coughing overwhelmed her.

'Mam, haven't you been taking your medicine?' Rose asked.

'I finished it two days ago,' Dora replied when she had at last got her breath. 'And I am feeling better. Stop fussing, Rose.'

Betty smiled at her as she got down off the chair. 'We'll

all have a great time. There's nothing like a party to cheer everyone up, Mrs Cassidy, is there?'

Dora nodded and smiled back. 'And I can't wait to see this fancy evening dress of Gloria's.'

Chapter Five

———◆◆◆◆———

By the time Saturday afternoon arrived Sal felt quite exhausted, although she wouldn't for the world admit it to anyone, least of all Harry. The whole house had been given a spring clean before the decorations had been put up and the furniture had been rearranged. Harry had set up the 'bar' in the kitchen with all the bottles and glasses and accountrements he would need. He had a good supply of beer, spirits and also many liqueurs for he specialized in making such cocktails as Singapore Slings, Black Russians, Blue Lagoons, Manhattans and many more. Gloria, Betty and Rose had helped Sal lay out the food, which had been delivered that morning by the various caterers. There was smoked salmon, Parma ham, venison and ham vol-au-vents, a variety of pâtés and cold meats, salads and canapés with shrimps and even caviar. There were fresh cream cakes, sherry trifle, fruit salad and fresh pineapple and peaches which had been delivered by Cooper's.

Harry had supervised them, making sure everything was laid out on the correct dishes and in the correct manner.

'Use more parsley for the garnish on that salmon, Betty, don't skimp,' he had instructed his daughter, before admonishing Gloria for not putting a fancy doily on the plate on which she was arranging the various crackers which were to accompany the variety of cheeses he himself had laid out on the cheeseboard.

Sal had heartily wished he would just go away and leave them alone; after all it would only be Sybil and Richard who would notice such things. The members of her family and the neighbours certainly wouldn't. She felt very relieved when everything had been done to his satisfaction and she went up to get washed and changed.

'He should remember that we haven't been trained to do stuff like that and neither has Mam,' Betty complained to Rose as they were getting changed in Betty's bedroom.

'But it all does look really nice, very fancy and posh, as usual,' Rose admitted as she pulled the dress she was wearing over her head. It was her best but it still looked a bit shabby even beside the plaid wool dress with the white broderie anglaise collar and cuffs that Betty had on. It would look awful compared to Gloria's frock.

'No one will care what it *looks* like. All everyone will want is for it to *taste* good,' Betty replied as she began to brush her thick short hair.

'Except your Aunt Sybil,' Rose reminded her.

Betty raised her eyes to the ceiling. 'I would enjoy myself more if she wasn't coming. I'm sure she watches me and I know she disapproves of everything I do and say.'

'Oh, don't let her put the mockers on things. We'll have a great time,' Rose replied, clipping back her hair with the fancy pink slide Betty had given her.

They were all ready and downstairs by half past seven. Gloria had persuaded Sal to let her go and have her hair set for the occasion and it had been finger waved which, with the ornate headband, made her look older.

'You really do look gorgeous, Gloria, very grown up. Doesn't she, Sal?' Dora said admiringly. Rose had escorted her next door and Sal had made sure she was seated in a comfortable chair that had been placed out of any potential draughts.

'I wasn't too sure about the hairdo at first,' Sal confided.

'I think it suits her,' Dora assured her. 'You're looking very nice yourself, Sal,' she added.

'Do you think these beads are a bit too much?' Sal asked, fiddling with the two long ropes of amber beads she'd put on for she'd felt her beige wool dress looked a bit plain.

'Mam, you look great and the beads just finish it off,' Gloria said.

Harry appeared, dressed as usual in a well-pressed suit, clean shirt and tie and highly polished shoes. He'd been doing a last-minute check of the drinks and glasses. 'They're real amber, not glass. I bought them in Lisbon,' he informed Dora.

'And you can tell, Harry. They really look smart.' Dora

smiled at Sal; she always enjoyed these parties: Harry certainly knew how to entertain, she had to give him that. The food was mouthwatering and she'd never even heard of some of the fancy drinks that were usually on offer, let alone tasted them. She was going to enjoy just sitting here and watching everyone: she wouldn't have missed it for the world. Usually she stayed until the end and helped Sal to clear up, but she didn't intend to stay too late tonight, she really wasn't feeling very well. The place looked lovely, she thought, with the Christmas tree and all the decorations, and there was a box of party hats and crackers, expensive ones too, she surmised. Harry wouldn't have anything he considered 'shoddy'.

Gloria was to be in charge of the gramophone, which would be used when her aunts Doris and Eileen were having a break from playing the piano. Both her mother's sisters were musical and played well and always took it in turns to provide the music at such functions. Her da always made sure they had the latest records and she was sorting them into some kind of order when Aunt Sybil and Uncle Richard arrived.

'Doesn't she look lovely, Sal? So elegant. Oh, I do like your hair, Gloria!' Sybil beamed at her niece before handing Betty her fur coat to take upstairs.

'Makes her look very grown up, don't you think? Now what would you like to drink? A cocktail?' Harry enquired. 'And for you, Richard?'

'Just a small Scotch for me Harry, please,' Richard Mostyn said affably. He couldn't honestly say he really liked his brother-in-law but they got on well enough – on the surface.

'I'll have a dry martini, Harry, if you have any olives,' Sybil said.

Sal could have hit her. Of course they damn well had olives and thinly sliced lemon and lime, ice, cocktail cherries and fancy cocktail sticks too. Pushing her annoyance to the back of her mind she went to open the door as more guests arrived.

'Do you think everyone's here now? I'm worn out running up and down with all the coats,' Betty said to Rose as they gazed at the pile of garments that now entirely covered her parents' bed.

'I hope so. Maybe we can get a drink now. I wouldn't mind some of that cherryade I saw in the kitchen.'

Betty nodded eagerly. 'I'll have some too and I hope it's not too long before we can eat. I'm starving. We only seem to have had sandwiches all day and some of the cakes look "divine", as our Gloria would say.'

'She looks "divine" too.' Rose giggled. 'But I can't say I like that frock your Aunt Sybil's got on.'

'I think it makes her look fat!' Betty rolled her eyes, thinking that the very wide black and white horizontal stripes of her aunt's long silk evening dress made her look bigger than she actually was.

Rose laughed out land. 'Let's hope your Auntie Doris doesn't go and say something like that to her. You know what she's like when she's had a few drinks.'

'Don't remind me! Do you think I'd better put Aunt

45

Sybil's fur coat in our Gloria's room? Just in case something awful happens to it?'

Rose nodded her agreement. 'We wouldn't want anyone to go off with it by mistake, not that it would be a mistake. No one else has got a fur coat.'

'Don't go saying anything like that downstairs, there'd be murder. I'll move it and then let's go down. We don't want to miss anything.'

The party was in full swing with Sal's sister Doris playing the piano enthusiastically. Some people were dancing and others were singing along to the old favourites Doris was playing. Great inroads had been made into the buffet, which had been voted the best they'd ever tasted, while Harry had been kept busy making the cocktails he'd urged many of his female guests to try. Gloria had basked in the numerous compliments she'd received and Sal was very relieved that things were going so well.

Rose and Betty had come to sit with Dora for as Betty admitted they were both suffering from the effects of far too many cakes and cherryade.

'Trust you to go and make a pig of yourself, Rose,' Dora said, shaking her head.

'Well, it's not often I get to eat so many cream cakes. It's a real treat for me to get just one,' Rose replied.

'Aunt Sybil made some comment to Mam about "greedy little girls" but Mam just laughed and said it was a celebration and everyone should enjoy themselves,' Betty informed them.

Dora didn't reply, she really wasn't feeling very well at

all. She kept going hot and then cold and she was finding it hard to breathe.

'Mam, are you all right? You don't look too well,' Rose asked, taking her mother's hand. 'You're freezing!' she exclaimed.

'One minute I'm shivering, the next I'm so hot,' Dora admitted.

Rose looked anxiously at Betty. 'Perhaps we should go home?'

'No. No, it's still very early,' Dora protested but only half-heartedly. She just wanted to crawl into her bed.

'I'll get Mam, see what she thinks,' Betty said, getting to her feet and going in search of Sal.

Sal was sitting talking to her sister Eileen but seeing Betty's anxious face she stopped. 'What's the matter? Do you feel sick? I don't wonder the way you've stuffed yourself.'

'No, it's not me. It's Rose's mam,' Betty replied.

'You know, Sal, I thought that woman looked far from well the minute I set eyes on her. She seems to have failed since I last saw her,' Eileen added.

Sal got up. 'She's had bronchitis and I don't think she's got over it.'

One look at Dora confirmed her suspicions. 'Dora, luv, I think we should get you home and to bed,' she announced.

'Shall I get Da to help you?' Betty asked.

'No. Leave him alone. Someone's got to look after the guests. We'll manage.'

Dora struggled to her feet and it was obvious that she really was ill. 'I . . . I've gone all dizzy,' she wheezed.

'Hold on to me and Rose. It's all been too much for you, Dora. The noise, the stuffiness in here, the cigarette smoke,' Sal said soothingly, thinking she really should have had more consideration for her friend's health.

'Do you think she should have the doctor again?' Rose asked. She was worried about her mother.

'He'd never come out at this time of night. If she's no better in the morning, we'll see,' Sal said.

'It's Sunday tomorrow. I can't be dragging the poor man out on a Sunday,' Dora gasped.

'Let's get you to bed and maybe after a night's sleep you'll feel better,' Sal urged. 'You'd better stay, Rose,' she added.

Rose nodded. She'd had no intention of going back to the party.

'I'll stay too, Mam,' Betty said firmly.

Sal nodded. 'Well, just for an hour or two, then you'd better come back home.'

'Mam, if Aunt Sybil wants to go home before I get back, her fur coat is in Gloria's room,' Betty called as her mother left. She didn't want her aunt making a scene if her coat couldn't be found.

The following morning Dora was no better, in fact Rose thought she was worse. Neither of them had had much sleep for the party had gone on until the early hours of the morning. She knew no one would be up early in Betty's house so she waited impatiently until ten o'clock before she ventured next door.

Sal was sitting in the living room in her dressing gown

with a cup of tea. The room was very untidy and reeked of stale cigarette smoke and drink. What little remained of the buffet was still on the table and the top of the sideboard.

'I knew I shouldn't have let Harry persuade me to have that nightcap. How's your mam, Rose?' Sal asked. Her head was thumping and she wasn't looking forward to all the cleaning up.

'She's no better, Mrs Jenkins. She didn't get much sleep. I've got her propped up with pillows, she can't breathe properly.'

Sal was concerned. 'I think we should get the doctor out, Rose. This has gone on too long.'

'Shall I go down to the phone box?' Rose asked although she was secretly afraid that they wouldn't take her seriously enough.

Sal got to her feet. 'No. I'll go. I wish to God they'd get a move on installing our phone. We could have done with it now. You go back to her and tell her I'm calling the doctor out.'

Rose had tidied up and made sure her mother was comfortable by the time Sal, now dressed and with her hair combed, came back accompanied by Betty.

'Is he coming?' Rose asked.

Sal nodded. 'He wasn't too pleased but I insisted. I said she shouldn't be left until tomorrow. I'll go back in and get the rest of them up but when he arrives you come for me, Betty,' she instructed her daughter.

Dr Foreshaw had had plans for this morning and he wasn't particularly pleased to have to cancel them.

'She just hasn't got any better at all, in fact she's worse,' Sal informed him as he examined Dora and took her temperature. She was very worried about her friend. She'd never seen Dora look so ill.

The doctor sighed. 'She's been taxing her strength too much. I'm afraid I think it's turned to pneumonia. You need to keep her warm. I'll leave you some medicine for her and I'll call again in the morning. If there's no improvement by then I'm afraid she'll have to go to hospital.'

'Oh, Mam!' Rose cried and Sal put her arm around the child's shoulder.

'Now, Rose, luv, don't go getting upset. You know we'll do everything that's best for her. You see Dr Foreshaw out.' She turned to the doctor. 'I'll see to her now and will you send your bill to me, please?'

When they'd left the room she helped Dora to sit up and gave her some of the medicine. 'Don't worry, Dora. Just rest as much as you can. I'll see to everything and Rose.'

Dora clutched her hand. 'Don't let him send me to hospital, Sal, please? I hate those places,' she begged.

'Don't go getting upset, luv. I'm sure it won't come to that. If necessary I'll come and stay here and nurse you,' Sal promised.

Dora looked agitated. 'But Harry . . . and it's Christmas.'

'To hell with Harry! He can put himself out for once,' Sal said firmly.

When she informed him of her intention to stay next door and nurse Dora, Harry was far from pleased. 'The woman's not at death's door, Sal! And if she's that bad then

I agree with Dr Foreshaw, hospital is the best place for her.'

'She won't go and I'm not going to tell her she should. With you away for so long she's become more than just a neighbour. She's been a good friend to me over the years, Harry. I think it's the least I can do and it will only be for a few days – or would you sooner I brought her in here? I could put her in Gloria's room and put Gloria in with Betty and we'd sort something out for Rose. I intended to have them both here for all their meals over the holiday anyway.'

Harry looked horrified at this suggestion. It would totally disrupt the household. 'No! No, I think it best if you stay there. The girls will cope here, as long as it doesn't drag on.'

Sal nodded. 'Right then. Get those two to start cleaning up and I'll get a few things together. If you need anything Harry, send one of them in to ask me. I would be very grateful if you could take some coal next door for me though. She really needs a fire in that bedroom, it's freezing.'

He nodded, feeling cross and put out. A fine Christmas this was going to be, he thought.

Chapter Six

———◆·◆———

WHEN THE DOCTOR CALLED the following morning Dora absolutely refused to go to hospital and at last, when his patience was exhausted, Dr Foreshaw agreed she could stay at home, providing she got proper care and attention. Sal informed him firmly that she would see to that so he left, promising to come back the next day. Despite Harry's annoyance at the situation Sal knew that he didn't object to paying the five shillings per visit the doctor charged. Rose was very relieved and thankful that Sal was staying; her mam had never been ill for this long before.

Betty and Gloria both made a big effort to keep the routine of the house as normal as Sal would have done for they were both aware that their father was far from happy with the situation and that didn't bode well.

'You take him Christmas shopping over the next few

days, Gloria. Rose's mam might be much better with Mam nursing her and I'll ask Mam what I can do about getting the Christmas dinner sorted out,' Betty suggested.

Gloria had readily agreed. She enjoyed shopping and in the few days left before the holiday the atmosphere in town was great. It seemed to have had a good effect on Harry's mood too, she thought as they boarded the tram laden down with parcels. For most of the journey home they had been entertained by the lively repartee between the conductor and some of his passengers who had obviously been 'celebrating' a bit early.

'You know, wherever you go in the world you always seem to find a Scouser with a dry sense of humour,' Harry said, laughing at the acerbic comments on husbands in general, and her own in particular, expressed by one of the flower sellers from Clayton Square who was on her way home.

'I suppose that's because so many men and boys from this city go away to sea,' Gloria had replied. Ships sailed for every part of the world from Liverpool. 'Do you think perhaps our Betty would like to go away to sea when she's older?' she mused.

'I doubt it. She's too much of a home bird to leave your mam and besides she's a bit too outspoken and independent to make a good stewardess. No, we'll have to think about something else for Betty,' he'd said.

Betty had been getting her list of instructions from Sal regarding the Christmas dinner.

'The turkey will be delivered by the butcher tomorrow

morning along with the sausages. If you bring it in here to me I'll stuff it and then you can take it back to cook.'

'What about the veg and potatoes? And what do I do with the pudding?' It was all a bit daunting for Betty but she was determined to make the best of it.

Sal was beginning to think it would have been easier for her to have nursed Dora in their house but she knew Harry wouldn't hear of it, especially not now that it was Christmas Eve tomorrow.

'We'll manage, Mam,' Betty promised. 'Rose will help me and our Gloria's doing her best.'

Sal nodded. 'Maybe Dora'll be well enough to come down for an hour on Christmas Day, just for her dinner,' she mused, although she didn't hold out much hope of that. Dora seemed very weak, even sitting up was an effort.

The following morning Dora was no better and the doctor firmly dismissed any idea that she might get up or be moved at all. After he'd gone Sal knew she had to make some sort of decision so she sent Rose to tell Harry she wanted to see him.

'I don't honestly know how we're going to manage tomorrow, Harry. She's no better and the doctor has forbidden her to get up, even for an hour. In fact he said she shouldn't be moved at all.'

Harry frowned. Things were going from bad to worse in his opinion. He was certain that the girls couldn't manage to prepare and cook a decent Christmas lunch. The house was untidy and this morning, to his utter chagrin, he'd found that for the first time since as far back as he could remember he didn't have a clean shirt to put on. 'I think, Sal, we should have another talk to Dr Foreshaw about her going into hospital. If she's not getting any better it's obvious that that's where she should be. You've been goodness itself to her, Sal, I have to say that, but you're not a trained nurse. He'll have to put his foot down. It's for her own good.'

Sal bit her lip, for there was some truth in what he said. 'I'm not having her upset, Harry, it will only make her worse, and she will be if she's carted off to hospital. Especially now on Christmas Eve.'

'Well, what *are* we going to do then? Those girls are doing their best but the lunch is going to be a disaster and you should see the mess in the kitchen! And I've no clean shirts,' he said petulantly.

'For heaven's sake, Harry! There are more important things than clean shirts and untidy kitchens,' she snapped. 'We have to do *something* to try and make tomorrow a special day for everyone. I can pop in and out and supervise things.'

Seeing she wasn't going to budge on the matter of Dora going to hospital, which to him seemed the only possible and sensible solution, he lost his temper. 'How can it be "special" with the lunch a disaster in the making, the place resembling a pig sty, the girls exhausted and miserable and you stuck in here? It won't even be a *family* occasion, not without you.'

'Just what am I supposed to do, Harry? Leave the poor woman alone and ill on Christmas Day? That's a very charitable thing to do, I must say! I'm sure God would be delighted to know that *that's* how we're celebrating the birthday of His son.'

He ignored the barb. 'She won't be alone. She'll have Rose and it will only be for a few hours.'

Sal was becoming increasingly angry herself. 'I had planned for that poor child to have her dinner with you and the girls.'

Harry glared at her. Because Dora Cassidy was hell bent on remaining so stubborn over a totally irrational fear of hospitals, everyone's Christmas was to be ruined. 'Well, if that's your attitude, Sal, stay in here and wait on her, don't worry at all about your own family! I'm going to phone Sybil. I'm sure when I've explained she'll have myself and the girls for Christmas lunch. We'll take the presents and open them there,' he snapped before turning on his heel and storming out.

She sighed heavily. There would be a huge row; she could see it coming. Sybil wouldn't be very happy about having last-minute and uninvited guests to start with, nor about having both her nieces – Sybil had, to Sal's fury, said that she just couldn't 'take' to Betty, she was untidy, ill-mannered and outspoken. Well, Sal refuted the latter two, but very probably Betty would refuse to go.

Oh, what a mess, she thought. Just for once couldn't Harry have made an effort to help the girls with the meal and welcomed Rose too instead of carrying on like this? So what if the meal wasn't perfect or the place was untidy, did it really matter? She just couldn't leave Dora on her own. Dora was her best friend – in fact she was the only person to whom Sal had ever confided the hurt and annoyance she felt at Sybil's dislike of Betty. Dora was very poorly indeed and she really was terrified of going to hospital. Dora had explained to Sal that her fear was all to do with having to go to Walton Hospital when Bill had been rushed there after the accident and watch him die there.

It wasn't long before Betty came rushing in, tears streaming down her cheeks. 'Mam! Mam! He belted me! I told him I wasn't going to Aunt Sybil's tomorrow. It will be *horrible*! I told him that and I said I hated going there and I hate her too! And he . . . he roared at me and he hit me,' Betty sobbed.

Sal took her in her arms. She was furious with him for taking his temper out on the child although Betty had obviously provoked him with her outburst. 'Oh, come here to me, luv. I know you don't want to go and he shouldn't have hit you. Mind you, you shouldn't have said you hated her. You shouldn't *hate* anyone.'

'She hates me, Mam. You know she does!' Betty cried.

'She doesn't. Oh, I know Gloria is her favourite but she doesn't hate you. Now, dry your eyes. I'll have a talk to him.'

'But will I still have to go?' Betty pleaded.

'Yes you will, luv. It's bad enough me not being able to be with you but if you don't go then the family will be even more divided.'

'What about Rose? She was going to come in to us.' Betty couldn't see why they had to go to Aunt Sybil's at all. They would have managed and it was only for one day, it was just one meal. She couldn't understand why her da was making such a huge fuss or why he was so angry.

'Rose will have her dinner with her mam and me. I'll cook it in here. Now, be sensible, luv. Go and make sure you have a clean dress for tomorrow and ask Gloria to wash a couple of your da's shirts. They'll be dry by tonight and then I'll iron them.' She ruffled her daughter's hair affectionately. 'It won't be that bad. Uncle Richard will be there too and you like him. He doesn't give himself all the airs and graces your aunt does.'

Betty nodded sulkily. She wished she could have stayed and had her dinner with Mam and Rose and Mrs Cassidy, although she didn't think Rose's mam would be eating all that much.

It hadn't been quite as bad as she'd anticipated, Betty thought as Uncle Richard drove them home the following evening. Her da seemed to have got over his bad-tempered outburst and when they'd arrived he'd laughed and wished them 'Happy Christmas' and kissed his sister on the cheek. Aunt Sybil's large lounge, as she called the living room, had looked lovely with very elegant decorations and a huge Christmas tree set in the bay window. Her da had congratulated her aunt on the dining table, saying the centrepiece was very tasteful, and the meal had been really great. Both she and Gloria had been allowed a small glass of champagne, which she hadn't really liked but which her da said was of an excellent vintage, whatever that meant. She had missed her mam but then they'd opened their presents and Aunt Sybil had actually bought her something she liked, which was unusual. It was a beautiful leather-bound copy of *What Katy*

Did, which was one of her favourite books. After that she
and Gloria had been allowed to sit in the morning room and
listen to the wireless, play the gramophone and look through
old photograph albums while the adults had stayed in the
lounge, chatting and drinking cocktails with some of her
aunt and uncle's neighbours who had called in.

When they finally arrived home the house was in darkness
but lights burned next door.

'Should we go and see Mam first?' Betty suggested.

'Yes, let's go and tell her all about our day,' Gloria agreed,
pulling her father in the direction of Dora's house.

'Have you had a nice quiet day, Mam?' Betty asked as
she hugged her mother.

Sal smiled. 'Yes. Rose and I have been playing all kinds
of board games.'

'We had a really lovely day. Aunt Sybil even let us have a
glass of champagne,' Gloria informed her.

'What, both of you?' Sal asked, looking at Harry, who
thankfully seemed to be in a far better humour.

'Both of them, although I think it was wasted on Betty,'
he replied affably.

'The bubbles get up your nose,' Betty said, pulling a face.
'How is your mam?' she asked Rose.

'Last time I went up to her she was sleeping fitfully,' Sal
replied, getting to her feet. 'In fact I think I'd better go up
and check on her.'

As she went upstairs she felt relieved that the day with
Sybil seemed to have gone well; even Betty hadn't complained. Dora was lying propped up with pillows and looked

to still be asleep. The room was warm thanks to the fire that burned in the small fireplace and was lit only by the bedside lamp.

'Dora, luv, are you asleep?' Sal said quietly, placing her hand gently on her friend's forehead. It was clammy.

Dora turned her head and struggled to say something but Sal was seriously worried by the strange gurgling sound she made.

'What is it, Dora? Do you feel worse?'

Dora reached out for Sal's hand. 'Sal . . . Sal . . . I'm not going . . . to . . . make it. I . . . I feel as if I'm sinking . . .'

'Dora! Don't talk like that!' Sal was now very worried indeed. Maybe she should have taken more notice of both Harry and the doctor. She'd seen enough of death in the past to realise that Dora was failing fast. All the signs were there.

'Rose. Look after . . . Rose . . . for me.' Dora could barely get the words out.

With a terrible feeling of shock and despair Sal realised that Dora was dying. What had started as bronchitis had turned to pneumonia, and pneumonia was a killer. 'Dora, luv, don't try to talk. Save your strength. Of course I'll look after Rose,' she pleaded.

'Rose . . .'

Sal rushed to the bedroom door and shouted for Harry to come up.

Realising by the urgency and hint of hysteria in her voice that something was very wrong, Harry took the stairs two at a time.

'Harry, for God's sake phone for an ambulance!' she

begged. 'I think she's going to die. You'd better send Rose up,' she added breathlessly before hurrying back into the room.

Harry quickly ran downstairs and after a quick word with Rose went next door to phone for an ambulance.

Sal sat beside the bed, holding Dora's hand, the tears falling slowly down her cheeks. She'd done her best but it hadn't been enough. Dora had been weakened by years of worry and stress, trying to making ends meet, and by not being able to afford to eat well or heat the house properly and she hadn't been able to fight off the illness. Now her dear friend was slipping away from her. Dora had been her friend, companion, confidante and shoulder to cry on for so long that she didn't know what she would do without her. When Harry went back to sea she would miss Dora terribly and poor Rose, how was she going to tell the child? And on Christmas Day too. Christmas from now on would be a time of such sadness for both Rose and herself.

Rose and Betty had crept up the stairs and when she'd caught sight of them Sal had beckoned to Rose to come closer. Betty had remained standing in the doorway, too shocked to take everything in.

Sal put her arms around Rose who had started to cry.

'What's wrong?' Rose wailed.

'She's not going to suffer any more, Rose. It's just as if she . . . she's going to sleep. She's very tired,' Sal tried to comfort the child, fighting back her own tears.

Rose couldn't believe it. Just a few hours ago she had been up to see her mam and she had smiled and asked what she was doing. She had been downstairs playing Ludo and Snake and Ladders while all the time Mam had been getting worse. 'Will . . . will they take her to hospital now?' she sobbed.

Sal shook her head. 'No, luv. I don't think so. I don't think there will be time. But hold her hand, Rose, and tell her how much you love her.'

Rose grasped Dora's clammy hand tightly in her own; she was trembling so much she could hardly get the words out. 'Mam . . . Mam, I . . . love . . . you. Don't . . . go, don't . . . go, Mam!'

Harry came up and took a stunned Betty downstairs but by the time they heard the clanging of the ambulance bell he knew it was too late. Dora Cassidy had breathed her last.

Chapter Seven

‒⊷⊷◦⊷‒

No one got much sleep that night and Betty thought it was one of the worst times in her life. She was very upset but she tried her best to comfort a heart-broken Rose. Sal had insisted that Rose stay with them. She hadn't wanted to; she'd wanted to stay with her mother.

'There's nothing you can do for her now, luv. She . . . she's gone to be with your da, she's happy and at peace,' Sal had said, leading the weeping child downstairs. She knew that the doctor would have to be called to sign the death certificate and then the undertakers would arrive and she didn't want Rose to have to see all that.

Sal felt drained and exhausted with shock and grief, yet she knew she had to try to keep some semblance of a routine. At least Harry was being helpful and considerate, she thought as, after they'd got the girls upstairs to bed, he brought her a cup of tea to which he'd added a drop of brandy.

'To help steady you,' he told her. 'Things will be better after we get today over, Sal,' he said. He'd never envisaged that Dora would die. People often recovered from pneumonia, especially those who weren't old.

'I wish I could believe that, Harry, I really do. There's the funeral to arrange.'

'I'll deal with the doctor and the undertakers. You'll have your work cut out with the girls. I don't suppose she had any kind of burial fund or insurance so we'll have to take care of the expenses too.'

'That's generous of you, Harry. She couldn't afford to pay into anything like that. You know how she had to scrimp and save and do without herself. She ate like a bird and that . . . that's what helped to kill her. She had no stamina.'

He nodded. He really did hate to see Sal so upset. 'Well, we couldn't do much about that but at least she won't have a pauper's burial.'

Sal sipped her tea and dabbed at her swollen eyes again. 'I couldn't let that happen to her even if I have to pawn all my jewellery. I really will miss her terribly, Harry.'

He nodded. 'I suppose you will, Sal. It's only natural.' He paused. 'I don't suppose you've had time to think about young Rose yet?'

She looked at him, not really understanding what he meant. 'Rose? What about Rose?'

'About what's going to happen to her now?'

'I promised Dora I'd look after her, Harry. The child has

no one else, except two distant cousins she's never even seen. She'll have to live here with us. Where else can she go?'

He nodded slowly. He'd have to keep Rose for the next few years until she started work. He wasn't very happy about that but there was nothing he could say. 'Of course. You realise that once we get the funeral over, and it will probably be delayed because of the holiday, I'll be due to sail again.'

'I know,' she replied, thinking how quickly the time had gone.

The funeral was indeed delayed and Sal was worried that the postponenent of over a week would have an adverse effect on young Rose. Once it was over and done with she felt the child could start to try to look forward. Obviously it was going to take a long time for Rose to get over her grief and loss. For the most part Rose still seemed dazed, unable to take it in, disorientated, listless and confused, but at night the realisation would hit her and she sobbed until she was exhausted and finally slept.

It wasn't easy for Sal to accept either. It had come as such a shock and there was so much to remind her of Dora. Still to come was the awful task of getting rid of all Dora's things, including the home her friend had struggled so hard to maintain. She couldn't subject poor Rose to that. She would keep a few small pieces for she was sure Rose would want them later on in her life, but most of the furniture would have to go. She had no room for it and it would cost too much to put into storage. The house, like their own, was only rented so it would have to be emptied before new tenants arrived and the landlord wouldn't want to leave it empty for very long. Her head ached when she thought of it all and Harry wouldn't be here to help either. She'd have to do it all on her own.

On the day of the funeral they dressed in their best clothes, with black armbands sewn around the sleeves of their coats. Both Betty and Rose were very near to breaking down in tears again.

'I still can't really believe it, Betty. It's just like a bad dream. I keep thinking that any minute she'll come in through the door looking for me. Asking me why I've been out so long.'

Betty nodded miserably. 'I know. But Mam says that after . . . after today, it should get better. We can all settle down then.'

'Do you really believe her?' Rose asked with a note of hope in her voice. Mrs Jenkins, or 'Aunty Sal' as Betty's mam had said she must now call her, had been so good to her. She'd held her in her arms when she cried and had reassured her that her mam was happy and at peace and that she wasn't to worry about anything.

Betty shook her head. 'I think it's going to take a long time, Rose. But at least I'll be here to help you get through it. We'll be going back to school soon and our Gloria will be starting work and Da will have sailed. Let's just try and get through today.' She took Rose's hand and squeezed it but after a moment found she was hugging her friend tightly as they both sobbed. It was some time before they both went downstairs.

Sal felt the day would never end. She couldn't hold back her tears and her heart had never felt so heavy as when she'd watched Dora's coffin being lowered into the ground. She already missed her terribly. It had been a very nice service though and the minister had spoken well of Dora. There had been wreaths from many of the neighbours as well as the one from Rose and themselves. Her friend was to have a decent headstone and she would make sure that Bill Cassidy's name was put on it too. It was something Dora had never been able to afford, to her great sorrow. In time it might help Rose knowing that both her parents were remembered in this way. She'd held the child close to her as she'd cried at the graveside and Betty had then taken Rose's hand to lead her back to the waiting car.

When they got back to the house Sal had sat Rose down and had taken her hands. 'You're going to live with us, Rose. This is your home now and I'm going to look after you. You're not to worry about anything, Uncle Harry will move all your things in here and you will be sharing a room with Betty. Things will get better in time, luv, I promise.'

Rose had nodded slowly, her eyes still red and puffy. 'But . . .'

Sal had gathered her in her arms. 'I promised your poor mam I'd take care of you, Rose, and I will. You're like another daughter to me, I wouldn't . . . *couldn't* let you go to strangers. You know that, luv. Now, dry your eyes and we'll all have a cup of tea and then you and Betty can start to sort that room out.'

She'd been grateful for Harry's support even though she

knew his mind was occupied with his imminent departure. He would have to report for duty early next morning and the following day he would sail. She would go to see him off and then she would have to start sorting out Dora's things. She felt bowed down with the immensity of the task but somehow she would cope. She always did.

It was a cold, grey January morning when Sal went to see Harry off. She had her usual cup of tea with him but not in the lounge this time; they were in his cabin as there were passengers aboard. She never lingered long for he was always busy on sailing day but today her stay was even shorter than usual.

'You'll be all right?' he asked.

'Of course I will. Take care of yourself, Harry.' There wasn't the formality of the 'Henry' and 'Sarah' charade. They were alone so there was no one to observe them.

'You've got the addresses of the shipping agents? Write and let me know how things are going. How Rose is settling down and how Gloria is getting on in the job.'

She nodded and kissed him on the cheek.

'I might even telephone you from Lisbon, now we've finally got our own phone,' he added, trying to lighten the atmosphere a little.

'You might have difficulty getting through, it's so far away, so don't worry if you can't. I'd better go now. I know you have a million and one things to see to.'

He accompanied her to the gangway where the taxi waited and waved as she got in. Then he turned away. He breathed deeply; the familiar odours of furniture polish mingled with the perfume from the fresh flower arrangements and the aroma of the coffee wafting from the lounge made him feel much better. What with one thing and another his leave had been rather fraught.

The next few days were hectic for Sal too as she got the girls back to school and Gloria off to start her new job. Then she steeled herself for what she knew would be the upsetting task of sorting out Dora's things. She'd chosen a few small pieces of furniture to keep and had then contacted a second-hand furniture company. They'd come and assessed all the rest and offered her an amount, a very small amount. She'd had no alternative but to accept it and she'd opened a Post Office savings account for Rose with it. A house clearance firm had taken the curtains and bedding and the kitchen things. She'd spent one afternoon going through old photographs and some letters from Bill that Dora had kept. She'd found them in a battered biscuit tin and with them she'd found a pawn ticket. It was from Stanley's on Scotland Road and was for a gold locket and chain and a pair of gold earrings. The date on the ticket had long expired. Sal hadn't been able to stop the tears then. 'Oh, Dora! Why didn't you tell me? It was the only bit of jewellery you had and it should have gone to Rose, she would have liked it. I would have given you the money, you know I would,' she'd said quietly to herself but she realised that Dora had had her pride too. Stanley's was miles away from here; Dora must have made a special journey to take the items. She'd put the photographs and letters together in the box to keep for Rose. Dora's few clothes had been donated to the Salvation Army. She was so relieved when it was all over for she'd never in her life done anything that had upset her so much. She'd managed to put a brave face on it all for the girls' sake but at night she felt utterly miserable and very alone.

Chapter Eight

———

1926

IT WAS THE FOLLOWING week when the new neighbours arrived. Sal had seen the van pull up outside the house next door but she hadn't gone out to speak to them as she would normally have done. It was hard to see another family moving into what she still thought of as 'Dora's' house.

Betty and Rose were also a bit taken aback to see the van as they walked down the road on their way home from school.

'It just seems so *odd*. Someone else moving into our house,' Rose said with a catch in her voice.

'Our house is your home now, Rose, I expect in time you'll get used to it.' Betty was trying to encourage her friend to look on the bright side of things.

'Who are they, Mam? Have you spoken to them yet?'

Betty asked as she and Rose went into the kitchen.

'I don't know. I've seen a woman and a man and I think there are two lads but I haven't spoken to any of them,' Sal replied. 'It must be a bit unsettling for you, Rose,' she added.

Rose nodded. 'I'll get used to it though. This is my home now.'

Sal smiled at her. 'Good girl. Now, we'll have a cup of tea and a slice of currant cake. That will put us on until Gloria gets in and then we'll have our supper.'

They were all seated around the kitchen table when there was a knock on the back door.

'That's got to be one of them. Shall I go, Mam?' Betty asked.

Sal shook her head, getting to her feet. 'No. We're going to have to get to know them sometime so I suppose sooner would be better than later.'

She opened the door to find a small, plump woman with fair curly hair and blue eyes, about the same age as herself, standing outside on the step.

'Sorry to disturb you, but I'm Elsie Taylor. We've just moved in next door and this is the first spare minute I've had, so I thought I'd come and introduce myself.'

She seemed pleasant enough, Sal thought as she smiled at her. 'Hello. I'm Sal Jenkins. Will you come in? We're just having a cup of tea and you're welcome to join us. It's such an upheaval moving house. You must be worn out.'

Elsie Taylor followed her inside and smiled at the two girls who were eyeing her curiously.

'This is Mrs Taylor, she's moved in next door,' Sal announced, getting out another cup and saucer. 'This is Rose and my youngest daughter Betty. Gloria, my other girl, is at work.'

The two girls said a polite 'Hello' and Betty cut another slice of cake while Sal poured the tea.

'I've two lads myself. Arthur, "Artie" as we call him, is seventeen and our Brian is thirteen,' their new neighbour informed them.

'Then he's just a year younger than these two,' Sal replied. 'Our Gloria is sixteen.'

Betty got up. 'Mam, if you don't mind, Rose and I will go and do our homework. We've got English and Maths to do.'

Sal nodded. She knew Betty was thinking of Rose and she could fully understand that Rose wouldn't want to sit and listen to the details of the family who had moved into her old home, at least not yet.

'Aren't they good? I wish I could get our Brian to do his homework without me having to nag him to death,' Elsie Taylor commented.

'They're not bad. I suppose you are all still at sixes and sevens?'

Elsie Taylor nodded. 'I can't find half the things I need. I said to George, my husband, it will take me weeks to get straight. Mind you, I'll be better off doing it on my own. Those two lads have been more of a hindrance than a help. George and Artie will be back at work tomorrow and our Brian is going to school. I can't stick another day with him under my feet.'

'What do they do, your husband and son?' Sal asked, pouring herself another cup of tea.

'They both work on the railway. George is a driver and Artie is an apprentice mechanic. George put in a word for him. I'm grateful they've both got good, steady jobs. There's so many unemployed these days. God knows what Brian is going to do when he leaves school, that lad can't seem to stick at anything. All he's interested in is kicking a football around.'

'He's only young yet. He'll settle down,' Sal said.

'I hope that our moving here will do him good. It's a much nicer neighbourhood than the one we've left. Some of the kids there were right little hooligans and he's too easily led.'

'It is nice here. It's quiet but people are friendly,' Sal agreed.

'What does . . . Gloria, was it? What does she do?'

'She's a clerk in the Inland Revenue offices. She's only been there a week.'

Elsie Taylor raised her eyebrows. That was a good job and not easy to come by. 'Does she like it?'

Sal refilled the woman's cup. 'She's settling in well, so she says.'

'Is Mr Jenkins in work?'

Sal nodded. 'He's a Chief Steward with the Porto-Brasilia Line. He's just sailed on the *Amazonia*. He'll be away for almost nine months. They go to South America and back.'

Elsie thought George would be disappointed that there wouldn't be a man to chat to next door or maybe go for a pint with once a week. 'That's a long time to be away. Don't you get lonely?'

Sal shook her head 'No. He's always gone away to sea. I'm used to it now but this time it will be a bit different for me. I won't have Dora. She lived next door.'

Elsie Taylor instantly looked sympathetic. 'I heard she died, poor soul, and she was a widow too, I believe.'

'She was. Rose is her daughter. I promised Dora I'd look after her.'

Sal Jenkins rose greatly in Elsie's estimation. 'That really was good of you. I mean you've your own girls to see to and it's not easy bringing kids up these days.'

'Betty and Rose have always been friends and Dora was a very good friend to me. Always ready to help out in times of trouble.'

'Well, I can tell you now that you can always rely on George and me for help should you need it. I really mean that.'

Sal smiled at her. 'That's very good of you, Elsie, and if there's anything I can do to help you get settled in, you've only to ask.'

Elsie smiled back. 'I think we're going to get on like a house on fire, Sal.'

When Gloria arrived home from work she took off her hat, coat and the jacket of her costume, took them upstairs and put them away. She brushed her hair, studying herself closely in the mirror. She certainly felt more grown up than she did when she'd first started work. That first day she'd felt totally out of her depth but she'd found her colleagues to be friendly and helpful and now she at least knew where everything was kept, although she was still trying to get to grips with the filing system. No doubt she'd master it in time. Giving her short bob a last flick with the brush she went down. Betty and Rose were already sitting at the table and Sal was putting out the evening meal.

'I'm starving, Mam. That smells great.'

Sal smiled at her, thinking Gloria looked very smart in the grey skirt and the cherry-red long-line jumper, set off by the long rope of black beads. 'Don't you eat at lunchtime? You're always starving.'

'I just have a cup of tea and a couple of biscuits,' Gloria replied.

Sal tutted. 'You need more than that to keep you going, especially these cold winter days. You'll get run down,' she reprimanded her, thinking of Dora.

'I'll put on weight if I do nothing but eat all day, I haven't got what you would call an energetic job, and Aunt Sybil says these modern styles look awful on fat people. You need a slim figure to show them to their best advantage.'

'You take far too much notice of what Sybil has to say and sometimes she talks utter nonsense. You're a growing girl and you need to eat properly,' Sal said curtly.

Gloria changed the subject. 'I see the new neighbours have moved in. What are they like?'

'I've only met Mrs Taylor, Elsie, but she's very nice. I think we'll get on well. She's got two sons.'

'Really?' Gloria looked interested.

'I saw the youngest one piling some tea chests in the yard,' Betty informed them.

'That would be Brian; he's a bit younger than you and Rose. Elsie hopes now they've moved he'll settle down.'

Betty and Rose exchanged glances. From their bedroom window they'd seen him carelessly dumping the empty chests into a corner of the yard. 'I've no intention of speaking to that Brian, he looks awful,' Betty announced.

'You're bound to see him at school,' Gloria reminded her.

'I won't. The boys' part of the school is separate to ours, even the playground, as well you know,' Betty retorted.

'Mr Taylor works on the railway, he's a driver,' Sal interrupted.

'What about the other one?' Betty enquired.

'He's an apprentice mechanic. His name is Arthur, they call him "Artie" and that's pretty much all I know about him, except he's seventeen.'

'I wonder if Mr Taylor will get on well with Da, when he's home that is,' Betty mused.

'He's bound to, nearly everyone gets on well with Da,' Gloria replied.

'I told Elsie that your da is away now for nine months and by the time he gets home we should know the Taylor family much better. So let's just get on with our meal,' Sal said firmly.

After the meal Betty and Rose were putting away the dishes and Sal was about to get out her sewing basket to put a few stitches in the hem of Betty's school skirt, which was coming down, so it was left to Gloria to answer the knock on the back door.

'Oh, hello,' she greeted the fair-haired boy who stood there looking a bit embarrassed.

'Hello. Er . . . I'm Artie from next door. My mam sent me to ask your mam if . . .'

'Who is it, Gloria?' Sal called. The draught from the open door was making the fire smoke. 'For heaven's sake bring them in and shut the door before we're all choked with the smoke from this fire.'

Gloria ushered him in. 'It's Artie Taylor, Mam.'

'Hello, lad. Can I help?' Sal asked.

'Mam said have you a frying pan she could borrow just for tonight? She can't find ours. She'll bring it back in the morning. Clean, like.' He looked at Sal helplessly. He hadn't wanted to come but his mam had insisted. It sounded so pathetic, he thought, not being able to find something as big as a pan.

'Of course. Betty, bring the frying pan out here, luv,' she called.

Gloria was studying him closely. He was quite a good-looking boy, she thought. His hair waved naturally, he had blue eyes and he was tall and slim. Of course he was obviously embarrassed at having to undertake an errand better suited to his younger brother but he seemed pleasant.

'Haven't we got a bag or something to put it in? He doesn't want to go walking around carrying a pan, do you, Artie?' she said, taking the pan from Betty and smiling at him.

'He's only going next door and he's not going around the front way, Gloria,' Betty said flatly.

'It's all right, really it is. I don't need a bag or anything, but thanks for thinking about it, Gloria,' he replied. He felt such a fool and she'd realised it and had been trying to put him at ease. He smiled at her. She was a very pretty girl with that thick dark hair and big brown eyes and she was so stylishly dressed too. He was very glad now that they'd moved here and that his mam had sent him on this errand.

Gloria blushed and smiled back. When he smiled he really was very good-looking and she decided she liked him. She hoped they would get to know each other better.

Sal looked at them both speculatively. 'Right, you'd better get back, Artie, or you'll all be getting your supper when it's time to go to bed. Tell your mam I'll see her in the morning. I'll be going to do my shopping so she can come with me if she likes?'

Reluctantly he tore his gaze away from Gloria. 'I'll tell her, Mrs Jenkins, and . . . er . . . thanks.'

'Goodnight, Artie,' Gloria said a little coyly as he left.

'Seems a nice enough lad,' Sal remarked.

'I thought he was very nice, Mam. A bit shy but . . . nice,' Gloria said.

Betty glanced at Rose. 'I hope you're not going to get all soppy about him,' she said.

Rose stifled a giggle.

'That will do, the pair of you. Have you finished your homework? If not you'd better get on with it,' Sal instructed firmly. It looked as though Gloria had taken a liking to the lad but of course they were both very young, she thought. Still, it was the first time since Dora's death that she'd heard Rose giggle, even if it had been in response to Betty's teasing. It looked as if the Taylor family was going to fit in well here. She certainly hoped so.

A week later Artie plucked up the courage to ask Gloria out. He caught up with her as she was walking home from the tram stop. Of course he'd seen her a couple of times since they'd moved in and she'd always stopped to chat and the more he got to know her, the more he felt drawn to her. She was so pleasant and vivacious, always smiling and laughing, and he especially liked the way her dark eyes sparkled when she smiled at him. Her smile made his heart turn over. He'd never met anyone quite like her before.

'Busy day, Gloria?' he asked, falling into step beside her.

She nodded. 'I think I've finally mastered the filing system, which I have to say is a bit complicated. You wouldn't believe the amount of stuff that has to be filed, Artie.'

'I suppose it's only natural, them dealing with all the tax forms and things. I . . . I was wondering, Gloria, if you'd like to go out on Saturday night, with me? We could go to the cinema or a dance.'

She looked up at him and smiled. She'd been hoping he would ask her out, she really did like him. 'I'd love to, Artie.' She felt a little flutter of excitement as he smiled back. It was the first time anyone had asked her out.

'I think there might be a dance on at the Aintree

Institute . . .' he suggested tentatively, thinking she might prefer to go dancing.

'If you don't mind, I think the cinema would be just fine. Mam might think I'm a bit too young to go to the institute.' She was aware that Sal probably wouldn't raise any objection at all but she didn't want to spend the evening on a crowded dance floor, she wanted to get to know him better.

They had reached Gloria's house. 'I'll find out what's on then and we can go to either the Palace, the Walton Vale or the Rio. Shall I call for you about seven?' Artie asked.

'Seven would be perfect. I'll look forward to it, Artie.'

'So will I, Gloria,' Artie replied happily.

Artie decided on the Palace as the other two cinemas were showing westerns and he was sure she wouldn't want to watch them. She looked very smart and attractive in a royal-blue coat and matching hat.

'You look . . . lovely, Gloria. That colour suits you,' he said a little shyly as she came to the door.

'Thanks,' she answered, her cheeks flushing at the compliment.

He paid for decent seats and bought some sweets and as she relaxed into the seat and the lights dimmed he reached for her hand. She glanced up at him and smiled encouragingly. He really was very nice and she began to wonder if he would kiss her goodnight. She hoped he would.

They held hands all through the programme and on the way home and Gloria was sure he would kiss her goodnight. As he helped her off the tram he hesitated.

'Is something wrong, Artie?' she asked.

'I was just wondering if we should walk for a bit beside the canal? There . . . there's not much privacy here with the streetlights and . . . things.' He didn't want to have to kiss her goodnight in view of half the neighbourhood and no doubt Brian would be lurking behind the bedroom curtains.

'I think that's a great idea. It will sort of . . . finish the evening off.'

They turned and walked up over the stone bridge and then turned on to the narrow towpath.

'I really did enjoy myself, Artie,' she said. 'I . . . I hoped you'd ask me out,' she confided a little hesitantly, wondering if she was being too forward.

'Did you, really? I wanted to ask you sooner but . . .' He put his arm around her shoulder and she snuggled against him, her heart beating a little faster. 'I really do like you, Gloria. I like you . . . a lot.'

She looked up at him. 'And I really like you, Artie.'

He kissed her gently on the lips and she put her arms around his neck, feeling a little dizzy as she kissed him back.

'Can I see you again, Gloria? Take you out, I mean?' he asked when he at last pulled away.

'Yes! Oh, yes, please, Artie,' she replied breathlessly. Her first real kiss and it had made her feel so . . . elated, as if she was walking on a cloud, she really didn't want to go home yet. 'You don't have to take me out, I mean we can go for walks. Just as long as I'm with you, I'll be . . . happy.'

He held her tightly. He hadn't felt like this before. 'We can see each other most evenings if you like. Get to know each other . . . better.'

'I'd really like that,' she murmured as they reluctantly turned towards home.

After that they did see more of each other and found that they liked the same things, modern music and the cinema amongst them. She knew he didn't earn a great deal as an apprentice but she told him that she was content with the occasional outing and Artie confided that when he'd finished this year of apprenticeship he'd have more money, enough to take her to shows and dances. He wanted her to have the best he could afford for she was so very special to him.

'Do you mean that, Artie?' she'd asked, feeling the now familiar fluttering of her heart.

'Of course I do. I've never met anyone like you, Gloria. You're so lovely and sweet and considerate and . . . Oh, I could go on and on about how wonderful you are and how much you mean to me.'

She'd clung to him, feeling so happy that she felt she would burst. She must be falling in love, she was *sure* she was.

When he'd got in that night both his mam and Brian had gone to bed, his father was smoking his pipe and listening to the wireless.

'There was no need to wait up, Da. I'm not a kid.'

George nodded and grinned at him as he switched the wireless off. He was a big man but was quiet, reserved and astute. 'I know, lad.' He placed his pipe on the mantelpiece. 'You're seeing quite a bit of Gloria lately. I take it it's getting a bit more serious?'

Artie sat down. 'I really do like her. You don't mind, do you?'

George smiled. 'Not at all, both your mam and me think she's a very nice girl. Sal's brought her up well. I just hope that when he gets home Harry Jenkins won't mind you two walking out.'

Artie frowned. 'So do I. I wonder what he's like? Do you think you two will get on?'

It was George's turn to frown. 'He's travelled far more than I have, he's used to dealing with all kinds of people, used to more or less running the whole catering side of things on that ship, according to your mam. She's always saying I should offer to take him to the pub when he gets home, get to know him, but I think I'll wait and see what he's like first. Sort of reserve judgement. I might not be able to stand him or he me. He might be all "gas and gaiters" as my old da used to put it – you know, full of himself and his own importance and that's something I can't be doing with. We'll wait and see. Now, the pair of us had better get some sleep.'

Artie had got up, hoping that his father and Gloria's da would get on, not that it really mattered but it would make things easier for himself and Gloria.

Chapter Nine

———◆———

BETTY WAS VERY THANKFUL that she wasn't going to have to accompany her mam down to the docks to meet the *Amazonia* this time. Sal had decided that she and Rose should be at school and Gloria would be at work. It didn't seem all that long since her da had sailed, even her mam said the time had flown by. She wondered what he would bring this time and if there would be anything for Rose. She'd decided that if there wasn't a home-coming gift for her friend then she would share whatever her da brought her with Rose.

'I thought we'd have got out early enough to have missed *him*,' she said to Rose as they left the house, staring in annoyance at Brian Taylor who was closing their gate.

'His mam must have put her foot behind him this morning,' Rose answered laconically. She didn't dislike Brian half as much as Betty did. In fact she really didn't mind him at all.

'You're out early this morning, Brian,' Rose commented as he fell into step beside them.

'Mam's got a bee in her bonnet over something. Your da coming home today, I think.'

'What's that got to do with her?' Betty asked sharply.

He shrugged and pushed his unruly hair out of his eyes. 'Dunno. Something about making a good impression, us not having met him yet and your mam telling her he's dead fussy about things.'

'It's his job to be fussy about things,' Betty shot back.

'There's no need to get all airyated with me, Betty! I was only telling you what me mam said,' he replied huffily.

'Oh, stop it, the pair of you. You'll meet him soon enough, Brian, and they always have a really great party when he gets home,' Rose intervened, thinking sadly that this time her mam wouldn't be here for it. She still missed her terribly but at least she didn't break down in tears as much now.

'Will we all get invited? Me as well?' Brian asked incredulously. He never went to grown-up parties.

'Of course. Most of the neighbourhood gets invited and you should see the food they have. I bet you'll have never seen or tasted anything like it,' Rose informed him.

'You'd just better behave yourself, Brian, or my Aunt Sybil will have something to say,' Betty warned, grimacing at the thought of her aunt.

'They've got pots of money and live in Formby but she's

a terrible snob,' Rose remarked. 'I wonder what she'll think about Gloria and Artie?' she added.

Betty frowned. 'I bet she won't be happy but Mam says there's nothing serious about it so there's no need to make a huge fuss.'

'Well, it looks "serious" to me. They're always kissing and cuddling when they think no one is watching them,' Brian said darkly, feeling greatly embarrassed by the behaviour of his older brother. 'He's a big soft dope is our Artie, especially when he's with your Gloria.'

Betty turned on him. 'You've been spying on them! You horrible little sneak!'

'I haven't and I'm not!' he protested.

Rose shot Betty a warning look. 'Stop it!'

Sal was just putting on her hat, standing in front of the mirror in the living room. The silver-grey light straw cloche with its pink ribbon rosette matched her pale grey costume and pink crêpe-de-Chine blouse and had been given to her by Sybil. It was an expensive hat, as were all the samples her sister-in-law brought home.

'Just popped in to wish you luck, Sal. You do look very smart. It's a lovely colour combination, grey and pink. Suits you too,' Elsie Taylor complimented her.

They were friends now and Elsie usually went with Sal to the weekly tea dances and they did their shopping together. It wasn't as close a friendship as Dora's had been, Sal mused, but then she'd known poor Dora for a lot longer than nine months.

'Thanks, Elsie. I'll miss having the girls with me today. Harry always likes us all to be there. Especially when he gives us our presents.' She tilted the hat to a better angle, scrutinising her reflection in the mirror.

'Well, it can't be helped, Sal. They've got work and school to go to,' Elsie reminded her. 'You'll be glad to have Harry home, I expect.'

Sal nodded. 'Of course but he . . . well, he really enjoys his first weeks at home but then he starts getting bored. I suppose he's so used to being busy. Once the party is over he always feels at a bit of a loose end.'

'I'll see what George can think up in the way of "diversions",' Elsie suggested. She was very curious to meet Harry Jenkins.

Sal nodded again. George Taylor was a quiet, well-mannered man and she liked him but she wasn't sure if he would have much in common with Harry.

'I'll be back just after dinnertime, Elsie, so I'll be here for the girls. Harry likes us all to have our evening meal together.'

Elsie nodded. 'We won't be bothering you tonight, Sal. Let the man have a bit of peace and quiet on his first night home. And I've told Artie not to call either.'

Sal frowned. She hadn't mentioned in her letters to Harry anything about the budding romance between Gloria and Artie Taylor. She was sure Harry would like the lad and they were only a couple of kids when all was said and done. There was no question of them getting engaged or anything. It could all have fizzled out in a few months' time.

Girls of Gloria's age tended to be flighty.

When Betty and Rose got in from school Sal had already set the table and was peeling vegetables.

'Go and get changed, the pair of you. I brought the things your da got you home with me but I don't want you to open them yet,' Sal instructed.

Betty looked at the nicely wrapped boxes on top of the sideboard; she also noticed that her mam was wearing a new pearl necklace. 'Is there . . . something for Rose too?' she asked tentatively.

'You know your da, Betty. Generous to a fault. Of course there are things for Rose. He wouldn't leave her out.'

Both Rose and Betty were surprised and pleased with their gifts. They had matching necklaces of coral and new wrist watches with real snakeskin straps. Gloria had a beautiful necklace and earrings made of gold set with the brilliantly hued wings of tropical butterflies.

'You should see them. The colours are amazing and some of them are as big as my hand,' Harry informed them.

'You'll be able to wear them for the party, Gloria. They'll go really well with that new dress you've got and I'll wear my new pearls,' Sal added, fingering her necklace.

'Wait until I tell that Brian Taylor that this strap is *real* snakeskin,' Betty said, admiring her watch.

'And I can tell Artie what you said about the butter-flies, Da. I'm sure he'll be interested,' Gloria added without thinking.

Sal glared at her and shook her head slightly.

Harry hadn't noticed. 'I can see you get on well with them all.'

'We do. I think you'll like George too, Harry. He's a bit on the quiet side but I know he's looking forward to hearing all about your travels. He told me it must be very interesting and . . . now, what was it . . . ?' Sal frowned trying to remember the exact words. 'Yes, broadening for the mind. That was it.'

'Sounds like a sensible bloke,' Harry replied. He always liked to talk about his experiences and the places he'd been to.

'Elsie suggested the two of you might go to the Blue Anchor for a pint one night?' Sal remarked.

'Good idea. Maybe towards the end of the week. We'll have to decide when we're going to have the party, Sal.'

Sal nodded. 'When we've decided I'll phone your Sybil and let her know.'

When all the girls had gone to bed Sal decided that she had better mention that Gloria and Artie had been going out together on a regular basis for quite a while now. 'Shall I put the kettle on, Harry, or would you prefer something stronger than tea?'

He got up and went to the sideboard. 'I'll have a small Scotch, Sal, and why don't you have a glass of Madeira?'

She kept quiet until he handed her the drink and then sat down. 'I've been waiting for you to get home, Harry, to tell you that our Gloria has been seeing quite a lot of young Artie from next door. I didn't want to put it in a letter.'

Harry frowned. 'She's very young. Is it serious? What kind of a lad is he?'

'He's a nice lad, quiet, pleasant, well mannered. He's an apprentice mechanic. They hit it off from the start and then he asked her out and . . . well, they see quite a lot of each other and sometimes they go dancing or to the cinema. He's only eighteen and she's seventeen so I don't think it's serious. I mean, you know what these young girls are like these days, a bit flighty.'

'I hope she's not going to turn into one of these "flappers". All much too modern and free-spirited for my liking, Sal.'

'No. No, she's not like that, Harry. She doesn't smoke and she only ever has a drink at a party, where I can keep my eye on her. Anyway I don't think Artie would even dream of taking her into a pub. He doesn't go himself, George would have a fit.'

'I should think so too. The pair of them are under age. Well, I can't judge the lad until I've met him but I hope you've had a serious talk to her, Sal. We certainly don't want her bringing any disgrace on us nor do we want her to ruin her life. She's an attractive girl and she's got a good job and I'd like her to make an advantageous marriage when the time comes, the way Sybil did.'

Sal was a little put out by this. As usual he was placing all the responsibility for Gloria firmly on her shoulders and although she too wanted her daughter to do well in life she also wanted the girl to be happy. 'She knows right from wrong, Harry. She won't do anything foolish and I just want her to be happy with whoever she marries. As long as he can provide for her and for a family I won't mind what kind of a job he has. But as I've said, I don't think anything will really come of this. It's just puppy love: She's only seventeen.'

Harry nodded, although he wasn't too sure she was right. 'Well, let's just wait and see, Sal.'

Chapter Ten

———◆◆◆———

I T WAS TWO DAYS later before Gloria managed to see Artie. She slipped next door after supper on the pretext of returning a recipe book that Sal had borrowed from Elsie.

'I've brought your recipe book, Mrs Taylor,' she announced as she went into the kitchen where Elsie was just folding up the tablecloth, George was reading the newspaper and Brian appeared to be attempting to do his homework. Artie smiled at her.

'Thanks, luv, but there was no rush,' Elsie said. 'Everything all right?' She'd met Harry Jenkins for the first time yesterday. He had been pleasant and friendly enough towards her; charming in fact.

'Yes, fine. Da brought me a gorgeous necklace and earring set.'

'Your mam told me.'

'I wouldn't fancy wearing a watch like the ones he brought your Betty and Rose. They were showing me them on the way to school. Horrible, creepy, slimy things, snakes,' Brian said.

Artie glared at his brother. 'Shut up, Brian. Anyway, the snake's not alive any more, is it?'

'Well, it wouldn't be, would it?' Brian replied unabashed.

George lowered his newspaper. 'That'll do, Brian.'

'Have they decided when the party is to be, Gloria?' Elsie asked.

'Probably the Saturday after next. Da will start doing all the organising next week.'

Elsie smiled. 'We're all looking forward to it. It sounds like something that shouldn't be missed, according to Florrie Henshaw next door. I promised your mam I'd come in and give her a hand with things.'

'Well, I'd better get back,' Gloria said, casting an imploring glance at Artie.

Artie instantly got to his feet. 'I'll see you back, it's dark out there and there's no knowing just what meladdo here has left lying around in the yard. I fell over his bike the other night.'

Before they reached the back door of Sal's house Artie took her in his arms.

She reached up and kissed him. 'Mam's told him about us.'

'And?' he asked, nuzzling her neck. She always smelled of roses, he thought, it was the perfume she wore. She was gorgeous and he loved her, he was certain of it. He'd not met anyone like her before and when he took her out he'd noticed the admiring glances cast in her direction, which made him feel so lucky.

'He didn't say I had to stop seeing you.' She had been so relieved when Sal had told her for she'd been terrified he would forbid her to go on seeing Artie and that would have been a terrible disaster. She couldn't have done it. Artie loved her, he'd told her so, and she was sure she loved him.

He held her more tightly. 'Thank God for that. I would still have kept seeing you, Gloria – I *couldn't* give you up – but it would have had to have been behind his back and I don't want to do that.'

'I know it's only been a couple of days but it's seemed ages. I'm so used to seeing you every day.'

He kissed her gently. 'Shall I come in now and meet him?'

'Yes, I think that's a good idea.

'Artie's come back with me,' Gloria announced, leading Artie into the room. 'He wants to meet you, Da.'

Harry got up and had to look up as Artie extended his hand. The lad was much taller than him. 'So, you're Arthur, "Artie" Taylor?'

Artie smiled shyly and shook his hand. 'That's right. I'm very pleased to meet you, Mr Jenkins. And welcome home.'

Harry nodded. 'Sit down, lad. I won't bite.'

Artie sat down on the sofa and Gloria sat beside him, smiling encouragingly at him.

'So, you have been walking out with Gloria?' Harry said, quickly appraising the lad. He was good-looking, tidy, appeared to be quiet and a bit bashful but that was no bad thing.

'We've been sort of "courting" now for quite a while. I hope you don't mind? I'm . . . I'm very . . . er . . . fond of her.'

'And I'm fond of him too, Da,' Gloria gushed.

'We all know *that*,' Betty muttered.

Sal glared at her. 'That will do, Betty.'

Artie ignored her comment; he suffered similar jibes from Brian.

Harry nodded. Sal had assured him it wasn't serious but it certainly sounded like it to him and Gloria was gazing at the lad like a moonstruck calf. 'How long exactly is "quite a while"?'

'Probably since just after we moved in next door. I liked Gloria the first time I met her and then about a week later I finally plucked up courage to ask her out.'

'So, that was shortly after I sailed. Almost nine months,' Harry said.

'I suppose it is,' Artie answered.

'That is quite a while at your age,' Harry mused.

'You don't object, Da, do you?' Gloria pleaded.

Harry shrugged and smiled wryly. 'It looks as if it's a *fait accompli* you're presenting me with.'

Artie stood up, not understanding the French phrase but thankful that Gloria's da was at least smiling. 'Thank you, Mr Jenkins. I'll be going now. Goodnight.'

'I'll see you out, Artie,' Gloria said, following him to the door.

Betty looked at Rose and mouthed the word 'creep' and Rose giggled.

'I would think that lad has enough to put up with from

their Brian without you adding your two pennyworth, miss!' Sal rebuked her, having caught her daughter's gesture. 'Well, I think he's got very good manners, don't you, Harry?'

Harry nodded but he made a mental note to keep a close eye on Gloria and young Artie Taylor. He wanted something far better for her than a mechanic on the railways.

Harry was soon fully occupied with the arrangements for the party, as was Sal, and as the time approached Elsie, Betty and Rose all became involved. Gloria had decided that the dress she'd intended to wear just wasn't fashionable enough and had persuaded her father to give her the money for a new one. She wanted to look her best and she wanted her Aunt Sybil to approve of Artie.

'You will make sure your suit is well pressed and that your shoes are polished, Artie?' she said the day before. 'I want us both to look really smart.'

'Is she really such a dragon? Your Betty says she is,' he asked. He didn't tell her exactly what Betty had said, which was that Sybil Mostyn was a stuck-up, snooty old biddy.

Gloria laughed. 'Of course not. Our Betty doesn't like her but she's very good to me. Of course they've got plenty of money and she's always terribly well dressed and goes to all the best places.'

'Do you think she'll like me? Approve of me?' Artie was a bit worried. This aunt seemed to hold a lot of sway over Gloria.

'Of course she will! What is there about you not to like?

Don't you go taking too much notice of anything our Betty says.'

He nodded. 'Mam's given Brian a good talking to. He's got to behave himself and not go making a show of us all.'

Gloria nodded. In her opinion Brian Taylor was still a bit of a hooligan. 'Rose seems to get on with him better than our Betty, I'll ask her to keep him out of trouble and it will take her mind off her mam not being here this year.'

'I don't envy her but I'm not going to worry about him.'

'I don't want you to worry about anything, Artie. We're going to have a great time,' Gloria replied firmly.

When the Taylor family arrived on Saturday night Gloria thought that both she and Artie looked great. He'd bought a new tie, he informed her, especially for the occasion and to her delight she thought how well it went with her dress.

When her aunt and uncle had divested themselves of their coats and had been given a drink Gloria propelled Artie towards them. He felt a bit apprehensive of the slim, dark-haired woman in the long black silk dress embroidered with silver beads and the distinguished-looking man in an obviously expensive evening suit and bow tie.

'Aunt Sybil, Uncle Richard, I'd like you to meet Artie Taylor,' Gloria announced with pride, her eyes shining.

'You live next door in what was Dora's house, don't you?' Sybil said, extending her hand.

Artie shook it and nodded. 'That's my mam and da over there, talking to Mrs Henshaw.'

Sybil looked across quickly at the Taylors before turning

her attention to Artie. They looked respectable; dull but respectable. 'And I take it you do work?'

'Yes. I'm an apprentice mechanic. On the railways.'

Richard shook his hand and smiled encouragingly at the lad. He could see he was a bit nervous. 'Steady job that. A job for life, I'd say.'

Artie relaxed a little. 'That's exactly what my da says.'

Sybil noted that her niece was standing very close to the boy and that her hand was on his arm. Gloria looked as lovely as ever, she thought. Her chiffon dress was in a vivid shade of turquoise, which suited her, and was set off by the lovely necklace and matching earrings that Harry had obviously brought. They had an 'exotic' look about them. 'Are you a friend of Gloria's?' she probed. He was quite a good-looking lad. Nicely turned out but of course the suit wasn't very well cut and she thought the tie a bit garish. It matched Gloria's dress but that shade of turquoise wasn't really a suitable colour for a tie. He seemed rather gauche and didn't have a great deal to say. He obviously wasn't going to set the world on fire.

'Gloria and me, we . . . we've been courting for almost nine months now,' Artie replied, wilting a little beneath the scrutiny of Sybil's dark, steady gaze.

Sybil's eyebrows rose. This was the first she'd heard of this. 'Indeed. *Nine* months,' she repeated.

'I liked Artie from the day they moved in,' Gloria informed her, smiling up at him.

'And I take it your mother approves?'

Gloria nodded. She couldn't actually tell from her aunt's

face if she approved or not, but surely she liked him?

'And you'll be a mechanic with the Railway Company?'

'In another three years I will. Then I'll be on a good wage,' Artie said with a note of pride in his voice.

Sybil's smile belied her feelings. She was going to have to speak to Harry about this liaison. Gloria would be a fool to throw herself away on Artie Taylor. She could do far better. 'That's excellent. Ah, I see your Aunt Doris has arrived, Gloria. I must go and have a word with her. Very nice to meet you, Artie.'

Sybil swept her husband away to greet Sal's sister and Artie looked at Gloria anxiously.

'Do you think she liked me?'

'Of course she did. She's always a bit formal and direct.'

'She makes me nervous. She looks as if she can see straight through you.'

'No she doesn't. You'll get used to her. Now, let's go and get a drink and then I'll introduce you to Mam's family.'

Artie let her lead him towards the 'bar' in the kitchen. He'd liked her Uncle Richard but he still wasn't very sure about her Aunt Sybil.

It was quite a while before Sybil managed to find her brother comparatively alone. He was getting drinks for a couple of their neighbours who, upon seeing her, quickly went back into the living room where the party was in full swing with Sal's sister Eileen at the piano.

'What's all this about Gloria courting that boy from next door, Artie Taylor?'

Harry shrugged, mixing her another dry martini. 'Sal

says it's just puppy love, nothing serious. She's had a good talk to Gloria.'

'I hope she's impressed on her that she can do far better. She has to set her sights a lot higher, Harry.'

'Sal doesn't think it will last and she is only seventeen, Sybil. He's the first boy she's been out with and he's not a bad lad. I find him quiet and well mannered and he's got a steady job.'

'Yes, he'll be a *mechanic* – eventually – but that's not good enough for her, Harry. You know it isn't.'

'I think you're taking it all too seriously, Sybil. She won't end up marrying him. There's no question of an engagement,' Harry said, feeling irritated that Sybil was making such a fuss. They were all here to enjoy themselves after all and he hadn't realised that Sal hadn't told his sister about this matter.

'I sincerely hope not,' Sybil replied with some annoyance. She could see he was losing interest, which was typical. He always pushed things on to Sal and in this instance it looked as though her sister-in-law wasn't taking the matter as seriously as she should. Gloria had been hanging on to the lad's every word and any fool could see she was infatuated.

'The longer it goes on, Harry, the more hurt and upset one or other of them is going to be when it comes to an end. It will all end in tears and I just hope they aren't Gloria's. Perhaps I should have a talk to her.'

'Leave it, Sybil. For God's sake, don't go ruining the evening,' he snapped. 'Sal's well able to deal with it all.'

Seeing she was getting nowhere Sybil walked away. She would have to put her mind to this. She was determined that Gloria should make a very advantageous marriage; it would be the girl's best chance of a better life with a much higher standard of living and social status, even if at the moment her parents didn't seem to be very interested in that fact.

Chapter Eleven

———•◦•———

THE FOLLOWING DAY ELSIE went in to help Sal clean up. George had gone down to the newsagent's for his paper and Artie and Brian were still in bed, for it had been half past two before they'd got to bed.

'We'll have a cup of tea before we start, Elsie. I always enjoy the party but the following day I always wonder if it was worth the mess?' Sal said.

'Are they all still in bed?' Elsie asked, frowning as she looked around at the untidy rooms.

'Harry's up. He's gone for a walk to clear his head.'

'He didn't have all that much to drink last night,' Elsie commented.

'He never does, but he's always up early when he's at sea so I suppose it's more of a habit now. I've left the girls to sleep on.'

Elsie nodded. 'Didn't Artie and Gloria look just great together? Very smart and they seemed to really enjoy themselves. Mind you, I had to get a grip of our Brian though. I caught him with a plate piled high with all kinds of stuff, including four cream cakes. I made him put most of it back. The greedy little pig, you'd think he'd never been fed. Mind you, Sal, I've never seen anything like it. I've never had smoked salmon or that ham stuff before, let alone canapés.'

Sal poured the tea. 'Harry says that really they should be served with the drinks, before the other food, but I ask you, could we do that?'

'I got on famously with both your Doris and Eileen, and George and Walter, your Eileen's husband, found they'd been at the same school so it was "all our yesterdays".' Elsie paused and Sal smiled knowingly.

'And Sybil and Richard?'

'Oh, he's very nice. A thorough gentleman. But, well, I have to say I just couldn't take to her, Sal. Very "standoffish". She made you feel you were laughing too loudly or using the wrong fork. Very elegant though. Does she never let her hair down and enjoy herself?'

Sal grinned. 'I've never seen her although I think she does enjoy herself in her own way. She always says she does and if she didn't I suppose she wouldn't come.'

'I got the feeling that she didn't really like the idea of our Artie taking Gloria out.'

'Did she say anything?' Sal asked. She'd formed that impression herself although Sybil hadn't said anything to her.

'No. It was just the way she kept watching them with that *look* on her face.'

Sal nodded. 'Well, as I keep saying, Elsie, they're both very young and they haven't known each other all that long.'

'I wouldn't mind at all, Sal, if it did get more serious. She's a lovely girl and I know she comes from a decent home and if she makes our Artie happy then I wouldn't ask for more. Now, we'd better make a start or we'll be here until midnight.'

Unbeknown to Sal, Sybil had telephoned three times to urge her brother to think more seriously about Gloria's liaison with Artie Taylor and Harry had at last begun to take more notice of his sister. He agreed with Sybil: he wanted only the very best for Gloria; and while he liked Artie and the Taylor family was hard working and respectable they were still very much working class and he wanted his daughter to do better. Not the upper class of course, that would be aiming far too high, but someone middle class: a doctor, lawyer or bank manager. Gloria would never have a home like Sybil's if she married Artie for he would never have as much money as Richard Mostyn. In fact secretly he hoped Gloria would do even better in life than her aunt. He hadn't mentioned any of this to Sal for she wouldn't understand his ambitions for his elder daughter; after all she'd said she just wanted Gloria to be happy, and she was firmly convinced that it wasn't serious.

'Do they ever have social events at work, Gloria?' he asked her one evening when Sal had gone out to see her sister

Doris and Rose and Betty were upstairs.

'Sometimes they do. Mainly at Christmas. Why?' she'd asked.

'It's just that sometimes it's good to widen your circle of friends. Meet other people socially.'

'They have a Christmas party which is usually good, so I've been told. I'll be going this year.'

Harry had nodded his approval. 'Good. I suppose you've made a lot of friends at work?'

Gloria had shaken her head. 'Not too many. I'm just the junior so most of them are much older than me.'

'So there's no special friend?' he'd probed, feeling a little disappointed.

'Rita is the nearest in age to me and she's nice. Sometimes we go window shopping in our lunch hour.'

'No young men?' Harry had asked.

Gloria had looked puzzled. 'Not really. Mr Thornton is the youngest and he must be at least twenty-five and he's engaged. The rest are positively ancient.'

'More my age?'

Gloria had grinned. 'Sort of. Sorry, Da. Anyway, I'm not bothered about other young men, I'm quite happy with Artie.'

Harry had been disappointed to learn that there was obviously no one at work who might supplant Artie Taylor in her affections. He would have to speak to Sybil.

He phoned her the following day and imparted this information to her.

'I'd hoped there would be someone more senior, or who

had the ambition to become senior, in the Revenue whom she might have taken a fancy to.'

'I'd hoped that myself, Harry, but no matter.'

'How do I get her to go out and meet suitable people, Sybil? Sal can't take her to any of the places where she'd meet a much better class of person.'

'It's not easy, Harry. She is still very young so a lot of places are off limits to her, but she'll be eighteen next year and then we'll have to put some serious thought into the matter. That's if the romance is still on.'

'But what about now and Artie Taylor?'

'All you can do for now is try to make sure she doesn't see him too often. Oh, I know it won't be easy with him living next door and you being away, but do try and impress upon Sal that it's important she doesn't get too involved and in the meantime I'll rack my brains for a solution.'

Harry replaced the receiver irritably. God, there were times when Sybil and her high-handed ways annoyed him. How could he advise Sal to do that and why the hell should he?

Sal could sense the change in him. 'Has something or someone upset you, Harry?' she asked pointedly that evening.

'No,' he replied curtly. 'It's just that I've been thinking more about Gloria and Artie Taylor.'

Sal sighed. 'I've told you, Harry, it's not serious. If we leave them alone I'm certain it will all fizzle out. She'll meet someone else. But if we try to part them it will only make her more determined.' She was going to add that sometimes Gloria could be as stubborn as him but felt it better not to.

'How is she going to meet anyone else when she never goes anywhere other than with him?'

'They're bound to have a Christmas party at work and she'll be invited to other parties,' Sal replied.

'She's already told me there's no one at work near her age.'

'She's friendly with that girl Rita. Maybe she could go to a dance at New Year with her,' Sal suggested, seeing he wasn't going to leave the subject alone and not wanting to antagonise him further.

'Maybe she could go to a lot more places with this Rita. She must be a decent girl otherwise they wouldn't have employed her.'

Sal sighed again. 'I'll suggest it to her, Harry,' she promised.

Meeting new friends was the last thing on Gloria's mind as she discussed the party with Artie a few days later.

'I really enjoyed myself, Gloria, we all did. Mam's hardly stopped talking about the food and the fancy drinks your da persuaded her to try.'

'I did too and I thought we looked so . . . *right* together.' Gloria smiled, thinking of how her Aunt Eileen had remarked what a handsome couple they made.

Artie took her in his arms. 'We *are* right together, Gloria. You're the only girl I ever want in my life and now that both our families have seen us together – as a couple – I suppose they'll realise that we're serious about each other.'

'Are we serious, Artie?' Gloria's eyes were shining.

'I'm deadly serious about you, you know that. We've been courting for nine months and I love you,' Artie replied sincerely.

'I love you too, Artie. I know Mam keeps telling me I'm still very young, that I've my whole life ahead of me and I should meet other people, make new friends, but I don't want anyone else. We get on so well together, we like the same kind of things . . .' She kissed him gently on the cheek.

'And we have the same ideas about what kind of future we want together, so I'd call that "serious", wouldn't you? We've plenty of time ahead of us, Gloria – a lifetime.'

Gloria nodded happily. At some time in the not-too-distant future she was sure he would ask her da if he could marry her and then they'd get engaged and after they'd saved up they'd get married and live happily ever after, just like girls in the fairy tales did. Maybe that was being a bit too optimistic, she told herself, married couples did have their ups and down, but she was sure life with Artie would be mostly happy. She sighed with pleasure. 'I'm so glad we're really serious about each other now, Artie. It makes me feel sort of content and . . . *settled*.'

George made a similar comment when he called in to see if Harry wanted to go to the Blue Anchor for a pint. He still wasn't too sure of what to make of his neighbour but Elsie had nagged him to make an effort to get to know Harry Jenkins and it was the least he could do to take the man for a pint, especially after the splendid hospitality they'd enjoyed at Harry's expense. Privately George thought that party had all been a bit too extravagant, a bit too exotic. It smacked to him of showing off. After all, it wasn't to celebrate an important birthday or anniversary or a wedding, just the fact that he was home from a rather long voyage and apparently he threw one every time he was home. To his mind that was wasteful; they were only working-class people when all was said and done.

'Just thought I'd pop in and see if you would like to come for a pint, Harry?'

Harry was a little surprised; he too was still forming his judgement of George Taylor. He hadn't had much contact with him so far; even at the party there had been little time for serious conversation. His first impressions of George were of a quiet and rather dour man and he'd caught the look of slight disapproval at the lavish buffet laid out. George had refused both the best brandy and malt whisky he'd been offered, sticking to pale ale and not many of them either. Even though his neighbour seemed pleasant enough Harry had the distinct feeling that George didn't approve of either his lifestyle or generosity. He nodded slowly. 'Right, I'll just get my jacket and trilby, George, then we'll look in for a pint or two. I don't know what the beer's like though. Even though it's just down the road I don't go in very often.'

That surprised George, he'd have thought Harry Jenkins would have been a regular when he was home. He'd have a captive audience for his tales of foreign parts. 'It's passable,' he replied.

'It looks as if our Artie and your Gloria are very taken up

with each other. I heard one of Sal's sisters saying what a lovely couple they made and I have to admit, Harry, she's a very attractive girl. Nice nature, too,' George remarked as they walked down the road towards the bridge and the pub.

Harry frowned slightly, wondering if Sybil had heard the same remark. 'Oh, she's still very young, George. I don't think there's anything serious between them.'

'That's not what Elsie thinks. She said she's never seen our Artie so taken with a girl before and he had a couple of girlfriends before Gloria. No, she thinks it's serious and I'm beginning to agree.'

Harry's frown deepened. This was not something he wanted to hear. 'I think – and Sal agrees – that Gloria should have a wider circle of friends. She's really very young and has never been anywhere or done anything and as you say, she *is* very attractive and quite bright and we don't want her to feel she's not taken advantage of every opportunity to broaden her horizons, so to speak, in the future.'

George didn't reply. Obviously Harry Jenkins had other plans and ambitions for his eldest daughter and they didn't include a future with Artie. Or did he consider Artie simply not good enough? Either way he felt as though both he and his son had been insulted, which certainly didn't bode well for any kind of friendly relationship with his neighbour or happiness for Artie, unless of course Gloria herself had other ideas. He wondered just how much influence Harry had over her. Did she have enough spirit to stand up to him? She seemed a rather docile, placid girl, unlike young Betty who certainly had more to say for herself. Still, Harry was away for most of the time and, according to Elsie, Sal wasn't averse to Gloria and Artie's courtship, far from it. Only time would tell, he mused, but he knew that this would be the first and last time he would be sharing an evening in the pub with Harry Jenkins. He had decided he didn't like the man. He was almost as much of a snob as his sister.

Chapter Twelve

———◆———

HARRY WENT FOR A walk the following morning to clear his head and to think. It had been a rather tense evening and to fill the awkward silences he'd drunk more than he normally did. Sal had been in bed by the time he'd got home and he'd been thankful. He hadn't wanted to try to explain that he and George Taylor had very little in common and that he felt the man utterly disapproved of everything he did, although nothing explicit had been said. Nor did he want to have to get into an argument about Gloria and Artie Taylor's relationship but he felt that the less they had to do with the entire Taylor family, the better, although he knew Sal wouldn't agree with that. Nor did he blame her, she got on well with Elsie and she needed company when he was away for months.

He bought a newspaper from the little shop just a few

doors away from the pub and returned home.

There had been no sign of him when Sal came down but seeing the empty glass in the sink and noting that his overcoat had gone she surmised that he'd gone out for a walk.

'I'll put the kettle on for tea,' she stated as he came in.

'I'd prefer coffee if there is any,' Harry said, sitting down and opening the paper.

'You know I always keep some in for you. I didn't hear you come in last night, you must have been late. How did you get on with George?'

Harry shrugged. 'To be perfectly honest, Sal, we haven't got all that much in common. I find him a bit on the dour side.'

She was surprised. 'I thought he would find all your travels and experiences interesting.'

'He never mentioned anything about my job, except to say he wouldn't fancy being away from home for such long stretches.'

'So what did you talk about?' She was curious, surely they hadn't spent the evening just drinking in silence? That certainly wasn't like Harry.

'This and that.' He shook the paper as a sign that he wasn't going to enlighten her further.

She sighed. Maybe she'd get more out of Elsie. 'Will you be going down to the ship later?'

'I'll put a couple of hours in to make sure the cleaners are not skiving,' he replied. The company employed cleaners to scour every inch of the vessel and teams of upholsterers and carpet fitters to carry out any repairs needed to furnishings or carpets. It was the usual practice of all the big shipping companies. Cunard in particular employed a small army of them as they needed to turn their ships around quickly. 'I'll be back home by half past four at the latest. I presume Betty and Rose will be in from school by then?'

Sal nodded as she handed him the cup. 'They will.'

He said nothing further and so she carried on with her chores.

Betty and Rose walked back from school together discussing the events of the day. When they went in they found Harry reading the *Journal of Commerce*.

Sal smiled at them. 'If you've got homework I'd get it done now, before we have supper,' she advised.

Harry looked up and put down the journal. Reflecting on Gloria's future had made him begin to think more seriously about Betty and Rose. 'How much longer exactly have you both got at school?' he asked.

'We'll be leaving next year, Da. Some of the girls are leaving as soon as they're fourteen, they've got to find work because their families need the money, but Mam says we're to stay on and hopefully get a better leaving report and therefore the chance of a better job. Why?' Betty answered.

He nodded thoughtfully. 'I think it's about time we thought about jobs for you.'

The two girls looked at him in surprise. It was the first time this had ever been mentioned although Rose had begun to wonder what she would do for a job. It had been good of Uncle Harry and Aunty Sal to take her in but she couldn't depend on them for ever, she would need to make her own way in the world.

'I don't belong to the Masonic Brethren so we can't hope for anything as good as Gloria has, but I might be able to get one of you into the company's office,' he announced, having given the matter some thought earlier in the day. It always helped if you could find work for your children and everyone tried to do just that. George Taylor had got Artie his apprenticeship and Richard had helped Gloria. It was an accepted practice.

Betty decided to take the bull by the horns. 'I don't think I could stick working in an office, Da, if you don't mind.'

Sal frowned at her.

'What *do* you want to do? Have you anything in mind?' Harry asked.

Sal breathed a sigh of relief. He didn't sound annoyed, just interested. 'You are always saying that it's a great life at sea, Da. Is it really?' Betty asked.

'The best but it's damned hard work. The hours are long and if you're on the big liners you often have a lot to put up with from the passengers, but there's a great camaraderie and you get to see the world and get paid for it too, although not very much to start with. Why?'

'I've been wondering if I'd like it too,' Betty answered, ignoring the startled look on her mother's face.

'You mean work as a stewardess?' Harry too was surprised.

Betty nodded.

Harry frowned; he hadn't expected this at all. 'You'll still have to find some other kind of a job to start with, Betty. Even at fifteen you're far too young, you'll have to be eighteen at least and you might well have changed your mind by then.' He turned his attention to Rose. 'What about you, Rose?'

'I wouldn't mind working in an office at all, Uncle Harry. I couldn't face the thought of going to sea.'

Harry nodded. 'So you'd be happy if I could get you a job?'

'I'd be delighted. It's more than I had hoped for. I was going to try for shop work or even something in a factory.'

'Good God! We couldn't have you working in a factory, Rose. Your poor mother would turn in her grave.' Harry shook his head and picked up the paper again.

No indeed, Sal thought, she too wanted better for Dora's daughter, and she was glad that at least Rose would have the chance of a decent job. 'You might think about going to evening classes, Rose, for book-keeping. You're good at maths,' she suggested.

'I could, Aunty Sal,' Rose replied agreeably.

'That's an excellent suggestion, Sal. She'd get a better job in the accounts department,' Harry added.

Sal smiled and went into the kitchen to prepare the meal. Well, that was young Rose sorted out at least but she was very surprised that Betty wanted to go away to sea. She'd never mentioned the fact to her; she'd thought that the pair of them would probably have found shop work. She was certain Sybil could put a word in for Betty in one of the big stores in Liverpool – with a bit of persuasion from Harry. He could appeal to Sybil's sense of duty to the family.

Harry was home each day by five at the latest and in the evenings he devoted a lot of time to Rose, encouraging her to spend time on her arithmetic in particular. He, too, was good with figures, it was part of his job to make sure that they weren't overcharged for the supplies he ordered. He checked every delivery advice and invoice carefully before it went to the accounts department.

'Will you really like working in an office all day and working with figures? Won't it give you a headache?' Betty had asked Rose.

Rose had laughed. 'No. I really don't mind and if your da can get me that job I'd be over the moon. I can't wait to earn money of my own. I'd give your mam something for my keep, that's only fair, she's been very good to me. But you! You never said you wanted to go to sea!'

Betty had shrugged. In reality she didn't know what she wanted to do when she left school but she'd thought it might be interesting to travel and her da seemed to enjoy his work. 'I thought it might be exciting to see the world and Da's always saying what a great life it is but I didn't realise I'd have to wait years before I could start.'

'So what will you do in the meantime?' Rose had asked.

'I don't know, but I couldn't stand being stuck in a stuffy office all day.'

Rose had sighed. 'Well, you've got until next year to think of something.'

Nothing more was said on the subject but before Harry sailed at the end of October he had a phone call from Sybil to say she had a plan in her mind for Gloria which she hoped to put into action next spring.

'Why next spring? Why wait so long?' Harry had asked.

'I need time to persuade Richard to help me – to help us.'

Harry was still mystified. 'What's Richard got to do with it?'

Sybil had tutted impatiently. 'Harry, stop being so *negative*. Gloria simply can't throw her life away on that boy from next door and she will if something isn't done about it. She deserves far better in life and I was talking to Mona Halliday at the golf club a few weeks ago and she put the idea into my mind. She was telling me about a friend of hers whose daughter had just got married in America. Apparently the girl met her future husband on the ship going over, she was going out to work as a nanny to a family there . . .'

Harry couldn't see where all this was leading and was becoming impatient. 'Sybil, what has all this to do with Gloria and Artie Taylor?'

'If you'd just listen, Harry, I'll tell you. The girl met and fell in love with this young man, who has a very good job and now apparently she will never need to work again and lives in a big house in New Jersey. A veritable mansion Mona called it, she'd seen a photo of it.'

Harry was still confused. 'Sybil, have you been drinking?'

'Oh, for heaven's sake, Harry! Just think about it! Where

will Gloria meet someone who can offer her a life of leisure, luxury and social standing? On a ship of course! On one of the big Cunarders. This girl was only travelling second class, but if Gloria were to go first class just think of the opportunities that would afford. It's not beyond the realms of possibility that she would meet someone, she's very attractive and vivacious—'

'Sybil, it would cost a *fortune!*' Harry cut in.

'That's why I need Richard's help. We couldn't let her go unaccompanied, I'd go with her. Sal has the other two girls to see to.'

Harry was shaking his head at the thought of the expense but he couldn't help wondering if Sybil was right. Those ships were like floating palaces and anyone who was anyone travelled on them; as Cunard's advertising slogan said it was 'the only way to cross'. Gloria would never come into contact with the wealthy elite in any other circumstances and he'd seen dozens of romances bloom on the Atlantic crossing. He'd seen them fade too – but it was certainly something to think about. 'You said you'd be looking at next spring?'

Sybil seemed relieved that he hadn't dismissed the idea out of hand. 'Yes. That would give me time to persuade Richard.'

'I might be able to help you out with some of the expense,' Harry offered.

'I'd be grateful if you could. She'll have to have an extensive new wardrobe for a start.'

'We'll talk about it again when I get back, Sybil. You

never know, the romance might all have come to nothing by then and the expense won't be necessary.'

'Or it might not and besides, Harry, I'm convinced we should go ahead anyway. It's her best chance of a much better life,' Sybil had answered firmly.

Chapter Thirteen

———◦◦◦◦———

1927

TO SAL'S CONSTERNATION GLORIA resolutely refused to
accompany Rita to any of the dances she had suggested
they attend and clung tenaciously to Artie. She insisted on
seeing him every day and they went out at least twice a week.
Artie had even gone to meet Gloria and escort her home
after the last year's annual Christmas office party.

'I don't want to go anywhere without Artie, Mam,' Gloria
stated firmly whenever she brought the subject up.

Even Betty had said that she was sure that they'd be
engaged by next Christmas. Sal was concerned about Betty
too, for the girl had said she really didn't know what she
wanted to do when she left school, seeing as it would be so
long before she could try for a job at sea. Rose was different.
She now went to evening classes for book-keeping and was

looking forward to leaving school. Harry had been as good as his word and had written to someone he knew well in the accounts department and Rose had high hopes of being taken on by the Porto-Brasilia Line.

'You know, Elsie, I'll be glad when Harry gets home. I don't know what to do about our Betty. She just doesn't have a clue what she wants to do,' Sal confided one morning as they walked to the shops. She didn't mention Gloria for she knew Elsie was quite happy with the situation.

'Don't give her a choice, Sal. George just told our Brian that he would be starting work as an apprentice the Monday after he left school and that was that. He's got him the job, same as he got Artie his. Just tell her she's to go and work in an office or a shop and that's that. They should all thank their lucky stars to have jobs these days. Will you be having the big party again?'

'I suppose so,' Sal replied.

She'd thought about Elsie's words for the rest of the day and when Betty arrived home she decided to tackle the subject again.

'Your da will be home in a couple of days, Betty, and he's going to ask if you've decided what to do when you leave school.'

'I know, Mam. I'll just have to tell him I don't know.'

'You'll have to tell him something.'

'But I don't know, Mam, so what can I say?' Betty cried.

'Well, miss, if you can't make up your mind I'll make it up for you. You won't work in an office so I'm going to ask your Aunt Sybil if she can put a word in for you in one of the shops in Liverpool. You've got to do something, Betty, and you're not qualified for much else,' she stated firmly.

Betty bit her lip. She supposed it wouldn't be bad working in one of the big shops; it was just that she'd be beholden to Aunt Sybil. There would be lectures about not letting her down in any way. She hadn't really given much thought to the future. She was still only fifteen, for heaven's sake. All she wanted was to work somewhere where she would meet people, make friends that she could go out with – along with Rose, of course – and start to enjoy herself. To find out what life was really all about. It wasn't any use saying she would learn to type, that could only lead to office work, the idea of which she still dreaded. And she didn't have any ambitions like Rose. Rose wanted to work her way up, maybe even one day become a qualified book-keeper. As for Gloria, well, she couldn't see her sister reaching any kind of senior position in the Revenue, all she was interested in was Artie Taylor. She'd just end up marrying him, having a couple of kids and staying at home.

'So?' Sal asked.

'So I suppose you'd better ask Aunt Sybil,' Betty replied sulkily.

When Sal phoned her sister-in-law she thought she sounded preoccupied. Sybil seemed far more interested in exactly when Harry would be home for she informed Sal that she intended to come and see him.

'He'll be home on Tuesday morning, Sybil,' she said.

'Good. Then I'll come on Wednesday afternoon, Sal. There is something important I have to discuss with him, with you both.' Sybil now sounded brisk and businesslike.

'Am I going to be given any idea what it is?' Sal asked. She was very curious to know what Sybil had on her mind.

'No. I prefer to wait until Harry is home. We'll discuss it then.'

'And you will ask around for Betty?' Sal pressed.

'I will, but don't expect it to be the likes of Cripps or Hendersons or the Bon Marche, she hasn't got the right attitude. Probably Lewis's or Owen Owen.'

'But not Blackler's or T. J. Hughes.' They were the really cheaper department stores and Sal knew Sybil's company did not deal with them but she couldn't resist mentioning them.

'Of course not. Don't be facetious Sal. I'll see you next Wednesday.'

When Sal informed Harry that his sister intended to visit them the following afternoon he didn't seem surprised. 'Aren't you curious to know what she wants to discuss with us? I am,' she said as she sat sipping her tea in the lounge of the *Amazonia* the following Tuesday.

'Not particularly. I just wish she'd left it a bit later. Let me have a day's peace,' Harry replied. He was fully aware of what Sal's reaction to Sybil's idea would be. 'So, Gloria is still courting?' he added.

Sal nodded. She wasn't going to tell him that things were getting more serious between his elder daughter and Artie. He'd find that out for himself soon enough. 'I've asked Sybil to help get Bet— Elizabeth a job.'

'Really?' he asked, indicating that the waiter refill Sal's cup.

'Seeing as she didn't know what she wanted I made her mind up for her. She has to do something. I'm not having her just hanging around the house.'

Harry nodded. At least that was one problem less. He frowned. 'I've been thinking, Sarah, about the homecoming party.'

She looked surprised, wondering what was coming next. 'What about it?'

'Perhaps this time we'll give it a miss. Look around as you go home, Sarah. There are ships lying up in the docks, there's not as much money around these days – or jobs.'

She was a little alarmed. 'It won't affect you?'

'No. Small lines like this are more profitable. We can keep more of a check on costs. There's a terrible amount of waste on passenger liners and high running costs and they can't afford to keep ships sailing half empty.'

She was very relieved. 'Perhaps you're right, Henry. It is an extravagance.'

'I know people will be disappointed but I'm certain when we explain they'll understand. I'll take Sybil and Richard, Doris and Edward and Eileen and Walter out for a meal, and us of course. Just family this time.'

She nodded, not wanting to mention Artie. 'That's a good idea and it will save me all the work of clearing up afterwards.' She gathered up her bag and gloves. 'I'll go now, Henry. You'll be home later?'

He nodded. 'I'll bring the things I've bought with me, Sarah.

126

Save you the trouble.' He hadn't been as extravagant this time for Sybil's plans were going to cost him quite enough.

Sybil arrived on time the following afternoon stylishly dressed in a spring suit of cream wool with a matching hat decorated with a large bow of russet brown satin. Sal had dressed up for the occasion and looked elegant in a pale green wool crêpe dress, the collar and cuffs of which were edged in a darker green braid. She'd already set the table for tea with her best china.

'I think we'll get straight down to business,' Sybil said, taking off her jacket to reveal a blouse of russet silk dotted with cream spots.

'I'm all ears,' Sal said, pouring the tea.

'I take it that this romance of Gloria's is still going strong?' Sybil said, picking up a sugar lump with the little silver tongs and dropping it into her cup.

'I'm afraid it is,' Sal replied. So this is what this visit is all about, she thought. 'I've tried to get her to go out with Rita in the hope that she'll broaden her circle of friends but she flatly refuses.'

'So she's getting more and more involved with Artie?' Harry was thinking aloud.

Sal nodded. 'She sees him every day and they go out at least twice a week. He's on better money now, although he's not out of his time yet.'

'She can't marry him, Sal. She would be throwing herself away and none of us wants her to do that, do we?' Sybil said firmly.

'I certainly don't want her to marry him,' Harry stated.

'She can do much better. She's a very attractive girl and I won't have her ending up stuck in a rented house with a couple of children, trying to make ends meet all her life. Which is what will happen if she marries Artie Taylor.'

Sal said nothing. Being 'stuck' in a rented house with two kids was good enough for his wife but obviously not for his daughter. She did want a good life for Gloria but she wanted her to be happy too. She had no real objection to Artie, she just thought Gloria was too young and hadn't had enough experience of what life could offer.

'She's never going to meet anyone else the way she's going on so what I propose is this,' said Sybil. 'I've had a long talk with Richard and with Mr Bateman at work and he is willing for me to take some time off so I can take Gloria on a trip to New York. We'll go as first-class passengers on the *Mauretania*. It will take five days to get there; we'll stay a few days and then come back, possibly on the *Berengaria*, which will take another five days. Travelling first class, she's bound to meet someone far more suitable than Artie Taylor.'

Sal was stunned. 'Good God, Sybil! That will cost an absolute fortune!'

Harry nodded. 'I'll help out as much as I can. I think it's a very good idea, Sal. I've sailed with Cunard remember – not as a first-class steward of course – but I've seen the type of passengers who travel with them first class and they really are very wealthy. She'll stand a good chance of meeting someone who can offer her a very good life.'

So that was why he was making economies, Sal thought.

'You knew all about this, Harry, didn't you?'

'Sybil mentioned it to me and I agreed with her. Even if you or I take her to dances and soirées and the like, at places such as the Adelphi, Sal, she still wouldn't meet very many suitable people. That's if she would agree to go in the first place. But she can hardly turn down a trip like this. You must agree that it's the opportunity of a lifetime,' Harry replied.

Sal was still struggling to take it all in but he was right. Gloria would refuse to go to such places and it would be left to her to try and drag the girl out, something she didn't relish at all. Nor was she really very comfortable in what she termed 'Society circles', whereas Sybil was. 'It most certainly is. Doesn't Richard mind the expense?'

Sybil shook her head, thinking of the hours she'd spent convincing him that it would be worth every penny if her niece managed to find herself a wealthy husband. 'It took a little persuasion. He mentioned it wasn't really fair on Betty, but he agreed it would be worth it.'

'But what if she doesn't meet anyone? We'll be back to where we started and will have wasted hundreds of pounds,' Sal said.

'She *will*, Sal. If Grace Harding, who was travelling second class to go to a job as a nanny, could meet someone, Gloria will,' Sybil said firmly. 'Grace Harding's mother is a friend of a friend of mine at the golf club,' she enlightened Sal.

Sybil was determined that not a single moment of this trip would be wasted. She would find an eligible young man for Gloria if it killed her. She was well aware of just how much money this was going to cost.

Seeing that both Harry and Sybil were set on this venture Sal turned her attention to the more practical things. 'She'll have to have a whole new wardrobe of clothes, Harry, including evening gowns.'

'I'm aware of that,' he replied.

'And it will all have to be of the best quality – but I'm sure we can get discounts,' Sybil added.

'And what about her getting the time off from work?' Sal asked.

Sybil had already thought of this. 'She's entitled to some time for holidays and I'm certain that when it's explained where she's going and the means of travelling they'll allow her the extra time off – unpaid of course as she is still a junior member of staff.'

Sal sighed. 'So who is going to tell her?' She didn't relish the task.

'I will,' Harry answered after receiving a quick nod from his sister.

'Of course we won't make any mention of the real purpose of the trip. Just that it's an enormous opportunity and a great treat,' Sybil added.

Sal was still very dubious about it. The whole trip would only take a couple of weeks; did they really think Gloria would meet and fall in love with a complete, if wealthy, stranger in that time? She had her doubts but seeing they were both set on it she said nothing. It *was* the opportunity of a lifetime for Gloria and she wouldn't deny her daughter this chance to travel, and travel in such luxury.

Chapter Fourteen

———

Harry decided to tell Gloria that evening and asked Sal if she could send Betty and Rose out to the cinema.

'They'll know there's something going on, Harry. They never go out mid week.'

'Just tell them we have something very important to discuss with Gloria,' he'd replied.

Both girls were surprised when Sal informed them that as a special treat they could get the tram to the Princess, which was near Walton Vale.

'Why are we being treated? Did Da give you the money because he didn't bring us very much this trip?' Betty asked suspiciously.

'He did and it's a treat because this time we're not having the usual home-coming party. We'll all be going out for a meal instead, just family, and there is something we want to talk to Gloria about,' Sal added, trying to sound offhand.

They discussed it on the tram as it trundled its way towards the main road and Warbreck Moor where the cinema was situated.

'I bet it will have something to do with her future,' Rose speculated.

'Probably her "future" with Artie. I bet she gets engaged at Christmas,' Betty added.

'If she does, she's mad. What's she done so far? Nothing much,' Rose said.

Betty shrugged. 'She's getting to be a real pain. She's always hanging around Artie's neck and I have to agree with Brian, it's sickening. Well, I'm certainly not going to go and marry the first boy who shows any interest in me and I'm certainly not going to get engaged at eighteen.'

'Me neither,' Rose agreed.

'It must be a serious discussion otherwise Mam would never have let us out and not to see Ramon Novarro.'

Rose sighed. 'He's just *gorgeous!* I wouldn't mind getting engaged to someone like him.'

Betty laughed. 'Fat chance either of us have of ever meeting anyone like him. Come on, this is our stop.'

Gloria was a bit annoyed when Sal told her that after supper she wasn't to go next door to see Artie and that she'd asked Elsie to stop him from popping into their house too. 'Your da has something very important to tell you, Gloria,' she'd informed her daughter.

'What's *that* important?' Gloria replied pettishly.

'Wait and see. Now take that look off your face, miss,' Sal instructed.

When Betty and Rose had gone out Gloria began to feel a little apprehensive. She prayed her da wasn't going to give her a lecture about her romance with Artie.

'Your Aunt Sybil called here this afternoon, Gloria, with some very good news indeed,' Harry informed her.

Gloria tried to look interested.

'Just you wait until you hear this, Gloria,' Sal said, smiling.

'She's going to take you on a trip. A very special trip. You're going to New York, Gloria, and on the *Mauretania* – first class.'

Gloria stared at her father and her jaw dropped. 'Me? I . . . I'm going to . . . *New York?*' she at last managed to stammer.

Harry laughed at the incredulous expression on her face. 'You are indeed. Just think of all the sights, the Statue of Liberty, Central Park, the skyscrapers, the—'

'The shops on Fifth Avenue,' Sal interjected.

'And that's only part of it. Travelling in luxury there and back, waited on hand and foot, and all the cocktail parties, the balls, the gala evenings, the fabulous food,' Harry enthused for her face had now lit up and her eyes were shining with excitement.

'And you're to have a new wardrobe of clothes too, with evening gowns and cocktail dresses,' Sal informed her.

'Oh, Mam! Da! I just can't believe it!' Gloria cried, her hands pressed to her cheeks.

'Your Aunt Sybil is going down to the Cunard Building tomorrow morning to book it. She'll telephone you in the evening to tell you all about it and exactly when you'll be sailing. Isn't it exciting?' Sal enthused.

'Why did she decide to take me now? I can't think of any special occasion. I mean I'm not twenty-one or anything,' Gloria asked.

'It's a treat. A very special treat. Both she and Uncle Richard think you should see a bit of the world,' Harry explained.

'How will I get the time off work? I'm only entitled to a week's holiday.'

'Don't worry about that. I'll make an appointment to see whoever is in charge of the office and explain,' Harry assured her.

A cloud of euphoria had enveloped Gloria but then she remembered Artie and some of her excitement faded. 'But I won't be able to see Artie for ages!'

'It's only for a couple of weeks, Gloria,' Harry said irritably.

'But what am I going to tell him? Oh, he'll miss me so much and I'll—'

'For heaven's sake, Gloria! Don't say you're even thinking about not going!' Sal interrupted before Harry could make any comment. 'It's the opportunity of a lifetime. I wish it had happened to me. Your aunt will be absolutely devastated if you refuse and it's going to cost a small fortune. Just a trip to New York would be fantastic but to travel in the lap of luxury – well! Words fail me.'

Gloria bit her lip. She was utterly torn between having to leave Artie for two weeks and the most exciting thing that had ever been offered to her.

'You can't turn this opportunity down, Gloria. I won't hear of it. I don't know of another girl who has ever been offered such a chance and your mam is right, Sybil and Richard would be so disappointed in you. I doubt they'd ever forgive you,' Harry said firmly.

'I'm sure when you tell Artie all about it he'll say you'd be mad not to go,' Sal urged. 'If he got the opportunity he'd seize it with both hands.'

Gloria nodded. She couldn't disappoint Aunt Sybil and Uncle Richard, it was more than generous of them to spend so much money and time on her and she really would love to go – and to have all those new clothes! And she really wouldn't be away *that* long. 'I'd love to go, really I would.'

Sal breathed a sigh of relief and Harry smiled. 'Well, you're going to be very busy these next few weeks – shopping,' he said.

The excitement was back in Gloria's face. 'Can I go and tell Artie, Mam?'

'As long as you're not there too long. We'd better get going on a list of everything you'll need,' Sal reminded her.

Elsie could see from the girl's face that she was delighted with something.

'You look pleased with yourself, Gloria.'

Gloria laughed. 'I am. Oh, Artie, wait until I tell you what Da's just told me.'

Elsie laughed. 'For heaven's sake, sit down. You're hopping up and down like a jack-in-the-box.'

'I'm so excited. I still can hardly believe it.'

'Believe what?' Artie asked.

Gloria looked around and knew she had everyone's undivided attention. 'He's just told me that Aunt Sybil is taking me on a trip to New York! And we're going first class on the *Mauretania*!'

Elsie stared at George in astonishment and Brian's mouth dropped open.

'That's great news, Gloria!' Artie cried, looking as astounded as everyone else.

'I really won't be away long. Just over two weeks, we're going to stay in New York for a few days to see all the sights.'

Elsie found her tongue. 'You really are a very lucky girl, Gloria.'

'Oh, I know!' She turned her attention to Artie. 'It's not something I could turn down, Artie. They'd have been so terribly disappointed.'

He smiled at her. 'Of course you couldn't have turned it down. Do you know when you'll be going?' He was glad for her, he really was, even though it would mean he wouldn't see her for a couple of weeks.

'I'll know tomorrow evening. She's going to book it tomorrow.'

Elsie's initial surprise was wearing off and she thought it very unfair of Sybil to shower so much on Gloria and nothing on Betty. She wondered if Sal thought that too. In fact, why was Sybil going to so much trouble – to say nothing of the expense?

'Can we all come and see you off, when you do go?' Brian asked. He'd seen the ship and it was huge and he knew people had farewell parties on board. Wouldn't it be just great to go on board a ship like that?

'I suppose so,' Gloria answered.

'We'll just come down to the Landing Stage to wave you off. Your mam and da and the girls will be there too so I don't expect there will be room in your cabin for everyone,' Elsie said.

'Oh, there's bound to be. We're going first class so I expect our cabin will be big and I'd love to have a Bon Voyage party,' Gloria replied happily. 'I'd better get back. I promised I wouldn't be long as we've got to make a list of all the new clothes I'll need.'

'That's going to cost your da a pretty penny,' Elsie remarked.

'I know. That's probably why we're not having a party this time he's home,' Gloria informed them.

Artie saw her back and before she went in he took her in his arms. 'I'm really pleased for you, Gloria, but I'll miss you.'

'And I'll miss you too. It's going to seem like ages,' she said, kissing him.

He smiled down at her. 'You won't forget all about me, will you? I expect you'll be dancing the nights away.'

'Artie! Of course I won't forget you! How can you think such a thing let alone say it when we've been courting seriously for so long?'

'I was only teasing, Gloria. You go and enjoy every minute of it,' he said but he hadn't been teasing. She was bound to find herself in the company of other young men, but at least her aunt would chaperone her.

'You must come on board to the Bon Voyage party,' she urged.

He grinned. 'I will but can you see your aunt's face at the sight of our Brian poking his nose into everything?'

'Well, I won't care. Promise you'll be there?'

'I promise, Gloria.'

Chapter Fifteen

———◆◆———

SYBIL HAD BOOKED THE trip the following day and Gloria
had listened with growing excitement as her aunt
described the state room she had booked on the *Mauretania*,
the suite at the Waldorf Astoria Hotel in New York and the
state room on the return trip on the *Berengaria*, which was
supposed to be even more luxurious than her sister ship,
having been the property of the Kaiser. She had been
confiscated at the end of the war and taken over by Cunard
to compensate for the loss of the *Lusitania*, which had been
sunk by a German U-boat.

Gloria had then read out the list of new clothes Sal
had made for her aunt's approval and arrangements had
been made for the first shopping expedition to start early on
Saturday morning. They were due to sail from Liverpool on

Saturday 16 April so there wasn't a great deal of time. Just over two weeks.

'She'll have poor Mam demented until she finally gets on board,' Betty muttered to Rose when Gloria came back in to relay her conversation with her aunt. They had both washed up and were putting away the dishes in the kitchen.

'She really is lucky, Betty, but I don't think it's very fair at all. What about you?' Rose stated. She was glad for Gloria but the amount of money that was being spent was enormous and Betty, as usual, was getting nothing.

Betty shrugged. 'Even if she had offered to take me too I wouldn't have gone, not without you. And besides, I don't think I could stand being stuck on a ship for five whole days with *her* and her airs and graces, let alone have to put up with her for two weeks. If I want to go to New York I'll pay for myself.'

'I have to agree that I couldn't stand her watching me like a hawk for all that time. I wouldn't be able to enjoy myself,' Rose added.

'I don't think our Gloria will either.'

'Of course she will. She gets on great with Madam High and Mighty and she's so excited about it all.'

Betty hung up the tea towel and leaned against the sink. 'I'm pretty sure she isn't being taken just to have a great time.'

Rose stared at her hard, puzzled. 'Why do you say that?'

'I think it's Aunt Sybil's way to "detach" her from Artie. I'm certain she doesn't approve of him and I know Da doesn't want Gloria to marry him.'

'Your da doesn't seem exactly fond of the Taylor family,' Rose mused.

Betty nodded. 'I think they're hoping our Gloria will meet someone else on this trip. Someone rich and "more suitable", as my dear aunt would say.'

'What makes you think that?' Rose probed. It sounded highly unlikely to her. If it was the reason then, in her opinion, they were certainly going to extremes.

'Well, you notice she didn't mention it until Da was home? If she's been planning it, and I think Uncle Richard would have needed a lot of persuading to part with so much money, why didn't she say something to Mam about it before this? No, I think she waited to get Da's support because I don't think Mam would have been very agreeable. She doesn't mind Artie, she just thinks they're too young.'

Rose thought about it and then nodded slowly. 'You've got a point.'

'So, our Gloria *will* enjoy herself but you can be sure Aunt Sybil will be pushing her into the arms of the first fellow she thinks suitable.'

'Do you think Gloria realises all this?' Rose asked.

Betty shook her head. 'Don't be daft. Our Gloria's not the brightest star in the sky and besides all she can think about are new clothes, luxury travel and the wonders of New York.'

'Should we say something?' If this was Sybil's plan Rose thought it was very underhand and sneaky and certainly not fair to either Gloria or Artie.

Betty pulled a face of mock horror. 'Are you mad? We'd just be accused of sour grapes, of being so jealous that we want to ruin the trip for her. No, we'll keep our mouths shut, Rose.'

141

*

Sal called in to see Elsie one morning early the following week, begging a cup of tea and a few minutes' peace and quiet.

'I'm worn out with it all already, Elsie, and by the time she's ready to go I'll be exhausted,' she confided.

'So, when are Betty and Rose starting work?' Elsie asked to change the subject entirely.

Rose had had her interview and had been offered the job in the accounts department in the offices of the Porto-Brasilia Line in the Royal Liver Building and Sybil had managed to get Betty an interview with Lewis's department store in Ranelagh Street. Betty had been offered a job in the haberdashery department. It didn't sound very interesting or exciting, she'd confided to Sal; she'd hoped for something in ladies' fashions or millinery or footwear, but she supposed it was a start. It was a big store on five floors and they had a restaurant and even a small zoo. Sal had donated a parrot to the zoo. Harry – in a fit of sheer lunacy, she'd thought at the time – had brought it home and the thing had been so noisy and messy that as soon as he'd gone she'd taken it to Lewis's zoo. Thankfully he'd brought no more.

'Rose starts next Monday and she's looking forward to it. She'll work Monday to Friday nine to five thirty and Saturday until lunchtime so she'll have finished work and be more or less "on the spot" to see Gloria off. I don't really think our Betty is looking forward to her job. The hours are long, eight until six Monday to Thursday and seven on a Friday and of course she works all day Saturday. She won't earn as much as Rose either, she's starting on twelve shillings a week and Rose is getting fourteen.'

'If she's working all day Saturday then she won't be able to see Gloria off,' Elsie remarked but thinking that maybe that wouldn't be so bad. She thought it quite scandalous that Betty as usual was being left out when so much was being lavished on Gloria. She couldn't understand Sal's attitude to all this.

Sal sighed. 'I know but she's going to ask can she have a bit longer for her lunch that day and if she can she'll come on board for a bit. Will your Brian be able to go?' she asked, knowing that Brian too was starting work the following week.

'He'll be working on the Saturday morning and, to be honest, Sal, I don't know if it will be a good thing or not to bring him.'

'Why?' Sal asked, surprised.

'I don't want him getting any mad ideas about going away to sea. He's got the chance to learn a trade, be a skilled man, and it's steady work. He's very, very fortunate but I don't think he realises it. I heard him asking Harry what it was like to work on one of those ships.'

'When was that?' Sal asked. It was the first she'd heard of it.

'The other day. Our Brian was leaning over the back-yard wall talking to him.'

'I hope Harry told him it was damned hard work, long hours and you get the height of abuse from some passengers. Harry worked on the big liners for seven years.'

'I think he did. Brian said he told him it was no picnic, especially if you started off as a steward or waiter in steerage class. But I still think it might be a mistake to take him. It is a great sight, Sal, all those paper streamers being thrown down from the decks, there's usually a band playing too and there's such an air of excitement, and then when they cast off, you'd be deafened by the noise of all the other ships in the river blasting off on their steam whistles.'

Sal nodded. She had to agree with Elsie. It was a great sight to see the departure of the big liners, one that was witnessed by Liverpudlians on a regular basis, although these days such spectacles were becoming less and less commonplace as ships were being laid up. 'I'll leave it up to you, Elsie.'

'Of course Artie's delighted that Gloria's being given such an opportunity but he'll miss her and I know he's a bit worried that she might meet someone else,' Elsie confided.

'She'll meet lots of people, Elsie, but I suppose what's to be will be. If Gloria really loves Artie then she won't be interested in anyone else. Don't forget the saying. "Absence makes the heart grow fonder".'

Elsie nodded slowly. 'I hope you're right, Sal. I'd hate to see the lad get hurt and he would be. He thinks the world of her.'

'I know, Elsie.' Sal got to her feet. 'Only time will tell. I'd better get back now, I'm expecting Sybil to phone about the hats.'

Chapter Sixteen

───◆───

S AL WAS VERY RELIEVED when the day finally came when
Sybil and Richard arrived to take Gloria and her luggage
down to the ship. The previous week had been hectic with
all the last-minute arrangements and the packing. Everything
had to be carefully folded with sheets of tissue paper placed
between – on Sybil's instructions – and then packed into the
new trunk and cases that had been bought. Harry had
ordered a taxi for himself and Sal, Rose would go straight
from work and Betty would get a tram down to the Pier
Head to spend a short time with her sister. Artie was to
accompany Elsie, George and Brian (who had insisted on
going too) on the tram to the Pier Head and then he would
go on board while the rest of the Taylor family would wait
with the crowds.

She had to admit that Gloria looked every inch a well-dressed, elegant young lady. She wore a silver-grey fine-wool tailored costume with a matching hat. Her plum-coloured pure silk blouse matched the broad band of ribbon that decorated the hat. Gloria's gloves and shoes were of pale grey kid, the shoes sporting an hourglass heel and a strap over the instep. Her clutch bag was also pale grey embellished with beads.

'Oh, very smart and stylish, Gloria,' Sybil said approvingly. 'Now, have you got everything?'

Gloria nodded, checking the angle of her hat for the last time in the mirror.

'Harry will give Richard a hand with the luggage. Will it all fit in, Sybil?' Sal asked a little anxiously.

'Of course it will,' Sybil replied firmly, ushering her niece towards the door.

Sal thought that Sybil had gone to town on her outfit too. Her sister-in-law wore a pale apple-green wool dress under a matching coat, the collar and cuffs of which were trimmed with pale beige fur. Her cloche hat was of pale green and beige and all her accessories were of beige kid. The pair of them certainly wouldn't look out of place at all in the first-class accommodation.

When they finally reached the Pier Head it was very crowded. The boat train had arrived at the Riverside Station and passengers had alighted and porters were sorting out the luggage and transporting it to the ship. On the Landing Stage itself Cunard officials were dealing with hundreds of passengers of all the various classes while porters and crew were manhandling luggage aboard. The huge black hull of the ship towered above everything, the four red and black funnels emitting trails of smoke.

Harry and Richard pushed their way through the crowd and secured the attention of an official and the services of two porters. Then Sybil, Gloria and Sal were escorted to the first-class gangway.

'Oh, Mam, isn't it *huge*!' Gloria marvelled as a steward led them along the wide, thickly carpeted companionway towards their state room.

'It's certainly a lot bigger than the *Amazonia*,' Sal replied. 'You'll have to mind you don't get lost,' she added.

Harry had had a word with the steward and they were given a quick tour of the main first-class lounge and dining room en route.

'Oh, isn't this elegant!' Sal remarked, gazing around the huge lounge. The centre of the ornately plastered ceiling was capped by a large domed skylight of leaded glass. Parts of the ceiling were supported by slender columns of marble and onyx. In the very centre of the room was a massive floral arrangement of flowers and palms, the fronds of which almost touched the centre of the glass skylight. The room was lit by dozens of crystal chandeliers and at one end there was a marble fireplace whose logs flickered realistically although they were lit by electricity. A large clock reposed on the mantelshelf above it. The carpet was a plain soft green, and the sofas and chairs were covered in green, pink and beige brocade, their arms richly carved and gilded. Highly polished occasional tables were secured to the deck and there were vases of flowers everywhere.

'It looks more like a drawing room in a country house than a lounge on a ship,' Richard commented.

The dining room was on two decks, the upper balcony supported by marble columns. The tables were already laid for dinner with crisp white damask cloths and napkins, silver cutlery, crystal glasses and fine china. The steward pointed out the Captain's table in the very centre of the lower deck, which featured another huge floral arrangement, the fronds of its palms reaching up as high as the balcony above.

'Oh, such style and . . . élan!' Sybil breathed rapturously.

Harry nodded. It certainly was very opulent but he wondered how the diners on the upper balcony would fare in rough weather. Probably be flung about a great deal, he surmised. Those who managed to face mealtimes at all. The ship might be the holder of the coveted Blue Riband for the fastest crossing of the Atlantic but he'd heard it was a bumpy crossing even in good weather. It was something to do with the length of the ship.

When they finally reached their state room Sybil was not disappointed. It was spacious. The carpet was blue, as were the curtains at the two portholes. The bulkheads had been wallpapered in a very modern art deco design. There were two single beds, not bunks, with white wrought-iron frames and blue and gold bedspreads. Between them was a marble-topped cabinet with a sink and a mirrored cabinet above for toiletries. In a compartment over one bed were two life-jackets, over the other a small brass plate containing the call buttons for the steward and stewardess. There were also two wardrobes and two dainty gilt-framed chairs.

'Your stewardess will be along once we've cast off, madam, to unpack,' the steward informed them. 'Will you be requiring anything further?'

'We'd like drinks bringing, if you please. For the bon voyage party. Champagne, I think,' Sybil instructed him.

'This is really gorgeous and so comfortable,' Gloria said excitedly, sitting on one of the beds and taking off her jacket.

'I should think so, too, at one hundred and thirty dollars each, each way,' Richard remarked, peering out of one of the portholes and gazing down at the crowds who seemed very far below.

Harry raised his eyes skywards. It was nothing short of exorbitant; he hoped it was all going to be worth it.

The steward reappeared with glasses and two bottles of champagne just as Rose and Artie arrived together.

'I came up the gangway with Artie but then we got lost. It's so big! There are miles of corridors; we ended up in a room they call the Verandah Café, all wicker chairs and tables and potted palms, then someone directed us here,' Rose informed them, gazing around.

The bottles were opened and the drinks poured.

'No sign of Betty yet?' Sal asked, looking anxious, hoping Betty had managed to negotiate the crowds and not get lost once on board.

Rose shook her head. 'Not yet.'

'Sit yourself down beside Gloria on that bed,' Sal instructed, sipping the fizzy wine. There seemed to be dozens of people going up and down outside the open door. 'Did

Brian come with your mam and da, Artie?'

Artie nodded. He'd been overcome by the sheer size and opulence of the ship and he hadn't liked the rather disdainful look Sybil had given him. He was also well aware that he had little chance of having a few minutes alone with Gloria to say their farewells. There were just too many people around.

'Harry, if Betty hasn't arrived in five minutes will you go and look for her?' Sal urged.

'Oh, she'll be all right, Sal. Someone will direct her here,' Sybil said, indicating that Richard replenish her glass.

Sal didn't look convinced but a few seconds later a flushed and rather windblown Betty arrived, her coat flying open to reveal her black shop dress beneath.

'It's sheer mayhem out there! First of all I had to fight my way up the gangway, then I was asked was I in the right place by a real snooty-looking feller in a uniform. Then when I told him the cabin number and the name he finally got a lad in a fancy suit with brass buttons down the front and a hat like a round biscuit tin to show me here.'

'That would have been a bellboy, Betty,' Sybil informed her, frowning at the girl's untidy hair and open coat and thinking it was no wonder her appearance in first class had been questioned.

'For heaven's sake, Betty, tidy yourself up!' Sal admonished, catching the expression on her sister-in-law's face.

'It's always windy down here, Mam, and I was rushing. I've got to be back in half an hour. I had to wait ages for a tram and I'll get no lunch and I'm starving!' Betty protested, plumping herself down on the bed next to Rose and her sister.

Harry pressed the bell on the wall and when the steward arrived he asked for some sandwiches to be brought.

'I wouldn't be able to find my way around at all, Gloria,' Betty said, eyeing the dainty sandwiches hungrily.

'Oh, I'm sure it won't be hard, not once all the visitors have gone ashore. It will be far less crowded then and things will be more leisurely,' Sybil assured Gloria.

'Do you think you'll be seasick?' Rose asked, sipping her drink.

'Of course she won't!' Sybil replied firmly, thinking that Rose was utterly without tact.

'You'll have every comfort in here if you are,' Artie added, trying to sound more cheerful than he felt. He'd seen quite a few young men as they'd made their way here and they'd all been extremely well dressed and full of the self-confidence that seemed to come with wealth.

'You'll find that the time flies, Gloria. There's so much to do,' Harry said. 'Do you know where you are docking in New York, Sybil?'

'Apparently at Pier number fifty-four at the Chelsea Dock,' she informed him.

He nodded. Cunard used Piers 53, 54 and 56, which were located between West 13th and West 15th Streets. 'You'll get a cab up to the Waldorf, I assume?'

Sybil nodded. 'Of course.'

'Ask the Purser to arrange it for you. There's no point in

having to join the free for all when you disembark,' he advised.

The sound of a gong being rapidly beaten and the cry of 'All ashore! All visitors ashore, please!' came from the companionway outside.

'Time to go,' Harry said as Sal gathered up her bag and gloves. Betty got up and fastened her coat, popping the last sandwich into her mouth.

'I won't be able to wait to wave you off, I'll have to get back,' Betty informed Gloria as she hugged her sister. 'But have a really great time. I know you will.'

Rose too hugged her and wished her bon voyage, as Richard kissed his wife farewell.

'Right then, girls, let's give Artie a few minutes alone with Gloria,' Sal instructed after she'd kissed her daughter goodbye. She and Harry and the two girls left to make their way to the gangway.

Sybil had no intention of leaving the pair alone but she busied herself unpacking her toiletries.

'Well, I'll see you in a couple of weeks, Artie. Take care of yourself,' Gloria said, casting a sideways glance at her aunt.

'Will you write, Gloria?' Artie asked. He wanted to take her in his arms and kiss her but knew that wasn't possible.

'I won't be able to post any letters until I get to New York, but I will write and I'll send postcards too,' she promised, gazing up at him.

'I'll miss you but have a really great trip, Gloria,' he said, bending to kiss her on the cheek.

'I know I'll miss you too, Artie,' Gloria said, her eyes misting.

'Last call for visitors! All ashore who's going ashore!' came the raucous cry from outside.

'We'll walk with Artie to the gangway, Gloria, so he won't get lost,' Sybil suggested pleasantly. 'Then we'll go up on deck. Put your jacket back on, dear. It could be chilly.'

Artie again kissed Gloria on the cheek before he joined the other visitors leaving the ship and Sybil then took her arm and they made their way up to the promenade deck.

There was great activity below on the Landing Stage as the gangways were removed and the hawsers were slipped from the bollards. They both jumped as the *Mauretania*'s steam whistle blasted out three times, the sound echoing across the waters of the Mersey. Hundreds and hundreds of coloured paper streamers were thrown from the decks down to the crowds below and the band of the Liverpool City Police struck up a military march.

Gloria clutched her aunt's arm, her eyes shining. 'Oh, isn't it just *wonderful*, Aunt Sybil!'

Sybil laughed delightedly. 'It certainly is.'

'Can you see Mam or Da or Artie?' she asked, peering down at the crowd and waving madly.

Sybil didn't reply for quite a few minutes because speech was impossible owing to the cacophony of sound that engulfed them as every ship on the river and in the docks on both banks sounded their farewells to the mighty Cunarder.

When some semblance of peace was restored and the ship drew slowly away from the Landing Stage, Sybil took her niece's arm. 'We'll go down now and oversee the unpacking; the crowd is starting to disperse. And Gloria, dear, I think that from now on if you are referring to your parents you should call them either "Father and Mother" or "Mum and Dad". It does sound so terribly common to say "Mam and Da" and that won't do at all, not in first class.'

Gloria nodded. She was going to have to watch her manners, she knew that, but it didn't detract from her feeling of excited anticipation.

Chapter Seventeen

————

B ETTY WONDERED JUST WHAT Gloria was doing at that
exact moment. She was dusting the tall cabinets that
held the dozens and dozens of boxes of buttons. It was
something she had to do every morning after making sure
the counters were tidy. They sold everything that was needed
for sewing: pins, needles, tape measures, thimbles, bias
binding, elastic, ribbons and everything else that fell into the
category of haberdashery. It was so boring, she thought, and
she wondered if her sister was having breakfast or was she
taking a walk on deck? Her da had told her that there was a
difference in time so she couldn't really work out what time
it was for Gloria.

It was only Tuesday, four more days to go until the end of
the week she thought, but Rose was going to call in after
work and wait for her to finish. Then they were going to the

Kardomah café for something to eat before returning home. Her lunch break didn't fall at the same time as Rose's so they couldn't meet up then.

The time seemed to drag interminably but at last she caught sight of Rose threading her way between the counters on the ground floor.

'Have you been busy?' Rose asked, pretending to scrutinise the selection of ribbons. Betty thought she looked smart in her navy-blue coat and hat, which was trimmed with a large pale blue bow. Rose could wear anything 'suitable' for work while she had to wear this awful black dress with the detachable white collar and cuffs.

'Not really. It wasn't too bad this morning but the afternoon has dragged. What about you?'

'The work's always steady but it gets busier on Thursdays. They do the wages then.'

'I wonder will there be a letter or a card from Gloria in the post today or tomorrow? They seem to have been gone ages.'

'I shouldn't think so, they don't arrive until tomorrow. Your da said the shipping agent takes the mail to post when they dock and then it comes back on the next ship that's licensed to carry the Royal Mail. It will be next week before we get any word.'

'Well, I bet she's having a more exciting time than we are,' Betty said gloomily. Looking up she caught sight of the floor walker. 'I'll have to measure out some ribbon to look as though I'm busy and not just chatting. Pick a colour.'

Rose pointed to a reel of wide scarlet satin ribbon and Betty began to measure it out.

'Give me another yard. I'll buy it,' Rose instructed.

'You don't have to. I can roll it back on again when he's gone off to annoy someone else.'

'No. I'll use it around the hem of that black dress I've got,' Rose informed her. It would only cost a few pence.

'What time is it now?' Betty asked as she cut the ribbon and folded it.

'A quarter to six. I'll just wander around for a bit. Go and look at the cosmetics and the fashions upstairs. I might even be able to afford a new blouse for work.' Rose was thinking of Alan Hopkins, one of the young men who worked in the same office as herself as she handed over the coins and Betty handed her the small brown paper bag. He seemed interested in her and she liked him.

'Thanks. See you later,' Rose said, walking away and flashing a smile at the middle-aged floor walker in his pin-striped trousers and black jacket.

She couldn't afford to buy herself anything yet, Betty thought. She would have to save up for a few weeks for by the time she'd given her mam something for her keep and paid her fares, there wasn't a great deal left of her wages. She sighed heavily as she replaced the roll of red ribbon. She couldn't honestly see herself sticking it here for long. The work was dull, the days long and the pay miserable. But what else was there? Office work, waitressing, factory work? Mam would have a fit if she so much as mentioned factory work. She thought again of the day her sister had sailed. It really would be great to travel and from what she'd seen of the ship that day it had looked luxurious. She'd heard that even in second class the accommodation was superior to anything they had at home. Even the *Amazonia*'s public rooms were lovely and that was only a small ship. She wondered again about the possibility of becoming a stewardess – but could she possibly stick working here until she was eighteen?

As they settled themselves at a table in the Kardomah café half an hour later, Betty decided to broach the subject with Rose.

'I hate that job, Rose. It's so boring and the pay is a pittance,' she announced after they'd ordered.

Rose frowned. 'You've only been there five minutes, Betty. Give it a chance.'

'It's not going to get any better, is it?' Betty protested.

'Can't you ask for a transfer to another department?' Rose suggested.

'I don't think there are any vacancies. They have a noticeboard in the canteen where they advertise vacant positions and I've only seen one and that was for a junior to work Saturdays.'

'Just keep your eyes open. Something might come up. Jobs are not easy to come by, Betty,' Rose advised, but she felt sorry for her friend. She herself had settled in well and she enjoyed her work.

The tea and toasted tea cakes arrived and Rose thanked the waitress.

*

Betty decided to broach the subject to her father again before he sailed. He was due to leave in two days' time.

'Da, I hate this job at Lewis's. It's so boring and the pay is really terrible. Are you sure I can't apply to be a stewardess? Couldn't I put my name down at least?'

Harry looked up from his newspaper. 'Betty, you've only just started that job. Give it a chance, since your Aunt Sybil was good enough to help you get it.'

Sal nodded. 'Your da is right, give it a chance. You'll get a rise in time.'

'But couldn't I put my name down on some sort of waiting list? I wouldn't mind carrying on at Lewis's if I thought in a couple of years I could do something a bit more interesting and exciting,' Betty persisted.

'They don't have waiting lists, at least not for so far in advance. A couple of months maybe but not years. The youngest I've ever heard of anyone being taken on is eighteen and most lines won't take you until you are twenty-one at least. And it's far from glamorous or exciting. Running around day and night after often bad-tempered and ungrateful passengers. Cleaning up after them when they're sick and when you feel like death yourself. You have to work even if you're seasick too. It's long hours, you even have to eat standing up, and if you get a couple of hours off in port you count yourself lucky. And the pay isn't great either. It's not until you work your way up to second and then first class that you start to get good tips, and that takes years.'

'But what about the Porto-Brasilia Line, Da? Their stewardesses don't have to work like that,' Betty persevered.

'They don't but you wouldn't even be considered until you were twenty-five and had suitable experience. And even if I put a word in for you, the competition is fierce.'

Rose thought that working on the big liners sounded awful. 'It sounds as if you're better off where you are, Betty.'

'She most certainly is,' Sal added emphatically. She didn't want the kind of life Harry had described for Betty. She'd be nothing but a skivvy. 'Just put it out of your mind, Betty. Give the job you've got more of a chance. You can't afford to go giving in your notice because you find it boring. You should be thankful you've got a job at all.'

Betty sighed. It looked as if she had no option.

Sybil leaned back in her chair and sipped her after-dinner brandy, which had so kindly been ordered for her by Bernard Hepworth, or 'Barney' as he'd insisted she call him. He'd introduced himself and his son, Grant, at dinner as they'd been sharing the same table, along with two other couples. He'd also informed her that he was one of the 'Hepworth Brothers', a firm of financiers with offices on Wall Street.

'How simply fascinating. How many brothers do you have, Barney, and are they all involved in the firm?' she'd asked.

'Just the one and he's more what you'd term a sleeping partner. He spends his time in the Caribbean. He has a nice place in Barbados. Not really very interested in the day-to-day business,' he'd confided. He'd gone on to tell her he lived in New York, in a large brownstone house near Central Park, and that he'd taken his son to London to meet some influential people at the Stock Exchange there.

Sybil's gaze rested on the small group of young people who were drinking cocktails at the bar and she smiled. Gloria appeared to be getting on very well with them all. There were three young men and just Gloria and another girl, but her niece was by far the more attractive and elegantly dressed of the two. Barney's son Grant, who she'd learned would be twenty-seven in a few months and who she thought seemed very well mannered and quite handsome, seemed to be taking a great deal of interest in Gloria. With his dark hair, small, neatly clipped moustache and beautifully cut dinner suit he looked every inch a gentleman.

Gloria sipped her drink slowly. It was called a manhattan and she wasn't totally sure she liked it. It was quite strong and she wasn't used to drinking and she certainly had no intention of making a fool of herself in front of all these sophisticated young people. The other girl – Delia something – had urged her to try it. She herself seemed to be enjoying hers; she'd almost finished it and the young man called Freddie had ordered her another.

'If you'd prefer something with a bit less of a bite, Gloria, I could get you a Blue Lagoon,' Grant Hepworth offered, having noticed that she didn't appear to be enjoying her drink.

Gloria smiled at him, thinking how observant and considerate he was. He was also quieter than the two other young men. 'Oh, yes, please. That would be lovely. I've tasted that before. My father can make a lot of cocktails and he always mixes them at the parties we've had.' She glanced in her aunt's direction. 'Aunt Sybil usually has a dry martini. I wonder: should I try one of those? What do you think, Grant?'

He shook his head, looking mildly amused. She was a rather sweet girl, he thought, and a bit out of her depth, especially beside Delia who was obviously very much a 'party girl' and would no doubt spend the evening propping up the bar. 'Much too "dry", Gloria. So "dry" in fact it would bring tears to your eyes, I'm sure.'

'Then I'll have a Blue Lagoon, please.'

He ordered the drink and when it was served, he handed it to her and leaned closer, lowering his voice. 'Do you think we should perhaps join your aunt and my father who seem to be getting along famously?'

Gloria nodded, feeling a little relieved. Keeping up with the others in the group with both drinks and conversation was beginning to be a bit daunting and Grant Hepworth seemed to be a much nicer person than the others. 'Yes, I think that's a good idea. It's still really quite early and I can't say I want to spend the entire evening drinking cocktails.'

Grant took her arm and guided her politely towards Sybil and Barney.

Grant smiled at Sybil. 'We thought we'd join you, if you don't mind. It's getting a bit loud over there.'

'We'd noticed,' Barney said, frowning in the direction of the group at the bar. 'Sybil was just telling me that it's your first visit to New York. That she's brought you on this trip to see a bit of the world, Gloria, broaden your horizons.'

'What a swell opportunity for you, Gloria,' Grant said, smiling and offering her a cigarette from his silver case.

'Thank you, but I don't smoke,' Gloria said, returning his smile. 'Yes, it's really wonderful for me. Aunt Sybil is so generous,' she added.

'Nonsense. Richard and I just want the best for you, dear,' Sybil replied sweetly.

Grant finished his brandy and turned to Gloria. 'I wonder, would you like to take a turn around the deck? It's quite a mild evening.' She was a very attractive girl and he'd be happy to get to know her better. If he was brutally honest with himself, he had to admit he was rather tired of the company of his father and the middle-aged stuffed shirts they'd been entertained by in London.

Gloria looked enquiringly at her aunt, not quite sure if she should accept the invitation. He was very nice, far more sophisticated than Artie, but of course he was older and had obviously travelled more.

'What a good idea. I'd get a jacket or maybe even a coat though, Gloria,' Sybil advised, thinking this was a very good start indeed.

'Another brandy or maybe a cocktail, Sybil?' Barney Hepworth asked when the younger couple had left.

'That's very generous of you. I think perhaps a martini, but just the one or I'll be tipsy,' Sybil tinkled.

'And may I ask what Mr Mostyn does?' he enquired after he'd given his order to the bar steward.

'He owns a factory. They make packaging. Cardboard cartons, things like that. Not very exciting I have to say, but it pays the bills,' she replied.

'Your niece is a very attractive girl,' he commented.

'She is but she also has a lovely nature. She's quiet and perhaps a little naive but very thoughtful and quite . . . biddable,' Sybil impressed upon him.

'A little naivety is no bad thing these days, Sybil. I don't approve of the antics of some of these modern girls.' He looked pointedly across to the group at the bar where that flighty young thing was now quite openly clinging to one of the young men. 'Nothing short of outrageous.'

'Oh, I quite agree. I can assure you that dear Gloria would never make such an exhibition of herself.'

Barney's disapproving gaze was still fixed on Delia Mayberry. 'An "exhibition" is an apt description, Sybil. That young lady might have money but she sure is showing a marked lack of both breeding and manners.'

Sybil nodded. 'I'm so glad Gloria and Grant decided to leave them to their own devices. Quite disgraceful for a young girl to drink like that. I wonder what her parents think?'

'Does Gloria have no parents?' Barney asked, offering Sybil a cigarette which she accepted.

'Oh yes, but her father, my brother, is away at sea for a great deal of the time so I do like to keep my eye on her.'

'Taken her under your wing, have you?' Barney produced a gold lighter.

She nodded. 'She has a younger sister but this sort of trip just didn't appeal to Betty. Anyway, if she'd come too it would have meant my sister-in-law would have been left on her own.' Sybil made no mention of Rose. 'Gloria works for the Inland Revenue. The tax people,' she added, anxious to divert his attention from her brother and his family.

'Smart as well as attractive,' he mused, smiling. 'Well, I hope the youngsters get to know each other better on this trip, Sybil.' He winked.

She smiled broadly at him. 'So do I, Barney.'

Chapter Eighteen

———◆·❖·◆———

GLORIA HAD GONE FOR her coat and had quickly checked her appearance in the mirrored front of the cabinet over the sink before she'd made her way up to the boat deck, which she managed to find more by chance than by design. She found Grant waiting for her, leaning on the ship's rail, smoking a cigarette. He quickly extinguished it and came towards her.

'I hope I haven't been too long? I'm still not sure which staircase to use. All this "forward" and "aft" is a bit confusing,' she confessed.

'Don't worry, you'll soon get used to it. Do you want to go down to the promenade deck? It's enclosed on one side. I'd sure hate you to be cold.'

'No. This is fine. As you said, it's quite a mild evening.'

She looked around; there seemed to be other people taking an after-dinner stroll too.

He took her hand and tucked it under his elbow. 'I find it can get quite stuffy inside and I don't just mean the atmosphere,' he said, winking.

She laughed. 'You mean Aunt Sybil and your father?'

'Well, maybe not your aunt, I haven't gotten to know her yet, but you're the first person I've met recently who is under the age of thirty. I seem to have spent all my time with some very up-tight guys.'

'I know what you mean. I work in the offices of the Revenue and anything to do with finance is taken very, very seriously indeed. There are some "up-tight" people there as well.'

'So we have that in common, Gloria. Now let's see what else we have.'

She'd asked him all about New York and he'd described his life there and his interest in baseball and football. He'd been a quarterback in his college days, he'd informed her, although she'd confessed that she didn't have a clue what that was as she didn't think they had them in football teams at home. He'd laughed and told her that American football and soccer were vastly different. She'd found him attentive, interesting and amusing. He made her laugh and then he said her laughter sounded like tinkling bells. She'd blushed at that but then she had begun to feel cold.

'You're shivering. I'll escort you back to your state room. We don't want you catching a chill, not on your first night at sea.' He'd put his arm around her shoulders and they'd gone back inside. She wondered with surprised detachment why she didn't mind his arm around her but when they'd reached her state room he hadn't made any attempt to kiss her.

'I'll see you at breakfast, Gloria. Then perhaps you'd like to have a game of shuffleboard or quoits. Weather permitting, of course.'

'I'd like that, Grant,' she replied.

'Great. I'll look forward to it. Goodnight, Gloria.'

'Goodnight.'

Sybil was already in her nightdress and was brushing her hair. 'Did you have a pleasant stroll?' she asked, trying to detect any sign that her niece had enjoyed young Grant Hepworth's company.

'I did. He's very nice.'

'I thought so too.'

Gloria took off her coat and hung it up, noticing that their beds had been turned down very neatly. 'I'm going to have a game of shuffleboard or quoits with him tomorrow after breakfast, if the weather is nice,' Gloria informed her.

Sybil smiled to herself. 'What a good idea. I was thinking of visiting the library and spending a quiet morning reading, but I'm sure you'd prefer the company of someone more your own age.'

Gloria hadn't thought her aunt might have made other plans. 'Oh, if you'd prefer me to stay with you—'

'Heavens no! I want you to enjoy yourself, Gloria, and Grant is a very nice young man. You'll have fun,' Sybil interrupted.

Gloria hung up her dress. 'He makes me laugh and he

says the nicest things. When I laughed at something he'd said he told me it was like hearing tinkling bells.'

Sybil nodded. She hoped this friendship would blossom.

As she lay in the narrow bed, aware of the slight rocking of the ship as it moved through the calm waters, Gloria thought how much she had enjoyed her first day. All the excitement of leaving the Mersey, the luxury and comfort of their state room, the palatial public rooms, the mouth-watering dinner and then finding herself in Grant Hepworth's company. He was really very charming and quite unlike anyone she'd ever met before. He seemed considerate and had lovely manners. She was glad now that he'd suggested they leave Freddie, Delia and the others. She hadn't really been very comfortable in their company. Grant hadn't seemed comfortable either, he was quieter, more reserved. Of course he was so very different to Artie and she vaguely wondered could that be what attracted her to him? She wondered what Artie was doing at this moment. Was he missing her? Very probably. With a little jolt she realised that she'd hardly had time to even think about him since they'd sailed, her mind had been so full of other things. This was such a different world to that she was used to, everything was new and glamorous and exciting. There was certainly nothing mundane about it or the people she was now mixing with; even Aunt Sybil seemed different, more relaxed and less stuffy. The rocking motion was sending her off to sleep and she drowsily thought she was looking forward to spending the morning on deck with Grant; she hoped the weather would be fine.

*

Gloria had been quite relieved when next morning Sybil remarked that the weather was exceptionally good for the time of year. There was very little wind and just a slight swell, and although it was cloudy, the waiter at breakfast had informed her rain was not forecast until perhaps later that afternoon. 'So you go and enjoy your morning with Grant and I'll pop along to the library and we'll meet up for lunch,' Sybil had instructed.

She had laughed a great deal as Grant showed her how to play deck quoits.

'I'll never get the hang of it! I either throw the quoit too hard so it goes spinning off the board, or not hard enough so it ends up just a few feet away.'

'Try again. It's much better not to throw too hard though or I'll spend my time running around the deck to retrieve it.' He grinned, thinking how pretty she looked in her soft knitted two-piece, her cheeks pink from the wind the movement of the ship generated and her eyes sparkling with amusement. He took her arm. 'Look, like this . . .'

To Gloria's delight the rubber ring landed exactly on the highest scoring square. 'Look! I did it, Grant! With your help, of course.'

'By the end of this trip you'll be an expert, Gloria.'

She laughed up at him. 'I think I should quit while I'm ahead of the game, to use one of your sayings.'

He still had his arm around her. 'Let's go for coffee – or would you prefer the traditional bouillon? It's a sort of beef tea.'

She pulled a face. 'That sounds like something you give an invalid. I'll have coffee.' She patted her flat stomach. 'I think I might have to play deck sports every day. I'll never fit into my clothes by the end of the trip, with the amount of food that is on offer at all hours of the day.'

'I'll be very willing to partner you, Gloria, but I don't think you'll have much of a problem with your weight. You have a lovely trim figure.'

She'd blushed, very aware that his arm was still around her shoulders as they walked towards the stairway that led to the Verandah Café. He said the nicest things and she judged by his tone that he was sincere.

That afternoon they'd strolled leisurely around the promenade deck and he'd asked her about her life in Liverpool.

'You've never had the inclination to travel before, Gloria?'

She'd shaken her head. 'I'd never really thought about it but now . . . well, everything is so different and *exciting*. I'm really looking forward to seeing the sights in New York.'

'They say travel broadens the mind and it certainly does. I know I now view all kinds of things in a different light and I enjoy visiting other countries and observing all the different customs and cultures. I loved London, all the really old buildings, the sense of history. I was surprised there are so many parks. If I ever get time I'd really love to do what used to be called the "Grand Tour". Paris, Vienna, Rome, Venice, Florence, Naples and of course Athens.'

'Do you think you will?' She found his enthusiasm catching and it surprised her. She'd never in a million years thought about even leaving Liverpool, let alone visiting the places he'd mentioned, but why not? Her da had.

'I sure hope so,' he'd said, smiling as he'd squeezed her hand gently.

After dinner that evening the wind had freshened and it had started to rain so a walk on deck was out of the question. Sybil and Barney had promised to join one of the other couples at their table for a game of bridge so Grant suggested they go to the ballroom where a dance band was playing. It was quite crowded and noisy so after a few dances they decided to head for a quieter bar or lounge.

'A cocktail or would you prefer champagne?' Grant asked as he settled her into a deeply upholstered chair in the chart room lounge.

Gloria had only drunk champagne once before, at Aunt Sybil's the Christmas Rose's mother had died. Her da always remarked that it was a total waste of time drinking the inferior stuff that was served in most hotels but she couldn't see that they'd have anything inferior here. 'Perhaps I'll try a glass of champagne.'

Grant ordered a bottle of the finest and after tasting it Gloria found that she really did like it. 'It's gorgeous but you really don't have to spend so much on me, Grant.'

'Only the best will do for you, Gloria.' The more time he spent in her company the more attracted he was to her. She was open and uncomplicated, not in the least self-centred or opinionated; in fact she didn't seem to be aware of just how attractive she was. She was delightful and there was nothing devious at all about her, which made a change from some of the girls he'd known – one in particular, one he'd sooner totally forget about.

She blushed, thinking he made her feel so special.

When he walked her back to her state room she felt a little shiver of anticipation run through her, wondering if he would kiss her and what it would be like. Would it be different to the way Artie kissed her? She mentally shook herself. What was she thinking of? Artie loved her and was waiting patiently at home for her to return. They were serious about each other.

'I'll see you at breakfast, Gloria, and thank you for a lovely evening. You're delightful,' Grant said before taking her in his arms and kissing her firmly but gently on the lips.

Despite herself Gloria responded, a feeling of tingling excitement and pure happiness filling her. She'd never felt like this before. She was a little breathless and confused as she drew away. 'Goodnight, Grant,' she managed to say before opening the door and leaving him.

Sybil was still out and Gloria sank down on the edge of the bed. What was happening to her? she wondered. She shouldn't feel like this but she couldn't help it. Did she really love Artie or was it just that she *thought* she did? Did she think so because he was the first boy she'd ever been out with? Grant made her feel *different*, more grown up, more *passionate*. She'd never felt like that when Artie kissed her. Oh, it was all so confusing. Maybe she'd confide in her aunt; perhaps she could help her sort out her feelings.

'I thought you would still have been with Grant,' Sybil said when she returned, having spent a very pleasant evening, which had been rounded off by Barney insisting on buying her a nightcap. 'What's wrong, dear? You haven't had an argument with him?' Sybil could see something was troubling her niece.

Gloria shook her head. 'No, just . . . just the opposite.'

Sybil sat down beside her. 'Then what's wrong?'

Gloria bit her lip. 'He . . . he kissed me goodnight, Aunt Sybil and I . . . It felt . . . so different to Artie.'

Inwardly Sybil breathed a sigh of relief. 'He is very different to Artie, dear. He's older and more sophisticated.'

'He makes me feel so special; he treats me like a princess. He told me only the very best will do for me.'

'You *are* special, Gloria. You don't realise what a truly lovely girl you are and I don't just mean in appearance, you have a charming nature.'

'And he . . . he's made me start to think about things . . .' Gloria continued uncertainly.

'What sort of things?' Sybil probed gently.

'Oh, my life. Until now I'd never even thought about travelling, visiting other countries, but Grant wants to and he makes it sound so interesting. Oh, I'm getting so confused, Aunt Sybil.'

Sybil knew she had to tread carefully now. 'You're bound to be confused but don't let it upset or worry you, Gloria. Just relax, enjoy being in Grant's company and see how things . . . develop. You're young and relatively inexperienced, as is Artie. People can sort of grow away from each other as they get older and widen their circle of friends and interests. It's just part of growing up. Now you should get ready for bed, it's late. Don't dwell on these confusing feelings. Just let things happen at their own pace.'

Gloria nodded. She hoped her aunt was right.

They saw each other at breakfast and lunch; they had afternoon tea together and spent the evenings in each other's company as well, and Gloria began to realise that what she felt for Grant was something far different, far deeper than what she felt for Artie. In fact she tried not to think about Artie now and seldom mentioned him.

For his part Grant too was becoming more and more attracted to her. He had begun to realise that he loved everything about her: her nature, her vivacity, her enthusiasm for everything, all her little mannerisms and her utter lack of duplicity.

On the last formal evening of the voyage Sybil hooked up the back of Gloria's midnight-blue devoré evening gown, thinking that of all the dresses her niece had worn this one made her look very glamorous. It was cut on a bias which made it cling to her, showing off her lovely willowy figure. She wore matching shoes with high heels and long white evening gloves. Her dark hair shone and she had clipped a dark blue headband adorned with white egret feathers over it. Earlier, the stewardess had delivered a beautiful corsage of white flowers, sent by Grant. It just finished off the outfit, Sybil thought.

'I haven't put on weight, have I?' Gloria asked. 'The food is just so fabulous that I can't refuse.'

'Of course not. There, you look lovely. Grant won't be

able to take his eyes off you and what a lovely gesture to send a corsage.'

Gloria smiled. 'It was. He's very generous.'

'I know he is very attracted to you, dear. Even his father has said so.'

Gloria's cheeks flushed. 'Did he really? I . . . I . . . do feel . . . deeply about Grant, Aunt Sybil. I . . . I don't want this trip to end.'

'Well, we will be in New York for a short time. Perhaps it won't be the end of your . . . friendship with Grant.'

'I hope not, I really do.' Gloria hoped her aunt was right.

'Now, we'd better go down. I promised Barney we'd meet them in the cocktail lounge for a drink before dinner.'

Sybil watched Grant's face light up as he caught sight of Gloria and she smiled as he came across and took her niece's arm.

'Would you mind, Mrs Mostyn, if we went and sat over there?' he asked, indicating the high stools at the bar.

'Not at all. Off you go. We want you both to enjoy this evening, don't we, Barney? After all tomorrow is our last full day on board,' Sybil replied.

She and Barney Hepworth settled themselves into comfortable chairs and he ordered her usual martini.

'I have to say they sure do make a very handsome couple,' he remarked. 'She looks like a movie star tonight.'

'And Grant could easily be taken for a matinée idol,' she added. 'It's such a shame that we only have one more day. I really do think she's become quite fond of him, Barney.'

'I know he's quite smitten with her and I'm pleased. I'll

confide in you, Sybil.' He leaned towards her. 'He was involved with someone, quite seriously, but his mother and I never liked her. She wasn't right for him; she'd have made his life a misery. She was one of these modern, self-willed, opinionated girls, full of her own importance. Everything was "me"! She was older than him, of course, and I suspected she was only really interested in getting her hands on his money and the fact that he could introduce her into New York Society. Eunice and I were not sorry when she found someone else although it upset him deeply. He kept it to himself but we knew he was hurting. He's over it now I guess but that's why I'm happy he's found someone like Gloria. She is exactly the opposite of the one who hurt him; she'll be good for him. I'm sorry you're not staying in New York for longer. You couldn't extend your trip?'

She shook her head. 'No. It's impossible, I'm afraid. We're returning on the *Berengaria* early next week.'

'Grant can take some time off to show you the sights, Sybil, and you and Gloria must come to dinner before you go back. I know Eunice will love to meet you and that you'll get along famously.'

She beamed at him. 'Thank you. We'd love that, Barney. Should we say Sunday evening?'

'Sunday will be just fine.'

'Now, tell me what kind of flowers Eunice likes. I can't come empty-handed.'

It all sounded very promising, she thought. Gloria could spend more time with Grant in New York; she'd insist on going off shopping on her own and then they would go to the Hepworths' for dinner on Sunday night. Barney had obviously invited them so that Eunice could meet Gloria.

'Roses. She loves roses, Sybil. Particularly yellow ones. She says they bring some sunshine into the house. Now she's getting older she hates the New York winters.'

'Does she really?' Sybil made a mental note to order a very large bouquet of yellow roses.

'It does get bitterly cold and she complains it makes her joints ache. I'm actually considering buying some land down in Florida and having a place built. I don't intend working for ever; I'd like to retire and take Eunice down there. The climate will be more beneficial to her health.'

'Really? How thoughtful and considerate you are, Barney. Have you told Eunice? I don't want to go putting my foot in it.'

'Oh, sure, she knows all about it. Once I'm sure Grant can handle the business, I'll start putting the plan into action,' he confided.

'And will Grant continue to live in New York or will you sell the house?' she asked.

'He'll stay in the city but if he feels the house is too big, we can sell it and he could get an apartment.'

It got even better, Sybil thought. In the near future Grant would be running the business and his parents would be down in Florida. If Gloria married him she would have no in-laws to contend with and would have a wonderful life with everything the city and the Hepworths' wealth could offer. She would just have to make a concerted effort to make sure Gloria spent as much time as possible with Grant. She was sure that Eunice Hepworth wouldn't find anything to dislike about Gloria. Perhaps they should say the roses were from Gloria and she'd take a good bottle of champagne.

Chapter Nineteen

———◆———

ROSE CONFIDED TO BETTY that Alan Hopkins had asked her out on Saturday.

Betty's eyes widened in surprise. 'And are you going? Where's he taking you?'

Rose began twisting a lock of hair around her finger, a habit she had when she was nervous. 'I said yes. We're going to the Rotunda. There are some good acts on this week.'

'Rose Cassidy! You dark horse. How long has this been going on?' Betty cried.

'There's nothing "going on" and I was going to tell you. I like him, he's nice and we get on well together. I think he's quite good-looking; he's rather quiet but that's no bad thing. I'm only going to the music hall. I was going to tell your mam tonight, ask if it was all right.'

Betty nodded in agreement. She didn't begrudge Rose a

night's entertainment nor the fact that Alan Hopkins had asked her out.

Sal was surprised when after supper Rose said she had something to tell her.

'Now what? What madcap schemes have you been dreaming up?' she demanded. She'd intended to write to Harry tonight so she could post the letter in the morning; he'd be arriving in Lisbon soon.

Rose grinned. 'Aunty Sal, is it all right if I go to the Rotunda on Saturday night? A lad I work with, Alan Hopkins, has asked me to go with him.'

Sal looked a little surprised. Rose had never mentioned this boy before but after all she would be sixteen next birthday. She was growing up; she and Betty both were. Lately she'd been so involved with Gloria and her future that she had almost overlooked the other two. 'I suppose it will be all right. Is he a decent lad? He won't keep you out late?'

'He's very nice. He's seventeen and lives in Walton and his father works for the Union Castle Line. I know that much about him.'

'Not another seafarer?'

'No. He works in the office.'

Sal nodded. 'Then go and enjoy yourself, Rose. He will see you safely home, I take it?'

Rose nodded. 'He will, Aunty Sal, and thanks. I thought I should ask before I gave him an answer, what with Mam not being here . . .' It still upset her whenever she thought of Dora.

'You did the right thing, Rose. Until you are twenty-one

you are our responsibility and even after that I'll always be interested in your welfare and happiness,' Sal said firmly. She looked on Rose as another daughter and she would do the best she could for her – for Dora's sake. Sal smiled. 'I've been so taken up with Gloria lately that I am forgetting you two are growing up. I suppose the next thing will be you getting asked out on dates, Betty.'

Betty shrugged. 'There's no one I've met so far who interests me at all.'

'Not even at work? There are plenty of lads who work there,' Sal stated.

'No. The ones I seem to come into contact with are all like that idiot Brian next door.'

'You're not feeling left out, are you? Not wishing you'd gone to New York with Gloria?' Sal probed.

'No, Mam. I wouldn't have gone even if I'd been asked, I couldn't put up with *her* for all that time.'

Sal sighed absently-mindedly. 'I don't suppose you could and if she'd have offered I would have had my doubts about the wisdom of it. Anyway she's not trying to find you a husband.' The minute she'd uttered the words she regretted them for Betty looked quickly at Rose and then grinned.

'I *knew* she was up to something like that! I said to Rose that she wasn't taking our Gloria just to enjoy herself.'

'Forget I said it, Betty. Don't you dare repeat it to *anyone*,' Sal instructed firmly.

'I won't, Mam. I promise. But what happens if Gloria doesn't want anyone else and comes home quite happily to Artie?'

Sal shook her head and sighed for Betty had expressed her own thoughts. 'I don't know but I do know this, neither your aunt nor your da will be very pleased, to say the least. Well, let's hear no more about it. We'll meet the obstacles if and when they appear.'

Rose made a special effort with her appearance on Saturday. She'd washed her hair on the Friday night and had pressed her good black dress, having smartened it up with the red ribbon she'd bought. She had a rope of red glass beads she'd got in Woolworth's in Church Street that matched it. It didn't go very well with her navy blue coat, she confided to Betty, who had suggested she borrow her black jacket.

'It's not that cold at night now and you'll be taking it off when you get inside,' Betty had said.

'Won't you want to wear it?' Rose had asked.

Betty said she wasn't going out so there would be no problem.

Rose was glad to see that Alan was waiting for her outside the theatre. It was a round building which was built on and around the corner of Stanley Road and Scotland Road and belonged to Bent's Brewery. It was a very popular place; four storeys high with ornate windows and stonework and topped with a large dome where its name was spelled out in big letters. On both sides were awnings over small shops and the entrance was brightly lit.

'I hope I'm not late, Alan,' she said a little shyly for it was the first time they'd met outside work.

He smiled at her, his brown eyes dancing. He liked Rose a

great deal. 'No. I got here a bit early. I bought you these.' He pressed a small tin containing fruit pastilles into her hand.

'Oh, you shouldn't have, Alan, but thanks.' After they'd eaten the sweets she would keep the tin as a memento, she thought as he took her arm and they went into the foyer. He was paying for their tickets and that would have been enough for her. He probably didn't earn much more than herself; it was generous of him, she thought. She glanced sideways at him. He looked very smart. He was wearing a different suit to the one he wore for work. He was a few inches taller than her and had brown wavy hair and what she thought of as an open, honest face.

'I'll get a programme, Alan. You were good enough to buy sweets,' she offered.

He guided her up the stairs and she realised he'd got seats in the Dress Circle, which were quite expensive. 'I'd have been quite happy up in the Gods, you know.'

'What kind of a lad asks a girl out and then expects her to climb hundreds of stairs and sit so far away from the stage that she can hardly hear anything?' he said, smiling at her. 'I think a lot more of you than that, Rose.'

She smiled back, pleased at his words. She was going to enjoy being with him.

Chapter Twenty

GLORIA WAS FEELING VERY nervous as she sat beside her aunt in the cab, holding a large bouquet of yellow roses on her lap.

'You are quite sure I look my best?' she asked Sybil for the third time.

Sybil patted her hand. 'I'm absolutely certain and before you ask again, Grant's mother will be as delighted with you as his father is. Stop worrying, Gloria. You'll get frown lines on your forehead.'

Gloria hoped she was right for she did want Mrs Hepworth to both like and approve of her.

She had spent so much of her time in the city with Grant, she thought happily. He'd taken her to see everything of interest and she'd marvelled at it all. In the evenings he'd dined with her aunt and herself in the hotel. He'd taken them both to see a show on Broadway and then for supper afterwards in a very expensive restaurant where he was obviously well known, and yesterday he'd insisted on buying her a solid gold compact decorated with bands of black enamel that she'd admired in the window of a jewellers on 5th Avenue. She had protested that it was much too expensive but secretly she'd been thrilled. It was gorgeous and so very 'right up to the minute', a favourite saying of his. The city had more than lived up to her expectations. It was so vibrant, so alive, the sidewalks crowded with people of all nationalities, and she would really be sorry to leave it and to leave him too. He'd captivated her completely. He was just so different to anyone she'd ever met, but then she told herself she had only ever met the likes of Artie, who now seemed so young and gauche and . . . ordinary.

The cab finally came to a halt outside a large three storeyed house that had steps leading to an ornate front door. The street was quite a wide thoroughfare but quiet and she noted that all the houses were large and well maintained. It was an affluent neighbourhood; there were no stores or bars or restaurants and there were cars parked outside quite a few of the houses, large, expensive-looking cars. She manoeuvred herself and the flowers carefully out of the cab while her aunt paid the driver.

'Chin up and smile, dear!' Sybil advised as they went up the steps and her aunt rang the doorbell.

The door was opened by a girl in a maid's uniform.

'Mrs Mostyn and Miss Jenkins, we're expected,' Sybil informed her.

They were ushered in by the maid. 'Indeed you are, ma'am. Will I be after taking your coats?'

Gloria smiled at her. She didn't appear to be very much older than herself and was obviously Irish. 'Whereabouts in Ireland do you come from?' she asked as she handed her coat to the girl.

'Mayo, miss.'

'I'm from Liverpool,' Gloria replied before catching the look on Sybil's face and biting her lip. Obviously it didn't do to be chatting to the hired help.

The room they were ushered into was huge with a large marble fireplace and two big windows heavily draped in dark green velvet. The furnishings were mainly of polished dark woods and expensive brocade and two large antique Chinese vases stood one on either side of the fireplace.

'Gloria! You look as gorgeous as ever,' Grant greeted her and, taking her hand, led her over to a chair where his mother was seated.

Gloria looked down into grey eyes that were appraising but held a hint of warmth. Eunice Hepworth looked to be the same age as her aunt but her well coiffed hair was grey. She wore a lilac-coloured dress and a single short strand of pearls which Gloria thought was a little old-fashioned compared to her aunt's very smart brown and cream striped suit and long rope of pearls.

She held out the bouquet and smiled. 'I brought these for you, Mrs Hepworth. Mr Hepworth said they are your favourite flower.'

Eunice Hepworth's features relaxed into a smile. 'That

was very thoughtful of you, Gloria. Grant, would you ask Mary to see to them, please?' She turned her attention to Sybil, taking in every detail. Barney had told her that Sybil had brought her niece on the trip out of sheer generosity and the desire to broaden the girl's outlook but she couldn't help wondering about that. Still, he'd also told her that Gloria was a charming and delightful girl, quite unspoilt and unsophisticated, and she hoped that this time her son had fallen in love with someone who would love him for himself and not his position and background as that dreadful creature he'd been involved with had done. She was glad of this opportunity to make her mind up about Gloria.

'I'm so pleased to meet you. May I call you Eunice? Barney has told me so much about you and I'm sure we'll get on famously,' Sybil gushed while Barney fussed around, getting them all drinks and making sure they were comfortably seated.

After a while Gloria began to relax. She could see that actually her aunt and Grant's mother were getting on well and Grant was being very attentive to her, as usual.

Dinner was a very well-cooked and -served affair in an elegant dining room on the other side of the hallway. Mary helped an older woman to serve while everyone chatted. Gloria gave the girl a smile as she passed her her dessert and Grant leaned closer and whispered, 'She's quite pretty but not nearly as gorgeous as you.'

By the time her aunt stated that they really should be getting back to the hotel, Gloria felt a little light-headed. A little too much champagne, she told herself, but it was a pleasant feeling. The only cloud on her horizon was the fact that tomorrow was their last day. They would board the *Berengaria* early on Tuesday morning and would sail at noon.

A cab was ordered, coats were brought and goodbyes were said. Mrs Hepworth told Sybil that it had been a real pleasure and that when she was next in New York she must most definitely call on them. Sybil in turn had thanked both her and Barney profusely, saying she would keep in touch by letter.

Grant accompanied them to the sidewalk and opened the cab door for Sybil before kissing Gloria on the cheek. 'I'm sorry I just can't get away tomorrow but don't worry, I'll be down to see you off on Tuesday,' he promised. 'And there's something important I want to ask you, Gloria,' he added.

Her heart began to race. 'What is it, Grant?'

'Not now, my darling girl. It's late and I'd like us to have a bit more privacy than there is out here on the sidewalk.'

She reached up and pressed her hand to his cheek. 'I'll be waiting for you on Tuesday.'

Eunice Hepworth settled back in her chair with a cup of coffee brought by Mary while Barney helped himself to a brandy.

'So, what did you think of her, Mom?' Grant asked as he too helped himself to a drink. He knew his father approved of Gloria, they'd had a long conversation before they'd retired on their last night aboard the ship, but his mother's approval was also very important to him for he'd decided to ask Gloria to marry him. He loved her, it was as simple as that.

Eunice smiled. 'I liked her, I liked her a great deal. She's charming and seems very genuine and sincerely fond of you, Grant.'

'I love her. I love everything about her,' Grant said.

'I don't want to put any kind of a dampener on things but you really haven't known her all that long,' Eunice reminded him gently. The last thing she wanted was for him to be hurt again. 'I'm just thinking of your . . . your feelings, Grant.'

He nodded. 'I know, Mom, but we spent so much time together that we got to know each other really well, probably better than if we'd been dating, just seeing each other a couple of times a week. I'm sure she's the girl I want to spend the rest of my life with.' He looked to his father for support.

'I think he's chosen well, Eunice, I really do. OK, so she's not very wordly wise or well travelled and I don't think her family are as affluent as we are but we can't hold that against her. She's well mannered and well behaved, she isn't one of these "flappers" – thank God – and she sure isn't what you'd call devious. She's a sweet-natured girl who I think will make him very happy.'

Eunice smiled at him. 'You can stop praising her to the skies now, Barney, I happen to agree. I thought her very open and honest, quite transparent really, and I mean that in a complimentary way.' She thought Gloria was possessed of a warm, generous nature and not in the least bit vain or self-obsessed. 'If it's what you want, Grant, then we won't raise any objections. Just as long as she makes you happy.'

*

Sybil settled back against the upholstered seat of the cab. 'Well, I think that went very well indeed, Gloria. A charming family. So friendly and hospitable. You know at first I thought I was going to have trouble making conversation with Eunice but she's really very entertaining and quite well read. She's a very nice person indeed. What was Grant saying before you got into the cab, dear?'

'That he'll be down to see us off on Tuesday morning and . . .'

'And?' Sybil pressed.

'And that he's got something important he wants to ask me.'

'Did he give you any idea what it was?'

Gloria shook her head. 'No, but I hope . . .'

'You really have become very fond of him, haven't you? I'm glad that you've been able to spend so much time together.' Sybil had insisted her niece spend as much time as possible with Grant, which meant she'd been on her own quite a lot but she hadn't minded.

'I think . . .' Gloria paused.

'What? You know you can confide in me, Gloria. I have your happiness at heart.'

'I really do think I've fallen in love with him, Aunt Sybil.'

Sybil held her breath for a few seconds. She had to tread carefully. 'But I thought it was Artie you loved?' she said quietly.

Gloria frowned. 'I thought so too at the time. I honestly did. But now . . . now I think it was just a sort of passing fancy. He was the first boy who had ever shown any interest in me. I really have never met anyone like Grant and since I left home I feel as if I've grown up.' She paused, trying to find the right words to express herself. 'I feel that now I am looking at things through very different eyes and that things have changed. That I've changed.'

'You seem to have become far more sophisticated, Gloria. Far more . . . discerning,' Sybil agreed, feeling so relieved. 'Do you think he is going to ask you to see him again? I mean to come over to New York again?'

'I hope so. I really feel so down about having to go back, I've had such a wonderful time. And I feel quite miserable about having to leave him.'

'I'm certain that between us we can arrange something, Gloria,' Sybil said consolingly. 'Don't get upset.'

The following day a bouquet of red roses arrived at the hotel for Gloria, with a note from Grant that read: 'Can't wait to see my darling girl on Tuesday. All my love. Grant'.

They were in the throes of packing but Gloria detached the card and slipped it into her purse, promising herself she would keep it for ever. It was such a shame that he just couldn't get away today.

There was just as much chaos at Pier 54 as there had been on the Landing Stage, Sybil thought as she at last managed to get the attention of an official and they were conducted towards the first-class gangway. The ship was as luxurious as the *Mauretania* she concluded when they reached their state room and she ordered tea to be brought. It was far too early for anything stronger, she told Gloria.

Grant arrived fifteen minutes later. 'There really should be some better kind of organisation down there. How are you this morning?' He kissed Gloria on the cheek and smiled at Sybil.

'I'm just "fine and dandy", as you would say, but Gloria is feeling a bit down in the dumps at having to leave,' Sybil replied, picking up her jacket from the bed. 'Well, I think I'll go and try to get my bearings. Find out where the dining room is and the lounge. I have to say this really is a lovely ship from the little I've seen so far. Quite splendid and *so* satisfying to think it was confiscated from the Kaiser.'

'I've heard that she's a lot less uncomfortable than the *Mauretania*, especially in choppy seas,' Grant informed her.

When she'd gone he took Gloria in his arms. 'I do wish you didn't have to leave, darling girl.'

'Oh, so do I,' she said, feeling really miserable.

He kissed her and she clung to him. 'I'll miss you so much, Grant.'

'And I'll miss you, too. I've gotten something for you.' He extracted a small box from his pocket. 'And you remember I said I wanted to ask you something important?'

She nodded. Her heart was beating wildly and she felt a little dizzy, as if she'd had too much champagne.

'You know I love you, Gloria. I think I knew it from the minute I saw you. Will you come back?'

She gazed up at him, tears sparkling on her lashes. 'Yes. Oh, yes I will! I promise. I love you.'

'And will you marry me?'

'Oh, Grant! Darling! You know I will. I really do love you!' she cried.

He kissed away her tears. 'Darling girl! I promise I'll make you so happy. You'll have the very best of everything. Nothing but the best will do for you.'

'Grant, I don't want to go. I don't want to leave you, especially now.'

'I intend to come over to England as soon as I can get away. To meet your folks and ask your pa for your hand – officially. But I want you to have this, just to remind you that you're all mine.'

She gasped as he slid the ring on to her finger. She'd never seen a diamond so big. This was her *engagement* ring! She was overcome with happiness. And he was going to come over to Liverpool soon! They wouldn't be apart for long and then she would become his *wife* and would come back here to live. It was just too much to take in. She dissolved into tears.

'Darling girl, why are you crying?' he asked, bemused.

'I'm just so happy, Grant!'

He handed her his handkerchief and then held her tightly. He really did wish she didn't have to go. He'd told his father of his plans yesterday and Barney had been delighted and told him to 'go for it'. His mother too had seemed pleased, saying she thought Gloria a very sweet, thoughtful girl. So he'd gone and bought the ring for he hadn't wanted to see her sail out of his life for ever.

By the time Sybil returned Gloria had dried her eyes,

powdered her nose and was sitting holding Grant's hand. Sybil smiled at him ruefully. 'I'm afraid I have to tell you they are getting ready to ask the visitors to go ashore.'

Grant got up, drawing Gloria with him. 'We have something to tell you, Mrs Mostyn, or perhaps I should call you "Aunt Sybil" too now. Gloria has just consented to become my wife.'

Gloria held out her left hand, smiling happily.

Sybil threw her arms around her. 'Oh, I'm so pleased and so happy for you both!' Grant in turn was embraced. 'Grant, congratulations, and of course you must call me Aunt Sybil!'

'I'll be coming over to Liverpool very soon. I have to ask her pa's permission.'

'Oh, dear. I'm afraid he is away and won't be back for months,' Sybil informed him but seeing Gloria's face fall she hurried on: 'But of course her mother will be delighted and I know I can speak for Harry, he'll have no objections at all.' She wasn't going to let him postpone his visit just because her brother was away. Things had worked out exactly as both she and Harry had hoped they would, so she was speaking the truth when she said he certainly wouldn't have anything to object to. 'I'll write and tell him as soon as we get home. In fact it might be possible to send him a wireless telegram. I'll sort it out with the shipping agents.'

Gloria looked very relieved and Sybil urged her to accompany Grant to the gangway as the now familiar sound of the gong and the shouted instructions for visitors to leave immediately sounded in the companionway outside.

Sybil sat down on the bed. Oh, she was so happy for

Gloria. She would have a wonderful life in New York, it was a far better outcome than she had envisaged. The Hepworths were very wealthy, you only had to see the size and style of the house and the size of the diamond on Gloria's finger to know that, and she was certain it would be the first of many expensive jewels her niece would receive. She would describe everything in detail to Harry when she wrote. Their trip had been well worth every single penny and she was sure Richard would agree with her.

Chapter Twenty-One

S AL AND RICHARD HAD come down to the Landing Stage to meet them. Sal had only had one letter from Gloria and that had obviously been written before she'd arrived in New York for she'd written mainly about the ship, the food, the dances and cocktail parties and the various ways she was keeping herself entertained. She had mentioned that she spent quite a bit of time in the company of a young American called Grant Hepworth, who was travelling with his father. They were on the same table in the dining room and Sybil, it appeared, had become quite friendly with Barney Hepworth.

She had hoped Gloria would write or at least send a postcard from New York but there had been no word from her since. That hadn't pleased Elsie either. She'd said that poor Artie looked so upset and disappointed when he came home each day and there was no letter for him.

'She's obviously having such a good time that she can't be bothered even sending a postcard,' Elsie had remarked sharply.

Sal had learned from Richard that Sybil had written that this young man seemed to have become very fond of Gloria and that she had high hopes of it developing into something more serious as he was, Sybil considered, very eligible indeed.

They didn't have to wait for too long before Sybil and Gloria came down the gangway. Richard kissed his wife fondly and Sal hugged her daughter and said she was glad she was home. Then there was the usual flurry of activity as the porters took the luggage to Richard's car and they all got in. He drove slowly up the floating roadway to the Pier Head.

'You must have had a really exciting time, Gloria. We did expect more than just the one letter,' Sal remarked as Richard turned the car into the Dock Road.

'Oh, Mam! I can't wait to tell you all about it.' Gloria drew off her gloves and held out her left hand. 'Look, Mam! I'm engaged. Grant is the most wonderful person I've ever met and I just *adore* him! You'll really like him too, I know, and he's coming over soon to meet everyone.' The words tumbled out and Gloria's eyes were shining.

Sal stared at the huge solitaire on her daughter's finger in utter amazement and for a few seconds was totally bereft of speech.

'You really will like him, Sal. He's a very nice young man

from a charming family. His father is a financier; they are very wealthy. It's just what we'd all hoped for,' Sybil said.

Sal found her voice. 'But you've known him for a much shorter time than you'd even known Artie! Are you sure you've done the right thing, Gloria? You haven't been blinded – *dazzled* by everything?'

'No, Mam! I needed to see things in a different light. I needed to travel, to meet other people, just as you told me I should. And Grant just swept me off my feet. He treats me like a princess; he calls me his "darling girl".'

'But, Gloria, you've only known him for *two weeks*. This all sounds like complete and utter madness to me. You're still only eighteen.'

'Sal, don't go getting upset,' Sybil intervened. 'When you meet him I know you'll approve of him. He idolises Gloria – and just think of the wonderful life she'll have.'

'Money and status aren't everything, Sybil. I'm not at all sure about her marrying a man she hardly knows and going to live thousands of miles away.' Sal was wishing that Harry was home but then she realised that in all probability Harry would agree with Sybil. He'd been in favour of this idea right from the start. She wasn't in the slightest bit happy about this situation. 'What about Artie, Gloria? What are you going to say to him? He's going to be very upset.'

Gloria frowned. 'I know now that I really didn't love Artie, Mam. I just thought I did. It was a passing fancy. I've outgrown him. I'll have to try to explain that.'

Sal sighed. The poor lad was going to be broken-hearted and she dreaded to think what Elsie would have to say about it. With a sinking feeling she knew that there was very little she could do to stop Gloria marrying this Grant Hepworth. Harry would certainly give his permission, urged on by both Gloria and Sybil, and at the end of the day she too wanted Gloria to make a good marriage. But she also wanted her to be happy. What she certainly didn't want was for her daughter to go and live on the other side of the world. All she could hope for was that now she was home, in familiar surroundings and away from the bright lights and glamorous lifestyle, Gloria would at least give some serious thought to her future.

When Sybil and Richard had left Sal told her daughter that she thought she should go and break the news to Elsie. 'At least she can give the lad a bit of warning because as soon as he gets home from work he's going to want to come straight in and see you.'

Gloria bit her lip. 'Oh, I don't think I can face her, Mam,' Gloria pleaded. 'I didn't want to hurt Artie, you know I didn't. I couldn't have turned Aunt Sybil's offer down and I really didn't intend to fall in love with Grant, it just . . . happened. But she won't see it like that.'

'I don't suppose she will,' Sal replied grimly. 'But you are going to have to face Artie, Gloria.'

Gloria nodded. It wasn't something she was looking forward to at all. 'I know so can't you go and tell her, please? It's going to be bad enough for me seeing Artie.'

'No, this is something you are going to have to do, Gloria. If you can't face telling both of them then I'd save what you have to say for Artie.' This wasn't the home-coming Sal had planned at all. She'd been looking forward to them all sitting down this evening and listening to all the details of Gloria's trip, Artie included.

Both Betty and Rose were astounded to learn that Gloria was engaged and as they examined the ring Betty blurted out the first thing that came into her head.

'So, Aunt Sybil's plans all worked out then.'

'What plans?' Gloria asked, admiring the way her ring sparkled with a myriad of colours in the light.

'That's why she took you on that trip in the first place. To find you a wealthy husband. She didn't think Artie Taylor was good enough for you.'

Gloria stared at her. 'No, she didn't! It was a special treat.'

'I honestly wonder about you sometimes, Gloria. You can be so *dense*! It cost a fortune, it had to be more than just a special treat.'

'What a horrible thing to say! You're just jealous, Betty!' Gloria cried. 'Anyway I love Grant and I'm going to marry him.'

Betty wasn't going to say anything more on the subject of Sybil's ulterior motive. It was obvious her sister didn't believe her – or didn't *want* to believe her – and she didn't want Gloria to think she was jealous because she really wasn't. 'Well, if you're happy, Gloria, then I'm delighted for you.'

'It's a gorgeous ring,' Rose added.

'When are you going to tell Artie?' Betty asked.

Gloria frowned. All afternoon she'd been trying to work

out what to say so that he wouldn't be too upset but there didn't seem to be any way to avoid that. 'This evening. I expect he'll come in to see me as soon as he gets in.'

Betty pursed her lips. 'Sooner you than me, Gloria. He's not going to be very happy, to say the least.'

Gloria nodded and slowly removed her ring – at least she could spare him the sight of that.

Just as Gloria had surmised Artie came in as Sal was starting to cook the supper.

'Go on into the living room, lad. She's in there,' Sal instructed kindly.

Betty and Rose instantly retreated upstairs.

'Mam told me you were home. It's seemed ages since I last saw you, Gloria. Why didn't you write? I was getting really worried.' Artie crossed to take her in his arms but Gloria remained seated, plucking nervously at the edge of her blouse, trying not to meet his eyes.

'What's wrong?' Artie was beginning to realise that she didn't seem overjoyed to see him.

'I . . . I've got something to tell you, Artie.' She took a deep breath. There was no easy way to do this; she just had to get it over. 'I met someone on the ship going over and . . . well, I love him. I've realised that what I felt for you wasn't . . . love, Artie. It was just a sort of "crush".'

The colour drained from Artie's face and he stood staring at her, shaking his head. It couldn't be true. It just *couldn't*. 'No! No, Gloria. You love me!'

'It's true. I'm so sorry, Artie. I've changed. I've grown up. Everyone told me I needed to broaden my horizons, meet new people, and they were right.' She still couldn't look at him.

Shocked as Artie was he realised it was probably one of those wealthy, well-dressed, confident young men he'd seen the day he'd seen her off. 'Why, Gloria? You know I love you and you swore you loved me!'

'I thought I did but I was wrong. I'd never been anywhere, never met many people. I . . . I've grown up and things . . . changed. I've changed.'

'I haven't! I still love you. You hardly know this feller,' Artie cried. She was lovelier than ever, he thought, and it hurt so much just to look at her. She'd cast him aside without a second thought. 'I suppose he's a rich American who's swept you off your feet, turned your head with all his fancy talk and expensive gifts. How can you do this to me, Gloria?'

'He hasn't turned my head, but he has "swept me off my feet", as you put it. I love him and we got engaged. I'm going to marry him and he's coming over very soon to arrange things,' Gloria answered.

'Write and tell him that you've changed your mind, Gloria. Please?' Artie begged, although he hated himself for begging.

She shook her head sadly. 'I'm really sorry, Artie. I never intended it to happen but it did. I never wanted to hurt you, really I didn't, but I won't change my mind, you can be certain of that.'

He stood staring at her in silence for a few seconds, fighting to control his emotions; then he turned away so she wouldn't see the pain, anger and desperation in his eyes. 'Then I'm glad you'll be going to live over there. I couldn't stand to see you living here with someone else, Gloria,' he said bitterly.

She didn't reply. There was nothing more she could say but she did feel very sorry for him.

Artie rushed from the room.

'I'm sorry, lad,' Sal said when he came back into the kitchen.

He nodded curtly and she could see the tears in his eyes. 'Goodbye, Mrs Jenkins,' he said.

'Goodnight, Artie,' Sal replied.

He didn't go home; he couldn't yet face the agony and humiliation of having to tell them that she'd dropped him like a hot cake for some fast-talking, rich Yank. Instead he walked the streets, trying not to think of the times they'd spent together, the kisses and embraces they'd shared, the promises she'd made of undying love. It hurt too much.

When he'd been gone for over an hour and a half Elsie decided to go and tell him that his meal was fast drying up and that they would have plenty of time to catch up now she was back, but by the look on Sal's face as she came into the kitchen she knew something was wrong.

'I came to see if he intended to come home at all tonight.'

'He's not here, Elsie. He's been gone for over an hour. Sit down, luv.'

'What's happened?'

'She told him it was … well, that it's all over between them. She met someone else on the ship.'

Slowly Elsie nodded and then sighed heavily. 'I had a feeling something like that would happen, Sal, and when she didn't write I began to think she'd found another lad. Oh well, they're both very young and these things happen.'

Sal was relieved that she seemed more disappointed than annoyed. 'I know, Elsie, and I also know she really didn't intend to hurt him. She says she loves this Grant Hepworth but I wonder: does she? Or has she been dazzled by everything?'

'It might just be a shipboard romance, Sal.'

Sal shook her head. She had to tell Elsie the whole story. 'I don't think so. He's coming over soon; they're engaged.'

Elsie stared at her in astonishment.

'I know, you could have knocked me over with a feather when she told me this morning.'

Elsie didn't know what to say but then she thought of Artie. 'And she told our Artie that? No wonder he hasn't come home, the poor lad. He must be devastated.' Privately she thought Gloria was a fool but she felt sorry for Sal, who had nodded in reply to her question. 'It must be a worry for you, luv, she's only eighteen.'

'It is but I'm worried about Artie too. Do you think he'll be all right?'

Elsie was wondering that too. 'I suppose so. He'll get over it in time, I expect, but he's bound to be feeling utterly miserable and wretched now. If he isn't back in half an hour I'll get George to go and look for him.'

A thought suddenly struck Sal. 'He won't go and do anything . . . stupid, will he?'

Elsie got to her feet. 'No. He's much too sensible. He'll be broken-hearted but young hearts mend. I'm sorry it hasn't worked out between them.'

'So am I, Elsie,' Sal said, wishing now that she hadn't let Sybil and Harry talk her into letting Gloria take that trip. She wasn't at all sure that Gloria was doing the right thing.

Chapter Twenty-Two

———◆◆◆———

TWO WEEKS LATER A telegram arrived for Gloria and she read it aloud.

'Oh, Mam! It's from Grant. He's booked his passage. He's sailing next Monday. He'll be here at the end of next week! I can't wait to see him again,' she cried excitedly.

'He's certainly not wasting time, is he?' Sal remarked, thinking that he obviously wasn't giving Gloria any time to change her mind – or maybe he really was missing her. Elsie had told her that Artie was taking it so badly that he was going to ask at work if he could be transferred to another depot, somewhere like Crewe where there were big engine-repair works. Elsie had told him to think a bit more about it, he'd have to stay in digs and living alone wouldn't help; she was sure he'd get over it without taking such drastic measures. Now, however, Sal wondered if a temporary move wouldn't be such a bad thing. At least the poor lad wouldn't have to see Gloria and Grant together.

Gloria had instantly phoned Sybil who had advised that he should stay at the Adelphi and promised to make all the arrangements, seeing as he hadn't mentioned accommodation.

'I wonder how long he's coming for?' Rose mused. She was getting ready to go to the cinema with Alan. This was the third week he'd asked her out and she'd bought a new blouse for the occasion, a pale green crêpe-de-Chine affair with a satin bow at the neck, and she'd had her hair trimmed. On two days this week they'd gone for a cup of tea together in their lunch break. She really liked him.

'I don't think she knows. She said Aunt Sybil asked her the same thing,' Betty replied. 'Maybe he'll write and give her more details. At least he isn't going to stay here,' she finished, thinking of Artie.

'There's no room and, besides, he's probably used to something a bit more luxurious. Not that there's anything wrong with our home but he'll be better off at the Adelphi,' Rose added. 'I wonder will they make all the arrangements for the wedding?'

'I suppose so. It's a long way to come just to visit,' Betty replied.

'You'll be a bridesmaid,' Rose reminded her friend.

Betty pulled a face. 'I'd forgotten that. Knowing Gloria I'll have to wear something I'll hate and you can bet Aunt Sybil will have a big say in everything. Anyway, she might ask you to be bridesmaid too. You are one of the family now.'

'Do you really think so? I wouldn't mind being a bridesmaid,' Rose confided.

Sal decided she should have a talk to Gloria about Grant's visit.

'I know he's coming to meet everyone but if you still intend to go ahead with things I suppose you will have to think about when and where you will have the wedding,' she said to Gloria, although she was still full of misgivings.

'Oh, yes!' Gloria clasped her hands together.

'Well, your da won't be home for months and I know he will want to give you away and meet Grant and his family.'

Gloria's face fell. 'Oh, Mam! I don't want to have to wait *that* long!'

'Don't you think it would be wise? It would give you more time to think and besides, weddings can't be arranged in a couple of days. The Hepworths will be expecting quite a grand affair, I should think, and that certainly can't be arranged in a hurry. And if your da isn't here, who is going to give you away?'

'Uncle Richard will. I really don't want to wait for ages, Mam.'

Sal could see she was determined. 'Let's wait until Grant arrives and see what he has to say. He might want to wait until the *Amazonia* gets back.'

That hadn't occurred to Gloria and she nodded, pouting a little. She was torn between wanting to get married quickly and leave for her new life with Grant and wanting her da to give her away and for the occasion to be very 'grand' as Sal had said. She certainly didn't want a hole-and-corner affair.

On the morning when Grant was due to arrive, Gloria dressed with more care than she had for the past few days. Both Sal and Sybil were to accompany her down to the Landing Stage where the *Aquitania* would tie up. Sybil had booked him into the Adelphi for a week and had also booked lunch for them all and a taxi to take them there. Richard was going to drop them off at the Pier Head.

'I'm getting quite used to coming down here to either see people off on big liners or welcome them home,' Sal remarked as they waited with the crowds. At least the weather was kind, she thought. It was a really beautiful May morning with a clear blue sky and a warm breeze. Even the waters of the Mersey looked less grey and turgid than usual. He would at least see the city at its best.

'There he is! Grant! Grant, we're here!' Gloria cried, catching sight of him and waving before pushing her way through the press of people towards him, followed by her mother and aunt.

Grant waved back and as she reached him, he swept her into his arms. 'Gloria! I've missed you so much.'

Sal looked on as he kissed Gloria, thinking she could see why her daughter had fallen for him. He was a very handsome young man and extremely well dressed, and he obviously was very fond of Gloria judging by the way his face had lit up when he'd caught sight of her daughter. Poor Artie hadn't stood a chance beside this matinée idol.

'Aunt Sybil, it's great to see you again and' – he turned to

Sal, smiling – 'this must be Mrs Jenkins.' He took her hand and kissed her on the cheek. 'I'm so pleased to meet you, mother-in-law-to-be.'

Sal had to laugh. 'Oh, don't! That sounds terrible. And "Mrs Jenkins" is so formal. Call me Sal, or Sarah if you prefer.'

He cocked his head to one side, studying her. 'I really think Sarah suits you better. You are a very elegant lady. I can see now where Gloria gets her sense of style from.'

Sal smiled. Oh, he was a charmer all right, she thought.

'I've arranged for a taxi to take us all to the hotel, Grant. I've booked you in for a week as we didn't know how long you intend to stay,' Sybil informed him as she ushered them all towards the waiting car and the porter followed with the luggage.

'That's fine and dandy. I can only stay a week, I'm afraid. But I'm sure it will be long enough for us to get acquainted and make some arrangements, and for me to see some of the sights in your fine city.'

Gloria was a little disappointed but she said nothing while Sal wondered what, apart from the Pier Head, St George's Hall and the Town Hall, there was for him to see? The eight miles of docks? The dock estates with their terrible slums; the barefoot urchins who played around the Steble fountain? Liverpool wasn't all gracious buildings, but then New York wasn't all skyscrapers either.

Over lunch Sal asked Grant if he had any particular date in mind for the wedding, informing him that Harry wouldn't be back until the end of December, providing they were not delayed on the way by bad weather.

'That's kind of not the ideal time of year to bring the family over. Mother hates the winter months and she's not terribly happy about travelling this far by ship,' Grant informed them.

'I can't say I blame her either, Grant. I wouldn't fancy crossing the Atlantic – twice – in the middle of winter,' Sal agreed as the waiter took away their soup dishes.

'I told Ma— Mother I really don't want to wait so long. I'll be utterly miserable separated from you for months and months,' Gloria told him.

He took her hand and squeezed it. 'What else can we do, Gloria?'

'I wonder would Harry mind terribly if Richard gave Gloria away?' Sybil suggested. 'I'm sure if we explain about Grant's family having to come so far at such an awful time of year he'd understand. After all, he spends most of his life at sea, he knows how rough a trip it can be.'

'I suggested that,' Gloria added eagerly, looking hopefully at her mother.

'Then we could set a date for, say, the end of August?' Sybil continued.

'Sybil, that's only three months away. Can we get things organised in time?' Sal asked, thinking that really Sybil should be thinking more of Harry's feelings. Gloria was the first of his daughters to be married.

Sybil was confident. 'Of course, if we put our minds to it. What do you think, Grant?'

'Well, if you really think Mr Jenkins won't be upset at missing such an occasion—'

'I'm sure he won't! All we want is for you both to be happy and for your family to travel in comfort and safety, don't we, Sal?' Sybil urged. She would make sure when she wrote to her brother to impress upon him the fact that she didn't want Gloria to have too much time on her hands. She just might start changing her mind or, worse still, meet someone else, or – horror of horrors – take up with Artie Taylor again.

'I'll write and explain. I'll tell him I just can't be apart from Grant until next year,' Gloria added.

Sal could see she was outnumbered. She nodded. 'So, we'll start to think about August. If we say the last Friday or Saturday in the month, do you think that will be enough notice for your family, Grant?'

'I'll send Pa a wire giving him the dates and he can work around that,' Grant replied happily. He hadn't wanted to wait too long either.

'It might be easier to make arrangements for the Friday,' Sybil suggested, thinking that possibly they could hold the reception here at the Adelphi. Grant's family would be bound to be staying here – it was by far the best accommodation in the city – and they did things with such style. That would only leave the church, flowers, cars, invitations and of course their outfits. 'You will be having the traditional white wedding?'

'Oh, yes, and with all the trimmings,' Gloria replied, looking both relieved and rapturous.

'Have you any sisters or cousins whom you might like to have as bridesmaids, Grant?' Sal enquired.

'Just one cousin, Iris, but I don't think it would be practical to ask her. There might be difficulties with her dress and so on, considering the distance involved.'

Sal felt quite relieved. He was right, it could cause endless problems.

'I'll have Betty and Rose as bridesmaids. Two is quite enough,' Gloria said.

'I'm sure they'll both be delighted,' Sal replied. It was thoughtful of Gloria to include Rose. She hadn't expected her to.

Sybil nodded, thinking that Rose would probably manage to look far tidier and behave with more decorum than her other niece. She raised her wine glass. 'I propose a toast. To the future Mr and Mrs Grant Hepworth.'

Gloria blushed and smiled happily at Grant. It sounded so wonderful. 'Mrs Grant Hepworth'.

A wireless message had duly been sent to Harry and Sal was very surprised when he telephoned. Long-distance calls were enormously expensive and the connections were not always the best, but Harry told her he thought it was a good idea not to postpone the wedding and that this young man sounded just the type of husband he'd wanted for Gloria. He impressed upon Sal that opportunities awaited their daughter that neither of them could have envisaged. Gloria should not be left with too much time to think, especially not with Artie Taylor right next door. After all the trouble and expense they'd gone to they couldn't risk Gloria changing her mind. He could also fully understand Grant's family not wanting to make the trip in the middle of winter. You certainly couldn't expect them to undertake two voyages that could turn out to be absolute nightmares. The weather on the North Atlantic would be atrocious in December. He wanted the best of everything for Gloria; the Hepworths must have no complaints at all. He didn't tell Sal that he was glad Richard would be giving Gloria away, he could be relied upon to see it was done properly, whereas his wife's brothers-in-law could be a bit slapdash about such things; nor did he say he intended to write to Sybil asking her to tactfully oversee the arrangements. It obviously wasn't going to be a huge 'Society' wedding but Sybil would ensure that it came as close to it as possible.

When Sal at last replaced the receiver she wondered if Harry had even given a thought to the fact that he probably wouldn't see his daughter again for possibly years and that he would have missed what should have been one of the happiest and proudest days of his life.

Chapter Twenty-Three

———

SYBIL HAD ARRANGED TO pick Grant and Gloria up from the hotel late the following afternoon. Gloria was to spend the next day with him taking him on a tour of Liverpool.

'Richard and I will pick you up and drive you out to our house; it's quite a pleasant drive along the coast,' she'd informed him. 'Sal will come out with Betty and Rose when they get home from work. The train runs along the coast too and we're just a couple of minutes' walk from the station.'

'I think she's got a flaming cheek, Mam. Uncle Richard is picking them up and driving them out to Formby, while we have to traipse there on the train,' Betty said as they made the short walk from Formby Station to Sybil's house.

'It wasn't too bad, Betty, and it's a nice enough evening,' Rose commented.

Sal gave her a grateful look. Trust Betty to be cantankerous. 'Let's hear no more complaints and tuck the collar of your blouse inside your jacket, Betty,' Sal instructed as they walked up the gravel path to the house.

Rose had never been here before and she looked around curiously as Sybil ushered them in. It was much bigger than Auntie Sal's house and the furnishings were far more elegant but it wasn't what you'd call 'homely', she thought. Everything looked in pristine condition and the furniture was polished to death.

Grant got to his feet as they came into the lounge. He greeted Sal warmly and then turned to the two girls. 'And which of you two lovely young ladies is my future sister-in-law and which of you is Rose?'

Betty glanced quickly at Rose. She could certainly see what Gloria saw in him. He was very good-looking and charming. She held out her hand. 'I'm Betty.'

He shook her hand and kissed her on the cheek.

'And I'm Rose.'

Rose was greeted in a similar fashion. 'And you are going to be our bridesmaids.'

'It seems like it,' Betty answered as Uncle Richard indicated that they sit down and went to pour them a drink. Sybil, Grant and Gloria already had glasses of what looked like champagne and she wondered did they never drink anything else?

'We've had a truly great day. There are some beautiful buildings in the city. Both your Town Hall and St George's Hall are magnificent.' Grant had been very impressed with both the interior and exterior of both buildings.

'Such a pity the cathedral isn't nearly finished,' Sybil said regretfully. 'It will be one of the biggest in the country when it is and quite splendid, I hear.'

'I just loved that quaint old graveyard at the foot of it: all those centuries-old headstones. Kind of spooky though,' Grant added.

'I think we should make the most of this opportunity to sort out some of the more pressing arrangements,' Sybil said briskly.

As her aunt and mother and sister began to discuss with Grant the church and the venue for the reception Betty sipped her drink slowly. He was all right, she supposed. Not the sort of person she would have chosen, he was a bit too glib, just a bit too charming, but Gloria was lapping it up. She wondered what it would be like going to live in another country where everything would be so different. Gloria obviously wouldn't work so what would she do all day while he was at the office? There was only so much shopping you could do. In fact her sister wasn't going to go back to her job at all. She'd already written to tell them so. She'd have far too much to do with the wedding, she'd told her mother, and Grant wouldn't expect his fiancée to work and certainly not for the pittance she was paid.

Rose had wondered whether she should apply for Gloria's job but then had realised that it would mean that she wouldn't see Alan every day. They usually spent their lunch break together. Now that the weather was warmer they took their sandwiches and sat in the gardens of St Nicholas's

Church, which was close to the Royal Liver Building and provided a haven of peace and tranquillity from the constant traffic and crowds at the Pier Head. Anyway, Sal had advised her to stay where she was, for she might find the Revenue office very 'stuffy'.

Betty suddenly realized that Sal had been speaking to her and dragged herself out of her reverie. 'Sorry. I was miles away.'

'I said, will it be a problem for you and Rose to have that Friday off?' Sal repeated.

'I'll have to ask. I suppose it will be better than asking for a Saturday off, that's our busiest day, but I won't get paid.'

'What about you, Rose?' Sal enquired.

'I don't think it will be too much of a problem.'

'Then, that's settled. Friday the twenty-sixth of August,' Sybil said firmly. 'Sal and I will make all the arrangements with the banqueting manager of the Adelphi.'

'And we'll go and see the vicar at the church and hope there won't be a problem with Grant being Episcopalian,' Gloria added.

'I think it's pretty similar to your High Church of England,' Grant assured her.

Betty began to fidget. These next months were going to be very tedious, she thought as she twisted the stem of her now empty glass between her fingers. She was already fed up with this wedding and it was only going to get worse. It was all they were going to hear from now until August.

*

Rose relayed everything to Alan as they walked hand in hand towards St Nicholas's Church at lunchtime the next day. As usual at this time the Pier Head was very crowded with office workers adding to the usual crowds, taking advantage of the mild weather. In the garden of the church the first roses were coming into bud and they sat down on a bench, the breeze from the river feeling warm on their faces.

'So, it's all arranged,' Alan said rather bemusedly. He'd found Gloria's whirlwind romance entertaining, as relayed by Rose who seemed enthralled by it all, although she'd confided that she would certainly have liked longer to get to know someone before agreeing to something as serious as marriage.

'In such a short time that it would make your head spin,' Rose replied, unwrapping her sandwiches.

'What's he like?' Alan asked. He'd never met an American, let alone a wealthy one.

Rose smiled at him. 'Actually he's very charming and he really does seem to love Gloria. She's asked me to be a bridesmaid, which I thought was generous of her.'

'And I bet you'll look just as lovely as the bride,' he said, smiling back. He thought Rose was very pretty and the more he got to know her the more he liked her.

'Oh, I hope not, Alan. It's her big day and no one should outshine her.'

He nodded. That was typical of Rose, always very considerate of other people's feelings. 'I presume she asked Betty too?'

'Of course. Oh, I do hope she's going to be happy, Alan.

It's such a long way away – to live, I mean. I don't think I could go so far from everyone. I know Betty wants to travel. As soon as she's old enough she wants to go away to sea like her da, but that's different. She will come home quite a bit.'

'So you'd be happy to stay in Liverpool all your life?' he asked, looking thoughtful.

Rose shrugged. 'I suppose it would depend upon certain things . . . who I'd be staying with or for.' She hadn't really given the matter much thought but she knew that one day she wanted to have a home of her own. Maybe it would be with him?

He nodded, brushing the crumbs from his lap. 'Rose, would you like to come for tea on Sunday afternoon? Meet my mam and da? Mam's been asking me when I'm going to bring you to meet her.'

Rose's heartbeat quickened and she blushed. 'I'd love to, Alan. You did tell them that I live with Aunty Sal, that Mam and Da are dead?' She felt a little emotional that she would never be able to introduce them to her parents but she was sure her mother would have liked him.

He took her hand and squeezed it. 'I did and Mam said it's all the more reason for you to come.'

Rose felt less apprehensive; Mrs Hopkins sounded nice.

When she'd told Betty about the invitation Betty had smiled knowingly. 'That sounds serious. You'll be the next one walking up the aisle.'

Rose had blushed. 'Don't be daft. I'm far too young and we haven't known each other all that long.'

'Do I have to remind you that all this fuss and performance

that's going on is because our Gloria managed to fall in love in two weeks?'

'I'm not Gloria and besides I'd have to save up a lot of money before I could think of getting married. I can't expect your da to pay for my wedding – if and when I get married,' she added.

'So you've actually been thinking about it!' Betty teased. 'Oh, don't get upset. Just go and meet them,' she added, noting Rose's expression.

Rose had taken a lot of care with her appearance but she still felt a little nervous as she saw Alan waiting at the tram stop for her.

'You look nice, Rose,' he greeted her, helping her off the platform.

'They haven't gone to a lot of trouble, have they? I mean your mam hasn't got the best china out or spent all yesterday baking?'

He laughed. 'You've been listening to Mrs Mostyn too much. No, it's just the usual Sunday tea, nothing fancy.'

Rose was relieved but she wondered it she had been taking too much notice of Sybil and her airs and graces. Alan's family were working-class people, just as her own parents had been.

It was a small terraced house in a quiet street quite near to Liverpool's football ground but it was obvious that everyone took a pride in their homes. All the windows were clean with crisp lace curtains, the front steps were all scrubbed, and the brass knockers were highly polished.

Mrs Hopkins greeted her warmly and Rose began to relax.

She was a small, plump woman with light brown hair and kind blue eyes; Alan resembled her greatly.

'Take your jacket and hat off, Rose, and sit down. Our Alan's told us so much about you that I wanted to meet you. Alan, you take her things while I put the kettle on. It's just sandwiches, scones and a Victoria sponge. I always say after a big Sunday lunch another hot meal is just too much, especially for me,' she fussed.

'Can I do anything to help, Mrs Hopkins? I always try to help Aunty Sal with the meals,' Rose offered, smiling shyly.

Alan's father had got to his feet and extended his hand. 'Nice to meet you, Rose. You're very welcome.'

Rose liked him instantly, he was a tall thin man with greying hair and a moustache and his eyes crinkled up when he smiled.

'You can help me bring in the plates if you like, Rose. Everything is ready, it just needs setting out,' Mrs Hopkins said, bustling into the tiny but spotless kitchen.

Rose picked up two plates of sandwiches as the older woman put the kettle on the small gas ring.

'You're the first girl he's agreed to bring home,' she confided, lowering her voice. 'Not that there have been very many others. He's a quiet lad is Alan, takes after his da.'

Rose smiled; she'd known he'd had a few other girlfriends but he'd told her they'd been very short-term things. 'My mam always said I took after my da, mainly in looks.'

Alan's mother shook her head sadly. 'Such a shame for you, Rose, to lose both parents so young, but I hear Mrs Jenkins has been very kind.'

'She has. Mam was a great friend of hers and I think of their place as my home, but I would like a home of my own – one day.'

'Of course you would. It's what every girl wants, what every girl needs. Now, let me just put the water in the pot and leave it to draw for a few minutes, and I'll bring in the scones.' Maisey Hopkins liked her. She seemed a pleasant, well-mannered lass who certainly hadn't had a very fair deal in life, but it didn't seem to have given her any kind of a chip on her shoulder.

Chapter Twenty-Four

BY THE AUGUST BANK holiday Betty was heartily sick and tired of all the fuss and the tears and tantrums. She felt sorry for her mam because Gloria went first to her aunt with every minor complaint and imagined disaster instead of discussing things with Sal first and it had reached the stage where Sybil had virtually taken over. The words 'Friday the twenty-sixth of August' seemed to have been etched indelibly into her brain.

'Well, there's not long to go now, Betty, and things can get back to normal,' Rose had consoled her. Since her first visit to Alan's parents she had gone each Sunday for tea and was delighted that Gloria had invited Alan to the evening reception. Both girls had also learned that Artie Taylor had gone to Crewe on a temporary transfer where he had made some new friends and seemed to be going out more.

'He's well out of all this fuss and performance!' Betty had remarked.

Gloria had chosen the style and material for the bridesmaids' dresses without even consulting either Betty or Rose. It was something that annoyed both Betty and Sal, although Rose had said that she really didn't mind. It was Gloria's big day and she was pleased she had been asked to be bridesmaid at all and the dress would be the most expensive she'd ever owned.

'You really are a good-natured girl,' Sal had said, smiling at Rose.

Betty hadn't taken the same attitude. 'She's too soft. I think our Gloria's got a flaming cheek. She should at least have discussed it with you, Mam. I don't mind the style of the dress but that particular shade of peach will look terrible on me.'

'She says it's called "soft apricot",' Sal had informed them, fingering the swatch of silk Gloria had pinned to the picture of the dress the seamstress at Drinkwater's was to copy for Betty and Rose. The choice of Gladys Drinkwater's dressmaking establishment, the finest and most expensive in Liverpool, had been suggested by Sybil of course and Gloria had readily agreed. Sal couldn't see why the dresses couldn't have been purchased at either Cripps, Hendersons or the Bon Marche, all three shops having good bridal departments, and she'd said as much to Elsie, who had curled her lip disdainfully and remarked acidly that Sybil would think it 'very common' to buy something 'ready-made'.

'Well, peach or apricot, it will still make the pair of us look insipid,' Betty had remarked cuttingly. 'But maybe that's the whole idea. Maybe she wants us to fade into the background so we won't steal any of her limelight.'

'Betty! That's a bit cruel,' Sal had reprimanded her.

'I don't think she thinks like that at all. I think she's just so intent on everything being perfect that she hasn't even given a thought to whether the colour will suit us. *She* likes it and maybe that's really what matters,' Rose had said, trying to lighten the atmosphere.

Gloria had spent hours discussing and agonising over her own dress with both Sybil and Sal but finally it had been agreed that she should have a dress very similar to the one Lady Elizabeth Bowes-Lyon had worn when she married the Duke of York four years ago, complete with a very long white silk veil, but Gloria's veil would be held in place by a small coronet of white wax flowers.

'Such a pity she couldn't have a small tiara,' Sybil had mused, studying the picture she'd obtained of the Duchess of York on her wedding day.

Sal had cast her eyes to the ceiling. 'For God's sake, Sybil! She's not marrying into the royal family.'

There had been many arguments over Sal's own outfit for she'd been absolutely determined she would choose it herself without any interference from her sister-in-law. She'd been encouraged by Elsie in this matter.

'*You* are the mother of the bride, Sal. Not *her*. Don't let her influence you. You choose it and never mind the cost, Harry's paying and you've certainly had to put up with enough from him over the years. You more than deserve an expensive outfit.'

Gloria had been very put out that her mother wouldn't hear of Sybil accompanying them on the shopping trip.

'But, Mam, she has such good taste!' Gloria had urged.

'Meaning that I don't?' Sal had replied cuttingly.

'No! You know that's not what I meant at all. You always look smart but this is such a special occasion. I want you to look stunning. Aunt Sybil says Grant's mother is so fortunate to have such a wide choice of elegant shops in New York—'

'And your aunt thinks I won't look as stylish or elegant as Mrs Eunice Hepworth?' Sal had snapped.

'She didn't say that, Mam,' Gloria had replied impatiently and with a note of pettishness in her voice. Why was Mam being so awkward? Both she and Aunt Sybil just wanted her to look her best.

'Just what *did* she say, Gloria?' Sal had demanded.

Gloria had bitten her lip, thinking of some of her aunt's words about which colours definitely would not suit Sal and which would look insipid. Remarks about the length of Sal's skirts being just a 'touch' old-fashioned and the right and wrong amount of jewellery to be worn. When Sybil had realised that she was not to be included in the shopping trip she had inwardly seethed but had calmed herself down sufficiently to give her niece a description of the style and shade of outfit that should be searched for – but with strict instructions that Gloria was not to mention this to her mother. She must let Sal think she had picked it out herself. 'She said just to make sure it was "elegant and suitable".'

Sal had pursed her lips at the reply. Sybil had almost

certainly said a lot more than that. She knew her sister-in-law of old. Well, she'd certainly avoid buying anything Gloria was over-enthusiastic about. Sibyl was bound to have primed the girl.

There had been problems with the flowers too. Sybil had insisted the roses were *exactly* the same shade of apricot as the bridesmaids' dresses but the harassed florist had said she couldn't possibly guarantee an exact match. Sal had then suggested that cream rosebuds be mixed with the larger apricot blooms and Gloria had agreed until Sybil said she thought pure white would be better and that Sal's suggestion that bows of apricot ribbon be attached to all the table decorations would detract from the classical design she had spent so long choosing. Nor would bows of ribbon be suitable for the floral decorations in the church, they would render them a little 'tacky'.

St Mary's Church, Walton-on-the-Hill, had finally been chosen. It was very High Church and had grounds where photographs could be taken and Gloria had been delighted when Sybil had pointed out that it was also very old and what Grant's family would call 'quaint' and very 'English'.

There had been endless meetings with the banqueting manager at the Adelphi Hotel and Sybil had requested their very best suites for Grant and his family, who were arriving on the *Berengaria* on the Monday before the wedding. Sybil had also arranged for both families to have dinner there on the Wednesday evening. Sal had thought Tuesday would have been better – not so close to the big day – but Sybil had said they would obviously need a day to unpack and recover from the voyage. No, an intimate family dinner on Wednesday would be best. Sal thought it wouldn't be very 'intimate' as not only Grant and his parents but two uncles, two aunts and three cousins were travelling over and with Sybil and Richard, herself, Gloria, Betty and Rose, plus her two sisters and their husbands, a party of twenty was definitely not small. It was going to be a very busy and probably also a very fraught week, she thought gloomily.

Betty had hoped to escape to the cinema with Rose that Wednesday evening but when Gloria informed them of the dinner party she realised that there would be no respite from all the fuss.

'I expect you want to choose what both Rose and I will wear,' she said sarcastically.

Gloria looked offended. 'There's no need to take that tone, Betty. I just want both of you to make a good impression and not let the family down.'

'You mean not let Aunt Sybil down.'

Gloria frowned. 'What's the matter with you, Betty? You said you were delighted for me but lately you seem to have changed.'

'It's not me who's changed, Gloria. It's you. You're getting more and more like Aunt Sybil every day. You're turning into a snob and you never think about other people's feelings. All you seem to be able to think about is yourself. I wonder if you even think much about Grant these days, you're obsessed with how you'll look, what people will think of you and your dress and the flowers and will the reception be grand enough for the Hepworths.'

Gloria's eyes filled with tears of hurt and anger. 'How can you say such terrible things? Of course I think of Grant. I love him, I think about him all the time and I'm *not* turning into a snob! I just want everything to be perfect, it's my *wedding* day!'

Betty relented. 'Oh, don't get upset, Gloria. I know you want it all to be "perfect" and I will miss you when you've gone to New York. So I'll make a special effort for Wednesday, I promise.'

She did. She had her hair washed and set in her lunch hour and she wore her newest dress with the new white kid shoes she'd been saving up for weeks to buy. Rose wore a pale blue linen skirt and jacket and a white blouse with a pale blue and white hat and Gloria happily complimented them both on their appearance.

'You've got to admit that she's certainly calmed down a lot since Grant arrived,' Rose remarked to Betty as they entered the hotel foyer behind Sal and her sisters and brothers-in-law. Grant had come straight from the ship to see Gloria on Monday and he'd spent as much time with her as possible since.

Betty nodded, smoothing out an imaginary crease in her navy and white nautical-style dress, which had a broad white sailor collar and a short pleated skirt. Sal had informed them that the dinner was to be held in a private room so they wouldn't be the object of the curious glances of the other diners.

'Don't they look sort of staid? The way Aunt Sybil has gone on I thought they'd all be dressed in the height of fashion,' she muttered to Rose as they entered the room and caught sight of the assembled ladies of Grant's family. The men all wore dark suits, as did her uncles Richard, Walter and Edward, but she had thought Grant's mother and his two aunts would be far more stylishly dressed. Their dresses were obviously expensive and the jewellery they wore was tasteful but compared to Aunt Sybil and her mam they did look rather matronly.

'Well, they are all rather old, apart from that girl who looks the same age as Gloria,' Rose whispered back.

Betty looked across to where a young girl with short auburn hair wearing a pale green silk cocktail dress was holding an animated conversation with two young men. 'She at least looks as if she's got a bit of life in her. She must be one of Grant's cousins.'

They were all introduced and Betty and Rose found themselves seated at the end of the table with Grant's cousins Iris and Ingram Hepworth and Teddy Chambers who was, he informed them, the son of Grant's mother's sister. Betty was particularly relieved that Gloria and Grant were seated at the other end of the table with Sal and Sybil and Richard. At least there would be no frowns or censorious looks in her direction from her aunt tonight.

Everyone seemed to get on very well and both Rose and Betty found the young Americans affable and highly entertaining and the noise level at their end of the table increased as the evening wore on. By the end of it Betty confided to Rose that she was beginning to think that she might well enjoy this wedding after all.

'I was always going to enjoy it – and the evening,' Rose replied happily.

Betty smiled back. 'I had begun to dread it but I'm changing my mind.'

'Something to do with Teddy Chambers?' Rose teased. He'd been paying a lot of attention to her friend.

Betty shrugged. 'Maybe and maybe not. He'll be going back next week and I'm not as impulsive as our Gloria, not where boys are concerned. Anyway I don't think Mam would be very happy losing another daughter to the delights of New York City.'

Rose nodded and glanced up the table to where Gloria sat smiling and holding Grant's hand, the large diamond of her engagement ring sparkling in the light of the chandelier overhead. No, Betty wasn't at all like her sister.

Sal had been a little wary of Eunice Hepworth to start with but she soon found the woman easy to talk to after she'd confided her doubts and worries.

'I have to agree with you, Sarah, I did think it was all very sudden and Gloria is so young.'

'But you feel they will be happy? I mean you do know your son far better than anyone else does.'

Eunice smiled. 'I think they'll be fine, Sarah. She's a delightful girl, I can't find fault with her at all. Believe me there were others I definitely had my doubts about, one in particular, but Gloria – no.'

'I'll still worry about her being so far away and not knowing anyone.'

'Of course you will but he'll look after her – we all will –

and she'll make friends, she's such an outgoing girl. I promise you he'll never let her down or do anything to hurt her, it's not in his nature, and if she does have any worries I hope she'll confide in me. I know I can never take your place but I hope, Sarah, that she'll look on me as a friend and confidante.'

Sal had smiled. 'That's a huge relief for me, Eunice, thank you.'

Grant's mother had placed her hand over Sal's. 'It's a pleasure, Sarah.'

Chapter Twenty-Five

FRIDAY MORNING DAWNED WARM and sunny. At first a hazy mist had hung over the garden but that had quickly been burned off by the sun and Sal hoped that it would not get oppressively hot later in the day for the wedding was to be at noon. It was now just after eight and she was extremely thankful that Sybil was not arriving until after ten o'clock. The last thing she needed was her sister-in-law imperiously issuing last-minute instructions and orders and making Gloria even more nervous.

As she was pouring herself the first cup of tea of the day Betty came into the room. 'Mam, Rose and I are going to help Gloria get ready so you can concentrate on yourself. You'll have plenty of time. We agreed you shouldn't be rushed; after all it's a big day for you too.' Betty helped herself to a cup from the pot; she'd already removed the pins from her hair and brushed it out, as had Rose. 'We've laid out our shoes, stockings, gloves and head-dresses on the bed and our dresses are on hangers behind the door. It won't take us long to get ready once we've sorted Gloria out. With a bit of luck we'll all be ready when "Madam High and Mighty" arrives so there will be nothing for her to start fussing about.'

Sal smiled grimly. 'You really shouldn't talk about her like that but it's good of you and Rose to be so organised.'

Sybil had wanted to come much earlier but Richard had said emphatically that he wasn't going to drive to Sal's at the crack of dawn and then have to wait, getting under everyone's feet, until half past eleven when they were to leave for the church. It was going to be a long enough day as it was and besides he was certain that Sal could more than cope. She had been very grateful for his intervention.

Betty grinned at her mother and then pulled a piece of paper towards her across the table. 'Right, let's check off the final things. Cars: arriving at eleven thirty. Flowers: due to arrive any time now. All outfits: ready. You *have* got everything, Mam?'

Sal nodded. She had checked everything last night.

'And a bottle of decent sherry and the best glasses for a drink to steady all our nerves before we leave,' Betty finished triumphantly, thinking the whole affair had been organised like a military operation. 'Aunt Sybil won't object to that, surely, and she can't turn her nose up either, it's a bottle of Croft's Original Pale Cream Sherry, none of your Empire rubbish.'

Sal got to her feet. 'Right, I'll take the bride a cup of tea and see what she wants for her breakfast. It's the last meal she'll be having in this house,' she added a little sadly. Gloria and Grant were staying at the hotel until they left for New York and once there they would travel on to Bermuda for the honeymoon. She didn't have much time left to spend with her elder daughter, she thought ruefully. Even though during these last few months there had been times when she could have cheerfully slapped Gloria, she loved her and was praying her daughter had made the right decision.

'I'll make some toast to start with,' Betty offered.

Gloria was awake and sitting up in bed.

'You're supposed to be having a lie-in this morning,' Sal greeted her, smiling as she drew back the curtains and the sunlight streamed into the room.

'I've been awake for hours, Mam. I'm so nervous. Oh, I really *do* know I'm doing the right thing. I love Grant and I'm looking forward to my new life but it's such a *big* step.'

Sal sat down on the bed beside her and took her hand. 'It is a big step, luv, but he's a nice person and he idolises you. He'll take care of you, he's promised me faithfully he will and you get on well with his family. I have to say I think his mother is such a kind and sensible woman that if you have any worries you can safely confide in her and that's a great relief to me. I had quite a long conversation with her before we left the hotel and she assured me that she thinks you are a delightful girl and that you'll be very happy with Grant. She hopes you will look on her as a friend and confidante. You really are very lucky, Gloria.' A whole new life lay ahead for her daughter, a life of comfort, wealth and social standing. It was a life Harry and Sybil had connived and schemed to secure for Gloria, whereas she had just wanted the girl to be happy and content. However, now it seemed as though all their wishes had been granted.

'I know I am but . . . but I will miss you, Mam. And Betty and Rose.' Gloria's eyes misted as she wondered how long it would be before she saw any of them again after she'd sailed for New York next week.

'And we'll all miss you, luv. Now, let's not go getting all weepy and sentimental. Betty is making you some toast but what else would you like?'

Gloria smiled. 'Just toast, Mam. I couldn't face anything else.'

Sal got up. 'I'll start running your bath. Betty and Rose are going to help you dress. I've been instructed to see to myself so you'll be done up in all your finery next time I see you.' She bent and kissed Gloria on the cheek, a little lump in her throat.

As she dressed and carefully applied her make-up Sal smiled to hear the laughing and giggling and exclamations of delight coming from Gloria's room. That was just as it should be, she thought. Harry was really a fool to agree to miss this very special occasion. Photographs just wouldn't do it justice.

Before she put on her hat she gave her hair one last brush and looked at herself appraisingly in the mirror. The jewel-bright sapphire silk of her dress suited her. She felt confident and somehow vibrant wearing it. It had short cap sleeves and a boat neckline, the edges of which were embroidered with a border of silver bugle beads. The skirt, which the sales assistant had assured her was the height of fashion when she had wondered was it too short, showed off her still shapely legs encased in pure silk stockings. Her shoes, which sported an hourglass heel, pointed toe and a strap with a bow across the front, had been dyed to match the dress. Her gloves and small clutch bag, to which her corsage of white roses had been attached, were of pewter-coloured kid and lay on the bed. On the dressing table in front of her reposed her hat: a very smart cloche of pewter silk, trimmed with sapphire. The brim was slightly turned up on one side and held by a small cluster of feathers that had been dyed silver. Carefully she placed it on and adjusted the angle. In her ears she wore the sapphire stud earrings Harry had brought a few years ago and which had given her the inspiration for her outfit. She nodded slowly. She was certain that not even Sybil could find fault with anything, not that she cared a great deal about her sister-in-law's opinion. She had just wanted to look her very best on Gloria's big day and when she'd shown her outfit to Elsie her friend's eyes had misted and she'd declared that she wouldn't look out of place at a Buckingham Palace garden party. Pushing the thought aside she got up; she'd better go and see how those girls were getting on for she'd have Sybil and Richard arriving before long.

To her relief all three of them were ready. Betty and Rose looked far from insipid, she thought, carefully spreading the cloud of white silk veiling around Gloria's feet. She placed both hands on her cheeks and sucked in her breath. She had never before seen Gloria look quite so beautiful.

'How do I look, Mam?' Gloria asked, a catch in her voice.

Sal crossed and took both Gloria's hands in her own. 'Oh, Gloria! You look even lovelier than the Duchess of York did! Your da will be so sorry he wasn't here when he sees the photographs and they can't possibly do you justice.'

'Oh, Mam!' Gloria's voice held a sob.

'Now don't start crying, you'll end up with red, puffy eyes, which will ruin the whole effect!' Betty urged.

Gloria sniffed and managed a smile.

'You look absolutely fantastic, Mam! Like someone in a fashion advertisement. Aunt Sybil will be green with envy,' Betty cried delightedly. She was certain her aunt wouldn't look half as gorgeous. 'What about us, will we pass muster?'

Sal nodded. Both girls wore circlets of apricot and white wax flowers over their shiny bobbed hair and although the dresses were quite plain they were extremely well cut. Their shoes were of white satin and the bouquets of apricot and white roses and stems of trailing dark green smilax lay on the bed beside Gloria's bouquet of white lilies and roses. 'You both look lovely.'

Betty became brisk and businesslike. 'Right, we'd better all go down before we have aunt and uncle in on top of us. Rose, you take her train and Mam and I will take this veil. It could be a bit of a problem on the stairs so go slowly, Gloria, and for heaven's sake take care you don't trip.'

When Sybil arrived it was to find, to her great surprise, all four were dressed and waiting quite calmly with a crystal glass of sherry in their hands.

'Good heavens! I expected there to be chaos but here you all are ready and calmly drinking sherry.'

'We *are* all very calm, Sybil. Betty, pour your aunt a drink,' Sal replied, feeling rather smug at the sight of Sybil's slightly disgruntled expression.

'Gloria, you look absolutely radiant, my dear! I count myself a very lucky man to be giving you away. Grant will be delighted with you.' Richard kissed his niece on the cheek.

'Da will be sorry he couldn't be here,' Betty added.

'He will,' Richard agreed.

Sybil sipped her sherry thinking that her brother would indeed be sorry to have missed this occasion. Gloria looked absolutely stunning and Betty and Rose looked very attractive too. She had to admit to herself that Sal had certainly chosen her outfit well, she couldn't have done better if she had been included in that shopping trip. She'd been a little worried when Gloria had told her the outfit was pewter and what she had described as 'royal blue'. It had sounded a little garish but it was actually more of a sapphire blue and looked very elegant and tasteful. And Sal had had the sense not to wear too much jewellery with it. Now Sybil was sorry she had opted for something 'light and summery', as she'd termed the pale eau-de-Nil and cream chiffon dress with its matching stole. Perhaps it really was more suitable for a summer cocktail party than a wedding. She'd gone to great lengths to match the shade of green to her accessories but now she felt as though there was just too much green.

It hadn't pleased her one bit that Richard had made some fatuous remark about it being bad luck to wear the colour green at a wedding, or so he'd heard.

'Don't be so ridiculous! Where on earth did you hear that?' she'd snapped.

He'd shrugged. 'Just something my mother used to say. She had two friends whose close female relatives wore green and within a year they were both widowed.'

'Utter nonsense! Pure superstition!' she'd replied huffily.

'Drink up, ladies. The cars have arrived,' Richard informed them as the shiny black Morris Cowleys, bedecked with white ribbons, drew up outside.

Betty thought the church looked really lovely as the sunlight streamed in through the big stained-glass windows and scattered a myriad of colours on the bridal party as they made their way up the aisle, the notes of the organ resounding through the church. Grant and his cousin Ingram, his best man, and the rest of the family were already assembled, as were her Aunts Doris and Eileen and their husbands. It was a small wedding by some people's standards but it was certainly very opulent and stylish.

As Gloria made her vows Betty squeezed her mother's hand and Sal surreptitiously wiped away a tear. Looking across the aisle she noticed that Eunice Hepworth was doing the same thing. She caught Rose's glance and smiled at her friend. 'You next,' she mouthed and Rose blushed.

To everyone's relief the whole day went without a single hitch. The ceremony, the photographs, the reception, the speeches and toasts, the cutting of the cake, all were 'just perfect', the new Mrs Hepworth confided to her mother at the end of the evening as she accompanied Sal and Betty and Rose to the hotel entrance where the car was waiting to take them home. Sybil and Richard had already left.

Betty smiled at her. 'And that photographer from the *Liverpool Daily Post* turning up was the icing on the cake. You'll have your photo and your names in the paper.'

Gloria smiled back happily. 'That was all Iris's doing. She said if we'd been married in New York we'd have been on the Society pages, so why not here?'

Sal turned and hugged her. 'It's been a wonderful day, Gloria. Now, you'd better get back to your husband or he'll think you've run off and left him already,' she joked. 'We'll be seeing you both before you sail.'

'Of course and you're having lunch with us the day before and will be coming to see us off too, Mam.'

'Try and keep me away,' Sal said, endeavouring not to think about having to say that final farewell. The ship was sailing at ten o'clock so neither Betty nor Rose could accompany her.

Gloria hugged first Betty and then Rose. 'I'll see you both before I leave, but you must write.'

'Of course we will,' Betty promised as they went down the front steps to the car, leaving Gloria standing framed in the light from the hotel foyer, her long white silk train cascading down the steps. Grant had come out to join her and, one arm around his new wife's waist, the other raised, he waved his new relations off.

'They look just like those figures you often see on the top of the wedding cake, except that Aunt Sybil wouldn't let them put anything so tacky on their cake,' Betty remarked.

'I suppose it was only a matter of time before you reverted back to your usual self, Betty,' Sal said with resignation. Then she smiled. 'At least you didn't put a foot wrong today, either of you.'

Betty grinned at Rose. Alan hadn't left Rose's side all evening and it was quite obvious that they were made for each other. When Rose looked at him it was as though a light had been switched on behind her eyes and he'd looked so proud and happy as they'd danced together. She hoped nothing would happen to make them drift apart. She sighed happily. It had turned out to be a really enjoyable day after all.

Part II

Chapter Twenty-Six

1929

G LORIA LOOKED AROUND THE lounge of the apartment and felt a thrill of happiness. It was a beautiful room, bright and airy, and she intended to decorate it in the art deco style that was so fashionable, in shades of cream and beige with accents of black and gold. This was truly the first home of their own – hers and Grant's – for up until now they had been sharing his parents' house. She walked across to the window and looked out; the view across Central Park was magnificent and she'd fallen in love with the place as soon as she'd seen it. Barney and Eunice were moving to Florida and their house had been sold and she and Grant had decided to buy an apartment. She'd found life here quite different and not a little daunting at first but Eunice had been a tower of strength and so of course had Grant, although she'd quickly found out that he worked long hours, which left her to her own devices a great deal of the time. She'd been a little homesick too at first, she missed Sal and Betty and Rose, but Iris had been instrumental in introducing her to friends who were more her own age than Eunice's companions. She and Iris had become good friends and they went for lunch together, to concerts, galleries, exhibitions and sometimes to the shows on Broadway. They particularly enjoyed going shopping and Gloria had opened accounts at all the best stores.

She turned away and looked at her watch, an anniversary present that Grant had bought her from Cartier's. It would be another hour before the interior designer arrived but Eunice had said she would stop by for half an hour to see how things were progressing.

She was scrutinising the swatches of fabric that the designer had left when the doorbell rang and she went to let her mother-in-law in.

'I can't stay long, Gloria dear. There's still so much to do. Barney's seen to most things but I still have to oversee the packing.'

Gloria kissed her on the cheek. 'I'll miss you both, you've been so good to me.'

Eunice smiled, thinking how fond she'd become of her daughter-in-law. Gloria was as attractive as ever and always smartly dressed and still slim. Eunice was aware that Gloria had hoped to have become pregnant by now but so far it just hadn't happened. Perhaps now that they would be on their own it might. There was plenty of time; Gloria was still young. 'Nonsense, we look on you as a daughter, you know that. Now, where are things up to?'

Gloria enlightened her as to what had been ordered and the colour schemes she had already chosen but Eunice felt that, despite her obvious enthusiasm for her first home, something was troubling the girl.

'It all sounds wonderful but do I detect a hint of . . . anxiety?'

Gloria nodded. Soon she wouldn't have Eunice to confide in and something *was* worrying her. 'I'm concerned about Grant. He works so hard, too hard, I think. He's never home until after eight, sometimes it's nine o'clock and even then he is often preoccupied.'

Eunice frowned. 'Have you spoken to him about it?'

Gloria nodded. 'He's tried to explain to me that he gets a great deal of satisfaction from making money both for the business and other people, but stocks and shares, bonds and gilts are all beyond me.'

Eunice nodded. 'Now that Barney has all but retired I think Grant feels as though he's got to show that he can keep everything on an even keel and indeed increase business. I think he's trying to prove that he is every bit as successful as his father. He takes his work very seriously.'

Gloria sighed. 'I know. Even when we have dinner with friends, the talk often turns to business. I'm not complaining, I just worry that he's working too hard and not enjoying life as much as he should.'

Eunice smiled. She hoped Gloria would find herself pregnant soon; a baby would really change her life and she would have little time to worry about Grant, who at this stage of his life was having to work very hard indeed – just the way Barney had done when they'd first been married. 'I'm sure things will ease off in a while, Gloria. Don't worry, I know Grant won't become so involved with work that he'll neglect you. Now, have you heard from your mother recently?'

Gloria felt more relaxed having voiced her concerns over her husband and took Sal's latest letter from her purse and read some of it out to her mother-in-law.

As Eunice was preparing to leave she looked thoughtfully at Gloria. 'Why don't you book a table at your favourite restaurant for this evening, for just you and Grant? Say for eight thirty – that will give him time to get home and change. Tell him it's a special treat as he's working so hard and needs to unwind a little.'

Gloria smiled, feeling happier still. 'What a good idea. I'll do that. In fact I think we should do it every week, make some special time just for us.'

Eunice gathered up her purse and gloves as the doorbell rang. 'Ah, that will be your designer person. I'll leave you to get on with getting this place fixed up.'

Betty could see that Rose was excited about something as soon as she came into the room. On Saturday evenings Rose always went out with Alan and on Sundays she went to his house for tea. They went out in the week as well although not as frequently these days, she'd noticed.

'You look pleased with yourself tonight,' she remarked,

putting down the magazine she'd been leafing through. Her da was home and he'd been listening intently to a play on the wireless while her mam was knitting.

Sal looked up at Betty's words. Rose did look flushed and excited, she thought.

Rose took off her coat and hat; it was nearly October now and the evenings were too cold for just a jacket. 'I've got something . . . important to ask you, Uncle Harry.'

'Turn the sound down, Harry,' Sal instructed, and then seeing the look of annoyance on his face she continued: 'Surely you've already guessed who the murderer is by now? I have. What is it, Rose?'

Rose smiled again at Betty. 'Can Alan come and see you tomorrow night, Uncle Harry? He wants to ask you something.'

Betty gave a little shriek of delight and jumped to her feet. 'He's finally asked you, hasn't he?'

Rose nodded.

'Betty, will you stop acting like a jack-in-the-box and let Rose finish,' Harry said sharply.

'He's asked me to marry him but he wants to come and ask you, as you're my guardian—'

'Did you say yes?' Betty interrupted impatiently.

'Betty, for heaven's sake will you let the poor girl finish!' Sal laughed. She knew what Rose's answer would have been. Rose and Alan Hopkins had been courting now for two years and she liked the lad and would be delighted to see Rose happy and settled. She knew that poor Dora would have been too.

'Of course I said yes. I love him. There's never been anyone else for me, you all know that.'

Harry looked pleased that Alan Hopkins would soon be taking the responsibility for Rose off himself and Sal. 'Of course he can come and see me, Rose, but if you are quite certain you want to marry him then we won't stand in your way, will we, Sal?'

'Of course not, Rose. I hope you'll both be very happy. He's a decent, hard-working lad from a respectable family.'

'We're not thinking of getting married for at least two years. We have to save up. I can't expect you to pay for my wedding, Uncle Harry, although compared to Gloria's it will be quiet and inexpensive. And we'll need to find somewhere to rent and buy furniture and things.'

'Very sensible, Rose,' Harry replied, thinking that the cost of Gloria's wedding had been ruinous. Still, Gloria and Grant now lived in what sounded like a very sumptuous apartment overlooking Central Park and Grant had recently taken over from his father in the family business and was doing well.

'You mean I've got to wait two years before I can be a bridesmaid again?' Betty laughed, pulling a face.

'It will give you plenty of time to save up for a decent wedding present for them,' Sal remarked. 'Of course we'll help out with the expenses, Rose,' she added, thinking of her promise to Dora. 'And in future you can give me five shillings less each week. That will be a bit of a help towards the savings. It's certainly not cheap to set up home these days.'

'That's really good of you, Auntie Sal, but I got a rise

when I turned eighteen and if I pass my next exam I'll get another one.'

Harry nodded. Rose worked hard and was doing very well at her job and it wouldn't hurt him to at least pay some of the girl's wedding expenses. She'd said it would be small and quiet. They could have the reception here and he would lay on a buffet and provide the drink, that wouldn't cost him much with his perks. And how would it look if he didn't contribute? People would think him mean-spirited and tight-fisted and that wasn't his style at all.

Rose and Betty spent the next hour discussing Rose's plans. Since Gloria had gone they didn't have to share a bedroom but often they would sit together in Betty's room for a chat.

'You might not have to wait the whole two years, Rose. Not if Da pays for some things and I don't mind paying for my own dress.'

Rose nodded. 'Thanks, Betty, but I'll wait and see what Alan says. I told him I'd start looking at the prices of furniture and things next week just to give me some idea of how much we'll need to save up.'

'Well, I wouldn't be looking at stuff in our place, it's quite expensive. Blackler's is cheaper for bedding and curtains and pots and pans and I'd try some of the smaller furniture shops for the big items.'

'We want to have at least enough for the basics. You can't expect to have a fully furnished home right away, it takes years to acquire a nice home.'

'Unless you're our Gloria, of course,' Betty added. Mam

had had letters full of detailed accounts of Gloria's shopping trips to furnish the new apartment. Her sister seemed to have the best of everything and all kinds of luxuries they'd never heard of, like an 'ice box' – whatever that was – and a shower and a laundry room. Not that Gloria ever used that. She had a maid and a cook. That was fortunate for Grant as her sister hadn't even been able to make a pan of scouse without burning it.

'I'm quite happy with Alan even though he doesn't earn a fortune,' Rose said emphatically.

Betty nodded. 'When will you be going for the ring?'

'Next Saturday. Alan's been saving up for it for months but I don't want anything too expensive. I think I might suggest we go to somewhere like Stanley's on Scotland Road. They sell unclaimed pledges and we might get a bargain.'

Betty tutted. 'You really don't want to take this economy too seriously, Rose. You only get one engagement ring, so for heaven's sake get something from a decent jewellers, like Brown's in London Road.'

Rose smiled. 'We'll see.'

After supper when Sal had gone next door and Rose was busy writing down and totting up the list of furniture prices she'd obtained, Betty felt restless and irritable, unable to settle at anything.

'What's the matter with you, Betty? You're like a cat on hot bricks,' Harry asked crossly. He was due to sail next week and was feeling bored and restless himself.

'I've been thinking, Da, that it's about time I did something about my future. I've been in that dead-end job now for two years and even though I've been moved to the soft furnishing department it's not much better and neither is the pay.'

Harry put down the *Journal of Commerce* and nodded. This had probably been brought on by Rose's engagement. 'Then I think it's about time you made some decisions, some changes, Betty.'

'Now that I'm eighteen I'm old enough to go to sea.'

Harry frowned. 'I've already told you, Betty, it's no picnic. You'd have to start at the bottom and do you think you've got the right temperament? There will be times when you'd have to bite your tongue and you're not very good at that.'

'I won't know until I try, will I? I've got to do *something* with my life, Da.'

Harry nodded. He was reluctant to encourage her but she was right. She was achieving nothing here. A seafarer's life was a hard one but it did have its compensations. He sighed. 'Well, give it a try, Betty.'

She smiled at him. 'Where do I start?'

'With Union Castle or Canadian Pacific. Cunard won't take you at eighteen. Go down to the offices and ask.'

'Couldn't you do something, Da? Ask around?'

Harry considered it. If she was determined then . . . well, he was acquainted with a couple of people at Canadian Pacific. They were a relatively big line sailing mainly between Liverpool and Canada, carrying both first class and emigrants. 'I'll see what I can do, Betty, but there might not be a vacancy. You might have to wait.'

'But could I put my name down?'

He sighed again. 'Can you get a half-day off before I sail?

I'll take you to the offices of Canadian Pacific.'

Betty nodded. If necessary she'd tell Lewis's she had a dentist appointment; she wouldn't mind losing a few hours' pay if it meant she might have a hope of changing her mundane lifestyle. She knew her mother wouldn't be very happy about it but Sal would still have Rose at home, at least for the next eighteen months. She now felt happier and far more animated than she had done for ages.

Chapter Twenty-Seven

———◦•◦———

SAL WASN'T AT ALL happy when Betty imparted the news to her and she was also far from pleased with Harry's involvement.

'What are you encouraging her for? You know she'll be little more than a glorified skivvy,' she demanded.

'If she sticks at it, Sal, she has a chance of promotion – in time. She's grown up a lot lately, become more sensible. What can she hope for working as a shop assistant? Head of the department at best. She might hate it, we don't know, but at least let her give it a try.'

Sal still wasn't convinced. 'What kind of promotion can she achieve? First class at best and she'll still be waiting hand and foot on the likes of your Sybil.'

'At least the tips will be good.'

'Not always. A lot of wealthy people are notoriously mean in the matter of tips.'

He couldn't argue with her on that but he wasn't going back on his word. 'She could make Chief Stewardess one day. Anyway, Sal, I've promised her now.'

'Chief Stewardess, my foot! She'll never stick it for *that* long,' Sal had retorted but she knew there was little she could do about it; she just hoped there would be no vacancies at the moment, so Betty would have time to give the matter far more serious thought.

Rose too was not surprised when Betty imparted her news. 'I know you've been thinking about it for years but are you sure? You'll have to start in steerage.'

'I know that, Rose, but I'm fed up being stuck in the rut I'm in now. I see the same people every day; I do the same boring things every day. I never go anywhere. I want to do something *different*. I want to visit different countries, the way Da does.'

Rose sighed. She could understand that. Betty's job was dull and she hadn't met anyone special the way Rose had, but she was aware her friend would find the life hard. She managed a smile. 'At least your mam will have me at home while you're away.'

Betty nodded. She had impressed that fact on her mother already.

'So when are you going to go then?

'I'm going to take Monday morning off. Mondays are quiet to say the least. Da is going to take me there.'

'Good luck then, if it's really what you want,' Rose said

affably. She hoped Betty would at least get an interview.

Harry had phoned his contact at Canadian Pacific and had managed to obtain an interview for Betty on Monday morning at ten thirty. He'd asked were there any vacancies and had been told that there were two for steerage. It was something he didn't mention to either Sal or Betty. Let Betty get through the interview first.

On Monday morning she made an effort with her appearance. Even though it was now getting colder she decided not to wear a coat. She'd had her best coat for over a year now and she thought it was looking a bit shabby. She'd intended to buy a new one but hadn't seen anything she liked at a reasonable price. Instead she wore her grey tweed costume with a fine black wool jumper underneath. It was very plain so she decided to wear a lemon, grey and white patterned scarf to brighten it up. Her black shoes were decent and she had a black handbag and gloves. Now all she had to do was sort out a hat.

'Should I borrow one of Mam's?' she asked Rose as she'd tried on the whole outfit on Sunday evening.

'You don't want anything too fancy,' Rose advised. 'Why don't you discard the scarf and just wear your gold cross and chain instead and borrow my black cloche. The one trimmed with that cherry-red velvet bow. That will brighten everything up without making it too fussy. It's plain but sort of elegant.'

Betty had tried it on and realised that Rose was right. She also thought it made her appear a bit older.

To her great relief it was neither blowing a gale nor

raining on Monday morning; at least she wouldn't arrive looking windblown or bedraggled and damp. They got the tram to the Pier Head, outside the Liver building, and walked across the cobbled expanse of Man Island to the imposing building with its twin clock towers on the top of which were perched the mythical Liver Birds, one facing towards the river, the other over the city.

'Now remember what I told you, Betty. Answer all questions honestly and slowly. Don't gabble or giggle and don't fidget or fiddle with your buttons or your nails. Put your bag down on the floor, sit up straight and don't cross your legs. You want to appear steady, polite and composed,' Harry instructed as they went through the swing doors and into the wide corridor with its black and white tiled floor.

The offices of the Canadian Pacific Steamship Company were on the fourth floor and as her da ushered her in she looked around. Ahead was a long counter of highly polished wood behind which sat three male clerks, all formally dressed. On the walls were large posters advertising specific voyages and she was surprised to notice one that was advertising 'Sunshine Cruises'.

'I thought you said they went to Canada and carried mostly emigrants,' she whispered to Harry.

'They do but in the winter months the Saint Lawrence river freezes over completely so they sail to the Caribbean islands out of New York and there is no steerage, just first and second class and mostly American passengers. So, they promote their steerage-class girls to second class just for the duration of the cruises. I think they return to the Canadian run about the end of March or early April.'

She hadn't known that and her excitement rose. New York and what most people called the West Indies. 'Really? That sounds fantastic and I could go and visit our Gloria.'

'You've got to get through the interview first,' Harry reminded her firmly.

Betty was ushered into a small office at the far end of the room and she shook hands with Albert Franklin, the man her father had spoken to on the phone.

'So you are Elizabeth, "Betty" Jenkins. Please sit down.'

Betty smiled and sat on the chair Mr Franklin indicated, dutifully placing her bag on the floor beside her and smoothing down her skirt. He seemed very pleasant and she answered all his questions confidently and truthfully.

At the end of half an hour Albert Franklin nodded and leaned back in his chair. 'Well, I think we can offer you a position as a stewardess, Betty. You seem hard-working, reliable and polite and pleasant. I take it you will have to give a week's notice to Lewis's?'

'I will, Mr Franklin, and thank you so much. I'm very grateful,' Betty replied, feeling both relieved and delighted. 'I'll tell them this afternoon.'

He pulled a sheaf of papers towards him, scrutinising the top one closely. 'The *Empress of Britain* is sailing a week on Wednesday for Quebec and Montreal. I'd like you to join her. Miss Lawson is the Chief Stewardess; you'll report to her. You'll have to have a Discharge Book and all the uniform, but I'm sure your father can help you there. You'll get the uniform at Greenberg's in Park Lane and your Discharge Book from the Pool at Man Island.'

He opened a desk drawer and brought out a stiff white card, quickly wrote on it and then handed it to Betty, smiling.

She took it from him and quickly scanned it. The words 'Canadian Pacific Steamship Company' were printed in black across the top, beneath which were the crossed red-and-white chequered flags, the company's emblem and then:

Name: Miss Elizabeth Jenkins
Rating: Stewardess Third Class
Ship: SS *Empress of Britain*
Port of Embarcation: Liverpool
Date of Embarcation: Wednesday 9 October 1929
Time: 08.00 hours G.M.T.

'Present that to Miss Lawson with your Discharge Book and good luck,' Albert Franklin instructed her.

She got up and, putting the card in her bag, thanked him again.

He accompanied her outside to where Harry was waiting. He gave a brief nod and Harry shook his hand warmly. 'I'm very grateful for your help, Albert. If I can reciprocate the favour at any time I will.' He ushered Betty towards the door before turning back and lowering his voice. 'There will be a case of something very drinkable sent to you, Albert. Here or at home?' he enquired.

'Home would be perfect, Harry. You know the address?'

Harry nodded. Some people would no doubt raise their

eyebrows and call it bribery but he called it 'helping one another out'. And it was a very standard practice amongst the seafaring community in this city.

'Oh, Da, I'm so *excited*!' Betty cried, clutching his arm as they left the building. 'In less than ten days I'll be off to Quebec! *Canada!* Oh, thanks, Da! I would never have got it but for you.'

'Well, mind you don't go letting me down. Work hard, do as you're told and don't argue. Now, let's get your Discharge Book sorted out. You can't sail without it.'

'What is it?'

'You could call it a seaman's passport. At the end of every trip this Miss Lawson will report on your work and behaviour to the Captain who will then write his comments in it. If he writes D.R. – Declines to Report – you won't get taken on for another trip. In fact you won't get another ship but you really have to have behaved very badly for that.' Harry grinned.

'What's so funny?' Betty asked.

'I've known blokes who've had a D.R. tell their wives it meant "Definitely Reliable".'

Betty laughed. She had no intention of getting a D.R. in her Discharge Book.

When they arrived home Sal could see by her daughter's face that she'd got the job. 'They took you on then?'

'They did, Mam! I'm sailing a week on Wednesday to Canada on the *Empress of Britain*. Look, I've got my Discharge Book and my joining instructions.' She took them both out of her bag and passed them to Sal.

Sal nodded. 'I just hope you know what you're letting yourself in for, Betty, I really do.'

'I know I'll have to work very hard and that I won't get much time off but I can cope with that. I'll have to leave you an allotment, Mam.'

'I know,' Sal replied, thinking that not only did the money "allotted" to the wife or mother mean that they were not left without any means of support but also, God forbid, should anything happen to the seafarer, they would get some compensation.

'We didn't have time to go to Greenberg's, Sal, so you'll have to take her. She's got a list of everything she'll need. Now, you'd better get yourself ready for work, Betty. You have to give your notice in and I have to get down to the *Amazonia*.'

When Rose got in later it was Sal who informed her of Betty's good news.

'I really do hope she likes it,' Rose said.

'So do I. You should see the list of stuff she's got to have and they don't provide it. Two blue uniform dresses, two white sharkskin dresses, four white caps, two pairs of white shoes, a navy blue bridge coat and a navy beret, plus two white belts and then there's stockings and she'll have to have underwear too.'

'That will be expensive,' Rose agreed.

'It will so she'd better not do one trip and then come home and tell me she's changed her mind. I said to Elsie it just might be the making of her, if she can take orders and keep her mouth shut,' Sal answered sharply.

Rose nodded and began to help Sal to set the table.

As Betty got off the tram after work Artie Taylor was walking down the street and she quickened her steps to catch up to him. She liked Artie and she still thought Gloria had treated him very badly although she knew that since he'd come back from Crewe he'd had other girlfriends. His mam had told Sal that it hadn't taken him all that long to get over Gloria.

'Hello, Artie.'

He smiled at her. 'Just finished another hard day, Betty?'

'Another boring afternoon but I won't be there for much longer, thank God. I'm going away to sea, Artie.'

He looked surprised. 'I didn't know you wanted to follow in your da's footsteps?'

'I've got a job as a stewardess with Canadian Pacific. I gave my notice in today.'

'How long will you be away for?' Artie asked, thinking that probably Harry had been instrumental in getting her the job. That was usually the way things worked.

'A few weeks. Liverpool – Montreal – Quebec – Liverpool.'

They'd reached Betty's house. 'Well, good luck, Betty. I hope you enjoy it. I mean that. I've heard it's not a bad life.'

She smiled at him. 'Thanks, Artie. It's got to be better than being stuck behind a counter in Lewis's.'

Chapter Twenty-Eight

———•◦•———

BETTY WISHED HER DA had still been home, he could have accompanied her this morning instead of her mother, she thought as they reached Gladstone Dock where the ship was berthed. He could probably have persuaded the police-man on the dock gate to let him take her as far as the gangway.

'You'll only be able to come this far with me, Mam,' she said as they halted beside the hut and she showed him her Joining Card.

'I know, luv, but you'll be all right. There seem to be plenty of people around.'

Betty put down her small case and hugged her mother. 'Goodbye, Mam. I'm not going to be away for very long really.'

Sal smiled. 'I know. You take care of yourself and work

hard. Now, why don't you go and catch up with that girl over there, she's wearing the same uniform as you so she must be a stewardess too.'

Betty picked up her case and quickened her steps until she reached the girl Sal had pointed out. 'Excuse me. I wonder could you direct me to Miss Lawson's office? This is my first trip and I was told to report to her. I'm Betty Jenkins, by the way.'

The girl smiled back. She looked to be a bit older than herself and had thick auburn hair and green eyes. 'Of course. I'm reporting to her myself. I'm Kate Duncan.'

Betty fell into step beside her. 'My da goes away to sea and I was fed up with my job so I thought I'd give it a try too.'

'What did you do?' Kate asked.

'I was a shop assistant at Lewis's.'

'You're going to find this a bit different, to say the least.'

'That's what I've been told but at least I'll get to see a bit of the world.'

They climbed the gangway and then Betty followed Kate along what seemed like miles of corridors and down three flights of stairs, passing numerous doors. 'It's almost as big as the *Mauretania*. I'll never find my way around.'

Kate laughed. 'You will and you'll be surprised at how quickly. Nearly there, one more flight down to D Deck.'

'What's she like, this Miss Lawson?' Betty was now feeling more than a little apprehensive, remembering the crowds of people who had been aboard the ship on the day Gloria and Sybil had sailed to New York.

'She's not too bad really. She's a stickler for all the rules and regulations and comes down on you like a ton of bricks if you don't do your work properly, but if you've got a problem or are in trouble she's great.'

Kate had finally stopped before a door bearing the title 'Chief Stewardess'; she knocked and was told to 'enter'.

They went in together and Betty quickly glanced around. It wasn't a very big room and there was no porthole but there was a bunk neatly made up, a narrow wardrobe, a washbasin with a cupboard beneath it and a desk set against the bulkhead. The desk was littered with papers and Miss Lawson sat behind it. She was older than Betty had anticipated, probably in her forties, she mused, with light brown wavy hair tucked neatly under a starched white cap and intelligent grey eyes.

'This is Betty Jenkins, ma'am. This is her first trip.'

'Thank you and welcome back, Miss Duncan,' Miss Lawson said with a smile as Kate handed over her Discharge Book and Joining Card and the Chief Stewardess duly ticked her name off a list. 'Welcome aboard, Miss Jenkins, I've been expecting you. I believe your father is Harry Jenkins, the Chief Steward on the *Amazonia*?'

'He is, ma'am,' Betty replied, taking her cue from Kate and passing over her own documents.

Miss Lawson became brisk. 'Then you will have some idea of what is expected of you. Miss Duncan will show you to your cabin but first things first. You will work a seven-day week while at sea. You will be on duty ten hours of each day but there will be periods for meals and rest, although you will still be expected to answer bells during those times. You will be expected to stand watch; everyone on board does. It will all be explained to you. I myself will supervise you at first, and then you will be under the direction of your section head. You will be expected to do your own laundry; your meals will be drawn from the galley. Lights out at 20.00 hours and – I must emphasise this fact – no men are allowed in cabins: ever! In fact no men are allowed near the stewardesses' quarters except to call for you if you are going ashore in port. You will work whilst in port, but Saturday afternoon, Sunday and Monday mornings you will have free.' She paused. 'You have, I presume, been informed of your wages?'

'Yes, ma'am. Eight pounds ten shillings a month,' Betty replied, trying to remember everything Miss Lawson had said.

'Have you made arrangements for an allotment to be left for your mother?'

Betty nodded. 'Fifteen shillings a month.'

'You will be given your section in steerage class. You will be looking after people who are emigrating and who often have very little money. Quite often they have less than you earn but they have paid their passage and are entitled to be treated with respect, even though at times they can be "difficult". You understand, Miss Jenkins?'

'I do, ma'am,' Betty replied, thinking that there would definitely be few tips at the end of this voyage if they were all so hard up.

'Have you ever sailed before?'

'Only on the Mersey ferries, ma'am, they don't really count.'

Miss Lawson smiled. 'No, they don't. Well, as it is October the weather will probably be rough and you will no doubt be seasick; nearly everyone is at first. However, you'll get used to it, and you will still have to work for there is no one to replace you or do your work. You will be expected to carry on – regardless! There will be a daily inspection by either the Captain or the Purser and woe betide you if there is even a hair out of place. I'm strict but I hope I'm fair and I expect my girls to be smartly turned out at all times. Now, have you any questions, Miss Jenkins?'

'None that I can think of, ma'am,' Betty replied.

'Then Miss Duncan will show you to your cabin. You will be sharing with her. You may count yourself fortunate, the men have to share with six or seven others. One last thing though, and I say this to all my girls when they start: you will soon find that you are answering bells with a smile on your face and hate in your heart, but it is something we all endure, I assure you. Good luck, Miss Jenkins.'

'What did she mean by that?' Betty asked as she followed Kate down the companionway, their heels tapping loudly on the uncarpeted metal deck.

'You'll soon find out,' Kate replied a little grimly.

The cabin she was to share with Kate was tiny. There were two bunks, one single wardrobe, a chest of drawers and a washbasin.

'Unpack your stuff and then I'll show you around. We'll go and get your emergency lifeboat number and final boat station. You're expected to learn both by heart. I'll show you the galley and the pantry where we take our meals – standing up. There's no crew mess.'

'I never thought it would be quite as bad as this.' The hours of work, the regulations and the thoughts of seasickness had begun to bother Betty.

Kate was holding up her dark blue uniform dress with its white collar and cuffs and double row of brass buttons and looking disgruntled. 'If the creases don't fall out I'll have to iron the damned thing again!' She grimaced at Betty. 'No one ever thinks it's like this. All they think of is the glamour and the chance to travel and get paid for it. It's work, work and more bloody work. Our passengers would often try the patience of Saint Peter himself and some of them are damned rude and ignorant. Some can't even speak English. They think they're entitled to have us running backwards and forwards all day long at their whim, that's what she meant when she said about answering bells with a smile on your face and hate in your heart. Those with nothing are the ones who do the most shouting and complaining. Those who have money are generally not like that. The first-class girls are the fortunate ones.' She hung the dress up in the wardrobe. 'Well, we'd better get going. We'll get something to eat first, we usually see one of the chefs all right, slip him ten shillings, that way we get decent meals, although half the time we don't get to finish them because of the damned bells.'

There had been no carnival-like send-off. No band, no crowds, no paper streamers or at least Betty didn't think so.

She'd been given her section and then the passengers had come on board and it had become very hectic. She hadn't even realised that they were moving until the ship was out of the shelter of Liverpool Bay and the weather began to get rough.

It had got worse as they'd left the coast of Ireland behind. The ship rolled and plunged in the heavy seas and the deck had sloped away beneath her feet and she'd slid with a bump against the wall of the companionway. The tray she'd been carrying had crashed to the deck. She'd picked up the broken crockery and mopped up the mess with a tea towel, gritted her teeth and headed back to the galley for replacements.

Next morning she had felt like death and was unable to keep even water down. Kate had dragged her bodily to her feet and forced her to get dressed.

'Oh, Kate! Just leave me alone and let me die,' she'd moaned.

'Get that idea out of your head right now. No one ever died from seasickness. There's no one to cover for you, you've got to carry on,' Kate had impressed upon her.

She never knew how she got through the next three days. It had been a nightmare for there was no let-up in the weather. The pitching and rolling never stopped and the effect of the motion was made worse by the ceaseless noise of the great turbines that drove the screws in the engine room below. Most of her passengers were sick and despite her own nausea she had to look after them as best she could. Cleaning up vomit as she forced down the bile in her own throat. Changing linen as her stomach heaved. Bringing them food and drinks only to be chastised for being late as she had to stop so often. All this while still parading for inspection and carrying out her normal duties. She had longed to return to the soft furnishing department at Lewis's.

On the day she began to recover Kate had suggested she go up on deck for some fresh air. 'You should have gone up top days ago. It helps. It's something to do with balance.'

So she'd stood huddled on the promenade deck in her bridge coat while the wind threatened to tear away her beret. She'd stared at the sea, cold and grey and menacing: such a vast expanse of water that it was hard to discern the horizon at all.

'It has many moods, Miss Jenkins. It can be dangerous and cruel and you will learn to respect it. Those who say they don't fear it are either fools or liars – or both. How are you feeling now?' Miss Lawson asked as she'd stood beside her.

'A lot better, ma'am, thank you.'

'You'll be fine now but I think you'd better go down, we don't want you catching cold.'

The following afternoon she'd felt back to normal and had gone to answer a bell when over the noise of the turbines she thought she heard a scream come from within the tiny cabin. She knocked loudly on the door and then went in. On one of the four bunks a young woman was lying with her knees drawn up, obviously in pain.

'Mrs McDonald, what's the matter, are you ill?' she asked, crossing to her.

'Oh, Miss Jenkins, I think it's the baby! Help me!' There were beads of perspiration on the woman's forehead.

Betty's eyes widened in shock. 'What baby? I wasn't informed that anyone in here was pregnant.'

Fiona McDonald clutched her arm and screamed again. 'I . . . We didn't tell anyone . . . in case . . . in case they wouldn't let me sail to join my Jimmy in Quebec. The baby wasn't due until next month. Oh, miss, please help me!'

'I'll go for the doctor!'

'No! Don't leave me, miss, please!'

'But you've got to have a doctor if the baby is coming,' Betty urged. She couldn't deliver a baby, she thought wildly. But then she remembered how calmly and sensibly Sal dealt with emergencies. She must keep calm and reassure Mrs McDonald. Her gaze fell on the bell push and she pressed it hard, leaving her finger on it.

It seemed ages before Kate appeared in the doorway. 'Betty, what's wrong?'

'Mrs McDonald is having a baby! She didn't tell anyone she was pregnant. For God's sake get someone, Kate, quickly!'

Kate fled while Betty tried to calm the woman who was rolling in agony on the narrow bunk.

At last Kate returned with Miss Lawson and one of the two doctors the ship carried. Betty stepped back as the Chief Stewardess took charge.

'Mrs McDonald, try to relax, please. Doctor has to examine you.' She turned back to Betty and Kate as the young man bent over Mrs McDonald. 'She'll be fine now. You can both get back to work.'

Once outside Betty breathed a sigh of relief. 'Oh, she gave me a terrible fright. I thought I was going to have to try to deliver it.'

'There will be hell to pay because she didn't inform anyone she was pregnant.'

'She was afraid they wouldn't let her sail to join her husband. It wasn't due until next month.'

Kate nodded. 'They wouldn't have. Well, I suppose when it's all over they'll take her – them – down to the hospital. Blast!' she finished as another bell sounded.

An hour later Betty was stripping off the soiled bedding when Miss Lawson entered the cabin.

'You coped very well, Miss Jenkins. Some girls would have become hysterical and panicked. I'm impressed and so is Dr Davies. I told him it was your first trip.' She rolled up her sleeves. 'Take the linen down to the laundry and change your uniform, it's stained. I'll finish up here.'

'What did she have?' Betty asked.

'A boy. A little on the small side but apart from that he's doing well.'

'Will she get into a lot of trouble, ma'am? For not telling anyone?'

Miss Lawson smiled. 'The Purser will have a few sharp words to say to her but she's not the first and she probably won't be the last. There have been babies born on this ship before.'

When they finally docked in Quebec Betty helped to get Fiona McDonald and her baby ashore to where her husband was waiting. She had made time to go down to the hospital to see her and the baby and on her way out Dr Davies had stopped her.

'Miss Jenkins? Could I have a word?'

She nodded. He was, she judged, about twenty-six or -seven and had dark curly hair, brown eyes and a Welsh accent. 'I just wanted to see the baby.'

'Miss Lawson told me you coped very well with the emergency on what is your first trip, I hear.'

She smiled. 'It is and, well, at least I didn't have a fit of hysterics and run off and leave her.'

'She really should stay in bed for longer but as we're docking tomorrow that's not possible.'

'But she will be all right?'

He nodded. 'As long as she takes it easy.'

'I'll come and help her,' she'd offered.

'I'm sure she'd appreciate that. Now, I'd better not detain you.'

She'd smiled to herself as she'd walked away. He was quite nice and it was good of him to thank her.

As she guided her passengers to the gangway she pulled the collar of her bridge coat up around her ears. A freezing wind was blowing in from the Gulf of St Lawrence. None of the crew was going ashore as they were due to sail for Montreal in a few hours. Below on the dockside there was great activity but high above the city in serene stillness rose the turreted Château Frontenac, the luxury hotel belonging to Canadian Pacific Railways that looked just like a real French château. She smiled to herself. This was Canada. Despite all the hardships of the trip she'd made it and now she felt a surge of excitement. She'd get time ashore in Montreal and Kate had promised she'd take her to see Windsor Street Station, the Bellevue Casino and the Indian Rooms, and then they'd do some shopping on St Catherine's Street before having something to eat at Joe the Greek's, which was a favourite haunt of the *Empress* crews. Her da had been right, it was damned hard work and long hours but there was a great camaraderie and a sense of 'belonging' too. She'd begun to think that she would enjoy this life, especially as after Christmas they'd be heading down to the West Indies.

When she returned to her cabin Kate handed her two letters. 'There are two for you; the mail has just been delivered.'

Betty turned them over in her hand. One was from her mother and the other was obviously from Gloria, judging by the stamp, but she wondered how her sister knew where she was. When she opened Sal's letter she found out. Sal had sent Gloria a telegram. 'Kate, you'll never guess! Our Gloria's going to meet me in Montreal; she's coming up by train from New York! I haven't seen her for two years. Mam thought she should know that I would be at least in the same part of the world.'

Kate grinned. 'That's great news, Betty, but it's a fair way from New York. It will take her days.'

Betty had opened Gloria's letter and was scanning the lines. 'She says Grant – that's her husband – has urged her to make the trip. Well, she's certainly got the time and the money. She'll get the train to Buffalo and then cross into

277

Canada and take the Canadian Pacific Railway up to Montreal. It will take her two days but she says Grant has organised it all – first class of course – and she'll come down to the ship to meet me.'

'Where's she staying?' Kate asked, thinking that Gloria's husband must be wealthy for the trip would cost a small fortune, just so Gloria could see her sister for a few hours.

'The Hôtel Grand Royal.'

Kate whistled. 'Is he a millionaire then?'

Betty laughed. 'I suppose he is.' She was thrilled. It would be wonderful to see her sister and catch up on everything.

Chapter Twenty-Nine

———◦•◦———

GLORIA LEANED BACK AGAINST the plush upholstery of the seat in the first-class Pullman car and looked out of the window as the train picked up speed. She had changed trains at the border at Niagara but unfortunately there had been no time to visit the Falls, which she'd heard were quite spectacular. She had been thankful when they'd left Buffalo behind for it had appeared to her to be a rather ugly little town given over to industry, but now they were travelling through lower Ontario towards Toronto. The countryside was beautiful at this time of year, she thought. The leaves on the trees had turned to vivid shades of red, orange, bronze and gold and she finally began to feel less apprehensive, excitement at the thought of seeing Betty taking over. It was the furthest she'd ever travelled on her own and when Grant had suggested she make the trip she had been very dubious.

'It's such a long way and I really won't be able to spend much time with her. She'll only have a couple of hours off,' she'd reminded him.

'But it would be such a shame to miss the opportunity to see her, Gloria. Don't worry your head about anything, I'll arrange it all and the trains are very comfortable and fast these days. You'll have your own private little compartment to sleep in, rather like a small cabin on a ship I'm told, and they have a dining car and a lounge. You'll be very comfortable and then you can take a cab to the hotel when you arrive in Montreal. I'll book the hotel too, one near the docks so you won't have to waste time travelling across the city. Nothing could be simpler.'

She'd still been unsure. 'But what about you, Grant?'

He'd grinned at her. 'What about me? I think I can look after myself for a few days. I sure have plenty of work to keep me occupied. So, no more doubts. Go and enjoy seeing Betty and hearing all her news.'

So she'd agreed and she had to admit that so far it hadn't been quite as daunting as she'd imagined. She had so much to tell Betty and she wanted to see if her sister had changed and how she'd managed on this her first trip, and she couldn't wait to hear all the news from home first-hand.

She'd found the journey rather tedious although very comfortable but eventually they arrived at Windsor Station and she alighted. A porter came to take her luggage and as she followed him to the cab rank on Dorchester Square she looked up at the building she was leaving. It didn't look like a station, she thought, it looked rather like a grand French château with an ornate tower that rose fifteen storeys, which seemed to be very high compared to the surrounding buildings, most of which seemed to have been built in what she assumed was the French style; there certainly were not as many skyscrapers as there were in New York. It looked more European than the cities she'd passed through.

The Hôtel Grand Royal was on the corner of Bonsecours and St Paul Streets and the cab driver informed her helpfully that she could easily walk to where her sister's ship would be docked. The hotel receptionist was equally helpful and, after making some enquiries, informed her that the *Empress* had already docked and that while Gloria settled in they would get a message to her sister.

'That's so kind of you,' Gloria replied. She hadn't expected the ship to be here already and felt a little flustered.

'Shall we ask her to meet you here in our small salon, ma'am? It will give you time to freshen up.'

Gloria nodded. 'Yes, please. I seem to have been travelling for days and I would like to get washed and changed.'

It seemed as though she had only just unpacked, washed and changed into fresh clothes when a bellboy arrived to tell her her sister was waiting in the petit salon on the ground floor.

'Could you show me where it is, please? I haven't had time to get my bearings yet.'

He grinned and nodded. 'Sure, if you'll follow me, ma'am, and would you like me to order you some tea or coffee?'

'Oh, tea would be lovely, thank you.'

Betty was sitting on one of the fragile-looking gilt chairs

gazing around avidly but when she caught sight of Gloria she leaped up and ran to her, throwing her arms around her. 'Gloria! Oh, it's really great to see you again!'

Gloria hugged her and felt tears prick her eyes; it had been two years since she'd seen Betty. 'Oh, I've missed you, Betty! I really have. Come and sit down. I've ordered some tea. I've only just arrived; I didn't think you'd be here already.'

They sat on an elegant brocade sofa, still holding hands. 'We docked three hours ago. I knew you were staying here, I got the mail in Quebec, and so I was going to walk up anyway. It's so good of you, Gloria, to come all this way. It must have taken ages.'

'Days, but it's worth it. Let me look at you. You look great, a bit older but still . . . Betty!'

Betty laughed. 'A bit older and a lot wiser after that trip!'

'Was it rough? Is it hard work? Do you think you'll stick at it?'

Betty grimaced. 'I was so sick at first, I thought I was dying, and I still had to work – but I got over it. It is hard work but it's all so . . . different. One woman on my section went into labour, no one knew she was pregnant.'

Gloria's eyes widened. 'Did you panic? What did you do?'

'Got a doctor as fast as I could.' Betty thought she glimpsed a shadow cross her sister's face. 'No sign yet of you being in the "family way"?'

Gloria shook her head. 'No, it just hasn't happened. Grant works very hard, Betty. Too hard, I sometimes think, and now Barney and Eunice have gone to Florida I sometimes feel a bit, well . . . lonely.'

'But you've made friends, you said so in your letters, and you seem to see quite a bit of Iris.'

Gloria nodded. 'I do and I'm not complaining at all but it's not quite the same as having your real family around you. I do miss everyone. Mam, you, Rose and even Da, though he was never there very much.' She smiled, not wanting to sound as if she was moaning about her lot. 'It's a pity you can't come back to New York with me. I'd love you to see our apartment and I could take you shopping and to see all the sights.'

Betty grinned. 'I'll be able to see everything and meet everyone after Christmas. The St Lawrence River freezes over so we go cruising to the West Indies and we sail in and out of New York.'

Gloria clapped her hands delightedly. 'Really? Oh, that's fantastic, Betty. We'll be able to spend time together then.'

The tea arrived and Betty poured. 'I've had plenty of practice at this, Gloria.'

'How is Mam? She always sounds so cheerful in her letters.'

'She is, she misses you and I suppose now with me away too she must get a bit lonely but Rose is still at home – although she's just got engaged.'

'Has she? To Alan Hopkins? When's the wedding?'

Betty nodded and sipped her tea. 'Yes, to Alan, but she says it will be two years before they'll have saved enough.'

'What about you, Betty? No one special on the scene?'

Betty sighed. 'No. You know me, I'm hard to please. I've been out with a few lads but none of them swept me off my feet, the way Grant did you.'

Gloria smiled happily. 'I still love him very much, Betty.'

'I know. Still, I'm only eighteen: I've plenty of time and right now I'm concentrating on my new career.'

'You're going to make a career of it?' Gloria asked.

'Why not? It's a great way to see the world and the girls I work with are very friendly. Kate who I share with was going to take me to see the sights here until I found you were coming, but I'll see them all next trip. I can't believe that a few weeks ago I was stuck working at Lewis's and now I've crossed the Atlantic, seen Quebec and a bit of Montreal and in the New Year I'll be gallivanting around the West Indies.'

'And New York,' Gloria added, thinking how enthusiastic Betty looked about the future. She was glad Betty seemed to be enjoying her new life although it was something she knew she couldn't have stuck at. 'How long have you got before you have to be back on board?'

Betty looked at her watch. 'Another five hours.'

Gloria stood up. 'Then we'd better make the most of it. Shall we go and do a bit of "exploring" ourselves and then maybe have something to eat? We can still chat while we do.'

Betty tucked her arm companionably through Gloria's. 'We can see some of the sights together and you can tell me more about New York and your apartment and your life. Then I can relay it all to Mam when I get home.' It would be good to share the experience of seeing a new city with her sister.

They'd taken a cab to St Catherine's Street and Betty had done some shopping for souvenirs – Gloria said she would have time to shop tomorrow for she was spending another day here before going back – then they'd gone for dinner at the Indian Rooms, which they'd both found fascinating as they were decorated with artifacts from the native tribes. Finally and reluctantly they'd returned to the hotel. Gloria insisted that Betty stay in the cab for she felt it was too late for her sister to be walking back to the ship alone.

Betty hugged her tightly. 'I've had a great time, Gloria, and it was so good to see you and spend time with you.'

'I'm glad I came, Betty, I really am. Take care of yourself and give my love to everyone when you get home,' Gloria instructed with a catch in her voice.

'I will and don't forget I'll see you again in the New Year. It's not that far off now. Have a safe journey home and give my love to Grant,' Betty replied as Gloria paid the driver and stood in the hotel doorway, waving as the cab pulled away.

When Betty reached the top of the gangway she made her way along the deck and then leaned on the rail to take a last look at the city before going down to change into her uniform.

'Have you had a good time ashore, Miss Jenkins?'

She turned to find Dr Davies standing a couple of feet away, also leaning on the rail. 'Yes. My sister travelled up from New York and we spent the afternoon and evening together. I haven't seen her for two years.'

'That was good of her; it must have been expensive to come so far.'

Betty nodded and smiled. 'It probably was but Gloria married . . . well.'

'And she's happy in New York?' He thought they must be close for her sister to make such a journey.

'Yes, she seems to be and I'll be able to see her more often in the New Year.'

He smiled 'Ah, indeed. The cruises. We all look forward to them. Blue skies, sunshine and warm breezes in January and February.'

'Much better than being at home in the rain and snow. And I've never been anywhere as exotic before.'

He grinned at her. 'And I doubt there will be any "unexpected arrivals" to deal with.'

Betty grinned back; he was teasing her but not unkindly. 'I hope not.' He was really very nice but of course it was definitely frowned upon for the crew to fraternise with the officers and he was a medical officer. Still, there was no harm in them just chatting. 'I thought I'd like to take a last look at Montreal.'

'It's a very pleasant city, very French, as of course is Quebec.'

'All the street signs and shop signs are in French. We had a bit of difficulty finding our way around,' she confided.

He wondered if they'd encountered the obstinacy some French Canadians displayed in replying to questions asked in English. He had come up against it on occasion; the looks of confusion followed by a reply in French or sometimes just complete silence. He'd found it disconcerting to say the least and he hoped she hadn't been subjected to it. 'I've found it helps if you try to learn a couple of French phrases. People then seem more inclined to be helpful.'

She laughed a little self-consciously. 'I don't think I could manage that.'

'Why not? You seem to be a very bright girl.'

To her dismay she found herself beginning to blush. Oh, for heaven's sake, stop it, Betty Jenkins! she told herself firmly. 'Thank you, Dr Davies. I'd better go down now or Miss Lawson will be on the warpath.'

'Goodnight, Miss Jenkins.'

'Goodnight,' she replied, her cheeks still flushed. She hoped that he hadn't noticed, he'd think her such a fool. Thankfully the lighting wasn't very bright.

Chapter Thirty

⸻

G LORIA STOOD GAZING OUT of the big picture window of her lounge that overlooked Central Park. The colours of the trees reminded her of those she'd seen on her way to Montreal. Next month there would be Thanksgiving and after that there would be Christmas. She'd quickly realised that winters here were bitterly cold with temperatures often plummeting to minus fifteen degrees or more even during the day. She sighed and turned away. After all the festivities were over January and February could be depressingly cold and dull, she thought. No wonder her mother-in-law had gone to live in Florida. She cheered up as she remembered that at least during those months she would see Betty again as she would be in and out of New York on a regular basis. She had enjoyed the short time she'd spent with her sister so much. Betty had become far more mature in her outlook on life than she'd previously been, but of course she had only just left school before Gloria had married Grant.

She wandered across to the large sofa in front of the ornamental fireplace and sat down. At least it was always warm in here with the central heating, something they didn't have at home in Liverpool. She glanced around the room and smiled. She loved this apartment. It was in a very select block and she felt she had furnished it comfortably but with great taste. Everything was brand new and in the art deco style.

She sighed, thinking of Grant. He still worked too hard and since her trip she had begun to think there was something bothering him although he swore there wasn't. When he talked about how well the business was doing and of how much money he'd made both for himself and others, he'd always been very animated – excited even – but these last couple of days he hadn't shown that same animation and she wondered if he was mentally tiring of the effort and energy he was expending in proving he was every bit as successful as Barney had been. Some nights when he came to bed he was so exhausted he fell into a deep sleep immediately. She frowned, remembering how he turned away from her when she reached out for him. They would never have a child if he continued to keep up this frenzied pace of work.

Carmel, her young Irish maid, entered, bobbing dutifully. She'd interviewed all three girls the agency had sent but she'd liked the young girl from West Cork best.

'Would you like tea or coffee, Mrs Hepworth, ma'am?

And Cook is after asking will Mr Hepworth be home early for dinner this evening?'

Gloria smiled at her. 'I think I'll have coffee but maybe we should wait until Miss Iris arrives. And you can tell Cook that Mr Hepworth will be home probably about eight.'

The girl left and Gloria picked up her latest fashion magazine and leafed through it until she found the page she was looking for. Grant's cousin Iris was due to call and she wanted to ask her what she thought of this accessory.

The picture showed a model wearing one of the latest little skull caps in gold tissue. She thought it was lovely and was certain it would suit her. She loved the latest fashions and there were so many good shops in this city. Skirts were just on the knee now and there were coats with bold geometric patterns and 'sporty' styles were popular too – for the country – and of course furs were not only fashionable but practical too for winter.

She got to her feet as she heard the doorbell, leaving the magazine open on the low table. Carmel would answer it and show Iris in.

Grant's cousin bustled in, carrying a box tied with ribbon. 'Gloria, wait until you see what I've bought for the Thanksgiving dinner!' she gushed, placing the box down on the sofa.

'Isn't it a little early yet?'

'I know but I just couldn't resist it!' Iris delved into the layers of tissue paper and held up a very short dress that shimmered in the light. It was white silk overlaid with white chiffon and almost entirely covered in silver beads.

Gloria took in the deep 'V' neckline of both front and back. 'It's gorgeous, Iris, but there isn't a great deal of it, it's much shorter than usual.'

'Oh, Gloria, don't be so prissy! Look, I bought this to go with it.' She held out a silver-tissue skull cap very similar to the one in the magazine. 'It will look perfect.'

Gloria smiled. 'It will. I was just looking at something similar and was going to ask you if you thought I'd suit one.'

'Oh, you would and they are so chic.'

Gloria nodded although she thought that as Iris intended to wear this outfit for Thanksgiving dinner maybe she should look for something else. She didn't want to look as if she was copying her.

As Iris replaced the dress in the box Carmel brought in the silver coffee pot and the Clarice Cliff cups and saucers. After she'd left Gloria poured them each a cup. 'Will you stay for dinner, Iris? I want you to give me some moral support.'

'What for?'

'I think Grant is working far too hard. You know that since he's taken over he's determined to show his father that he can make Hepworth Brothers even more prestigious and successful than it already is, but just lately I think he's getting very tired and I feel there is something he's not telling me.'

Iris nodded as she sipped her coffee.

'So I'm going to suggest that we take a vacation after Christmas. Go down to one of the Caribbean islands for a week or two. It's so cold and depressing here in January. We could even book a cruise on Betty's ship and I'll still have time to meet up with her each time they dock here.'

'I think that's a swell idea. Everything goes so flat then, unless of course you go to Aspen for the skiing. Do you think he'll agree?'

'If you back me up it will help. I think it would do us both the world of good to spend some time lying on a lovely warm beach.'

'I wouldn't mind a vacation then myself but I wouldn't want to spoil your romantic getaway. I'll ask Ingram if he'll take me somewhere.'

'Thanks. I do appreciate it.'

'Have you heard from your folks recently?' Iris asked, putting her coffee cup on the table and leaning back, crossing her long, slim and silk-clad legs.

'Yes, I had a letter yesterday. They are all fine. They had a party for Rose and Alan before Dad sailed again.'

'When Betty is in New York we'll have to take her out, Gloria.'

Gloria laughed. ' "On the town" – aren't you forgetting about Prohibition? Surely you weren't thinking of taking her to one of those dreadful speakeasies?'

Iris giggled. 'If you haven't been to one, you haven't lived.'

Gloria looked alarmed. 'Iris, you haven't? Grant says the stuff they serve is positively lethal. People have *died* from drinking it. And think of the disgrace if there is a police raid.'

'I know and I promise I only went once, just to hear this new music craze – jazz.'

'For goodness' sake don't mention it to Grant, he'll be horrified. He thinks they just encourage crime.'

Iris nodded and smiled wryly. 'I won't. I promise.' Gloria seemed to worry a great deal about Grant's welfare, she thought, but then she supposed if you loved someone it was only natural.

At dinner Gloria thought Grant seemed rather pre-occupied which didn't bode well for her plans. 'Is there something worrying you, Grant?'

'Just a hard day at the office, Gloria. Nothing for you to worry about.'

'Thank goodness it's Friday so you'll have the weekend to relax. You work too hard, Grant. I was saying just that to Iris this afternoon.' Gloria sipped her mineral water.

'You should take a vacation, Grant,' Iris added.

'I agree. After Christmas I think we should spend a couple of weeks in the Caribbean or maybe book a cruise on Betty's ship,' Gloria added brightly.

Grant frowned. 'I'm sorry to be a killjoy, Gloria, but I just couldn't spare two whole weeks to go on vacation. And besides, Betty will be working, she won't have time to spend chatting to us.'

'Grant, the business won't fall apart without you. You have excellent staff,' Iris said. 'I was thinking of asking Ingram to accompany me on a trip somewhere. It's a great time of the year to go.'

'Please, Grant? It would do us both good to get away,' Gloria urged.

Grant relented, seeing the look on his young wife's face.

He really hated to deny her anything and they hadn't had a vacation for a long time. 'Well, maybe I could spare a week – tops. The problems we had with the market yesterday seem to have been halted. We'll see how things are after Thanksgiving.'

Gloria didn't understand much about finance or economics at all but she smiled happily. A week would certainly be better than no vacation at all. She'd call into a travel agency first thing on Monday morning.

But over the weekend she couldn't rid herself of the feeling that something was worrying Grant badly and on Monday morning there seemed to be a very strange atmosphere in the city, she thought as she walked along the crowded sidewalk. Even though she felt excited at the prospect of obtaining some travel brochures, she noticed that people seemed anxious and even a little tense and edgy.

The staff in the travel agency hadn't been very helpful either, she thought irritably as she left. They too had seemed preoccupied and vague. It was all very disturbing. She decided she would call in and see Grant; it was something she seldom did but it would soon be lunchtime and maybe she could persuade him to join her for something to eat.

As she walked further along Wall Street the atmosphere got worse. People were shouting to each other and there was definitely a sense of panic in the air. Ahead of her a crowd had gathered and she tried to push her way through it; feeling decidedly uneasy she caught the arm of the man nearest her.

'What on earth is going on? What's happened? Why is

there such a crowd? Has there been some sort of incident?'

'Lady, haven't you heard? The stock market has crashed. Billions of dollars have been wiped out.'

She stared at him in disbelief. 'How? Why? I don't understand, my husband said things were recovering.'

'They were until about a couple of hours ago and then it all fell apart. People have lost entire fortunes in minutes, companies have gone bankrupt, and a couple of guys have jumped from the top floor of the building ahead. That's why there's such a crowd.'

Gloria felt the panic rising in her as his words began to sink in. The building he had spoken of was where the offices of Hepworth Brothers were situated. She uttered a strangled cry and pushed her way forward, elbowing bystanders aside in her panic until she finally reached the front of the crowd where three police officers were trying to keep the people back. She heard the screaming of an ambulance siren drawing nearer.

'Please, let me through! Please, I'm Gloria Hepworth! Grant Hepworth is my husband! I *have* to see him!' she begged, grasping the arm of the officer nearest her.

He looked down at her, his own shock and horror evident in his eyes as he caught her by the shoulders. 'Ma'am, I can't let you through. I'm sorry. Jesus Christ, I'm so very sorry . . .'

Gloria looked at him in horror. 'No! No, please, please tell me he hasn't . . . hasn't . . . He . . . can't have . . .' The noise of the siren drowned out her words as the ambulance screeched to a halt.

Gloria forcibly tore herself away from the policeman and took a few steps forward before he grabbed her and dragged her back, but she had caught a glimpse of the crumpled and broken figure lying on the blood-spattered sidewalk ahead. She instantly recognised him and then she started to scream.

Chapter Thirty-One

———————

THE POLICE HAD BROUGHT her home but she could remember very little about anything after she'd been dragged away from that horrific scene. The officer had explained what had happened to a stunned and disbelieving Carmel who had helped Gloria to the bedroom, taken off her coat, hat and shoes and eased her down on to the bed. Then the weeping girl had gone to telephone the doctor and Iris Hepworth.

Iris had heard the news that was sending shock waves throughout the entire country but she hadn't known that her cousin had committed suicide. She arrived at the same time as the doctor and it was he who had informed her of the tragedy.

Iris's knees buckled and Dr Wiseman had to help her to a chair.

'Take it easy now, Miss Hepworth. I'll give you something for the shock and then, when you feel up to it, perhaps you'd better get in touch with your uncle.'

Iris nodded, although she was having trouble in assimilating his words.

'I'll go through and see his poor wife – widow,' he amended, shaking his head. It beggared belief. The crash had happened so quickly and totally without warning and he'd lost a lot of money himself, but for a young man to take his own life because of it – it was utterly unbelievable.

Carmel brought in a cup of hot, sweet tea and, like someone in a dream, Iris took the tablet the doctor had given her.

'Oh, miss! 'Tis shocking, 'tis *desperate*! I can't believe it! Will . . . will we telephone them in Florida?' Carmel wiped her eyes with her apron.

Iris looked at her bleakly. Everything was just so *unreal*. 'I . . . I can't face it. I just *can't*.'

Carmel twisted her hands together helplessly. She couldn't face it either. 'Will we ask Himself, Dr Wiseman, to do it? She needs someone – family . . . but . . . older . . .'

Iris nodded. 'I'll ask him when he comes out. Surely he must understand . . .'

The doctor understood perfectly although he didn't relish breaking the news to Barney. He'd known both Barney and Eunice for years, which made it worse, but he reluctantly agreed and went into the hall to make the call.

Both girls looked up as he re-entered the room.

'They'll be here as soon as is humanly possible. I advised

Mr Hepworth to send for a doctor before he broke the news to Eunice. I hope she can stand the shock.'

'But they *are* coming? Will Uncle Barney break the news to Dad? He'll have to come up to New York too,' Iris asked.

'He didn't say but I assume at some stage he will have to tell him that they are both ruined financially, although in the light of Grant's . . . death I don't think either Barney or Eunice will be thinking about that. Barney thought the sun shone out of that boy and he was so proud of him.'

Iris nodded miserably, wishing her Uncle Barney and Aunt Eunice and her own father and mother were here now.

Gloria awoke the following morning feeling as though her head was full of cotton wool. She felt slightly sick and very dazed and confused as she tried to think why she felt so awful. Then slowly, through the fog that seemed to be clogging her mind, she began to remember. Grant lying like a broken doll on the sidewalk, the terrible screams that had filled her ears, her own shrieks, the officer dragging her away and bundling her into a police car. Then Carmel, taking off her coat and shoes, Dr Wiseman's sad, shocked face and then . . . nothing. She sat up slowly, her whole body shaking. Grant was *dead*! He was never coming home to her again. She'd never hear his voice again. She'd been his 'darling girl' but he had left her alone.

Deep, racking sobs convulsed her and then both Iris and Carmel were beside her and Iris had her arms around her.

'What happened? What happened to him, Iris? I don't understand why he's . . . dead!' she sobbed.

'Oh, Gloria! He . . . he jumped. He . . . he killed himself. I know we've all lost everything, that we're *ruined*, but so are other people. He just couldn't face the shame and guilt of it all.' Iris didn't say they'd heard that Grant wasn't the only one who had leaped to his death, unable to face the enormity of the calamity that had overtaken them.

Her words didn't register with Gloria who only sobbed harder. 'He looked so . . . broken! My poor darling Grant!'

'Shall I call Dr Wiseman?' Carmel asked timidly.

'I think you'd better. Then maybe she'll be a little bit calmer by the time Uncle Barney arrives tomorrow.' Iris hoped so; she didn't know how to cope with Gloria's grief as well as her own.

When Gloria awoke next time the room was in darkness except for one small lamp on the dressing table. She could faintly hear voices. Shaking her head to try to clear it, she raised herself up on one elbow. Why was she always asleep? They obviously had company; she must get up. She struggled out of bed and pulled a robe over her nightdress and went unsteadily to the door.

'Gloria!'

She stared uncomprehendingly at Eunice Hepworth who came forward and took her in her arms. Eunice looked drawn and ill and so much older, she thought. And then everything came rushing back and she cried out.

'Hush now, dear. I'm here and so is Barney. You're not alone now.' Eunice turned to her husband who had also aged terribly in the past forty-eight hours. 'Barney, help me with her, please.'

Between them they got Gloria back to bed and Eunice sat holding her as she sobbed, tears falling down her own cheeks. Oh, things were bad, they had virtually nothing left of their fortune, but surely, surely they would all have coped. Nothing was bad enough for Grant to have felt there was only one way out. The waste, the terrible, terrible waste and pity of it. She would gladly live in a hovel if she could have her son back, she thought broken-heartedly.

Days and nights passed, all seemingly jumbled together, and Gloria was overwhelmed with her grief and shock, but towards the end of the week she had at least stopped sobbing and felt a little calmer. Eunice had been so good, so patient and supportive, even though Gloria was beginning to realise that these feelings were not restricted to her. Her mother-in-law had patiently tried to explain that Grant must have felt the burden of responsibility for plunging the family into disaster and ruin, to say nothing of the hundreds of other people it affected, so overwhelming that he hadn't been able to face it. It had clouded his mind and his judgement so much that he'd seen death as the only way out.

'I wouldn't have cared that we had no money! We would have managed. I'd have worked; I worked before we were married,' Gloria had cried pitifully.

'I wouldn't have cared either, Gloria,' Eunice had replied truthfully.

Somehow Gloria had got through the funeral. That day too was blurred, and at the end of it as she had sat holding tightly to Eunice's hand she realised that it was her mother she wanted most now. Her world suddenly seemed dark and empty and frighteningly insecure.

'I . . . I don't want to sound ungrateful, but . . . but I'd like to go . . . home,' she said with a catch in her voice.

'Don't you think it's a little bit soon to be thinking of travelling, dear?' Eunice asked gently.

Barney was staring into the depths of the untouched glass of brandy cupped in his hands. 'It's not the time to be making big decisions, Gloria honey.' A telegram had been sent to Sal earlier in the week.

Gloria shook her head. 'I . . . I want my mother.'

Eunice looked anxiously from Gloria to her husband. 'It might help her, Barney, to spend some time with her family away … away from this apartment and all the memories. She doesn't have to go permanently.'

He didn't reply at first and then he nodded slowly. What was left for Gloria here now? Grant was gone; the apartment would have to be sold. New York would always hold very painful memories for the poor girl, as it would for both himself and Eunice.

Gloria's tearful gaze was pleading. She didn't want to stay here now, without him; and she longed to flee the memories.

'I'll sort something out, Eunice,' he promised, sighing heavily, knowing there would be no first-class travel for Gloria this time.

Sal brought the telegram into the kitchen and sat down at the table, wondering just who it was from: Harry, Gloria or Betty. She hoped it was nothing serious. She opened it and scanned the lines and then tears of disbelief and sorrow began to trickle slowly down her cheeks. Oh, poor Gloria! Poor Grant! The newspapers were full of the financial disaster – it had badly affected the London Stock Exchange too – and they were forecasting a recession, but surely things couldn't have been so bad as to drive the poor lad to suicide? How was her poor daughter coping with it all? She'd have to write to Gloria, but what could she say? How could she hope to comfort her from three thousand miles away? She'd have to write to Harry as well, although when he'd receive the letter was anyone's guess. She'd phone Sybil too. What a homecoming it would be for Betty after her first trip. She would write to Eunice and Barney too; her heart went out to them. They'd lost their only son and now there would be no chance of grandchildren either. It was a terrible tragedy for them all.

Wiping away her tears she got up and went to the phone. Sybil would be home from work by now.

'Sybil, I'm afraid I've got some terrible news.'

'What's wrong, Sal? What's happened? Is it Harry?'

Sal told her sadly what had happened and heard the gasp on the other end of the line.

'Oh, my God! How did he die?'

'He was one of those who jumped from the office building, Sybil. We read about it in the paper. God help him, he must have been out of his mind with it all.'

'I . . . I can't believe it, Sal. He . . . he was such a nice young man. Oh, poor, poor Gloria. How is she taking it?'

'I don't know but you can be sure she will be heart-broken.

I just got a telegram from Barney Hepworth. I'm out of my mind worrying about her, Sybil.'

'I can believe it.' Sybil paused. 'One of us should go over, Sal. She can't cope with this on her own.'

'She's not on her own, Sybil. If the telegram is from Barney then both he and Eunice are with her.'

'But that's not the same thing, Sal. They're not blood relations, just family by marriage.'

'And you can be sure that the rest of Grant's family will be there. By the time one of us could get there the poor lad will have been buried and besides, Betty is due home in a couple of days and she doesn't know and I'm not going to break the news to her in a message while she's at sea.'

'Then it had better be me, Sal.'

Sal bit her lip. 'No, Sybil. If anyone should go it should be me, I'm her mother. I think it best if I write to Eunice and ask her if Gloria would like to come home,' she said firmly.

'I think that's a very sensible idea, Sal. She'll be better off at home with her real family and away from the shock and horror of it all – and the memories.'

'I'll write now and post it first thing in the morning but I can tell you Sybil, it will be the hardest letter I've ever had to write.'

'Such a tragedy, such a terrible tragedy and we all had such high hopes for them both. They were doing so well,' Sybil replied, still shaken by the news.

As Sal replaced the receiver on its cradle she thought she hadn't cared how much or how little money Grant had had.

She'd just wanted Gloria to be happy and she had been – until now. And Harry wasn't here to shoulder any of the burden. She sighed heavily. As usual when there were big decisions to be made or projects to be undertaken or problems to be solved she was on her own.

Chapter Thirty-Two

B ETTY FELT A REAL sense of achievement the night before they were due to dock in Liverpool. She'd completed her first trip and despite everything she had enjoyed it. She felt she now understood why her da said he could never settle to a shore job. Every day brought something new and she'd really enjoyed the time she'd spent ashore with Gloria in Montreal.

Kate and the other girls had all been to New York and the islands of the West Indies before and were looking forward to going back again. Each seemed to have their own favourite island. Kate had said Martinique was lovely, very French-colonial and picturesque. Anne Haywood had plumped for Antigua, saying she loved the white sands and turquoise water and that English Harbour was great for a day out, while Sue Frobisher had said it was Haiti for her; it was very different to the other islands, mysterious and exotic. While anchored off Port-au-Prince you apparently could hear the sound of the voodoo drums in the hills beyond the Cul-de-Sac plain. Betty had said she couldn't wait to visit them all.

The weather on the way back had been mixed, with a few very rough days, but this time she hadn't been sick at all. As she'd cautiously made her way along the companionway, hanging on to the rail on one side with one hand and clutching a pile of fresh linen tightly to her with the other, she'd grimaced at Kate who had been coming in the opposite direction. 'Here we go again,' she'd laughed and Kate had cast her eyes skywards in resignation.

'They'll be ordering more crockery and glasses when we dock. Roll on the New Year and the gorgeous flat blue waters of the Caribbean,' Kate had replied.

Finally she reached her cabin. Kate was already there and was folding her uniform dresses, her case on top of her bunk. 'I'd pack as much as you can tonight, Betty. That way you won't waste any time in the morning. We'll be ready as soon as we get rid of the passengers and Miss Lawson lets us go. Is anyone meeting you?'

Betty nodded. 'Mam will be; Rose will be at work.'

'There's usually a gang of my relations, all waiting to see what I've brought them.' She grinned. 'My da would go mad if I didn't bring him my "docking bottle".'

'I've got the things I bought for Mam and Rose,' Betty added, taking her own uniform dresses from the wardrobe. 'There was no point in getting anything for Gloria, she's got so much already and on my wages I couldn't afford anything expensive. I didn't bother getting Aunt Sybil anything either, she would only look down her nose at whatever I'd bought for her. Da always brings really expensive things but then he earns far more than I do and he's away longer.'

Kate nodded knowingly. 'And don't forget his perks, I bet he gets a lot of them. Chief Stewards always do. See whose damned bell that is, will you, Betty?' she added.

Betty stuck her head out of the door. 'We've been summoned. It's Miss Lawson.'

Kate grinned. 'The Discharge Books must have come back from the old man.'

They both went to the Chief Stewardess's cabin together and were handed their documents.

'Another good report, Miss Duncan. And also for you, Miss Jenkins. I have been pleased with your work and your conduct on this first trip.' She smiled. 'I think we'll make a good stewardess out of you. You may go back to your sections now and I look forward to seeing you again next trip. I'm sure you will both be pleased to know that we have only two more trips to Canada. The ship is going into dry dock to prepare her for cruising next year, so we'll all be home for Christmas.'

'That is good news, Miss Lawson,' Kate replied. Usually they didn't get back to Liverpool until after the holiday. 'What she didn't say was that we don't get paid while the ship is laid up,' she informed Betty when they were outside.

The following morning there was the usual chaos as the ship tied up at the Landing Stage where the passengers disembarked. There were always last-minute panics, Kate said. Luggage missing, kids disappearing, personal belongings being lost and this after the entire crew had worked late into the night cleaning for it was a strictly held tradition that you never took a dirty ship into port. Even after the passengers were all ashore the cleaning went on as the crew stayed aboard until the ship was berthed in the Gladstone Dock.

It seemed like a mass exodus, Betty thought as she joined everyone else going down the gangway. She got separated from Kate and when she reached the dockside she found herself walking towards the dock gate beside Dr Davies. Since that evening in Montreal she'd seen him a couple of times when she'd gone up on deck for some fresh air and they'd chatted. It hadn't seemed like a 'crew and officer thing' at all, he been interested in her background and her plans to stay at sea.

He smiled at her. 'We meet again, Miss Jenkins. So, your first trip went well and you'll be back again?'

'I'll definitely be back, and I did enjoy it. Have you been with the ship long?' She'd meant to ask him that last time she'd spoken to him but they'd seemed to have spent the time talking about her.

'Nearly a year and I enjoy the life too.'

'I was terribly sick on the way out. I wished I'd never set eyes on the *Empress*.'

He grinned. 'I was myself on my first trip. It's an occupational hazard.'

'Mam will probably be waiting with that lot,' she replied, nodding in the direction of the small crowd waiting at the dock gate. 'Have you far to go? You're Welsh, aren't you?'

He nodded. 'I am. I have an aunt and uncle here in Liverpool so I usually stay with them the first night ashore. My parents live in Denbigh so I'll travel on tomorrow and of course I'll spend Christmas with them while the ship is laid up.'

'I'm really looking forward to cruising,' Betty said as they reached the gate.

'Me too. Well, no doubt I'll see you next trip.' He smiled at her again, his dark eyes twinkling. He liked her, she was easy to talk to and totally unassuming and natural.

'Bye, Dr Davies,' she replied as he skirted the crowd and walked towards the couple of taxi cabs that were waiting. She peered intently into the crowd, searching for Sal.

'Betty! Betty, over here!' Sal cried, waving and thinking that this was a far cry from the way she met Harry, but then this was a much bigger ship with a crew that were counted in hundreds and not dozens.

Betty grinned and pushed her way towards her.

Sal hugged her. 'Welcome home, luv! How was it?'

'Da was right. It's hard work and very long hours and there were times when I could have cheerfully murdered some of my passengers – and I was sick. Oh, was I sick! But I got over it.'

Sal nodded as they made their way to the tram stop. She didn't intend to tell Betty about Grant Hepworth until they got home. It wasn't the kind of thing that could be announced on a tram. Instead she asked Betty who was the young man she'd walked to the dock gate with and Betty relayed the story of Fiona McDonald and the baby, going on to tell Sal all about her friendship with Kate Duncan and the minutiae of her first trip to sea. Of course she recounted her meeting with Gloria in Montreal; so engrossed was she that she didn't realise that her mother had said very little about Gloria.

When they reached home and Betty had unpacked and shown Sal the things she had bought for Rose and had given Sal the silver brooch shaped as a maple leaf she'd bought for her, Sal thanked her and made a pot of tea.

'I think Gloria might be coming home, Betty,' she announced, slowly stirring her tea.

'For a visit? She never said anything to me about a visit when I saw her. She said we'd see each other when I go to New York.'

Sal shook her head. 'Not for a visit, Betty. For good.'

Instantly Betty realised that there was something very wrong. 'Why, Mam? She was fine when I saw her.'

Sal told her the terrible news and that she'd written asking if Gloria wanted to come home.

Betty shook her head in disbelief. She'd heard some people talking of the Wall Street crash but hadn't taken much notice; she'd been too busy and too preoccupied. 'Poor, poor Gloria. Oh, Mam, it must be awful for her.'

'It must be awful for them all. He was so young, now they're devastated not only by his loss but by the fact that everything they had has gone.'

Betty nodded slowly. How must it feel to lose everything overnight? She just couldn't imagine it and the Hepworths had been very wealthy. 'Do you think she'll come, Mam?'

'I hope so. What is there for her there now? She'll be

better off here with us, at least until she's in a fit state to think about her future.'

'When do you expect to hear?'

Sal shrugged. 'I don't know. She'll have had my letter by now. I expect someone will send me a telegram or she'll write, if she feels up to it.'

Betty wondered if Gloria would arrive before she sailed again. She hoped so. She would try her best to comfort her and she knew Rose would too.

'Rose has sent a lovely card and she says that if or when Gloria comes home she won't go mentioning anything about weddings and the like.'

'Rose is very thoughtful and she knows what it's like to lose someone very close,' Betty replied, thinking that this news was something she hadn't expected to come home to at all.

Rose had hugged her and asked her how she'd liked her trip but Betty hadn't gone into any great detail; she felt that it was all too trivial beside the great tragedy that had befallen her sister.

'I still can't take it all in . . . about Grant.'

Rose nodded sadly. 'I don't think any of us can and I know your mam feels so helpless being so far away. I do hope we'll hear soon if Gloria is coming home.'

'So do I,' Betty had readily agreed.

Later that evening she went next door to see Elsie and George.

Elsie turned the wireless off. 'So, you got home safe and sound, Betty. We got your postcard.'

'I did. I brought you this. Just a little souvenir, nothing expensive.'

'That was good of you, Betty. How was it? Will you be going back?'

Betty nodded. 'It's a far from glamorous life, hard work and long hours, but I enjoyed it. I've made a few friends amongst the girls I work with.'

'I suppose you know about your Gloria's husband?' Elsie ventured.

Betty nodded. 'Mam told me when we got home.'

'It's a terrible business, an awful tragedy,' George said.

Elsie agreed. 'And my heart goes out to his poor mother. It must be shocking to lose a child and in such circumstances.'

Betty wondered if her mam had told Elsie that she'd written asking Gloria to come home. 'Well, I'd better get back now. I just popped in to give you your gift. I'll be glad of an early night and a lie-in tomorrow. I'm exhausted.'

As she returned home she wondered what Artie thought about Gloria's tragic loss. He'd seemed to have got over that ill-fated romance but he must feel sorry for her just the same, he wasn't the type to harbour grudges.

Chapter Thirty-Three

———

To HER IMMENSE RELIEF Sal received a letter from Eunice Hepworth informing her that both she and Barney thought it would be the best thing for Gloria, at this present time, to go home. They were both very shocked and absolutely heart-broken – she doubted that she would ever get over Grant's death – and they had decided that they would go back to Florida, sell the house and find something much smaller and live modestly. Barney hadn't the heart to try to salvage anything of the business, although his brother was talking about maybe even trying to build it up again. They just wanted to leave New York and go south and try to live with their loss.

Gloria was a little calmer, although 'dazed' would be a more apt description, Eunice thought. Barney had booked her passage on one of the smaller Cunard ships, the *Scythia*, and she would be travelling second class, which meant she would have to share with someone else but at least she wouldn't be totally alone.

'When will she be arriving, Mam?' Betty asked, feeling as relieved as her mother when Sal had read the letter aloud.

'In ten days. Eunice says she will need time to help Gloria sort out her things. They are going to try to sell some of her jewellery so she will at least have a bit of money to bring home with her.'

Betty looked crestfallen. 'I won't be here, Mam. I'll have sailed. And I really did want to see her.'

'I know, luv, but it can't be helped. She . . . well, she might be feeling a bit better when you get home next.'

Betty nodded. Christmas wasn't going to be a very happy affair this year. Not for Gloria or her in-laws, and nor for themselves either. She'd have a look for something special in the shops in Montreal next trip, something to try to express her concern for her sister, although she knew it really wouldn't help Gloria in these terrible circumstances. Yet she felt she had to try to do *something* to express her own sorrow.

Betty had said there was no need for her mother to accompany her to Gladstone Dock this time. Gloria was due to arrive the following day and she knew Sal had more than enough to do. 'I know my way around now, Mam. I'll be fine,' she'd said emphatically.

She met up with Kate and Anne on the dockside that damp and misty November morning.

'I saw you when we disembarked, chatting away to our handsome young Dr Davies, Betty.' Anne laughed, but on seeing Betty's expression she stopped, frowning. 'Sorry. Is something wrong?'

Betty told them and both girls looked horrified and expressed their sympathy.

'So she's coming home. I'd hoped to see her before I sailed but she's coming in on the *Scythia* tomorrow afternoon.'

Kate looked around and shivered. 'If this gets any worse they could be late in and we could still be stuck here tomorrow. Fog is about the only thing that keeps us from sailing. Still, at least there's only one more trip after this so you'll be able to spend time with her then, Betty.'

Betty nodded. 'I know but after Christmas we'll be off cruising and I won't see her for three months.'

'When we get home at the end of March she should be feeling a lot better, Betty,' Anne added.

Betty sighed. 'I was so looking forward to cruising but this has sort of put a damper on it all.'

'When is your dad due home?' Kate asked, thinking it was going to be hard on Betty's mother.

'Not until next June. Mam's written to him but I know she wishes he were coming home sooner. She's going to have to cope with our poor Gloria on her own.'

'What about your aunt?' Kate asked tentatively. Betty had informed her of her own opinion of her aunt and of Sybil's influence over Gloria.

Betty looked grim. 'The last thing Mam needs is Aunt Sybil visiting by the minutes and fussing and going on about how wonderful Grant was and how sad and unfortunate everything is. I still think that if she'd left our Gloria alone she might have ended up marrying Artie Taylor and so wouldn't have been in the state she's in now. To my mind *that* one should mind her own business and I hope Mam tells her so!'

Gloria stood on the promenade deck of the *Scythia* clutching her coat tightly to her as the ship made its way slowly down the Mersey. She was pale and thin and the black coat and hat made her look wraith-like. Her face was pinched and there were dark circles under her eyes for the weather had been bad and she'd been very sick, and even when that had passed she hadn't slept well at all. She'd kept remembering her first trip with Sybil and the luxury they'd travelled in. The trip she'd met and fallen in love with Grant. Every time she thought of him it was like a knife being twisted in her heart. She was physically and mentally exhausted asking herself the same questions over and over again. Why had he done it? Why? Hadn't he thought about her and what his death would do to her? Hadn't he loved her enough to spare her that? Why had wealth and position been so much more important than trying to live without them? His parents seemed to be managing. He hadn't been alone. Many other people faced the same situation but they hadn't all killed themselves. She was dazed, grief-stricken, frightened, dis-orientated and tired, so very, very tired. Ahead of her the buildings of the waterfront were coming into view through the damp mist that drifted like shifting, wispy clouds over the grey turgid water. She'd never thought she would be sailing down this river towards home in such tragic circumstances. Not after she'd left in such a blaze of glory as the new Mrs Grant Hepworth. She shivered and turned away. She had better go back down to the cabin and collect her belongings.

Sal too drew her coat closer to her and shivered as she waited on the Landing Stage with the small crowd of relatives and friends that had gathered. She didn't expect Gloria to have a great deal of luggage this time, but she'd secured the services of a porter just the same and they'd get a taxi home. She had no idea what kind of a state her daughter would be in but she was certain Gloria wouldn't be in any condition to travel on public transport. Sybil had said she was sure Richard wouldn't mind taking a couple of hours off to drive them but Sal had politely and resolutely refused for she knew her sister-in-law would accompany him. And the last person she needed beside her here today was Sybil.

At first she barely recognised Gloria as the radiantly happy girl, dressed to the nines, she'd waved off two years ago. She was shocked by Gloria's appearance. It wasn't the plain black mourning clothes, it was the thinness and the haunted, frightened look in her eyes as she came down the gangway, like that of a terrified deer. She rushed forward and folded the girl in her arms, tears pricking her eyes.

'It's going to be all right now, Gloria. You're home, luv. Mam's here. It's all right.'

Gloria clung to her desperately, sobs shaking her. 'Oh, Mam! Mam! I need you so much!'

'Of course you do. Now, let's get your luggage sorted out and there's a taxi waiting. We'll soon be home.'

Gloria's sobs had ceased on the journey to Aintree but she'd remained silent and Sal hadn't tried to make conversation. She'd just sat holding her daughter's hand tightly. The driver helped them in with the luggage and after stirring up the fire and putting more coal on, Sal put the kettle on.

'We'll have a nice cup of tea and then I think you can try and get some rest. You look worn out, luv.'

Gloria nodded slowly. 'I am. Sometimes I don't know what day it is. Time seems to have stood still. Everything has been so *confusing*. I was terribly sick on the way across, Mam, and I couldn't have cared less whether I lived or died. The woman I had to share with was sick too. It was awful. Even when it passed I just couldn't face a meal in that dining room, sitting and having to make polite conversation with all those strangers.'

Sal shook her head sadly. 'You poor luv. No wonder you're so thin.'

Gloria sipped her tea slowly. Nothing seemed to have changed here, she thought, and that brought her some comfort. Here there was a sense of security and stability, something she hadn't felt for weeks now. 'I haven't been able to sleep properly either, since . . . since it happened. Apart from when I was heavily sedated. I keep asking myself the same questions. "Why did he do it?" "Didn't he think of me?" "Didn't he love me enough to want to go on living?" And there's no answer to them, Mam. At least I can't find any answers that comfort me.'

'I'm sure he did think of you, Gloria. And he *did* love you but his poor mind must have been so disturbed by everything that had happened that . . .' Sal struggled to find the right words. '. . . that he just wasn't thinking straight at all. That it seemed the only way out for him.' She honestly thought the lad must have been at his wits' end. He'd lost his mind completely and hadn't known what he was doing.

'That's what both Iris and Eunice said, but I don't know . . . The few days before he . . . died, I felt there was something bothering him but he swore he was fine. But he wasn't, I *knew* he wasn't, and I keep wondering if he suspected it was going to happen and the fear and guilt just kept building in his mind. Oh, if only he could have confided in me, Mam!'

'You'll have to make an effort to accept it all as a fact, Gloria. The shock and the grief will get better as time goes on, I know it will. Now, let's get you upstairs to bed. You need to rest and recover your strength. I've never seen you look so terrible.'

As she lay in the comfortable bed in her parents' room Gloria felt the waves of tiredness wash over her. She was home and she felt safe. There was no rolling and pitching deck beneath her, no loud and frightening crashes as the waves hit the side of the ship, like a hammer beating against a tin tray. She was home with Mam and somehow Mam would help her get over the terrible sense of loss, the ever-present grief and the shock of her world falling apart. She could let go and sleep deeply at last.

Elsie had seen the taxi arrive and had watched the driver

help Sal in with the luggage. She'd caught a glimpse of Gloria, pale and thin in her widow's weeds. She'd wondered if Sal had told the girl to come home or had Gloria begged to come? She sighed as she turned away from the window. She'd wait a while and then she'd go in.

Sal had been expecting her. 'I knew you'd see the taxi, Elsie.'

Elsie nodded as she sat down opposite Sal. 'How . . . how is she?'

'Utterly exhausted. I've sent her to bed. The shock, the grief, the voyage: all have taken a terrible toll on her, Elsie. She's so thin. Thank God I wrote and asked her to come home. At least I can keep my eye on her and look after her. I dread to think what would have happened to her over there.'

'It must have been hard for her, Sal. They would all have been in a similar state. I . . . I have to agree with you. I would have done the same thing in your place.'

'It will be a long time before she gets over this, Elsie, and it will have changed her. I can see the change in her now. She's not the same person who left here two years ago. She was a slip of a thing of eighteen then, Elsie, with a husband who idolised her; she was dazzled by the life that lay ahead. Now she's two years older, wiser and infinitely sadder.'

Elsie told Artie the news later that evening after George had gone down to the Blue Anchor for a pint. Brian was out.

'Gloria's home. She arrived this afternoon on the *Scythia*.'

Artie nodded. When he'd heard the terrible news about Grant Hepworth he had wondered what she would do. He felt sorry for her, it must have been an awful shock. 'Have you seen her? How did she look?'

'I just got a glimpse as she came up the path. She looked pale and thin. I did go in to Sal's but she'd sent Gloria to bed. She's exhausted; apparently the weather was bad on the crossing on top of everything else . . .'

'Has she come home for good or just until she feels . . . better?'

'She's home for good,' Elsie replied.

Artie nodded. It was two years ago now since Gloria had gone off and he'd got over the hurt and disappointment. They'd just been a couple of kids then but he still felt very sorry for her. He could understand that for Grant Hepworth losing a fortune must have been catastrophic but it wasn't the end of the world. Hundreds of thousands of people lived in far more straitened circumstances than the Hepworths now found themselves in but they didn't go committing suicide. He'd occasionally wondered how Gloria was finding her new life; he heard the odd snippet, mainly from Betty. Was there more to Grant Hepworth's suicide than the loss of a fortune? he mused. Maybe Gloria hadn't lived up to his expectations? She might not have really fitted into his circle; she had been very young when he'd married her. 'Do you think I should go and offer my condolences? I mean it's only manners.'

Elsie looked thoughtful. 'I'd leave it for a while, Artie. Give her some time to get . . . settled. I don't think the poor girl knows what day of the week it is. Leave it until Betty's home next.'

Artie nodded. That would give him time to try to think what to say to her. But what on earth could anyone say in the circumstances?

Chapter Thirty-Four

⬦━━⬦━━⬦

THEY DIDN'T SEEM TO be as busy on this return trip, Betty thought, but then she supposed that if you had the choice you really would avoid sailing at this time of year. If you had any sense you'd travel during the summer months and anyway they were never as busy going back to Liverpool.

'I passed through the second-class dining room on my way down and they are damping the tablecloths and taking all the glasses off the tables, so you know what that means?' Kate informed Betty who was setting a tray in the pantry.

'We're heading into bad weather. I didn't think it would be long before it changed.' So far they had been blessed with cold, bright, sunny days and clear, freezing nights and therefore no wind to speak of, but she'd known it wouldn't last. They had three more days ahead of them before they reached the comparative shelter of the Irish Sea and Liverpool Bay.

'We'd better draw extra linen; most of them are bound to be sick sometime during the next few hours. We'll not get much sleep tonight. I often pray that one day someone will invent a pill or something that will stop seasickness.'

Betty nodded her agreement. 'It would certainly make our lives a lot easier. Still, only another month before we're off to the sun. I'd better go and take this tea tray along or that flaming passenger will be ringing the bell again.'

'Don't forget to tell her to put it on the floor when she's finished or it will end up in bits. In fact tell all of them in there to put anything breakable on the floor,' Kate called after her.

As Kate had predicted they were called on many times during the next few hours as the weather worsened. One of Betty's passengers was a seasoned traveller and had recommended that all the ladies in her cabin take a glass of port and brandy mixed. It was a well known remedy for seasickness. She asked Betty to bring the drinks.

'I've heard that before, but I don't know if it's true or not. You'll have to go up to one of the bars for it. You know we don't keep wines and spirits in the pantry down here. We might get so desperately fed up we'd drink it ourselves,' Kate said laconically.

'Oh, damn! I hate the stairways in bad weather,' Betty complained.

'I know. Just hang on for dear life. Tell the bar steward to mix it and give you it in one bottle; it's easier to carry in one hand. And don't bring any glasses. They can use the cups from the pantry, they're not as fragile or dangerous. If they complain, tell them it's not them who has to carry glasses and risk getting a nasty cut and anyway, they should be going up to the bar for it themselves.'

Betty steadily made her way to the nearest bar which was situated on B Deck, three flights up. The higher up in the ship she got the worse the rolling and pitching became and she was constantly thrown from side to side against the metal bulkheads. 'God! I'll be black and blue at this rate,' she exclaimed as she finally reached the bar, which was virtually deserted.

'What's brought you up here, Betty?' Tommy Mac, the bar steward, asked her, grinning.

Glancing at an elderly gentleman at the other end of the bar Betty dropped her voice. 'Flaming passengers! They want port and brandy, so I have to get battered and bruised coming up here to get it. Mix it for me and put it in one bottle will you, Tommy, please?'

He nodded and started to measure out the brandy. 'How many glasses, Betty?'

'None. They can use the cups from the pantry.'

He grinned again. 'You'll get a rollicking from the Dragon if they complain.'

'I won't and she's not a Dragon. She won't be very happy if she finds out I've had to come up here. If they want alcoholic drinks they're supposed to come and get them themselves. Tea, coffee and soft drinks are all we serve. And hot drinks are bad enough to cope with in weather like this.'

He handed over the small bottle. 'Take care with it going back down, you don't want to have to make the journey again,' he advised as she wrote the cabin number and signed the docket for the drinks.

She had made it as far as E Deck stairway without slipping but as she started to descend the ship lurched violently to port and she lost her footing, falling from top to bottom, the bottle falling from her grasp and smashing. As she landed in a heap at the bottom a terrible pain shot through her left arm and she screamed in agony, trying to drag herself into a sitting position.

A steward came stumbling towards her, his feet slipping on the pitching deck. 'Jesus! That was some fall! Are you hurt, luv?'

'My arm!' Betty gasped. 'I . . . I think it's broken.'

'Don't move. Don't try to get up. Stay there. I'll go for a doctor. Who's your section head?'

'Kate Duncan. Oh, I've never been in pain like this before,' Betty gasped.

He disappeared and she tried to edge back and rest her back against the bulkhead. Now she felt dizzy and seemed to be aching all over. She prayed he would hurry up; she didn't like being here alone and in such pain.

Kate arrived first. 'Oh, my God! Billy Watkins said you'd been thrown headfirst down the bloody stairway. He's gone for a doctor and I told him to get Miss Lawson too.'

'I was. It's . . . it's my arm, Kate. I think it's broken. I'm in agony.' Betty's face was pale and drawn with shock.

Kate was visibly shaken. 'That bloody woman and her

port and brandy! You could have been killed! This is the worst storm I've ever experienced. I should have stopped you; they're supposed to go to the bar themselves. Let them risk their own damned necks.'

Waves of pain and dizziness were sweeping over Betty as Kate crouched down beside her, her eyes full of concern, and she was very thankful when at last the Chief Stewardess and Dr Davies arrived.

'She thinks her arm is broken, doctor, and she's got a few cuts and is probably bruised all over too,' Kate informed him as he bent over Betty, frowning.

'Can you move it at all, Miss Jenkins?' Hewel Davies asked kindly.

Betty tried but the slight movement caused her to cry out.

'All right, stop,' he instructed. He looked up at the two women. 'We'll have to get her down to the hospital. It's broken but I don't know how badly and she's very shaken up.'

As gently as they could they helped Betty to her feet and with Kate's and Miss Lawson's arms around her for support and preceded by Hewel Davies, very slowly they got her down to the hospital.

'Oh, I feel terrible,' Betty groaned as she was eased on to a bed.

'You are bound to, Miss Jenkins. That was a dreadful fall. Headfirst down the stairway so the steward told me,' Miss Lawson said. Thankfully the hospital was in the bowels of the ship and the movement wasn't nearly as bad as on higher decks. She turned to Kate. 'Miss Duncan, would you go back to your section now, please?' Her expression became grim. 'And would you kindly inform the ladies in cabin D204 that I will be along very shortly to see them.'

Kate nodded. 'Please don't blame her, ma'am. She was only trying to be helpful and I should have stopped her,' she said before she left.

'What was she doing?' Hewel Davies asked as Dr Mathews, his superior, arrived back from attending to a passenger who had been thrown from a top bunk but who had fortunately sustained no serious injuries.

'Fetching port and brandy from the bar for passengers who are well aware that they are supposed to go up and get it themselves,' Miss Lawson informed him. Well, she'd certainly have something to say about this. Betty Jenkins was only eighteen and could have been killed. She wasn't having her girls put at risk like this because of the sheer selfishness of some people. People who didn't want to risk their own safety but were willing to risk a young and still inexperienced girl's.

Dr Mathews examined her thoroughly and declared that she was bruised and shaken and that thankfully the fracture was a clean break.

'I'll give you an injection and then we'll set it and Dr Davies will put a cast on it. We'll keep you down here tonight, Miss Jenkins, and see how you are in the morning, but I'm afraid you are not going to be able to work for the rest of this trip.'

Betty bit her lip, dimly realising that she wouldn't be fit for work next trip either.

Despite the injection it had still hurt but she'd clamped her lips together to stop herself crying out. Dr Davies had given her some painkillers and a mild sedative and as the nurse mixed the plaster of Paris for the cast she began to feel better. A little sleepy but better.

'Thank you so much, doctor. I'm sorry to be such a nuisance; you must be busy, with the weather so bad.'

'You're not a nuisance at all, Miss Jenkins. I think you've been very brave,' Hewel Davies reassured her. 'And so were your actions in attempting to keep your passengers happy in the worst storm we've been through all year. You've had quite an ordeal. What is your Christian name? I can't keep calling you "Miss Jenkins".' He'd begun to admire as well as like her. She certainly had spirit.

'Elizabeth – Betty,' she replied, trying to keep her eyes open.

'Well, you were very fortunate, Betty, that you only have a broken arm and cuts and bruises. It could have been far, far worse. Those stairways are steep. Why didn't you take the lift?'

'I'd be terrified of getting stuck. And it . . . it happened so quickly. One minute I was at the top of the stairway, then . . . then I was falling. How long will the plaster have to stay on?'

'Six weeks. I'm afraid you won't be much use to Miss Lawson for the remainder of this trip.' He tried to sound cheerful. 'Still, we'll be in Liverpool in a couple of days.'

'Then I definitely won't be sailing next trip,' Betty murmured.

'I'm afraid not, Betty, but let's look on the bright side, you should be fit and well for the cruises.'

'I . . . I'm so . . . glad,' Betty murmured as the pain finally eased and she drifted off to sleep. He'd been very kind.

Sal was relieved that Gloria was slowly feeling less confused.

'It's as if I've been living in a dream these past weeks, Mam- or rather a nightmare,' she confided to Sal the day before Betty was due home.

'It has all been a nightmare for you, luv. Each day things will get a little bit easier; I've seen an improvement in you already. You are sleeping better now and starting to eat.' Sal paused. 'Your Aunt Sybil was on the phone earlier, asking when can she come and see you.'

Gloria's expression clouded. 'I . . . I don't know, Mam. I don't want her fussing over me and asking me about things.'

Sal reached across the table and took her hand. 'You don't have to see her now if you don't want to, we can put her off. But we can't put it off for ever.'

Gloria nodded. 'I know. Perhaps . . . it would be best if I do see her.'

Sal nodded. 'I'll phone her, tell her she can come for a short visit.' She thought to herself that she would make it quite clear to Sybil that she would not tolerate any kind of pep talk or discussions about Gloria's future and no questions at all about Grant's state of mind before the tragedy.

It was a brief and rather one-sided call but Sybil agreed to call that afternoon 'just for an hour' and then maybe she'd make a longer visit next week. As Sal was about to impart this news to Gloria she heard the door knocker. It was the boy from the post office with a telegram and as she took it from him she wondered if it was from the Hepworths.

Gloria looked anxiously at the telegram as Sal returned to the living room.

Sal opened it. 'Oh, Lord!' she exclaimed.

'What is it now?' Gloria's voice was a whisper.

'It's Betty. It's from the C.P. office. They must have had a wire from the ship. Betty's had an accident. She's broken her arm. Could someone meet her?'

'How did she do that?'

'It doesn't say. I'll have to go and meet her, Gloria. She won't be able to manage her luggage on her own and she won't be going back next trip.'

'Do you . . . do you want me to come too?' Gloria asked, although she felt she couldn't face the crowd of happy relations of the *Empress*'s crew who would be waiting at the dock gate. She never wanted to see another ship again – especially not a transatlantic liner.

'No, luv. There's always a big crowd down there, I'll go by myself.'

Gloria nodded thankfully.

Sybil arrived just after lunch, as usual smartly but sombrely dressed.

'Don't go upsetting her, Sybil, she's still very fragile,' Sal whispered as she let her sister-in-law in.

Sybil nodded curtly. When she caught sight of her niece sitting in an armchair beside the fire looking so pale, thin and lost, all her carefully chosen words of sympathy went out of her mind. She crossed to Gloria and hugged her tightly. 'Gloria, dear! You're home! How are you feeling now?' Her voice was full of sincerity.

Gloria managed a smile. 'A bit better. It was good of you to come, Aunt Sybil.'

Sybil smiled ruefully. 'I've been as worried about you as your mother has. I wanted to come to see you as soon as you arrived but realised it wouldn't be a good idea. Better to let you recover from the journey.'

Sal relaxed a little. Obviously Sybil had taken her instructions to heart and she was genuinely concerned about Gloria.

True to her word Sybil only stayed the bare hour but as she was leaving Sal invited her to come with Richard on Sunday afternoon. She also informed her of Betty's accident at which news Sybil had shaken her head, tutted sympathetically but made no comment at all.

Chapter Thirty-Five

S AL ARRIVED AT THE dock early and explained to the policeman on the gate, showing him the telegram.

'Go on through then, missus. They'll probably either let you on board or have someone to help her off with her things.'

Sal thanked him and hurried towards the ship, which towered above her. The enormous white hull was now streaked with rust from the storms, parts of her rails had been torn away and two of her lifeboats were badly damaged. They'd certainly taken a battering, Sal mused. There was an officer standing at the bottom of the gangway, from the master-at-arms's office she presumed. They were responsible for security on board.

She handed him the telegram. 'I've come to meet my daughter, Miss Betty Jenkins. She's had an accident.'

He nodded. 'There were quite a few casualties but she was

very lucky she only broke her arm, Mrs Jenkins. I heard it was a bad fall, that she went from top to bottom of a stairway. Mind you, it was blowing a storm force ten at the time.'

His words shook Sal. By the sound of it Betty had had a lucky escape.

'Go on up. Someone will take you down to her cabin.'

She didn't have to go any further than the top of the gangway for she spotted Betty coming towards her, her right arm in plaster, a graze above one eye and yellowish purple bruising starting to appear on her cheek. Beside her was the young man she'd seen her daughter talking to last time she'd disembarked.

'Betty! Are you all right? I had word from the office and I got here early and they let me on board.'

Betty managed a grin. 'Apart from my arm and some bruises, I'm just great, Mam. This is Dr Davies. He's been very kind. He and Dr Mathews patched me up.'

Hewel Davies shook Sal's hand. 'Nice to meet you, Mrs Jenkins. She's been an exceptional patient. No complaints at all. But she was lucky. It was a nasty fall that could have been avoided.'

Betty grimaced. 'I've already been told that by Miss Lawson, in no uncertain terms.'

He grinned at her. 'I know but I bet it was nothing compared to what she said to the ladies in cabin D204. Now, remember what I said. Take things easy and if you have any worries about your arm see your GP. And he'll be able to arrange for the cast to be taken off in six weeks.'

'I think I'll have him out to see her, doctor, if you don't

mind.' It wouldn't do any harm for him to see both her girls, Sal thought.

'Not at all. It will put your mind at rest.' He turned to Betty. 'Look on your time off as a bit of a holiday, Betty.'

She smiled wryly. 'A holiday without pay but I'll try to. And thank you again.'

He escorted them both down the gangway, carrying Betty's case, which he then handed over to Sal. He waved as they walked off towards the dock gate. He'd go and see her before the next trip, he decided. Miss Lawson would have her address and he wanted to make sure she was all right. And he liked her. He liked her a great deal.

'He's a very nice young man,' Sal remarked.

'I know. How's Gloria, Mam?'

'She's better than she was when she first got home. She was in a terrible state then. Rose tries to cheer her up.'

'And I'll be able to help her,' Betty added, hoping this accident of hers hadn't alarmed or upset her sister. 'But I'm not going to be much use to you around the house with this arm.'

'We'll manage, Betty. We always do.'

Betty was relieved that her sister wasn't prostrate with grief as she'd expected her to be. She hugged her but was concerned at how thin Gloria was. She'd always been slim but now you could feel her ribs. 'It's great to see you, Gloria, and to have you home, but I think we'll have to fatten you up, won't we, Mam?' She smiled.

'Betty, are you all right? Your face is a mess.' Gloria was taken aback by Betty's appearance.

'It looks worse than it is. I was thrown down a stairway; the weather was really awful on the way back.'

'You only had to see the state of the ship to realise that,' Sal added.

'But it has its good side. I'll be home for a while now.'

Over the next few days Gloria seemed to improve a little more and Sal thought that Betty's company and that of Rose was having a very beneficial effect on her. She was brighter in herself, although Sal still heard her crying sometimes at night. She was taking more of an interest in things and her appetite had improved with the result that she was looking much better.

She had persuaded both girls to go out for a walk. It was cold but bright and sunny. 'It will do you both good. You don't have to go far, walk up to the canal and along the bank and then back. That should put some colour in both your cheeks and you won't see many people.'

Betty laughed. 'Don't you think I've got enough "colour" in my cheeks already, Mam?'

'The bruising is starting to fade now.'

Betty grinned. 'What you really mean is you are fed up with having us under your feet. Come on, Gloria, let's give her half an hour's peace. Go and get your coat.'

Elsie came in when they'd gone. 'I saw them go out, Sal, and I have to say Gloria's looking a lot better. How is Betty's arm?'

'Mending slowly. They are both a worry to me, Elsie.'

Elsie nodded. 'I came to tell you, Sal, that our Artie was

asking if it would be all right for him to come in to see Gloria tonight, after supper? To offer his condolences. I said I'd come and ask you.'

Sal nodded. 'That's thoughtful of him, Elsie. Tell him to come about half past seven.'

Sal mentioned it to Betty when the girls got back.

'Why are you telling me and not Gloria, Mam?'

'I really don't know. I suppose I was wondering how it will affect her.'

'Mam, that little romance was over years ago. It was over the day she met Grant and Artie's over it too. They've grown up.' Betty frowned. 'You know I sometimes think that if Aunt Sybil and Da had left Gloria alone she might have been quite happy with Artie. It was Aunt Sybil and her fancy ideas about "marrying well" that turned our Gloria's head. Oh, I'm not saying she didn't fall in love with Grant. He was very charming and handsome but, well, she was young and very impressionable.'

'She was and that trip with Sybil, meeting Grant with all he could offer her, must have been exciting, especially as she wasn't used to it all.'

'And he just swept her off her feet. It must have seemed like a fairy tale to her,' Betty added.

'And now it's all over and at some time she's going to have to think about her future. Well, this time she'll decide things for herself without any influence from those two,' Sal said firmly.

'Good for you, Mam,' Betty agreed.

Sal smiled at her. It seemed as though Betty too had grown up a lot lately.

Betty was helping Sal in the kitchen when Artie arrived, looking a little apprehensive.

'Mam said it would be all right if I came in to offer my condolences.'

'Go on in, lad. She's in the living room,' Sal urged.

Gloria was sitting staring into the fire and she didn't turn when he went in. He stood for a few seconds studying her. He hadn't seen her, not to speak to, for over two years. She was thinner and the black wool dress emphasised how pale she was but there was something else. She looked . . . lost, and as if all the brightness and vivacity that he remembered about her had gone. Was it any wonder, he thought, the terrible shock and grief she'd suffered. Her world had been turned upside down, to say nothing of her miserable voyage home. She looked older, wiser and very much sadder.

'Hello, Gloria,' he said quietly, not wishing to startle her.

She turned and for an instant she didn't recognise him, then she smiled slowly. 'Artie.'

'I just came to say how sorry I am about . . . what's happened to you.' He'd thought very carefully about what he would say; he didn't want to upset her further.

She nodded. 'It's kind of you to come in. Sit down.'

He sat awkwardly on the edge of the sofa. 'Are you feeling any better now? Mam told me it was a bad crossing.'

'A little. Some of the sense of . . . unreality is fading and it *was* a bad crossing. I never want to set foot on a ship again. I thought I was going to die and at the time I wished I was. I don't know how Betty stands it.'

'She's been in the wars herself, I see,' he said.

Gloria nodded. 'And she says as soon as her arm's better she's going back.' She shuddered.

'She must enjoy it, although I can't see there's much fun in being flung all over the place.' There was a brief silence and then he stood up. There really wasn't anything else to say and he didn't want to intrude on her sadness. 'I'd better get back now, I told Mam I wouldn't be long.'

'Thank you, Artie, for coming in. It was thoughtful of you.'

He nodded, wondering if he should say that if there was ever anything he could do to help her she only had to ask, but then he thought better of it. It was the sort of thing people said at times like this but it wouldn't be of any comfort to her so it would be pointless.

He turned as he opened the door to see that she was once again staring sadly into the flames and his heart went out to her. Feelings he hadn't experienced in years were stirring in him. Feelings he'd thought had long since faded. Obviously he'd been wrong. As he left he felt confused. Had his visit been a foolish thing to do?

Gloria didn't even hear the door close behind him; she was once more enveloped by the overwhelming heaviness of grief.

Chapter Thirty-Six

T HEY HAD ALL WONDERED how Artie's visit would affect Gloria but it hadn't seemed to have upset her. Gloria had said it was thoughtful of him to call but she hadn't enlightened any of them as to just what had been said.

Sybil and Richard were due on Sunday afternoon and as Betty helped Rose with the dishes from lunch, as best she could, they both wondered how the afternoon would go.

'I expect she'll come dressed entirely in black, which would be her style. Even though she really didn't know the Hepworths that well. Everything for show,' Betty remarked.

Rose frowned. 'Do you think she'll start going on about how terrible, how tragic it is and wanting Gloria to tell her all the details?'

'She didn't last time, so Mam said, but I'll kill her if she does today. We've all worked so hard to help Gloria try to get over it and settle back into life here and you have to admit, Rose, that she's a little better now.'

'She is. I felt so terribly sorry for her when she first arrived but she's got a long way to go yet and she doesn't need any setbacks.'

'No she doesn't,' Betty agreed. 'Oh, I wish I could have this plaster cast off, my arm is so itchy and I can't scratch it. It's driving me mad!'

'It must be getting better. Ask Aunty Sal for one of her knitting needles,' Rose suggested.

'What good will that do?' Betty demanded.

Rose laughed at her friend. 'Honestly, Betty! It will fit between the cast and your arm. Then you can get at the itchy bit.'

'And I can poke Aunt Sybil with it if she starts her antics,' Betty added, grinning mischievously.

There were the usual preparations that a visit from Sybil necessitated. Sal got out her best china. Rose had already spread one of the embroidered tablecloths over the table and Betty had managed to bring in the milk jug, sugar basin and a plate of sandwiches on a tray with her good hand. There was no need to tell Betty how to set things out now. There was a lace doily on the plate and the silver tonges were beside the sugar basin.

'I really don't know why we have to make such a fuss when she comes to visit,' Betty muttered to Rose. Both girls had changed their dresses and Rose had helped Betty with hers. It was a fine wool crêpe in a shade of green that suited her but it had a row of small buttons on one shoulder that she couldn't manage with her left hand. Rose wore a dark blue pleated skirt and a long-line fine jumper of cream wool edged with dark blue. She was forgoing her usual visit to Alan's parents; instead he was having tea with them.

'Because we don't want her to look down her nose at us,' Rose reminded her. 'Those beads really do go well with that dress, Betty,' she added, indicating the long string of amber beads Betty had borrowed from her mother.

'It would all look even better without the cast,' Betty added ruefully. The cumbersome cast limited what she could wear and got hot and itchy during the night. She couldn't wait to get it off but she still had some weeks yet before that happened.

Gloria had made more of an effort than usual. She wore a long rope of jet beads over her black dress and matching earrings, but she was still very pale and had made no attempt to apply rouge or lipstick.

Richard's car drew up outside at half past two and Sybil checked her watch. Her dark grey coat sported a wide collar of black fur and her hat, also dark grey, was trimmed only with a band of black velvet ribbon. It was an outfit she considered smart but entirely suitable for the occasion, she thought. 'We're not too early, Richard, are we?'

Richard Mostyn was pulling on his gloves, preparing to get out of the car. 'I don't think so, Sybil. She didn't give a specific time, did she?'

'No. Just a minute, Richard, there's something on your coat.' Sybil brushed the offending piece of fluff off. 'We won't stay too long. We don't want to overtax poor Gloria –

and don't make any of those fatuous remarks about that green dress I wore at her wedding to poor, tragic Grant.'

Richard frowned at her. 'As if I would be so tactless, Sybil! And I honestly do think that you shouldn't keep referring to him as "poor, tragic Grant". That *will* upset her.'

Sybil tutted in annoyance and waited for Richard to come round to open the car door for her.

'Who is that young man? He looks as if he's going to Sal's house,' she hissed as she got out and caught sight of Hewel Davies about to open the gate, a posy of flowers in his hand.

'Are you visiting Mrs Jenkins too?' Sybil asked him a little curtly.

'Miss Jenkins, actually. I have got the right address?'

Sybil nodded, feeling very put out. Sal hadn't mentioned that Betty was expecting a visitor and the timing was spectacularly bad, which was just typical of Betty.

Before Sybil had a chance to knock on the front door it was opened by a very startled-looking Betty.

'Goodness, I didn't think I'd see you again until after Christmas! How did you know where I live?' Betty cried, but her eyes were shining. She had hardly been able to believe her eyes when she'd spotted him opening the gate. She'd been looking out for the car, intending to have a few words with her aunt in the hall.

'Miss Lawson gave me your address and I thought I'd call and see how you are,' he answered, smiling at her. She looked very attractive out of that rather severe uniform, even with the cast on her arm. 'Oh, I brought you these. I thought they would cheer you up.'

344

Betty took the posy with her good hand. 'Thank you. You'd better come in. You'd *all* better come in.'

'I was wondering when you would deign to notice us,' Sybil snapped. Really, the girl had no manners at all. She hadn't uttered a single word of greeting to them or made any attempt to introduce this young man who, Sybil thought, looked much older than her niece.

'Sorry, do come on in,' Betty apologised, her cheeks flushing pink as she ushered everyone into the hall. She was really delighted to see Hewel Davies again and surprised that he'd gone to the trouble of finding out her address. And he'd brought her flowers! No one had ever done that before, it made her feel special.

'Gloria, dear! How are you?' Sybil hugged her niece.

'I . . . I'm getting stronger every day, thank you,' Gloria replied.

Sal's eyebrows rose in surprise as she caught sight of Hewel Davies. 'Rose, would you take everyone's coats. Betty, you didn't tell us you were expecting a visitor.'

'I wasn't,' Betty replied, glancing first at Rose and then at Hewel. Rose's eyebrows had also risen and Hewel looked rather uncomfortable.

'I'm very sorry, Mrs Jenkins, to descend on you like this. I had no idea you were expecting company.'

'Oh, Sybil and Richard aren't "company", they're family. Sybil is my husband's sister,' Sal informed him, indicating he should sit down.

Sybil was far from pleased that Sal didn't seem at all put out that this young man had arrived unannounced. And it seemed to her very insensitive of Betty to encourage him to visit, particularly in the light of her sister's situation. The fact that he'd brought flowers obviously meant that Betty was courting at last.

Gloria too felt a little pang of curiosity. Betty had never mentioned a young man but then she supposed her sister thought that she would be upset. She wasn't. He looked very nice and Betty deserved to meet someone.

Sal beamed at Hewel. 'You are very welcome. Now, Betty, I think you really should introduce him to everyone. After all, apart from you and me, he doesn't know who anyone is. Then we'll all have tea.'

Betty smiled a little shyly at him. 'This is Dr Hewel Davies. He's one of the medical officers on the *Empress of Britain*. He was very kind and looked after me when I had my accident.'

He smiled back at her. 'She is by far the nicest patient I've ever had so I couldn't wait until she returned to duty to see her again.'

Rose glanced quickly at Sybil and then at Sal and had to purse her lips tightly to stop herself from laughing out loud at the look on Sybil Mostyn's face. Oh, good for you, Betty! she said to herself.

Sybil was utterly at a loss for words. He was a medical officer – a *doctor*! And he was obviously very attracted to Betty; he'd even brought her flowers. It was utterly unbelievable.

Chapter Thirty-Seven

1930

CHRISTMAS HAD BEEN A very subdued affair that year, Betty thought, but thank God the snow had gone at last. She looked out through the bedroom window at the grey sky wondering if might return. She sincerely hoped not. She shivered; at least tomorrow she would be sailing away from it all. At the beginning of December it had snowed heavily and then frozen, and more snow had followed, making life difficult for everyone.

She'd received a Christmas card from Hewel, who was with his parents in Denbigh, and then a letter in which he'd written that he hoped the snow had gone by the time he was due to rejoin the ship for at the present time they were virtually cut off. She'd been very dismayed to learn that for she was looking forward to seeing him again. He'd called at the end of his last trip, bringing a large box of chocolates to cheer her up and all the news from the ship. He'd given her his address and asked her to write when the plaster was off and she felt she could manage a pen and she had written one very short letter, finding it painful at first.

She smiled to herself. Rose often teased her about him but she really didn't mind. Rose hadn't been able to go to see Alan's parents on Christmas Day as there were no trams running and Alan had told her it was much too far to walk but he had valiantly trudged the long miles on Christmas morning to see her and to give her her present. Christmas was always a bitter sweet time for Rose and he was aware of it. Mam had made him have something to eat and a tot of brandy before he'd set off for home.

They'd all realised what an effort Gloria had made. In tears, she'd confided to Sal that she was desperately trying not to think of last Christmas but she couldn't help it. Sal had hugged her and told her that the first Christmas, anniversary and birthdays were the worst times and that no one expected her to be happy and cheerful.

'But I don't want to be a killjoy; I don't want to ruin it for everyone else. Both Betty and Rose have so much to look forward to,' she'd said, wiping her eyes.

'You may not think so right now, luv, but you have a future too and you certainly won't ruin anything. We're all just glad you're here with us,' Sal had consoled her.

Artie and his parents had come in on Christmas night, ostensibly to wish all of them season's greetings, but Betty had noticed that Artie paid more attention to Gloria than his parents did, sitting talking to her quietly as the glasses of sherry were passed round. She'd even seen her sister smile once at something he'd said. It had made her wonder if he really had got over Gloria. He'd called once or twice since but he never stayed long.

She was in the middle of her packing but somehow there was just far too much stuff to fit into her case and she shook her head in frustration.

Gloria came into the room carrying a pile of freshly laundered underwear. 'Mam asked me to bring these up for you to pack.'

'Oh Lord! I'd forgotten about them. Gloria, I'm never going to get everything in,' Betty wailed.

'Honestly, Betty, you haven't got a clue. Here, let me try and sort it all out.' Gloria put the clothes down on the bed and began to take out the things Betty had already put into the case. 'I know you are going to be away for three months but do you really need all these things?'

Betty sighed. 'I suppose not, I can wash and iron, it's just that I don't know what I'll need.'

Gloria smiled at her. It was a big adventure for Betty going so far away and for so long. Sadly she remembered the excitement she'd felt the day she'd sailed on the *Mauretania*. It seemed like a lifetime ago now, something that belonged to another world. She sighed, neatly folding and repacking Betty's uniform dresses. 'You certainly won't have any room for the things you buy on your travels.'

Betty nodded. She'd wanted to ask her sister which were the best shops – for her budget – in New York but that would have been very tactless and probably Gloria wouldn't know anyway, she'd only ever shopped at the expensive stores. She'd ask Kate, she would know.

'I'll miss you all but I'll write and send postcards. Rose has promised to send me all the . . . news.' Rose had promised she would write with the details of the wedding plans and their flat-hunting, for she and Alan hoped to get married next year, after they'd found and furnished somewhere to live.

'We'll miss you too. Mam's got used to having you at home, but she said now your arm is better you'll be much better off working. There, isn't that better and you've still got room for a couple of these summer dresses.'

'Gloria, you are a genius!' Betty said, giving her sister a quick hug and thinking that with each week that passed her sister was gradually becoming more like her old self.

Gloria wasn't going to see Betty off and Betty hadn't expected her to do so – there would be too many painful memories of the day Gloria had left Liverpool as a new bride. Rose would be at work and so it would be just herself and Mam who would go down to Gladstone Dock in the morning. She'd already had a lecture from Sal on not drinking any water in the places she would visit in the West Indies, being very careful what she ate there too and making sure she washed her hands thoroughly and often. The diseases they had in some of those places were very nasty and could kill you, Sal had said emphatically. 'But I'm sure that nice Dr Davies will keep his eye on you,' she'd finished. Betty had laughed but she hoped that she would see some of those places in his company.

Before she'd left for work that morning Rose had hugged her and told her to enjoy herself. 'It will seem an awfully long time before I see you again, Betty.'

'I know but I promise I'll write.'

Gloria too had hugged her and echoed Rose's words. 'You'll love New York, Betty, I know you will. Have a great time,' she'd added.

Sal knew how much it cost Gloria to say that for she caught a glimpse of the tears on Gloria's lashes. 'Right, we'd better be going, this is one trip you don't want to be late for, Betty.'

When they'd gone Gloria stood at the window and sighed heavily. The days would seem even longer now without Betty and she wondered what she should do to try to fill the time and keep the memories at bay. It was hard to even think about the future – her future, but she knew she would have to soon. There was a saying, 'Life goes on', and it was true. She couldn't just sit at home for ever. She turned away and began to tidy up. It would take an enormous effort to try to make any kind of plans and she just didn't feel up to it yet.

Sal had hugged Betty and given her instructions to take care of herself and to write; then she stood waving as she watched Betty walk towards the ship, its hull now newly painted its usual dazzling white. Of course she'd miss her but she was used to long periods of absence, it was only a third of the time that Harry was away and Betty would enjoy it – well, she'd enjoy the time ashore. And for the next three months she would be elevated to the status of a second-class stewardess. As she turned away, making for the tram stop, she wondered if the ship would only be half full for these cruises. Many Americans didn't have the money they once had; things were not good over there and they weren't much better here. There were more and more people out of work and she sincerely hoped it wasn't going to get worse.

When she arrived home Gloria informed her that Sybil had been on the telephone.

'What did she want? To come and visit, I suppose.'

Gloria nodded, pouring her mother a much needed cup of tea. 'She said she wanted to have a talk to you.'

Sal sipped her tea and frowned. 'Did she give you any idea what about?'

'No. She just said she would call tomorrow afternoon and then Uncle Richard could collect her on his way home from work.'

It must be something important, Sal thought, for Sybil to get the train here on a winter afternoon. 'Did you tell her I'd gone to see Betty off?'

'Yes. She said she hoped Betty would see more of that nice Dr Davies. She said Betty certainly shouldn't let him slip through her fingers.'

Sal raised her eyes to the ceiling. 'Trust Sybil to say something like that.'

'I think she's still quite astounded that Betty has managed to attract the interest of a doctor.'

Sal glanced at her eldest daughter and wondered whether she had any inkling of just how much Sybil had interfered in her life, but Gloria was smiling and it was the first big, genuine smile Sal had seen on her face since she'd come home.

Sybil arrived after lunch, muffled in her fur coat with a matching hat and wearing fleece-lined boots. 'Oh, it's raw out there! That wind is bitter,' she commented, pulling her chair closer to the fire after divesting herself of both coat and hat.

'This should warm you up, Sybil.' Sal handed her a cup of tea and Sybil sipped it gratefully.

'Did Betty get off all right?' Sybil asked. 'At least she's sailing off to the sun. Such a pleasant young man that Dr Davies; she should cultivate him, Sal.'

Sal ignored her comments. 'Now, what is on your mind? It has to be something important to bring you all the way out here on a freezing day like today, Sybil.'

Sybil placed her cup and saucer on the side table. 'Gloria, you are looking so much better, dear, but I'm still worried about you, as is your mother.' She glanced quickly at Sal. She was choosing her words carefully but she genuinely had her niece's welfare at heart. 'The days must be very long for her, Sal, and now that Betty has sailed, perhaps she should try to think about what she is going to do?'

'It's still very early days, Sybil.' Sal could see where this was leading and she wasn't at all sure that Sybil was being helpful.

'I know, but surely, Gloria, if you had something to help occupy you it would help. It might take your mind off . . . things.' Sybil wanted to say that she couldn't stay at home grieving for ever, she was still only a young woman with her life ahead of her, but she refrained from doing so.

'You mean, if . . . if I went back to work?' Gloria asked hesitantly.

Sybil nodded. 'And jobs are getting increasingly hard to find,' she said gently. According to Richard there were worryingly very difficult times ahead with unemployment rising daily. It was all to do with the crash of the Stock Exchange in New York, it was being felt worldwide and she didn't want her niece to eventually realise she needed to work and then find herself unable to get a job of any kind.

'I . . . I suppose I will have to think about it. I can't expect Mam to keep me for ever.' Gloria was trying to focus on her aunt's suggestion.

Sal was outraged. 'Gloria, this is your home! There is no question of you having to go back to work to pay for living here!'

'She knows that, Sal, but I'm thinking of her wellbeing, in the long term,' Sybil said placatingly. She hadn't meant her suggestion to be viewed in such a light.

Gloria frowned. 'I couldn't go back to the Revenue office. Everyone would be asking about . . .'

'No, of course not. However, there might be a place for you working with me, part time to start with but later on full time.' Sybil smiled ruefully at Sal. 'I'm not getting any younger and Richard is always urging me to retire.'

'Is that wise, Sybil, if things are getting so bad?' Sal queried. She had never really understood why Sybil had insisted on working, after all she didn't need to, Richard had the business, but maybe now things were not looking quite so rosy.

Sybil shrugged. It would mean a loss of a certain amount

of independence on her part but she would willingly train Gloria to take over her job if it would give the girl some purpose in life.

Gloria was thinking about her aunt's offer and she knew that she really didn't want to spend so much time with Sybil. She viewed her aunt in a different light now. Once Sybil had had great influence over her and she'd admired her, thought her so sophisticated and knowledgeable but now . . . She supposed she'd grown up. 'I . . . I don't want to sound ungrateful, Aunt Sybil, but I don't think I'd enjoy being in the millinery trade.'

Sal sighed with relief. Thank God for that, she thought. She didn't want Sybil to keep on trying to influence her daughter for the rest of Gloria's life. She'd had far too much say in it so far.

'Is there anything you *would* like to do, Gloria?' Sal asked, before Sybil could speak and ignoring the look of surprised indignation that had crossed her sister-in-law's face.

Gloria thought about it. 'I think I'd like to work with people, people who don't know me or what . . . happened.'

'In a different office or . . . or a shop?' Sal probed.

'I think I'd prefer a shop. I'd see different people every day.'

Sybil had recovered herself, pushing her disappointment to the back of her mind. This discussion wasn't about her, it was about Gloria's future, she told herself firmly.

'One of the better-class shops, of course. We can't have you working in Woolworth's or Blackler's. I'll make some enquiries and see if there is anything in Hendersons or the

Bon Marche. I've known the millinery buyers in both for years,' Sybil informed them.

'Are you really sure you're up to this, Gloria?' Sal asked anxiously.

Gloria nodded slowly and sighed. 'I have to do something with my time. I have to try to think about the future.'

Sybil nodded her agreement. 'There might not be anything at the moment, but I do honestly think it's wise to start looking now, before things get worse.'

Sal was relieved. Perhaps Gloria would have a while yet before she had to try to pick up the pieces of her life. It was going to be hard for her, very hard indeed, but she could see the sense in Sybil's thinking.

Artie called that evening, enquiring if Betty had got off without any mishaps.

'A bit of a fuss over the packing, but Gloria soon sorted that out, didn't you, luv?' Sal replied before absenting herself to make a pot of tea.

'Isn't she the lucky one to escape to the West Indies? I suppose you'll miss her, Gloria.'

'I will. We all will, Artie.'

'Mam said your Aunt Sybil called this afternoon, she saw your uncle's car at teatime.' Artie still had misgivings about Sybil. Lately he'd been thinking a lot about the time he and Gloria had spent together. He couldn't deny that his feelings for her were growing again and he'd begun to wonder if it had been Sybil's plan all along to separate them all those years ago. Gloria had been very impressionable and very excited about going to New York, but then he supposed she had loved Grant Hepworth; his death had devastated her.

'She did call and . . . and she's made me realise, Artie, that I can't just stay at home grieving for ever. I have to try to think about my future,' Gloria confided.

He was concerned. 'Are you sure it's not too soon, Gloria?'

'Perhaps it is but I have to *try* to do something. She suggested I go and work with her but . . . but I don't think I want to do that.'

Artie nodded. He didn't think it a good idea either. 'What do you want to do, Gloria?'

'I said I'd prefer to work in a shop where I'd see different people every day. I think that would take my mind off . . . things, just chatting to complete strangers. I couldn't face going back into an office.'

'What did she say?' Artie was glad at least that Sybil had made Gloria think about the next step in her life.

Gloria smiled wryly. 'That she'd try and get me something in either Hendersons or the Bon Marche. You know Aunt Sybil. It wouldn't do for me to work in Woolies, would it?'

Artie smiled back. 'If it would help to make you just a tiny bit happier, Gloria, then Woolies wouldn't be bad at all.'

'Thanks, Artie. It is good of you to call in to see me.'

'We're friends, Gloria.'

She nodded. 'We are, aren't we, Artie?'

Chapter Thirty-Eight

I T WAS NEARLY A month later when Sybil phoned to say she
had finally heard from the person she knew at Hendersons
for she'd already ascertained that the Bon Marche were not
taking on any staff for the foreseeable future. There would
be a vacancy in the cosmetics department at the beginning of
March as one of the assistants was leaving, she being in what
was delicately termed 'the family way'. Sybil had obtained an
interview for Gloria later in the week and was prepared to go
with her if required.

'I think I would be better on my own, Mam,' Gloria had
told Sal who had nodded her approval.

'Do you think you will like selling cosmetics? You won't
find it boring?' Sal had enquired.

'I won't know until I try, will I?' Gloria had replied.

It was finally decided that Sal would go with her, at least

into town. Gloria would go alone for the interview and would then meet her mother somewhere for a cup of tea. She had only ever attended a couple of interviews when she'd left school and she felt nervous. It seemed such a big step for her to take, the first one towards a new life, a new future. Since she'd come home she had only been in the company of family and friends; now she would have to face the world again.

'You look very smart, luv. Now don't be worrying that you won't get the job. If you don't it's not the end of the world,' Sal said as she gave her a quick hug and watched her daughter go through the doors of the large department store on Church Street, the commissionaire nodding politely as he held the door for her. Sal sighed; she had a few things to get and then she'd head for the Kardomah café in Lord Street. She prayed Gloria would get the job for her self-confidence would be seriously undermined if she didn't and that wouldn't help her on the long road to recovery.

As soon as Gloria walked through the door of the café and smiled Sal knew she'd been taken on and relief flooded through her. Gloria already seemed far more poised and confident than she had been earlier.

Sal beamed at her. 'You got it! I can see by your face.'

Gloria nodded, taking off her gloves. 'They were very nice, Mam. Aunt Sybil had told them my . . . history and Miss Anacott, who is going to train me, said it helped to have what she called a more "cosmopolitan" background. I think she meant it helped that I'd lived in New York.'

'So, when will you be starting?' Sal ordered more tea from a passing waitress.

'Next week. I'll have a week's training. I was taken on a tour of the different counters and there does seem quite a bit to learn. Different products and prices and brands. Coty, Helena Rubinstein and Goya. I have to learn what all the different products do, or are supposed to do. Just what something called "mercurising wax" does I have no idea.'

'You'll soon get the hang of it all, Gloria, and I'm sure you'll enjoy working there.'

Gloria nodded slowly as the fresh pot of tea arrived. She had once enjoyed shopping for the products she would now be selling so at least she would find it interesting and hopefully her days would be full and busy, not endless and empty as they had been.

Rose was as delighted as Sal that Gloria had found a job, and one that Rose thought would suit Gloria down to the ground. 'Won't it be great, working with all those lovely creams and potions and helping people choose the right shade of lipstick and rouge. You'll love it and you'll be good at it.' She smiled ruefully. 'Of course I can only afford to buy Pond's cream and lipstick but I don't mind.'

Gloria thought about it. 'You could still come in and see me and I suppose they must have samples. I could give you a few to try.'

Rose said she'd love that and listening to the two girls Sal thought that Gloria really did seem to be more animated than she'd been for a long time, and she thanked God for it. She even made a mental note to thank Sybil.

Gloria's training week went smoothly and she soon settled into her new routine. On her way home one day Gloria met Artie and they walked from the tram stop together.

'So, how is the new job going?' Artie asked. He was interested in everything she did.

'Fine. I'm having to learn quite a lot but it certainly occupies my mind. The day just seems to fly by.'

'You look better, Gloria, you've got more colour in your cheeks,' Artie commented, thinking she didn't have that air of despair about her any longer.

Gloria smiled at him but refrained from saying that she was once again wearing rouge, something she hadn't bothered with for months. But she had to look smart and well groomed, it went with the job. She couldn't turn up for work looking drab and untidy: what kind of an advertisement would that be for the products she was selling?

He changed the subject. 'Have you heard from Betty lately? She must be nearing the end of her trip now.'

'We had a postcard last week, from Kingston, Jamaica, but I think it's taken a while to get here. She's got a couple of weeks left before they head home but she seems to be having a great time.'

They'd reached Sal's gate and Artie raised his hand in a wave of farewell. 'Keep up the good work, Gloria,' he said. He was joking but this job did indeed seem to be helping her and he was glad.

Betty had managed to get on deck for a few minutes as they approached Port-au-Prince in Haiti. The sun was hot on her face and she squinted in the bright light. They were nearing the end of this last cruise and in some ways she was sorry, in others she was glad for she had missed her family. The time had flown by and the work hadn't been nearly as hard as it had been in steerage. Most of her passengers had been very pleasant and easy and she'd made good tips. She'd gone ashore in New York and Barbados and Puerto Rico with the girls but Havana, Antigua, Grenada, Trinidad, Martinique and Curaçao she'd visited with Hewel.

She leaned on the rail and gazed down at the turquoise waters of the Caribbean, thinking back to those trips. In Havana they'd wandered the hot, narrow streets of the older part of town and she'd bought a lace evening shawl for Rose. It hadn't been cheap, a hundred pesos, but Hewel had assured her it would have cost far more in some of the smart shops. Then they'd gone for a cool drink in a café with a tiny courtyard where there had been a tinkling fountain and bougainvillea, wisteria, jasmine and Spanish moss had cascaded from the walls, filling the air with perfume. She'd told him it was heavenly and he'd laughed and said it was just a taste of things to come. He'd kissed her and held her for a long time that night before they'd gone back on board and ever since she had counted the hours until she could spend her free time with him again.

She sighed and pushed a stray strand of hair back under her cap. Over the past three months they had got to know each other much better and she was sure she loved him. She now knew how Gloria had felt about Grant Hepworth and could understand more fully how devastated Gloria had been at his death. It had been at their last port of call, Willemstad, Curaçao – a picturesque little Dutch town – when they'd sampled the liqueur named after the island and had walked slowly along the palm-fringed beach that he'd told her he couldn't imagine life without her now.

'You're so very open and generous, Betty, and honest. If you have something to say, you say it, there's no beating around the bush. No innuendoes, no hints, and I like that. You make me laugh and I feel as if I've known you all my life. I don't want this trip to end. It's been so wonderful sharing the experience of exploring all these places with you. Look at us now, walking together in what is something akin to paradise.'

She sighed again but with pure pleasure. Ahead of them were Haiti and the Dominican Republic, two halves of the same island, and then finally St Thomas in the Virgin Islands. Then they would head back to New York before crossing the Atlantic to Liverpool and home. But at least the dark days of winter would be over.

Kate appeared beside her looking flustered. 'I've been looking everywhere for you. You've a message from your doctor friend.'

Betty turned and took the note from her, scanning the lines. He'd meet her on the dockside at Port-au-Prince when they docked in Haiti as the ship had to anchor offshore and they'd have to use the tenders; he had a surprise for her. She must let him know what time she would get off. She smiled at Kate. 'He's going to meet me on the dockside.'

Kate frowned. 'I don't want to be a killjoy, Betty, but your little jaunts together have been noticed and you know company policy about "officers and crew".'

Betty frowned. They'd tried not to be seen together too often but obviously they'd failed. She bit her lip, wondering whether she should tell him they would have to forgo spending time together exploring Haiti.

Kate looked sympathetic. 'I know it's a stupid regulation and I also know how much you like him. I can't say I blame you, he's very nice, but I'm just warning you, Betty. Now we'd better go back down or we'll both be for the high jump.'

She decided that she would go to meet him but she would have to tell him that their outings had been noticed. She'd finally got aboard a tender at six o'clock and saw him waiting in the shade of a warehouse. Her heart turned over, he looked so handsome. He was tanned and wore a short-sleeved white cotton shirt, a tie and beige trousers. Then she remembered Kate's warning and a little of the brightness seemed to go out of the evening.

'You look lovely, Betty. So fresh and cool.' He wanted to take her hand but couldn't do so until they'd cleared the dockside. 'We're going to have a really special evening. Everything is arranged.'

She was glad she had taken time to iron her white cotton dress with its pattern of blue cornflowers and she wore her white shoes with the hourglass heel and a very lightweight white straw hat decorated with a blue flower. She decided to put Kate's words to the back of her mind, seeing as he'd planned a 'special' evening.

He'd hired a horse-drawn cab which was more like a carriage. 'It's a better way to see the sights of Port-au-Prince than taking a traditional cab which, believe me, is a bit of a nightmare experience. The drivers are like lunatics behind the wheel!' he laughed as he helped her up.

She'd glimpsed the white pavilions of the presidential palace as they sailed past Gonâve Island but as they turned from Rue Roux into Grande Rue she saw them at close quarters. 'Don't they remind you of a fancy iced cake?' she asked, turning to him.

'Like a wedding cake? I thought that the first time I saw them.'

She twisted and turned as he pointed out buildings, until they passed the Café Savoy-Vincent and finally stopped in front of a colonial, two-storeyed white building that proclaimed itself to be the Hotel Excelsior.

'Here we are,' Hewel informed her, paying the driver. 'I've booked a table for two for dinner.'

'It looks gorgeous and very expensive. You really don't have to spend a fortune on me, Hewel. I'd have been content with something in a quiet little café.' She was taking in the pathway flanked by perfumed shrubs and flowers and then the magnificent reception hall with its floor of green and white marble, French furniture and huge marble urns filled with flowers and palms.

'I know you would, Betty, but I told you I want this to be "special".'

She felt a little overawed as the maître d' approached, his handsome black features impassive and a little arrogant, she thought. His black frock-coat and high white winged collar added dignity to his bearing and she remembered what the guidebook had said, that Haiti was the first black republic in the world. As he led them into the dining room she was forcefully reminded of the Salle Jacques Cartier dining room, the first-class dining room on the *Empress*. It was magnificent.

'I feel like one of my own passengers, Hewel,' she confided as she was seated and a handsome mulatto waiter appeared with the menus. A coloured orchestra sat on a raised dais flanked by palms at the furthest end of the room.

He leaned closer towards her. 'Confidentially, the food here is better than anything you'd get there, believe me. They excel in authentic Creole dishes.'

The food was unlike anything she'd ever had before. Crayfish in white wine sauce, turtle eggs, seafood in parcels of light puff pastry, mangoes, breadfruit and papayas and cocktails of white rum and fresh fruit juices.

They sat on the hotel verandah with their coffee. The mountain-banded bay reflected the deep velvet blue of the sky with its thousands of stars glittering like diamonds. Gonâve Island lay beyond, cloud-capped and misty. To the north-east stretched the Cul-de-Sac plain, gridded with sugarcane. Beyond that Hewel told her lay the great salt lake of Saumâtre, which in daylight shimmered ghostly white.

'Would you like a liqueur, just to round off the evening?' Hewel asked, feeling a little apprehensive. He'd made up his mind that tonight he would ask her that all-important question.

'Lord no, thank you. If I drink anything else you'll have to carry me back to the ship and then there will be hell to pay from Miss Lawson.' The thought of the Chief Stewardess brought back to her mind Kate's warning and she frowned.

'What's wrong?'

'I was just thinking of what Kate said to me when she delivered your note. That our "outings" have been noted, so I expect I'll be hauled over the coals by Miss Lawson anyway. But I don't care, Hewel. I don't want to stop seeing you.'

He reached for her hand and nodded seriously. 'And I've no intention of avoiding you, Betty. It's a stupid rule and I've already been warned about breaking it.' In fact it was his superior's words on the subject that had been instrumental in him reaching his decision.

Betty bit her lip. 'You've had a "proper" warning?'

He nodded. 'That's why I booked dinner for us here, why I wanted this evening to be special – one we'd both remember.' He paused, taking a deep breath. 'I can't see that they could find any reason to object to an officer and his fiancée spending their time ashore together, do you?'

Betty stared at him blankly until his words finally sunk in. Her eyes widened and she gasped. 'You . . . you . . . mean . . . me? Your . . . fiancée?'

'I do, if you'll have me, Betty. I love you and I can't imagine my life without you by my side.'

Tears were stinging her eyes and her heart was racing but she'd never felt so ecstatically happy in her life before. 'I love you too, Hewel, so much! Of course I'll "have you" as you put it. I'll be overjoyed, delighted . . . Oh, look at me! I'm such a fool!' Tears were trickling down her cheeks.

He got up and drew her to her feet and held her close. 'Oh, Betty! I was so afraid you'd turn me down.' Gently he kissed away her tears. 'We'll get the ring in Charlotte Amalie, they sell beautiful Colombian emeralds there.'

'I don't want this evening to end, Hewel. This place is just like paradise and I feel as if I'm really in heaven I'm so happy.'

'We'll come back one day, I promise,' he murmured into her hair.

It was very hard but they both agreed they would not go ashore together in Santo Domingo but would wait and go for the ring in Charlotte Amalie on St Thomas.

In the second jewellers they visited Betty fell for a square-cut emerald and when she refused the owner's offer to gift wrap it in its box, saying it was so beautiful she couldn't bear to take it off, Hewel kissed her and all the assistants crowded around to wish them well. They left holding hands, their eyes shining with happiness, and headed for the nearest hotel to have a drink to celebrate.

As he handed her a flute of champagne he smiled ruefully. 'I know I really should have asked your parents' permission, Betty, but . . .'

'How could you when we're thousands of miles away? Anyway, I can't see them objecting.' She grinned. 'It's getting to be something of a tradition in our family. Gloria went on a trip abroad and came back engaged and I think Mam is going to be just as astonished when I get home.'

'I just hope she won't be upset or offended.'

Betty smiled. 'No, she'll be delighted, I promise.'

When she got back to the ship Kate was already changing into her uniform. 'You've been summoned. She wants to see you and I think you're in for a dire warning.'

Betty held out her left hand. 'Can she object now?'

Kate shrieked and then hugged her. 'Oh, Betty Jenkins! You dark horse! Congratulations!'

'He proposed in Port-au-Prince.'

'And you never said a word!'

Betty laughed. 'I'd better get changed and go and see her.'

She twisted the ring around on her finger as she went to the Chief Stewardess's cabin, feeling excited, happy and a little apprehensive too.

'You wanted to see me, ma'am?'

Miss Lawson looked up from the paperwork on her desk. She could see that the girl was flushed and obviously delighted about something.

'I did, Miss Jenkins. You are aware of company policy regarding officers and crew fraternising and it has been noted that you and Dr Davies have been ashore together on numerous occasions.'

Betty nodded. 'We have, ma'am, and today we . . . we got engaged.' She held out her left hand, almost shyly. 'I . . . I hope that's not against regulations.'

Miss Lawson leaned back in her chair and a smile spread slowly over her face. She liked Betty Jenkins and now she'd managed to do something that many of her girls dreamed of doing. 'Not at all. Congratulations, Miss Jenkins, I hope you will both be very happy. He is a very pleasant and conscientious young man.'

'Thank you, ma'am. I know we will.'

'You do realise that once you are married your career at sea will be over. Married stewardesses are not employed by the company.'

Betty nodded. 'I know but I'll be happy to stay at home as a wife.'

Miss Lawson became businesslike. 'I'd advise you not to wear your ring while on duty; you don't want to damage it in any way and cleaning bathrooms etc., could scratch it. Emeralds are quite soft stones.'

Betty smiled at her. 'I won't and thank you, ma'am, for the advice.'

Chapter Thirty-Nine

———◆·◆·◆———

To Betty's delight both her mother and Rose came to meet her when they arrived in Liverpool on a bright but chilly early April day. News of their engagement had quickly got around the ship and they'd both been congratulated by everyone, including the Captain himself, who had said it was highly irregular but he wished them every happiness.

The downside was, however, that one of them would have to be transferred to another ship, most probably Betty as she was of the lower rank. She had been dismayed when she'd learned this but Hewel had said that it wouldn't be for ever as he intended to look for a position in general practice at home in North Wales, which was only a few hours from Liverpool by either bus or car so when she was home they could spend time together.

They had agreed to meet at the top of the gangway and break the news to Betty's mother together.

'Rose has come too, Hewel, that's a nice surprise,' she commented as they struggled with their luggage.

'It's Saturday, she only works a half-day,' Hewel reminded her.

Sal hugged Betty and then shook hands with Hewel. 'It seems such a long time since you left but it's not nearly as long as your da's trips.'

Rose could see that Betty was bursting to tell them something. She looked flushed under the suntan and her eyes were sparkling. 'What have you been up to, Betty?' she laughed.

Betty looked up at Hewel. 'We . . . we got engaged.'

For a second Sal just stared from Hewel to Betty, then a wide smile spread across her face. 'Well now, taking a leaf out of Gloria's book, I see!'

Hewel looked relieved and Betty showed them her ring.

'I have to say I'm surprised but I'm also very pleased. Now, we'd better move, we're causing a bit of a hold-up standing here.'

They moved away and stood to one side. As Rose examined the ring and enthused over it Sal found she was glad that Gloria had had to work so hadn't been able to come too. She wondered momentarily how her eldest daughter would take this news, although Gloria was much better in herself.

'Have you told your parents yet, Hewel?' she asked.

'I wrote to them and there was a reply in the mail when we docked here. They both want me to bring Betty to meet them as soon as possible. So I'll stay with my aunt and uncle for a day or two, as usual, and then I'll take my new fiancée home to meet her future in-laws.' He looked pleased and proud; the letter had been encouraging. They hadn't met Betty yet but he'd told them a great deal about her in his letters.

'Right then, we'd all better get going. We'll have to get a taxi because we'll never get on the tram with all that luggage. What have you been spending your money on, Betty?' Sal asked, eyeing the case and the three bags her daughter seemed to have acquired.

Betty grinned. 'Souvenirs and presents. It's almost obligatory for a seafarer to bring them; you should know that, Mam.'

'I'll take the case and I'll walk to the rank with you, then I'll be off,' Hewel said.

They said their farewells, Hewel promising to come to see Betty the following day to make some arrangements for Betty's trip to Denbigh, and Sal settled back, smiling as Betty chattered nineteen to the dozen to Rose about the whole trip. Betty seemed to have grown up yet more and she was happy for her. He was a very nice young man and Betty had known him for far longer than Gloria had known Grant before they got engaged. They must have spent a fair bit of time in each other's company. The first thing she would do when they got home was phone Sybil, she thought with some satisfaction. Unlike Gloria, Betty had found a very eligible young man without any help from her aunt.

The gifts and souvenirs were duly given out and exclaimed

over and after a cup of tea Betty went to unpack, accompanied by Rose.

'So, tell me your latest news, Rose,' Betty demanded as she dumped her case on the bed.

'I wrote telling you our plans so far, but actually we're going to have a look at a little house that's for rent tonight. It's in Smithy Lane, it runs at the back of the church where Gloria was married.'

'St Mary's-on-the-Hill?' Betty queried.

Rose nodded.

'I thought you weren't getting married until late next year?'

'If we can afford the rent we can start to furnish it. We've got enough to buy the bare essentials and then we *might* be able to bring the wedding forward.'

Betty sat on the bed. 'That's great. How *is* Gloria, Rose? I know Mam wrote and said she's enjoying her job and that she's much better but . . .' She shrugged.

'She *is* a lot better now. I think getting out of the house, being busy and meeting people is the best thing she could have done. She won't be over it for a good while yet, not properly, but she looks more like her old self and she doesn't mention Grant as often or sit for ages, not speaking, like she used to do.'

'That's a relief. I . . . I hope she won't get upset about Hewel and me.'

Rose smiled. 'I don't think she will.'

Betty could see the change in her sister the minute she walked in. Gloria was smartly dressed; she'd put on weight and she was wearing make-up again. Nor did she have that dull, dead look in her eyes.

Gloria's face lit up as she hugged Betty and exclaimed that she looked older and had a lovely suntan.

'And that's not all, Gloria. I've got some good news,' Betty said a little hesitantly.

'What?' Gloria pressed.

'She and young Hewel Davies have got engaged,' Sal announced, watching Gloria's face intently.

Gloria felt a pang of sorrow as she remembered how she'd announced her engagement to Grant, but she quickly fought it down and managed a smile. 'Betty, that's wonderful! He's very nice.'

'I think so,' Betty replied, determined not to make a huge issue out of her news.

'Let me see your ring?' Gloria was happy for her sister, even though Betty's news had stirred some painful memories. Betty held out her hand and Gloria examined the emerald. 'It's beautiful.'

'Hewel bought it for me in the Virgin Islands, they seem to specialise in emeralds.' Then Betty became brisk. 'Now, Gloria, you haven't even taken your coat off yet and you must be dying for a cup of tea.' She was determined there would be no further discussion about her engagement or wedding plans. They'd not made any themselves yet and when they did she hoped that her sister would be stronger emotionally.

Sal smiled to herself. Betty was being very considerate and tactful. She certainly had grown up a great deal in the months she'd been away.

*

Betty looked around with interest as they alighted from the bus in Lenten Pool. It hadn't been a long journey, a couple of hours and they'd changed at Mold, and once they'd left the towns behind she'd enjoyed the countryside they'd travelled through. Denbigh was a pretty little market town surrounded by fields and farms and with a ruined castle on the hill above it. The Davieses lived on Ruthin Road, which Hewel had told her wasn't much of a walk from where the bus ended its journey but his father was meeting them with the car so they wouldn't have to struggle with the cases.

Dr Davies senior came towards them, smiling and waving, and Betty thought how like him Hewel was.

'Welcome home, Hewel! And this must be Betty? I'm so glad to meet you. He's told us a lot about you.'

Betty smiled up at him, relaxing. You couldn't help but like him, she thought. His eyes twinkled, his smile was genial and his handshake firm. 'I'm very pleased to meet you too. It must have come as a surprise – our engagement.'

'Indeed it did. Never thought this boy of ours would settle down. Thought he'd be roaming the world for years but now he informs me he's looking to go into general practice.' He took Betty's case and Hewel's bag. 'The car's just over there and I've instructions not to be getting distracted chatting to people, I've to get you home directly, your Nain and Taid have come over from Pentrefoelas for the occasion.'

Hewel smiled at Betty who was looking mystified. 'It's Welsh for Grandmother and Grandfather,' he explained.

Betty smiled back. It certainly was going to be a family affair.

Hewel's home was a Georgian town house on a rather steep hill but Betty loved its elegant lines, deep sash windows and the fanlight above the door. There was a brass plaque beside the front door with Hewel's father's name on it. He'd told her that his father held his surgery in one of the downstairs rooms and that the other room was used as a waiting room; they 'lived above the shop'. As she climbed the wide staircase she felt a little nervous; she hadn't expected to meet his grandparents as well but if they were as warm and welcoming as his father she wouldn't have anything to worry about.

The room she was ushered into was large and bright and furnished with good but comfortable, well-used pieces. There was a large fireplace with a marble surround and vases of flowers were set on side tables, filling the air with their perfume.

Hewel was hugged and fussed over by his mother, a small, plump woman with red-gold hair and grey eyes, dressed in a lavender-coloured knitted two-piece, and then she turned to Betty.

'So this is Betty, from Liverpool. And your father is a seafarer too, I hear. A steward, is it?'

She was smiling as she took Betty's hand but Betty noted that the smile didn't reach her eyes and with a sinking feeling in the pit of her stomach she realised that this woman didn't like her. The grey eyes were cold. She obviously didn't think she was good enough for Hewel. She had wanted someone far better than a lowly stewardess with a Scouse accent as a daughter-in-law. 'He's the *Chief* Steward on the *Amazonia*,' she corrected quietly, determined not to be cowed by this far from warm welcome.

'You must forgive me, I get so confused by these unfamiliar titles. It's a mystery to me why Hewel wanted to go to sea at all, he's a country boy, isn't he, Arwel?' She looked at her husband for support.

'Born and brought up in Denbighshire but it's done him no harm to travel, Marjorie, now has it? And he's found the right girl for himself in Betty.' Dr Davies beamed at them both and Betty wondered if he was ignoring his wife's remarks or whether he really didn't know that she disapproved of her son's choice of future wife.

Hewel introduced her to his grandparents, who greeted her politely enough but she felt that they too found her unacceptable. Was it just her working-class background, she wondered, or was it the fact that she was not Welsh?

After she had unpacked her overnight things and they'd had tea, during which Marjorie Davies prattled on about friends from the golf club and the country club who were well known to Hewel and his father and grandparents but not to herself, she felt decidedly miserable and left out, a feeling compounded by the fact that his grandparents often spoke to each other in their native tongue, which she found incomprehensible and felt was extremely rude.

Hewel had noticed that she was very quiet and as it was a fine evening said they would go for a walk; he would show her the castle.

'What's the matter, Betty? You're very quiet,' he probed as they walked hand in hand up the hill.

'They don't like me. Your mother doesn't think I'm good enough for you and I can tell your grandparents aren't happy with the fact that I'm not Welsh.'

He put his arm around her. 'Take no notice of them, Betty. The old folk are like that. They can't see why I wanted to travel. They think I should have stayed here and married an unassuming and unadventurous country girl. Chapel like themselves and speaking nothing but Welsh. They are very narrow in their outlook. But that wasn't what I wanted at all. I wanted to see something of the world and I have and then I met you and I love you.'

'And your mam?'

'I know she had hopes of me marrying the daughter of one of her golfing friends so I suppose she's disappointed, but that really was a non-starter and it was one of the reasons I wanted to get away. I won't have her running my life, Betty.'

'I like your dad.'

'He's easy-going, sometimes a bit too easy-going, particularly where Mam is concerned.' He bent and kissed her on the cheek. 'You're marrying me, Betty, not my family, and when Mam gets to know you better she'll come round.'

'What if she doesn't?' Betty pressed miserably.

He shook his head. 'Then it will be her loss not ours.'

'I really wanted them to like me and accept me, Hewel. I know I come from a very different background but—'

He stopped and took her in his arms. 'I don't care what

kind of a "background" you come from. It's something I didn't even give a thought to. I fell in love with you and I'm going to marry you. We don't have to live here, I can go into general practice in Liverpool. I know Dad will be disappointed, I think he wanted me to take over from him eventually, but your happiness comes first. We can always visit them, say once a month. They've got used to me being away at sea so they can get used to me living in Liverpool.'

Betty clung to him feeling relieved and yet sad that he would be disappointing his father. Arwel Davies appeared to be a thoroughly nice man and she wondered how he had managed to marry someone as disagreeable and snobbish as Marjorie, but then she thought of her Aunt Sybil and Uncle Richard and stopped wondering. All she wanted was to marry the man she loved and live happily with him and she felt sure that things would work out well for them, providing they didn't live too near to his mother. At least he had been adamant that Marjorie Davies was going to have no say in how he lived his life and she took a great deal of comfort from that fact.

Chapter Forty

IT WAS A VERY hot day when Sal went down to meet the *Amazonia*. The river was flat calm, the azure blue of the cloudless sky reflected in the water. As usual she'd dressed with care, wearing a pale blue crêpe-de-Chine dress and a large white straw picture hat which was the latest fashion, according to Sybil. All her accessories were white and she hoped she looked cool and elegant; at least that's what Elsie had said when she'd popped in earlier. She was alone for Gloria was working and Betty had sailed on the *Empress of France* last week.

Thankfully she didn't have to wait long in the sun before she was ushered aboard with the usual formality.

Harry greeted her, looking tanned and smart in his white uniform as it was high summer and very warm. 'Sarah! You're looking well and very fresh and cool.'

She smiled. 'Do you think we could have tea in your cabin, if it won't be too inconvenient, Henry? There is such a lot to talk about.' She felt that for once they could forgo some of the stiff formality.

'That can certainly be arranged.' He wondered if there was another disaster in the offing. He sincerely hoped not.

The china, silver, damask napkins and sandwiches were duly transported to Harry's neat cabin-cum-office and after the tea had been poured Sal took off her hat and gloves and the pearl earrings that were pinching her earlobes.

'How are you, Sal? Life has been "eventful" to say the least while I've been away this time. How is poor Gloria?'

Sal sipped her tea. 'She's doing well. Oh, Harry, it would have broken your heart to have seen her when she first came home.'

He nodded sadly. 'It was tragic, Sal. A fine young man, such a terrible waste of a life. The whole thing is appalling and depressing. But she's young, she's her life ahead of her and thank God Sybil got her that job.'

'It's been the making of her, Harry, it really has. I was at my wits' end but I think in time she'll get over it all and I hope she'll marry again too. She can't live her whole life without love.'

Harry nodded as he stirred his tea. 'And talking of marriage, Betty has done far better than I could have expected.'

Sal smiled wryly. 'That's more or less what your Sybil said, but she's happy and he's a thoroughly nice young man, you'll like him. She sailed last week on the *France* but she'll be home next week. She wasn't very happy about changing ships but it's company policy. Hewel is still aboard the *Britain* and he'll be home in a few days. He's looking for a position in Liverpool.'

Harry looked surprised. 'He's giving up the sea? It's a good job, Sal; they don't do a fraction of the work a doctor ashore has to do.'

'Maybe not on this ship, Harry, but I think he's kept busy and when they get married Betty will have to stay at home and he says it's not really fair on her for him to be away so much.'

'We've managed, Sal.'

She helped herself to a cucumber sandwich. 'We have but when we were first married, if you remember, you weren't away for months at a time. I think they'll be happy. He'll make a good GP: he's got a nice manner with people. Mind you, Harry, it didn't go down well with his family. Betty was a bit upset when she got back from visiting them. She said his mother doesn't like her, doesn't think she's good enough.'

Harry frowned. 'Is that a fact? Well, she'll have a wedding to equal Gloria's and then we'll see if they change their tune.'

'His father is very nice, she said, but the grandparents are very narrow-minded and spoke Welsh to each other.'

Harry raised his eyebrows. 'Such lovely manners! That's the height of ignorance in my book.' He dismissed the subject. 'And Rose and Alan?'

'They went to look at a house in Smithy Lane but Alan

said he wasn't paying six shillings a week for what he termed "the street with a roof on". Apparently, according to Rose, it was a tiny one-up, one-down with a flagstone floor and a communal privy in the yard and it was opposite the Beehive pub so would be very noisy. I think Rose had hoped they had found the right place at the right rent but . . .'

'Something will come up, Sal, don't worry.'

She nodded. 'How was the trip?'

'Quiet. We had no passengers coming back, which is unusual, but I've heard rumours that the company is struggling and might be looking to lay people off.'

Sal was alarmed. 'Not you, Harry? Not with all your years of service?'

'No, but there is a rumour they will be taking the *Hildebrand* out of service for a trip.' He didn't think it wise to tell her that it looked as if they would be laying off some office staff too. He didn't want her worrying about Rose, she had enough on her plate with Gloria.

Sal was very relieved.

'So, no party again this time, Sal. We'll have two weddings to pay for at some time in the future.'

Sal nodded. It made sense not to waste money on a party and it didn't look good in the light of the fact that there was so much unemployment and that the Porto-Brasilia Line was taking a ship out of service.

Harry was very relieved that his eldest daughter seemed to be getting over her tragic loss and when Hewel Davies docked in Liverpool he came to meet his future father-in-law and they got on like a house on fire, discussing their lives at sea and the places they'd been to. Sybil had also paid a visit that day and had remarked to Sal that Hewel would be better looking for a place in a good practice in somewhere like Southport. In fact she would ask Richard to make enquiries amongst the members of his Lodge.

'I'm sure his mother would be much happier if he was living and working somewhere more . . . cultured.'

Sal had shaken her head. 'Mind your own business, Sybil. Betty is not Gloria and Hewel Davies will stand for no interference in his life. That's why he went away to sea in the first place. His mother was interfering too much.'

Sybil had tutted. 'I was only trying to be helpful, Sal.'

'That's very probably what his mother thought too,' Sal had replied flatly.

Sybil had changed the subject. 'Have you any plans for the August Bank Holiday Monday, Sal?'

'Betty will be home and she hasn't seen Harry for months so we'll probably go for a meal somewhere. Rose told me she and Alan were thinking of going on a day trip to the Isle of Man.'

'And Gloria?'

'Will be coming with us.'

Sybil had smiled. 'I know, why don't you all come out to me for dinner? I could then see Betty's ring and hear her plans; Harry tells me she's to have a big wedding.'

Sal had been taken aback. Sybil had never taken much of an interest in Betty up to now and she wondered if there was some kind of ulterior motive. Well, if Sybil thought she was going to play a big part in Betty's wedding, the way she had in Gloria's, she was very much mistaken. 'We might do that, Sybil, although Hewel won't be with us – he'll have sailed and I know Betty won't upset her sister by having every detail tactlessly discussed. Besides, I don't think they've even set a date yet.'

Gloria hadn't even thought about the forthcoming Bank Holiday, although she would have an extra day off that week. It was only when Artie brought the subject up when he called in to see her that she remembered her mam saying they'd all been invited to dinner at Sybil and Richard's house.

'Do you want to go to Sybil's, Gloria?' Artie asked. He felt it was time Gloria had a day out and he intended to take her to Southport. First of all he'd thought of asking her to go to New Brighton but then he remembered she'd said she never wanted to set foot on a ship again and they'd have to take the ferry across the Mersey to the small seaside town on the opposite bank.

'I don't know, Artie. I suppose it will be better than staying here on my own.'

'I . . . I've been thinking that maybe you'd enjoy a day in Southport, with me. We could go on the train, look at the shops on Lord Street, stroll along the promenade and the pier and then have something to eat. It would do you good, Gloria, to have a break. You spend all your time either at work or here at home.'

She frowned, uncertain what to say.

'Just friends, having a day out together?' he urged. His

feelings for her were growing but he knew it was far too soon for her to even contemplate anything more than friendship.

She smiled, feeling relieved. 'Yes, I think I would like a day out, Artie. I haven't been to Southport for years and years.'

Sal was very surprised when Gloria told her but she said nothing. He was still fond of Gloria, that much was very plain, even Elsie had commented on it. But although Sal did hope that one day Gloria would see how considerate and caring he was, she knew – as well as Artie did – that it would be a long time before Gloria would think of him as anything but a friend.

Thankfully the Bank Holiday Monday dawned bright and sunny and as Artie and Gloria got to the station it was clear that many other people had had the same idea. The train was crowded but he found her a seat and when they finally alighted and walked out into Chapel Street, he asked her should they make for Victoria Park? 'I ought to have realised everywhere would be very crowded. It's not too far, we'll walk to the end of Lord Street so you can see some of the shops.'

Gloria felt a stirring of happiness for the first time in months as they walked along the elegant thoroughfare with its Edwardian buildings. The shops were too expensive for her budget but she could window shop. Artie hated shopping, even window shopping, but he grinned and suffered in silence. He was just content to be out with her and to see her smile.

The park wasn't too busy; most people had headed for the

promenade and the pier so they walked and admired the flower beds and then went for a cup of tea in the park's café.

'If you want to brave the crowds we could go back. We could walk further along, by the Marine Lake. There will be a bit of a breeze there.'

Gloria shook her head. 'It's much nicer here. With all the trees and bushes and flowers, it reminds me a bit of Central Park. That's much bigger of course but . . .'

She had never mentioned New York to him before and he knew he had to tread carefully. 'You liked New York as a city, Gloria, didn't you?'

She nodded. 'Everything was so . . . different.' She paused, thinking it was the first time she had thought of that city without being overcome by painful memories. 'You know, Artie, I'm beginning to feel as though everything there was just a dream. As if it didn't really happen. It was such a different world. But then . . . then I remember our apartment and everything in it and Iris and my Irish maid Carmel and . . . Grant, and I know it wasn't a dream. It was real.'

He reached across and took her hand. 'I'm sorry, Gloria, if I've upset you by mentioning it.'

She shook her head. 'No. I have to learn to talk about it all, Artie. It will get easier in time but I have to try to start now.'

'You're sure?'

'I am. I can tell you all about the city and the sights, if you'd like to hear it, but not about the people I was close to. Not yet. Maybe in a few months' time.'

He smiled at her; he understood. 'I'd love to hear about

the city, Gloria.' He wanted to add that he had all the time in the world to wait until she was ready to confide in him further, but he didn't.

She had enjoyed the day, she thought as they sat on the train going home that evening. She'd been able to describe New York without breaking down and he'd listened avidly and asked questions. She'd even been able to tell him that the loss of the luxurious lifestyle she'd enjoyed there no longer seemed to matter. She was content to work in Hendersons and live with her family; they had been so supportive that she didn't know how she would have coped without them. All this had been a revelation to her and he had helped to bring it about. She turned to him. 'Thank you, Artie, for a lovely day. I've enjoyed it. And thank you for . . . for being so considerate. You're a true friend, I mean that.'

'That means a great deal to me, Gloria. Let's hope we can enjoy more days or evenings out together.'

She nodded. 'I hope so too, Artie.'

He closed his eyes briefly. It was a start at least. A step in the right direction.

Chapter Forty-One

'BETTY, YOU REALLY WILL have to stop spending your money on gifts, luv. You need to start saving up now,' Sal admonished gently as she examined the lace-edged tablecloth and matching napkins Betty had brought home from her latest trip.

'I know but I just couldn't resist it and it's for Rose. You know how hard she is saving to try to get a home together and I won't find it as much of a struggle, you know that,' Betty replied. She had to admit that she wasn't enjoying her work so much now. She missed Hewel terribly and was having a hard time settling into a new ship with a new crew and a Chief Stewardess who was an absolute martinet about rules and regulations.

Sal folded the tablecloth and wrapped it up in its tissue paper. 'You might well do at first, Betty. A young doctor starting out in general practice won't earn a fortune. Have you heard how he's getting on in that respect?'

'Just one letter, the mails seem to cross mid-Atlantic. He's hoping to hear something very soon and it won't be soon enough for us both. At least if he's here in Liverpool, I'll see him when I'm home.'

Sal sighed. It was difficult for them both being on different ships with itineraries that were seldom in tandem. 'I was wondering, Betty, should we invite his parents over one Sunday for lunch while your da is still home? They have a car and it's not too far to drive.' She was very anxious to meet Marjorie Davies to ascertain for herself just what kind of a person she was and if she was indeed the snob Betty swore her to be. Well, she'd had plenty of practice dealing with Sybil. If they visited the woman could at least see what kind of a family and home Betty came from and it was only manners to invite them.

Betty pulled a face. 'Do we have to, Mam? She'll spend all day looking down her nose at everything.'

'What is there for her to find fault with, Betty? We have a comfortable home, not as big as hers maybe and only rented, but tastefully furnished and you know very well that it will be an excellent meal with all the trimmings, your da will see to that. She won't find fault there. And we have to meet them sometime, it's only polite.'

Betty nodded; her mother was right. 'Maybe you could invite Aunt Sybil and Uncle Richard too.' Safety in numbers, she thought, and Aunt Sybil would be more than a match for her future mother-in-law, especially once she got going on

Uncle Richard's business, the golf club and her posh friends. For once her aunt's presence might prove useful.

Sal was debating the matter and a possible date with Harry when Rose arrived home from work. 'Good Lord! Is that the time already! I'll have Gloria in soon and no supper even started.'

Harry could see that there was something wrong, for Rose was very pale and Sal hadn't misjudged the time, Rose was home early. 'Rose, you're early. Is something wrong?'

Rose sat down and covered her face with her hands.

Betty was instantly beside her, her arm around her shoulder. 'Rose, what's wrong? What's happened?' Rose's shoulders were shaking with sobs.

Sal went to put the kettle on, the poor girl had obviously had some kind of a shock.

Rose made a huge effort, dabbing at her eyes with her handkerchief. 'I . . . I've lost my job! They . . . told me . . .' She broke down again. It was as if her world had suddenly tilted. With no job she would have no money and all her hopes and dreams of a little home of her own were fading rapidly.

'Oh, Rose, no! Why? You were doing so well! Did they tell you why?' Betty cried. Poor Rose, she thought. Why now, when she'd been hoping to bring her wedding forward?

'I'd heard a rumour that there would be cuts in the office staff,' Harry said quietly. 'Was that what they told you, Rose?'

Rose nodded, still wiping away her tears. 'They said I was the one who had been there the shortest length of time, so . . . Oh, I'll never get another job now. Who is going to employ me? Everyone seems to be out of work!'

'Last in, first out,' Harry said as Sal came in with the tea.

'And I'm worried sick that Alan will lose his job too. He hasn't been there very long either, just a year longer than me, and then what will we do? We'll never be able to afford to get married.' Rose broke down again.

Sal looked anxiously at Harry. 'Isn't there something you can do?'

He sighed and shook his head. 'I can perhaps find out if there is a chance Alan might be laid off, that's all. Times are getting harder, Sal, for everyone.'

Betty felt desperately sorry for Rose; she'd lost both her parents and her home and now, when a home of her own with Alan had been all she dreamed of, that dream looked to be in danger of being snatched away. 'I wish I could give you my job, Rose. We seem to be busier than usual, so many people are emigrating, and I won't need it once I'm married and Hewel is working in Liverpool.'

'I . . . I couldn't do your job, Betty, but . . . but thanks for the . . . support.' Rose sniffed unhappily. She would be terrified constantly sailing the oceans of the world in all weathers.

'What did Alan say, Rose? He does know, I take it?' Sal asked, handing Rose a cup of very sweet tea.

Rose nodded. 'He's coming here straight from work. I know he is worried too.'

'Good. We'll try to sort something out, Rose. Drink your tea, luv, and try to calm down a bit,' Sal advised.

Rose had pulled herself together by the time Alan arrived and the family tactfully left them alone together to talk, Betty informing Gloria of Rose's bad news as she came into the kitchen and looked mystified at it being so unusually crowded.

'Poor Rose, life is so unfair,' Gloria commented sadly.

'Uncle Harry said he could try to find out if . . . if your job is safe or not,' Rose informed Alan, after she'd cried in his arms.

He'd been very shaken by the news and all the way here on the tram he'd wondered what they would indeed do if he lost his job too. Unemployment was rising daily. On every street corner you passed in the city there were groups of men and boys hanging around looking dejected and desperate. Men far older than him and with families to keep had no work; ships were lying up in the docks; there were fewer and fewer cargoes for the dockers to load and unload. Money was becoming very tight and in America he'd heard it was worse; they were even setting up soup kitchens for people were starving.

'I'd be very grateful if he could, Rose. I mean that,' he said, wondering if it would indeed be better to know the worst or was 'ignorance' really 'bliss'?

'I'll tell him, Alan. If we *know*, we can try to make some plans. Betty said she wished she could give me her job, she won't need it when she gets married and she said they at least are busy, so many people are emigrating. I couldn't do it, though. I'd be terrified and I know I'd be sick. I was bad enough on that trip to the Isle of Man and it wasn't even rough.'

Alan stroked her fair hair and smiled. 'I couldn't see you running up and down stairs on a ship that was rolling and pitching, Rose. No, we'll wait and see what Mr Jenkins can find out. Hopefully, we won't have to alter our plans very much.'

'But how can we afford to save or to buy things or even live on just your wages?'

'We'll manage, Rose, you'll see. Other people are managing on less and they've got kids to feed and clothe too. Don't worry, things will work out.' He hoped he was right but Betty's words on the increasing number of emigrants stuck in his mind.

Harry was as good as his word and went next morning to the company offices, but as he left and crossed Man Island to get the tram home he was worried. Things were worse than he had imagined. There would be more cuts to the office staff and it looked as if the *Amazonia* too would be laid up after the next trip. For how long it had been impossible to ascertain, although it was being mooted that the five ships of the Porto-Brasilia Line would be laid up on a rota basis so as not to put everyone out of work. He'd never known times to be so hard.

Sal looked grim when he imparted his news. 'We'll all have to pull our horns in and tighten our belts, Harry. Thankfully, we've got a bit saved up to tide us over and at least you are not going to be laid off permanently. But it does look as if young Alan is. It's such a shame, they were doing so well too.'

Harry nodded. 'And I think Betty will have to forgo the big wedding too, unfortunately.'

'I don't honestly think she'll mind that. She's already told me she couldn't go through all that fuss and palaver the way Gloria did, not even to impress Hewel's mother. Perhaps Alan should start now to look for something else.'

Harry looked grim. 'There's very little out there, Sal. Especially for a junior accounts clerk.'

Alan echoed his words that evening when Harry told him the unwelcome news. He'd walked to the tram stop to wait for the lad, not wishing to impart the news in front of Rose and hoping to give Alan some time to compose his thoughts.

'All you can do is try, lad,' Harry urged.

'I've been thinking all day about something Betty said to Rose,' Alan confided. He hadn't been able to stop thinking about it and the more he thought the more convinced he'd become that this was the only course open to himself and Rose if they were to have any kind of future together.

Harry frowned. 'What did she say?'

'That they were busy with people emigrating.'

Harry stopped and looked at him intently. 'It's true numbers are on the increase but—'

'I think it's what Rose and I should do. Make a new life in a new country. Things are getting worse here, Mr Jenkins, you know they are. Skilled men with years of experience are losing their jobs now and we're only junior clerks, what hopes have we got of a home of our own and a decent life?'

Harry nodded slowly. There was a lot of truth in the lad's words. 'Have you talked this over with anyone else? Rose, your da?'

Alan shook his head. 'No, I've really only just made up my mind.'

'It's an enormous decision, Alan,' Harry warned.

'I know and I will discuss it with everyone, I promise,' he replied, wondering how his parents would react, to say nothing of Rose.

Rose took it far better than he had envisaged, after he'd explained that it was almost certain he would lose his job in the very near future. He told her that he'd be very hard pressed to find another, and that the only way he could see them having a future to look forward to was by starting married life in a new country. A fresh start, a new beginning. They were both young and healthy and could work hard and he was prepared to try his hand at anything. They had their savings so even after they'd paid their fare there would be something left over to help get them on their feet.

'Have you thought where would be best, Alan?' Rose asked. Even though this idea had come as a bolt out of the blue she had infinite faith and trust in him. He hadn't just thrown his hands up in despair at the circumstances that now faced them, he had thought seriously about their future. A better future. And why not go? She would miss everyone terribly for she looked on them as family but at the end of the day she really didn't have a family. She and Alan would start their own family in a new land where there would be new opportunities for everyone.

'New Zealand. Canada is bound to be affected by events in America. New Zealand is not as big. I'll find out more about it and how we go about emigrating.'

'What about your mam and da? Will they be upset?' Rose pressed.

'They might be at first but when I've explained, I'm sure they'll understand. There's not much of a future here for us, Rose. With no work we'd never be able to afford to get married or have a family of our own.'

Rose nodded. That was her dearest wish and if she had to go to the other side of the world to achieve it she would.

Sal, Betty and Gloria were stunned when she told them.

'But, Rose, it's thousands of miles away!' Sal exclaimed. Further even than New York, she thought.

'We'll never see you again!' Betty cried, stricken.

Only Gloria seemed to understand. She smiled. 'A new life, a new beginning, a new country, Rose. It's exciting and you'll enjoy it and I know you'll be happy. I . . . I was. Seize the opportunity while you can.'

Sal stared at her, thinking of how the exciting adventure had ended for Gloria, but then Rose's circumstances were very different: no luxury trip, no whirlwind romance, no wealthy lifestyle in a huge, ultra-modern city, no close family to leave behind. Gloria was right, it would be a wonderful adventure for Rose. And her daughter's words showed Sal how far Gloria had come in getting over her loss. Sal was proud of them both.

Chapter Forty-Two

———❖———

ALAN'S IDEA HAD COME as a shock to his parents and their initial reaction was one of horror. But he doggedly persisted with his arguments and persuasion until at least his father agreed that it was probably the best thing they could do.

'I suppose your mam and I are just being selfish really, wanting you to stay here, but at the end of the day, we've had our lives, you and Rose have yours ahead of you. Times are getting harder, I've never known things to be so grim. I was reading today that the miners up in the North-east are really in a bad way. There's talk of them marching from Jarrow to London, demanding the Government does something to help. Whether anything will ever come of it I don't know. It's a hell of a long way to walk but I suppose when you see your family starving you'll attempt anything. You go, lad. You're young enough to make a new life,' he'd urged reluctantly.

Alan had found out as much as he could about New Zealand and, helped by Harry, had enquired about the necessary procedures for emigrating. He and Rose duly filled in all the forms and obtained the necessary documentation and when they learned that there was a berth on a ship leaving the first week in September, they decided to take it.

'But it's so soon! Just a couple of weeks away, Rose!' Betty protested. Even though she was coming to terms with the fact that she would be losing her oldest friend, she'd thought it would be months, not weeks before Rose left.

'I know, but we have to take this opportunity. There's no reason to delay. And we've decided to get married before we go. We couldn't deprive Alan's parents of that too and I want Uncle Harry to give me away. I've no one else and he's due to sail a few days after we will have left. It's only going to be a very small, quiet wedding. I'm not even going to have a long white dress. I'll get something I can wear again. We need every penny and that would be a total waste,' Rose confided.

Betty had shaken her head. It just didn't seem right that Rose should be deprived of a decent wedding when she had planned to have something grander. It must be a huge disappointment on top of everything else.

She said as much to Sal after Rose had told her of her plans and Sal had agreed. 'Quiet and small it might be but that girl is going to have a proper dress, veil and bouquet. How could I face poor Dora in the next world if I let Rose get married in anything less? We'll have the reception here. Just our family and his. Will you be here? And what about Hewel?'

Betty stood up. 'I think we'd better get a pen and paper, Mam, and get Rose too. This is her wedding after all.'

All Rose's protests about the waste a traditional dress would be fell on deaf ears as Sal told her that her poor mother would turn in her grave to think her only daughter was thinking of getting married in an ordinary linen costume with a fancy blouse beneath. No, no huge amounts would be spent but a traditional dress, veil, head-dress and bouquet would be paid for by herself. It was her wedding gift. Fortunately Betty would arrive home that very morning – barring all disasters – and so would be able to be bridesmaid and as Hewel had actually obtained an interview for a position in Everton, which, should he prove suitable, he intended to take, he was taking unpaid leave. After that Rose felt as though events took place at breakneck speed, making her head spin and waves of nervous excitement course through her.

Gloria had kept Artie up to date about Rose's plans for they occasionally went to the cinema or for a walk together. He'd been dismayed when she'd told him that Rose had lost her job, Alan too was soon to be let go and even her da would be on unpaid leave after his next trip. It was a fine late summer evening and they were walking on the towpath beside the canal.

'Things are really getting desperate, Gloria. Do you think you'll be all right?'

'I hope so, Artie. I enjoy my job. It has been a bit quieter of late although some people still seem to have money to spend on clothes and cosmetics.' She was thinking of her Aunt Sybil, who had called in the previous day to take her to lunch and show her the new evening dress she intended to purchase. 'What about your job?'

'We'll have to wait and see but Da says they'll always need mechanics to service the engines and keep the railways running. Our Brian might be laid off, though, he's still an apprentice and there are quite a lot of them. So, what will Rose and Alan do?'

'They're emigrating. They're going out New Zealand. I hope everything goes well for them. Rose deserves some good luck and a home of her own.'

They paused to watch a heron take flight. Artie remembered that the house he lived in had once been Rose's home, before her mother had died, and he nodded his agreement. He liked Rose.

They walked on. 'They've filled in all the forms and are going at the beginning of September. They're getting married before they go. She wants Da to give her away.' She could remember now without overwhelming sadness her own wedding day. 'I often wish it had been Da and not Uncle Richard who gave me away, but at least he will be here for Rose and then later Betty.'

'It won't . . . upset you, Gloria? Rose getting married, I mean.'

She shook her head. 'I don't think so, Artie. I just want Rose to have a day she will always remember, the way I did.

Although it seems so long ago now.' She sighed. 'Da never even met Grant and it seems strange now that I was married and had a whole new life and Da saw nothing of it and he's mellowed so much too, which is just as well seeing he's being laid up.'

Artie nodded thoughtfully. She was obviously getting over Grant Hepworth. She talked less and less about her life in New York now and they were going out more frequently too. He hoped things would develop further.

'Would you . . . like to come as my guest, Artie? It's going to be a rather quiet affair, just family . . . but you've been so thoughtful . . .'

He felt his heart miss a beat. This looked hopeful. 'I'd love to come as your guest, Gloria. I really would,' he answered happily.

'Rose, if you don't sit still I'm going to end up sticking these pins in your head,' Betty warned as she struggled to secure Rose's head-dress to the veil.

'I can't help it, I'm just so nervous and excited,' Rose replied as she sat on the stool in front of the dressing table. The ivory taffeta suited her complexion, she thought. The style wasn't fancy; she'd wanted something plain, but the high neckline with the mandarin collar, long tight sleeves and short train showed off her slim figure.

'Of course you're nervous and excited. There would be something wrong with you if you weren't. Getting married and sailing off to a new life. Oh, blast!' she finished as she dropped the pin.

'Let me try, Betty. You're just making things worse,' Gloria intervened, taking the packet of pins from her sister. Both she and Betty were wearing what were termed 'afternoon dresses' of patterned crêpe de Chine in lilac, blue and white. Their hats, wide-brimmed white straw with clusters of blue and lilac flowers attached to one side, lay on the bed. Gloria deftly attached the veil and stood back. 'There. You look lovely, Rose.' She turned quickly to hide the sadness in her eyes. She couldn't entirely forget how she had looked and felt on her wedding day but she wasn't going to upset Rose in any way.

Betty glanced at her sister and then at Rose. 'Now what's the matter, Rose?'

'Everything *is* under control downstairs?'

Betty raised her eyes to the ceiling. 'Of course it is. You know Da, when he organises something it's always perfect. Stop worrying.'

Sal bustled into the room looking smart in a violet moiré dress and matching jacket, a mauve and violet hat in her hand. 'Are you girls nearly ready?'

'Nearly, Mam,' Betty replied as Rose got to her feet.

'Good, because the cars will be here soon and your da is getting a bit agitated.' She paused and took both Rose's hands in her own. 'Oh, Rose! If your poor mam were here she'd be so proud of you.'

Rose smiled a little sadly. 'I hope she's looking down on me and that my da is too.'

Sal nodded. Dora would have approved of Alan Hopkins. 'I'm sure they are.'

Impulsively Rose kissed her. 'Thank you, Aunty Sal, for everything and Uncle Harry too.'

Sal brushed away a tear. She had been determined that Rose would have a day to remember, the way Betty would when the time came. 'Well, "Uncle Harry" will be like a cat on hot bricks if we don't go down soon. You two put your hats on, Betty bring the bouquets and I'll help you, Rose, with your veil. Hook that train over your arm so you don't trip up.'

'Don't forget your own hat, Mam, and where are your gloves and bag?' Gloria asked, thinking she looked very elegant as she stood in for Dora. Her da was all done up in his best uniform to give Rose away, standing in for the long dead Bill Cassidy.

'Is Artie going straight to the church?' Betty asked her sister as they went downstairs.

Gloria nodded. She was glad she had asked him. She was gradually becoming aware that his feelings for her were more than just those of a friend but she wasn't yet ready to reciprocate. She would have to think carefully and deeply about her feelings for him. Yet she knew she was becoming fond of him again. One thing was certain: she had no intention of hurting him again. He deserved far better treatment than that.

'The cars have arrived,' Betty announced.

Rose took a deep breath and then slipped her arm through Harry's.

He smiled at her. 'Feeling all right?'

She nodded. 'Nervous and excited but looking forward to . . . everything.'

'You're both going to be very happy and you'll do well too. Right, I know it's customary for the bride to be late but we don't want to worry the poor lad, do we?'

Betty smiled happily as she caught sight of Hewel as she walked down the aisle behind Rose and her father. He looked so handsome in his uniform with the gold and red epaulettes on the shoulder that denoted his rank as a medical officer. She loved him so much and she prayed that he had been offered the position at the practice in Everton. As he caught sight of her he winked and made a thumbs-up sign and her smile widened with sheer delight. Now they'd be able to see more of each other and next year it would be her turn to walk down the aisle on her father's arm.

Gloria slipped into the pew beside Artie and smiled shyly at him, studiously ignoring the look of surprise on her Aunt Sybil's face. She was no longer an impressionable girl but a young woman and she would make her own decisions in future.

As Betty and then Harry slipped into the front pew beside her Sal smiled. She felt a great sense of achievement as Rose, blushing and a little nervous, made her vows. She'd fulfilled her promise to Dora; Rose's future was secured. And her own daughters? Betty was to marry a very fine young man and Gloria seemed to be far happier and more confident about her future, although whether there was a place in that future for Artie Taylor remained to be seen. She sincerely hoped so. She slipped her hand into Harry's.

'We've not done too badly, have we, luv? All three of them will be all right now.'

Harry smiled at her. '*You've* done a great job, Sal,' he said, giving her all the credit for once. She really was one in a million, he thought fondly, and whatever lay ahead of them they'd face it together.